Elena...Suddenly Jamie was looking into the deep green eyes again, feeling the painful physical awareness of her presence. He must forget her, think only of his wife—the woman who even now was bringing his child into the world...

Elena woke with a start. Another dream, of Jamie's lips, warm and searching, on her own. Dreams were all that remained of the aching instant of ecstasy they had known—and of the passion that had promised to free her from the dark curse of the past...

Love's Broken Promises

SHARON WAGNER

A BERKLEY BOOK
published by
BERKLEY PUBLISHING CORPORATION

DEDICATION

To Dorothy Wagner, my mother, with thanks.

ACKNOWLEDGEMENT

I wish to acknowledge the work of Bernard L. Casey who not only furnished the historical background of this book, but also collaborated in its entire creation.

Chapter 1

ELENA SIGHED AND moved restlessly in the stiff chair. Her small square of embroidery was fast becoming wrinkled as her hands grew damp with the effort of making the tiny stitches Dona Isabella insisted were necessary.

From beyond the windows came the sounds of the peasants who worked the estate lands, and the light breeze brought the scent of the blossoming orange trees that were a part of the sprawling lands her father had purchased when he came to Spain from France. It was definitely not a day to remain inside with no more entertainment than a square of rapidly greying cloth and a needle that all too often ended its brief journeys in her fingers instead of the cloth.

Elena glared at the empty chair beside her. "Where is Celeste?" she asked for the second time in an hour.

"She said that she was not feeling well and begged to be excused from your lesson today," Dona Isabella said, not looking up from her own work—which was so large a frame had been constructed to hold it steady for her busy fingers. "Since she has a fine touch with handwork already, I saw no reason why she shouldn't rest."

1

Elena squirmed again, not liking the reminder that her paid companion was far more gifted at the arts of a "proper Spanish maiden" than she. Though Celeste was her best friend and dear to her as a sister, in the four months since her mother's remarriage and the arrival of Dona Isabella, Elena had been made to feel terribly inadequate.

"If my father was here..." she began resentfully.

"Your good father is dead, child," Dona Isabella said gently, "and my dear brother has come to do his best to make a new life for both you and your mother, and it is his wish that you become a proper Spanish maiden. As your *duenna*, the training is my responsibility."

Bitter words rose in Elena's throat, but she held them back, well aware that they would do her no good. Her father's death had been so awful, and the six months of mourning afterward had seemed endless. But then her mother had suddenly decided that she couldn't manage the vast estates, and so soon... much too soon, Hernan Valdez had come into their lives, marrying her mother and changing everything.

"Hold the cloth gently," Dona Isabella said, pushing back her grey-streaked hair. "It is a thing of beauty you wish to create, not an animal you are seeking to subdue."

Elena shook back her dark brown hair, which in the dim room showed none of the auburn highlights that burned in it under the blazing Spanish sun. Her eyes, which could flash green when her temper blazed, were hazel now beneath her long dark lashes. "I would do better if it were a horse," she said softly. "This is a day to be out riding and..."

Dona Isabella gasped, her brown eyes scandalized. "No more of that," she said. "I've told you often enough that young ladies of proper family don't go racing about the countryside like *muchachos*. You are a lady, and your place is here until a proper marriage can be arranged. You will soon be seventeen. It is shameful that so little has been done about your future."

Elena blinked back tears and went on with her embroidery. Four months of this had taught her that, though the world might have moved in a free and forward-looking manner in this year of 1739, her new stepfather and his sister Isabella were determined to keep to the ways of the past. It was no wonder that Celeste seemed so different now, so distant. She sighed.

"I know this has been difficult for you, Elena," Dona Isabella said in a softer, gentler tone. She seemed so old with her dark clothes and quiet ways, yet Elena knew that she couldn't be more than a year or so past forty—her father's age when he was thrown from the pale stallion and the rock... She pushed the thoughts from her mind.

"Our ways are different from those your parents knew in France," Dona Isabella went on, warming to what seemed to be her favorite theme. "To be a true part of the life of Catalonia, you'll have to be like the young girls of the other families in this area. You must become a part of the proper class or your chances of a good marriage will be poor, even though you are growing to be most attractive. The fact that your only friend is a paid *companera* from France is most unsuitable, and..."

Her *duenna*'s voice went on, but Elena tuned it out, pretending an interest in her embroidery that she didn't feel. She thought of the days when she'd ridden with her father. What use had she for sitting around the dim *salas* of the big *haciendas* that dotted the rich land that edged the Ebro River? It was far more pleasant to ride along inspecting the carefully tended groves of orange trees, the vines that grew on the rockier slopes and gave them grapes for wine; or even to ride the hills of the estate, where the men and dogs watched over the endless flocks of sheep.

Besides, Celeste was a perfect *companera* and friend, far better than the few dull, silent creatures she'd seen when she went out with her parents. Celeste knew how to laugh, and... Her mind slowed and she frowned. It had been a long time since Celeste had laughed, she realized suddenly. In fact, it had been a long time since she and Celeste had shared more than their meals and lessons.

She glared at the now-silent *duenna*, wanting to blame her for the rift, but honesty kept her from such thoughts. She and Celeste had been close when Dona Isabella came to rule over their small area of the huge house, and they had stayed that way, plotting ways to evade the *duenna*'s endless supervision, and giggling together over the foolish rules she seemed so determined to enforce. When had it stopped? she asked herself.

No single date stood out in her mind, yet she knew it had been a long time, several months at least. In fact, as she cast her mind back, she could remember nothing they'd done together in the old way since the gigantic *fiesta* that had welcomed her mother and Hernan Valdez back to the *hacienda* after their short journey to meet a few members of his family and visit his estates following their marriage.

Had something happened that night? Elena pondered, trying to remember. It had been fun and exciting, there had been strangers on the grounds and filling all the extra bedrooms of the vast house. She and Celeste had been allowed to attend many of the activities and had even slipped out later—after Dona Isabella retired—and...

A tap on the door interrupted her thoughts and a young man came in to announce that her mother was in the garden and desired her company.

Elena leaped to her feet at once, her tall, slender body like a quivering sapling, too full of energy to be contained by the dim room and the silence. "May I be excused to go to her, Dona Isabella?" she asked belatedly.

Dona Isabella rose slowly and came over to inspect her embroidery first, then shook her head. "You might as well," she said. "Your work grows no better. I don't think you listen to anything I say to you."

Elena started for the door, eager to escape, but Dona Isabella called her back. "You must take a shawl," she said. "Your arms and hands are still far too dark for good taste. Your skin should be like milk, but the sun has darkened it much too much."

Elena controlled her impatience, dismissing the maid, then went to her room as she was bid. It took only a moment to pick up a shawl, but when she emerged, Dona Isabella had disappeared and the room seemed lighter without her presence. Elena started for the door, then turned back, heading for the room that Celeste occupied. She tapped lightly on the door and, when there was no response, opened it and peeked in. The room was empty and the bed was smooth as when it had been made in the morning. Celeste was not resting.

Frowning, Elena left the suite of rooms that were home to her, Celeste, and now Dona Isabella, and made her way through the long corridors and down the stairs to the interior *jardin* where she knew her mother would be strolling in the shade awaiting her. It was the best part of the day now, she thought sadly, the only time she was allowed to escape the ever-watchful eyes of Dona Isabella—and that was only because her mother insisted that she be allowed to come alone or with Celeste for company.

As she slipped through the door to the *jardin*, Elena was frowning, her thoughts still on the empty room upstairs. "Have you seen Celeste?" she asked her mother as soon as she'd greeted her.

Her mother started rather strangely. "Celeste? Wasn't she with you?" she asked, her hazel eyes evading Elena's.

"She's been acting very strange lately," Elena said, sensing that her mother was hiding something. "Is there something wrong with her, or with her family in France?"

"She hasn't said anything about her family, has she?" her mother asked, looking positively upset.

"What do you mean?" Elena asked.

"She hasn't been writing to them or... or anything, has she?"

Elena looked at her mother, noting that she looked lovelier than usual now, with her fair hair done simply and her eyes brighter than they'd been since her father's death. It seemed obvious that she, at least, was happy with the new kind of life her marriage had brought to the *hacienda*. "I don't know if she writes to them," Elena admitted. "But why shouldn't she? You've always complained that she doesn't write often enough. I thought that her mother was your best friend when you were growing up outside Paris."

"Nadine and I were very close," her mother said, "but... I don't want to talk about Celeste."

"Something is wrong, isn't it?" Elena asked, ignoring her mother's words. "Something has happened to make her sad all the time. What is it? Please tell me. She's my best friend and I want to help her."

Her mother looked dubious, and for a moment Elena was afraid that she would get up and move away down one of the narrow paths or even order her back to her embroidery. But after a few minutes of silence, her mother sighed and leaned back against the bench.

"I believe that Celeste will soon be marrying," she said quietly.

"What?" Elena stared at her mother in disbelief. "But..."

"She is a little older than you," her mother said softly, her eyes on a distant flower. "She has talked of it before, you know. Last year when you were spending more time with your father, she was lonely and..."

"She told me all about Juan," Elean admitted, "but I thought... You said that the match was unsuitable, that he was only a miller's son with education and manners above his station and..."

"It seems that I was wrong." Her mother said the words without belief. "Things are different now."

"How?" Elena demanded. "What has changed?"

"Hernan says that the match will be acceptable. They . . . they will be traveling to New Spain to live, and there Juan will be accepted among the better families because of his manners and education."

"New Spain?" Elena stared at her mother in disbelief. Since she had been educated well beyond the amount acceptable for a girl, Elena had seen maps of the distant lands and heard tales of life there, but to think that Celeste . . . "Why didn't she tell me?" she asked. "Why does it make her so sad?"

Her mother rose abruptly. "There are things that aren't proper for you to know," her mother said firmly. "Things that I don't wish to discuss with you. Celeste is to be married in a few weeks, and she will be leaving at once for the coast to board a ship to the new world. That is all you need to know. If she seems sad, perhaps it is because she is reluctant to leave us."

"I don't believe that," Elena murmured to her mother's back. "I just don't believe it."

Her mother whirled, her hazel eyes darkening a little as she glared at Elena. "You must believe it," she said. "You'll only make things worse if you don't. Now go to your room and stay there till time for *cena* to be served. Think about what I've told you and accept it. That's all you can do to help Celeste now."

Elena opened her mouth to protest, then closed it when she saw the anger in her mother's face. Whatever was going on, it was plain that her mother didn't plan to tell her anything about it. With no way of arguing with her, Elena sighed and left the *jardin*, going back inside; but heading for the rear of the house, not the stairway that would take her to her room. It was still a long time till the evening meal would be served.

She'd hoped to find the cook in the kitchen, but it was empty. She was ready to turn away when a flash of movement caught her eye near the stable, which was just across the broad rear yard from the kitchen area of the house. Juan was going into the stable. Curious, Elena slipped out of the rear door and hurried across the open area, hoping fervently that Dona Isabella wasn't looking out a window where she might see her.

The stable was dim, but the voices came to her clearly. "I'm here, Celeste," Juan said. "What is it you want?"

"To see you. To talk to you." Celeste sounded subdued, even near tears. Elena frowned and moved deeper into the shadows, aware that she had no right to listen but equally determined to know what was hurting her *amiga*.

"There is nothing to say," Juan said, his voice flat. "I've agreed to the marriage, what more do you want?"

"You said once that you loved me," Celeste murmured, her voice choked. "Once you *wanted* to marry me."

"I wanted to marry a pretty *muchacha* who laughed and behaved as a lady should . . . or so I thought. You were always so proper with me. A stolen kiss or two, that was all you allowed me. I believed that it was because you were innocent, and I respected that."

"I *was* innocent!" Celeste said.

"And now?"

"I told you the truth."

"But not the name of the man." The tone was full of accusation.

"What good would it do for you to know?" Celeste sounded sick and weary.

"I would kill him."

"And what purpose would that serve? You'd be killed in turn, you know."

"Is it better for us to go to the new world carrying that reminder of what we are leaving behind? Or maybe you want the reminder? Maybe you love this . . . this secret man who gives you his child and then refuses to marry you."

Elena's gasp was too loud, but she couldn't help it. Not knowing what else to do, she turned and fled quickly to the house, slipping inside before she even dared look back. There was no one visible in the doorway of the stable, but she had no way of knowing whether or not eyes were watching her from the dim interior.

"Was there something, senorita?" the cook asked, causing her to jump guiltily.

Elena turned to look up at the worn, friendly face, remembering that she'd come here to talk to Margo, to ask her what was wrong with Celeste. But now she knew . . . She shuddered slightly at the shock of what she'd overheard. "Nothing," she whispered. "Nothing at all, thank you." She turned and hurried from the kitchen and Margo's too-knowing eyes. Once out of her sight, she raced along the corridors and up the stairs, not stopping till she lay on her own bed.

Celeste carrying a child? Her head spun. It seemed impossible—something she would have just laughed at last week or even this morning—but now the words continued to echo in her ears. He had actually said it, and there'd been no denial from

Celeste. And he was going to marry her, take her away so that no one would know, but...

She shook her head, not wanting to accept the new knowledge and all it seemed to mean. Not Celeste. A thousand late-night conversations filled her thoughts. They'd talked about marriage and what lay beyond it for them, even speculated a little after having accidently seen a stallion and a mare in the corrals; but to think that Celeste and some man... someone she refused to name...

For a moment she tried again to deny the whole ugly situation, then her rational mind told her she couldn't. It explained everything only too well—Celeste's silence, the distance that had suddenly grown between them, even her mother's strange behavior and reluctance to talk about it.

Elena sighed. Her father would have told her, she thought bitterly. He would have let her help Celeste instead of keeping her ignorant as a child. She turned over and looked up at the ceiling. So now she knew, but what could she do? How could she help Celeste?

Chapter 2

A LIGHT TAP announced Dona Isabella. Elena sat up, trying to arrange her face into an acceptable smile of welcome, though her thoughts were still on what she'd overheard. "You don't look very pleased," her *duenna* said, frowning. "The idea doesn't please you? Your mother seemed so sure that it would."

Elena forgot her pretense and frowned. "Pleased about what?" she asked.

"She didn't tell you?" Dona Isabella looked disconcerted. "I wouldn't have mentioned . . . She told me this morning that she would tell you this afternoon and that I wasn't to mention it to you before then, as she wanted to surprise you yourself."

"Perhaps she just forgot," Elena said. "We were talking about Celeste."

Dona Isabella's smile faded slightly. "Well, it is your mother's wish . . ."

"Please tell me," Elena said. "You've already said too much. It isn't about the wedding, is it? She told me about that, but . . ." She stopped herself, aware that she couldn't repeat what she'd overheard, even if she wanted to discuss Celeste with this stern-faced woman.

For a moment Dona Isabella seemed reluctant, but then her face softened again. "We are going to go on a journey," she said. "We're going to Mallorca."

"Mallorca?" Elena caught her breath in surprise.

"The island off the coast," Dona Isabella explained. "We have cousins there and Hernan would like you and your mother to get to know them."

"Are we all going?" Elena asked.

"Of course. It will be wonderful! to see Esteban and Maria." For the first time, Elena heard a sound of genuine joy in her *duenna*'s voice. "It has been years, but we were all educated together when we were children. Maria was my dearest *amiga*. Estaban saw her first when she came to sit with me in the *jardin* of our *hacienda*." Her eyes narrowed a bit, but her lips were still touched with humor as she added, "He fell in love with her as he watched her working on a tapestry that hangs even now in their private rooms."

Elena subdued a giggle at the idea that a tapestry might have spawned a marriage, forgetting for a moment what she'd heard outside the stable. "Have you ever been to Mallorca?" she asked, fascinated at the idea of actually being allowed to see some of the world beyond the boundaries of the estates and nearby villages. Her one dream had been to make the journey to France with her parents, but her father's death had ended that hope, so till now . . .

"Not for many years," Dona Isabella said. "When I was younger I traveled there a few times with my family, but then my father became ill. I cared for him, and later for my mother during her last illness, so of course I couldn't leave our *hacienda*."

Elena looked at the rather wistful face before her and felt the first pang of pity for the woman her stepfather had brought to guide her. The words hadn't been spoken in complaint, she realized, yet the picture they painted was of a life even more restricted than hers had been since her mother's remarriage. It also explained why Dona Isabella had remained unmarried in spite of her position and the fact that her face still retained the vestiges of beauty. A sigh brought her attention back to the present.

"There is so much we must do," Dona Isabella said. "So much you must learn if you are to be accepted in Esteban's home. They have a daughter near your age, so you must not shame Hernan with your ignorance. Is that clear?"

"Yes, Dona Isabella," Elena murmured, trying to look properly submissive in spite of the excitement she was feeling.

They were still discussing her many shortcomings when a discreet tap on the door brought a maid telling them that it was nearly time for *cena* to be served. Dona Isabella rose at once from the chair near the door. "You must change," she ordered. "Your gown is a disgrace. I'm sure that Hernan will be with us this evening, eager to discuss our journey, so you must be ready." She hesitated, then added, "I only hope that your mother will not be displeased with me for having told you the news before she did."

Elena smiled at her. "I'll tell her that I made you tell me," she said. "That it wasn't your fault."

"You'll do no such thing," Dona Isabella said coldly. "A proper Spanish girl would never do anything like that. The decision was mine. If she is angry, I will accept the blame. Now hurry and change—it would be very bad form to be late." Her back was ramrod straight as she left the room.

Elena changed quickly, not bothering to summon a maid to assist her. As soon as Dona Isabella left, her thoughts went immediately to Celeste and all her quick excitement about the trip vanished. Would the trip come before Celeste was married? Was it part of a plan, perhaps decided upon just to take her away while the unhappy wedding was arranged?

That thought shocked and angered Elena and she stiffened. If that was the way of it, she would refuse to go, she decided firmly. Celeste was her *amiga* and she needed her. Whatever had happened...whatever was behind that scene in the stable...She would help her. She *must* help her.

With that in mind, she quickly finished her dressing and crossed the small sitting room to tap on Celeste's door. A muffled reply admitted her and she saw the slender girl lying on her bed—her brown hair fanned out, unbound on the pillow, her blue eyes red-rimmed from crying.

"I'll not be dining with you tonight," Celeste said softly. "Please make my excuses to your parents."

"I'll have a tray brought up," Elena said, crossing the room cautiously, wanting to touch her friend, to soothe her, but feeling clumsy-tongued and unsure of herself.

Celeste's eyes met hers, then the girl turned away. "Don't even look at me," she said.

"Why not?" Elena asked. She was sure now that Celeste had seen her fleeing from the stable, but could not think how to approach the subject without making matters worse. "You're my *amiga*, Celeste, I care about you."

"Don't." The word was cold. "I can't bear your pity. It was better when you didn't know. I..." A sound behind Elena stopped the words and she turned to see Dona Isabella entering the room.

"Are you not dining with us, Celeste?" the older woman asked, her tone cold.

"I was just asking Elena to make my excuses to her parents," Celeste said, her face impassive. "As you can see, I am again not felling well."

"We shall do that," Dona Isabella said. "Come along, Elena. We shall just be in time if you hurry."

"I'll be back later," Elena whispered to Celeste, this time reaching out to touch the cold hand that rested almost lifelessly on the side of the bed. "I have to talk to you, Celeste."

There was no response, and she was forced to leave the girl as Dona Isabella called to her again from the door that opened into the corridor. Feeling torn between her loyalties, Elena followed her *duenna* through the halls and down the stairs to the dining room. She was, she thought, going to hate the long evening meal—and the thought of Celeste alone upstairs made it seem even worse.

To her surprise, however, *cena* proved to be far more pleasant at first than any meal she'd known in the four months since Hernan and Isabella had come to the *hacienda*. Her stepfather seemed more alive, talking about Mallorca, his dark eyes flashing, his handsome face easing into smiles as he told a few tales of the adventures he and Esteban had shared as boys. His eyes even rested on Elena for a change.

"You will enjoy the visit there, Elena," he said, smiling at her. "Esteban has a daughter called Teresa who is near your age. You have had too few friends here, and even those are most unsuitable. Teresa will introduce you to some of the better families on Mallorca, and once you are accustomed to such company we will do the same here. There may even be families from this area in Mallorca to enjoy the sea. It would be an ideal way to become acquainted with them."

"Is it a special gathering there?" Elena asked, smarting at his reference to Celeste as an "unsuitable" *companera*, yet too frightened of him to protest.

"When old friends are together, it is special," he said. His tone had turned cold, warning her that she had, somehow, asked the wrong question.

Feeling her mother and Dona Isabella's eyes still on her, Elena spoke again. "I only wondered why so many families from this area should choose to go there at the same time," she explained, hoping to change his expression; but his dark eyes only hardened and he was no longer smiling even in a polite manner.

"Such affairs are not for women to discuss," he said firmly. "You will go to enjoy the sun and the sea and to meet my family; surely that will satisfy your unending curiosity. And you will, I hope, have learned by then not to ask questions about things that do not concern you."

Elena wilted under his icy tone, her cheeks blazing with shame though she was still unsure just why her question had made him so angry. If her father had been here . . . If she'd asked *him* such a question . . . She pushed the thoughts away, fighting tears as she remembered how happy the meals had been when her father sat at the head of the table. They'd laughed then, and he'd told her all about whatever was being done on the estate, talked about the future with her as if she were a son . . .

"Don't slump," Dona Isabella said in a too-loud whisper.

It was too much. Whispering her excuses, Elena rose and fled the table to hide the tears she could no longer control. Behind her she heard her mother's worried tone, quickly silenced by her stepfather's angry voice. She ran up the stairs, half-expecting to hear Dona Isabella's steps behind her, but they didn't come. She reached the small sitting room still alone with her tears.

Too hurt even to flee to her room, Elena dropped into the shadowed corner of the biggest chair, her sobs now slowing to mild sniffles. He was cruel, she thought. He didn't care about her at all. He simply wanted her to be a silent submissive daughter so that he could arrange a marriage and then conveniently forget her.

The idea of marriage turned her thoughts away from Hernan's cruelty, and Elena's eyes turned toward the closed door on the other side of the room. Had he treated Celeste this way? she wondered. Or had he simply listened to the story from her mother or Dona Isabella, then made his decision and let them tell her? She hoped fervently that it was the latter, for surely her mother—or even Dona Isabella—would be kinder than Hernan Valdez.

Thinking about Celeste reminded her of how little she really knew about what had happened, and she stirred, drying the remnants of her tears on her petticoat and reaching for the shawl she'd discarded earlier. It was cold up here now that the sun had set and no fires were laid. It was time she and Celeste...

Before she could get up, the door across the way opened and Celeste came out, tiptoeing. Elena opened her mouth to call out to her, then closed it again, caught by the furtive way the girl was moving. Celeste never even glanced in her direction, but headed directly for the door, paused to look both directions, then slipped out into the dim hallway. Without thinking, Elena followed her.

Celeste moved quickly, turning away from the front of the house and descending the narrow, dark back stairs, making her way through the deserted corridors of the servants area of the *hacienda* and finally slipping out into the night. Elena, close behind Celeste, pulled her dark shawl around her shoulders and followed her friend out into the cool night air.

Celeste moved more slowly now, plainly not heading anywhere. Elena followed her for a moment, then took a deep breath. "I still think we have to talk, Celeste," she said. "I really want to help you, if I can."

Celeste jumped fearfully, squeaking a little, then she faced Elena angrily. "What are you doing here?" she demanded. "You should be in the dining room. *Cena* can't be over so early."

"I wasn't hungry," Elena said, not wanting to go into what had happened. "I didn't stay."

"So you followed me instead." It was almost an accusation.

"I know something terrible has happened to you," Elena began, "but if you'll tell me what you want, perhaps I can..."

Celeste's laugh was bitter. "Can you make the rape not have happened? Can you take the child I'm to bear? Or will you make Juan love me again? What is it you can do for me, little Elena? What do you know of the world? You are still a child. I am now a woman, and no words or kindness can change that."

Elena winced from the words, the ugliness they evoked. "I didn't know," she murmured inadequately.

"I suppose you thought, like your dear mother, that I went

out seeking someone, that I went willingly to his arms; that I cried only when I found out that I was to bear his child. Well, you can ask Margo; she found me. She took the knife from my hand before I could kill myself with it."

"Celeste! No, I didn't...I know you love Juan, that you wouldn't..."

"Juan." The word sounded like an oath. "My *gallant lover*. He talks only of knowing the man's name, so he can avenge my honor. He has no thought of me, no love left. When he looks at me, I know he sees only another man between us."

"But he is going to marry you," Elena protested, frightened by the anger in her friend's voice, the venom in her eyes. "My mother said that..."

"Did she tell you the price of this wedding?"

Elena could only shake her head, shivering not from cold, but from the shattering effect of being here with a person she scarcely recognized. This wasn't the Celeste she'd known, loved almost as her sister. This was a hard-faced stranger whose words were full of hatred, devoid of the gentleness and love she'd always given so freely.

"I'm his future in the new world. That's what he's always dreamed of. He'll be quality there, a man of property. People will look up to him and his properly-raised wife, and they'll treat us as they treated your father and you. He has the education and the manners of the aristocrats, so why not? All he lacked was the money, the gold to buy passage and to purchase a proper estate once he arrived. Now he has it. And all he has to do is take me and my child with him."

"But if you no longer love him..." Elena began, then stopped as she saw the way Celeste winced from the words.

"You know nothing of life, do you?" Celeste demanded, her tone rough with a fury that Elena didn't understand. "You don't see the ugliness of it. Or perhaps it is laughable, only I can't laugh, not any more."

"I...I don't understand," Elena admitted softly, wishing now that she hadn't followed—that she hadn't forced this conversation, since it seemed to bring them both nothing but pain.

"That's because you've never loved anyone," Celeste said, and for just a moment her face was as soft and lovely as it had always been before. Then the pain and the hardness returned. "You've never loved anyone who can no longer love you." She turned away, hiding her face in her hands while Elena watched her friend's shoulders shake with sobs.

"Perhaps later, when the baby has come and you're in a new place . . ." Elena began, without much confidence. She wanted to console her, to reassure her, but nothing she'd ever known . . .

"Nothing can ever be the same," Celeste said. "Be careful, little Elena. Never trust a man, not any man. Don't believe them when they talk of love and caring. Perhaps, in the end, the rapist is the most honest man. He takes all that he wants and walks away without looking back."

"Oh, Celeste, don't talk that way. It will be all right; it has to be . . ." Rising hysteria made her voice shake and she realized that she, too, was crying. "Please, Celeste . . ."

"Leave me alone, Elena. If you truly feel anything for me, just leave me *alone*. I can't bear to have you here."

The words had the ring of genuine pain, and Elena—not sure what to do—could only stare helplessly at the girl before her. She saw that she was shivering and, without words, she took her shawl and slipped it over the slender shoulders. "Whatever happens, I love you, Celeste," she said, "and I do want to help if only you'll tell me what to do."

Cold fingers clutched at her hand for a moment, then Celeste was gone, hurrying across the hard earth in the direction of the shadowy trees shading the drive that led up to the house. Elena watched her till she disappeared from view, then went slowly, wearily, back inside—carefully retracing the route she'd followed before. She wanted very much to be in bed, feigning sleep, when Dona Isabella came up from the dining room.

Chapter 3

JAMIE WOKE SLOWLY, sensing an unfamiliar bed even before he opened his eyes. Then he remembered and sat up, fully alert and eager. Today was the day! As soon as they'd eaten something and said their farewells, he and Ian were leaving for London.

"So you're awake, are you?" Ian asked from across the room, where he was carefully putting things into a pack.

"You could have called me," Jamie said, though a glance at the narrow window told him that it was not yet dawn.

Ian shrugged. Just past thirty, he seemed an old and wise man to Jamie, and Jamie was glad that he had been the one chosen to take him to his father. "We'll not be leaving for an hour yet," Ian said. "Your uncle will have some words to say to you before you leave his lands after all these years."

Jamie's excitement faded a little at the thought of leaving Scotland behind. His uncle had raised him as another son, and these highlands were his home. Just coming here to the southernmost of his uncle's estates had been an adventure. To think now of continuing on, of finally joining his father...

"It's never easy to say goodbye to those who've been close to you," Ian said, seeming to read his thoughts, "but 'tis time you were with your father and learning his ways. Your uncle has plenty of sons to manage his lands; your father has only one."

"I'm surprised he finally remembered that," Jamie said, hiding his uneasiness with bitterness. "Five years it's been since his last visit here. Perhaps he has other sons no one here knows about."

"He'll not seek another wife," Ian said, his blue eyes glowing. "'Twas your mother only that he loved; and when she died giving you life . . . I feared for him, lad. Followed him about even when he bid me leave him. 'Twas only for you that he stayed his hand from joining her."

"And left me for someone else to raise," Jamie reminded him, no longer moved by the story that he'd heard far too often through the seventeen years of his life.

"And what would a young man do with an infant? Your aunt had just lost a child and was eager to care for you. Your father knew his brother would care for you as his son, so he went out to seek a new fortune—and from what I saw last time I was in London, he's done well for a younger son. 'Tis into the court circles you'll be moving, so you must be proud. You're of the Clan McDonald, remember."

Jamie opened his mouth to reply, but could think of nothing to say. His memories of his father were dim after five years, and he'd never been beyond the fringes of his uncle's holdings. Ian had told him stories of London and the court, but they were like his tales of battles . . . he couldn't always be sure what was true and what came from the ale that oiled Ian's memories.

Fortunately, he was too busy to give it much thought. His belongings had to be packed to tie behind his saddle, and there were the painful goodbyes to be said. His Uncle Liam's hard arms hurt his shoulders as he hugged him.

"You remember now: if you've too much love of the Highlands to live in London, you're to come back," Liam said. "The lands are large and there's plenty here for you to share, Jamie. Fergus has chosen his way and he seems happy in the service of the English, but a true Scot of the Highlands . . ." He let it trail off, but Jamie stiffened a little at the implications.

"I thank you, Uncle Liam" he said, "but my father wishes me to join him and I'm sure he has a place for me in London."

Liam's arms still held him. "Of course he wants you," he said.

"What father wouldn't want his son beside him. But you've been like a son to me, too, lad, and I don't like sending you so far away." His rugged features softened a little and his blue eyes warmed. "I always hoped that Fergus would come back to stay, you know that. While you were here..."

Jamie nodded, feeling a prickling behind his grey eyes that shamed him a little. "I'll ask him," he said, proud that his voice didn't show his weakness. "But now I think we should go. Ian tells me it is a very long ride."

Wails from his aunt stopped further conversation, and with the hugs and kisses of his cousins and friends, he was soon hustled out into the sharp, cold morning to the place where Ian awaited him with the horses. Only one pair of arms held him for an extra moment; Edwina's kiss left his lips burning for another, and her light blue eyes were shining with tears as she whispered that she'd wait for his return.

Ian grinned at him as they cantered out of the circle of people and across the open grassland toward the trail that would take them south. "Hard to leave that little one, I'd guess," he said.

"If my father hadn't sent for me, I would have been taking her to wife," Jamie admitted, too sore at heart to hide his feelings.

Ian sighed. "You could do worse," he said. "But you're much too young to think of a wife. A man needs to live before he takes on a single woman and the raising of bairns. After you've tasted the life of London, little Edwina may seem a bit like the heather—blooming fair, but too soon just another bush to ride by."

Jamie slowed his horse and glared at the older man. "Is that why you've never taken a wife?" he asked.

Ian laughed. "Why should I make one poor lass unhappy when there are so many to give joy to?"

Jamie shook his head, his flare of anger forgotten. "No wonder my uncle warned me about you," he said.

"Warned you?" Ian looked injured, but Jamie sensed that he was secretly pleased. "What would he be saying about me?"

"Just that I should remember the lessons taught in the kirk each Sunday and not let you lead me into evil ways." Jamie grinned at him, his grey eyes as deep and placid as the highland lakes under a cloudy sky. Nearly eighteen, he was taller than Ian or his uncle, and his wide shoulders—still slightly bony—gave promise that he would be a large, strong man when he finished filling out. His dark gold hair fell in easy waves about a handsome face, and the beginning of a silky beard covered his firm jaw and stubborn chin.

"And do you plan to listen to that warning?" Ian asked, his tone teasing now.

"My uncle is a wise man," Jamie said, then turned his attention to the way ahead. "How long will we be riding?" he asked. "How many days to London?"

Ian laughed. "Such impatience," he said. "We'll be many days on this trail, but there's much to see along the way. By the time you reach London, you'll be a man, not a lad, Jamie, if I have my way."

"What do you mean?" Jamie asked, uneasy again. "I'm near a man now. I can fight with the best of them—even the dueling, thanks to you—and I trained this stallion myself, did I not?"

Ian's eyes narrowed slightly. "A man of the Highlands," he said, "but the city is different, my lad. I warned your father that you should join him when you were twelve or thirteen, but he was afraid that you'd be tainted by what goes on in the court. He wanted you to grow up on the land as he did, but now..."

"I don't understand," Jamie said.

"And I'm not the one to explain it to you," Ian said. "'Tis your father's work. I'm only to bring you to him safely."

"Did you live with him in the city?" Jamie asked, aware from past experience that he'd get no more from Ian by direct questioning. The only thing to do was to get him talking and then try to steer the conversation to the things he wanted to know.

"Aye, for four years, till you were old enough to need a man like me around you."

"What is London like?"

"Like nowhere else on earth. 'Tis never silent as the Highlands are. There are people everywhere, and buildings like you've never seen. The streets are worse than any market day and they go on and on, twisting and turning like worms in a fresh-dug clod. And the goods... 'Tis said you can buy anything in the whole world on the streets of London, if only you know where to look."

Jamie stared out at the rolling hills, the familiar lands that he'd known all his life, but he no longer saw them. Instead he tried to picture the scenes that Ian was describing. He'd been to town on market days, wandering happily through the crowds with his cousins, occasionally pausing to buy a gift from the allowance that his father had settled on him before he left the Highlands. He shook his head, unable to really visualize what Ian was saying. The towns he knew had few streets, and the land was always open and free just beyond the last small hut.

"Edinburgh will give you a taste," Ian went on. "'Twill be the first real stop on our journey. Till then we'll be camping along the trail."

The excitement faded for Jamie as they rode on. Ian was a good companion, telling him tales of the land they passed through, the battles fought on every foot of the Highlands, and those won by the Clan McDonald. But Edinburgh was a disappointment—the inn small, the streets crowded but only a bit more numerous than the towns he'd seen before. Still, he felt hemmed in there, and was glad when they could ride on south leaving the strange scents of crowded life behind once again. He liked hearing the cries of the birds and seeing the distant flashes of wild things disappearing into the trees.

There were more inns as they left Scotland and traveled on English soil, but Ian still seemed reluctant to stay in them too often, muttering about the thieves that might be under the same roof and the lice that lived in the never-aired bedding. "Better the hard earth, lad," he said, "and the clean scent of the breeze."

"I doubt that my father would agree with you," Jamie said, chafing under the boredom of the long journey. "As I recall, he's not even fond of riding for more than a few hours. He came most of the way by ship when he visited five years ago."

"Aye," Ian agreed, "and was ill a good bit of the time, as I recall. If the good Lord had wished us to travel on His seas, I think He would have given us fins and the ability to breathe beneath water. Till He does, the solid earth is good enough for me."

Jamie laughed. "Well, I hope you'll find an inn that suits us soon," he said. "I have entirely too much of the solid earth on me now, and I'd like to wash a bit of it off in water that doesn't come directly from the icy depths of the earth."

"There be a place in York," Ian said. "Tomorrow's ride should take us there, and I've some old friends in the area, too— Men I served with long ago. They be posted nearby. I've sent word ahead that we would be riding this way, so with luck ..."

York, though unimpressive, was still a change from the countryside, and Jamie looked around with real interest as Ian

led the way into the courtyard of the Golden Rooster Inn.
Shouts came almost at once as two rather sloppily dressed men
came out of the inn's main room. Ian was dragged from his horse
and pounded and hugged till Jamie wondered if he should draw
his sword and drive the two off. Finally, however, the hubbub
eased and Ian, panting slightly, turned to make the introductions.

The smaller of the two was Robbie; the elder, a vast bear of a
man, was called Tiny—and they were both well into their
drinking. Neither seemed to hear Jamie's mild protests as they
dragged him into the inn along with Ian, and in a few moments
they were seated at one of the damp tables and a bright-eyed
wench was bringing them tankards of ale.

At first Jamie felt a bit stiff in the company of the men as they
talked of times he'd never heard of before. He sipped the ale, not
truly liking the taste, but thirsty from his long ride and needing
something to do. However, as his tankard was emptied, refilled,
then filled again, he found himself relaxing and laughing at the
stories that seemed to grow wilder and wilder.

Ian shouted for food and the same pretty wench with dark
eyes and long curling dark hair brought great platters for them.
Jamie ate hungrily, then thought again of the bath he'd planned
to take. However, the idea seemed far less interesting now as the
men began talking about his father.

"You knew him, too?" Jamie asked, eager to learn more
about the stranger who waited at the end of his journey.

"We all followed him into more than one battle," Ian assured
him. "And a noble fighter he was, too, not so ready to make
concessions and compromises then."

"'Tis the influence of old Walpole," Tiny said, his tone filled
with distaste. "Peace, peace, peace, 'tis all that Englishman
knows. A man can lose his taste for honest battle serving that
kind of master."

Jamie tensed at the words, not liking to hear his father
slandered though he had no experience to refute the accusations.
Ian, however, was ahead of him. "A man serves by keeping his
armies strong and letting others bleed," he observed. "'Tis the
wisdom that comes with age, I'd say. Age and seeing too many of
your good lads lying about your feet, never to fight again."

"To them," Tiny said, lifting his tankard. "To all our fallen
comrades."

They drank solemnly, then the stories began again and Jamie

listened attentively, hoping that he would remember all the battles so he could ask his father about them when they were finally together. As the day grew later more travelers came to the inn, and soon the other tables were filled as well. A second serving wench and the inn's owner were both in the room helping with the serving.

The room grew warm and the smoke that rose from the hearth became thick and burned his eyes. He found the stories harder and harder to follow. Several times he caught himself almost falling asleep even as he tried to keep his head up.

"Lad," Ian said after a while, "why don't you go on up to our room." He waved to the serving wench. "I'm sure this little lass will not mind seeing you safe to your bed. I'll just drink a few more rounds with Tiny and Robbie. Then I'll be joining you."

Jamie tried to protest, not wanting to seem like a child, but the pretty wench was already at his side, her bright eyes smiling into his, her red lips slightly parted. "This way now," she said, taking his arm and pressing it against her side.

Jamie tried to say something to the three men, but his tongue was disobedient. In the end, he merely waved a hand as the girl guided him away from the table and across the crowded room to the stairs which led to the sleeping rooms above. Jamie studied the stairs, then shook his head. "Outside first," he managed.

"A turn about the courtyard," the wench said. "Perhaps it will help. Your friends are very fond of the ale."

"They're soldiers," Jamie said proudly. "They served my father and they were telling me about all the battles they were in."

The girl laughed. "And planning the ones that you'll be in?" she asked, moving his arm so it pressed lightly against the heavy curve of her breast. "I'll wager there will be many before you're done," she said, lifting her ripe lips and pouting at him. "A handsome young man like you will conquer more than armies, I know."

Jamie stumbled a little. His mind focused on the appealing lips. It was easy to bend down, pull her close, and kiss her in the shadows just beyond the inn door. The cold night air cleared his head a little, making him more sharply aware of the full, warm curves of her body as she pressed herself against him.

For a moment he thought of Edwina—the few kisses they'd stolen in the shed behind the house, and in the woods as they walked together. His longing made him hold the girl even more tightly. She giggled a little when he finally loosened his grip.

"I think you've had enough air," she whispered, tossing her long black hair back with a flip of her head. "Shall we try the stairs now?"

Jamie hesitated. He was feeling much better, but he dreaded the moment he'd have to let the wench go. "You'll help me?" he asked, pretending doubts that he no longer felt.

"As much as you like, sir," she said with a sauciness that made him kiss her lightly again.

"I'm Jamie McDonald," he said.

"And I'm Rosie," she replied, taking his arm more purposefully.

They climbed the stairs easily enough. Rosie led him quickly past several doors and unlocked the final one. "'Tis a private room you have here, Jamie McDonald," she said, closing the door behind them.

Jamie stopped in the darkness. "A candle?" he asked.

"Do you need one?" Rosie asked. Her hands moved warmly across his chest. "I can help you out of your clothes easily enough. There's naught near us but the bed and it be just a few steps from here."

Excitement banished the last of the ale-mists and Jamie lifted his own hands to cup the full breasts. "You'll help me undress?" he asked. "And what if I do the same for you?" He tugged at the shoulder of her low-cut dress and felt it slide away, leaving her naked to the waist.

Rosie giggled. "I think perhaps you've not had as much to drink as you pretend," she said, but her fingers moved on, unfastening his clothing and slipping it away with an ease that intrigued him. Her own dress seemed to have vanished with a twitch of her round bottom. In a moment he felt her moving against him.

For a heartbeat he thought only of his uncle's warnings about the evils of loose women. Then his head was pulled down and he was kissing Rosie as she guided him the few steps to the bed. She fell back on it, pulling him with her, giggling as they tumbled. Still he hesitated, unsure of what he should do. His aunt had kept a strict household, so there'd been no more than stolen kisses and caresses.

Rosie, however, seemed to feel no restraint. Her hands were liquid fire moving over his body, caressing and guiding him, driving him till—panting and throbbing—he claimed her. Only when his first burst of passion was spent did she slow her urging and begin again—tantalizing and teasing, taking time to suggest and guide him, staying with him till he slept once more, exhausted by her insatiable need and his own fulfillment.

Chapter 4

JAMIE MOANED AND STIRRED, reaching out a little to seek Rosie's warmth. His fingers brushed rough cloth and, at the same moment, he became aware of a loud snorting. Opening his eyes, he saw that Ian lay beside him, snoring and moaning in deep sleep.

Blinking, he looked around for some sign of Rosie, but there was none. In the dim light he could see that his clothes now hung neatly from a wall peg and a candle stump sat on a small table on the far side of the door. Had it all been a dream? he asked himself. He'd had so much ale, been so tired and confused...

He turned his head and caught a scent of flowers, the same scent that had come in a cloud from Rosie's body. He smiled in spite of the pounding in his head, and felt a swelling of desire. He looked guiltily at Ian.

The Scotsman still slept. Jamie slid out of bed and went to wash in the cold water that stood on the table beside the candle stub. Beyond the tiny window he could see the bright light of a new day and he was suddenly anxious to be on his way.

As his mind cleared he had another thought. Fearfully, he

crossed to his clothes and checked for his money pouch. Relief made his knees weak as he found it still there. A quick count told him that all the coins were inside. He was immediately ashamed of having suspected Rosie.

Should he have offered her a coin? he asked himself, remembering only dimly the way he'd finally collapsed into sleep. He'd not even heard her donning her gown to leave, thanks to the ale and the pleasure she'd given him. She must think him a real dolt to have behaved so, he thought, bitterly ashamed now.

After a moment's consideration, he took one of the coins from the pouch and, after pulling on his clothes and smoothing his hair and beard, he left his snoring friend and went down to the inn's room seeking Rosie and something to eat. Just as he'd expected, he found both.

Rosie brought him a large portion and smiled at him shyly. "Did you sleep well, sir?" she asked, her dark eyes peeking at him from behind a veil of sooty lashes.

"Better than I ever have." He smiled at her. "Thanks to the ale, I fell asleep before I could offer you this," he said, slipping the coin into her hand carefully so that no one else in the sparsely populated room saw it.

Her fingers closed quickly over the coin, but her smile faded. "It is not necessary, sir," she said rather coldly. "I'm not for hire by any man who comes in here. I went with you by choice and because I liked you, not for what you carry in your money pouch."

Jamie winced under the words, aware that he'd insulted the girl and feeling miserable. "I didna mean it that way, Rosie," he said quickly. "I thought only to buy you a gift, but I'm afraid I'll have no time. We must be off to London as soon as my friend recovers from last night. Anyway, I thought you could choose better than I would." He hesitated, then added, "It was only my way of saying thank you; last night I slept too soon."

The doubt and anger in the dark eyes faded and a bright glow of pink touched the girl's cheeks. "You're a fine gentleman, Jamie McDonald," she whispered, bending close so that her full breasts brushed his fingers. "I'm only sorry you'll not be here another night."

Before he could say anything a loud voice cut through the soft chatter of the few diners in the room. "Jamie, my lad, so there you are. Order me a portion, too, and a bit of ale to still the beasts in me head. I'll be joining you soon as I order the horses readied."

Rosie gave Jamie another quick smile, then slipped away to get the food and ale, leaving him feeling both pleased and regretful. He, too, was sorry that he'd not be spending another night at the inn.

The rest of the journey south passed quietly enough. They stayed more frequently in the inns. Occasionally, Ian would introduce him to someone that he recognized in the public rooms, but there were no more nights like the one he'd spent with Rosie.

Ian said nothing about that night and Jamie kept his peace, too, unsure whether Ian would be pleased or angry if he knew what had happened while he was drinking with Robbie and Tiny. It made him feel more a man of the world.

But as they reached the outskirts of London, his confidence began to fade. The city was like nothing he'd ever seen before.

"Where is my father's house?" he asked, looking around dubiously.

"'Tis a long way yet, my lad," Ian said. "Your father's town house is not far from the houses of Parliament and the palace. His service makes it necessary that he be easy for Mr. Walpole to contact."

There was something in Ian's tone that made Jamie turn to look at him, but the man's face was unreadable, as usual. "You didn't want to come to London, did you?" Jamie asked, remembering things that had been said through the years he'd taken Ian's company for granted.

"A true Scotsman feels at home only in the Highlands," Ian said, "but a man does what he must, my lad. Your father has need of you now, so it is only right that we come."

"What do you mean, he has need of me?" Jamie asked.

Ian straightened in the saddle. "How would I know?" he asked, but his tone was not convincing. "Perhaps it is just that he feels you should be near him now that you are a man."

The streets were very crowded and the noise and congestion grew worse the further they rode. Jamie's horse pranced nervously as the people crowded unheedingly close to him. Urchins scurried about almost beneath his hooves and dogs came out to bark or snarl at each other, paying little attention to the heavy hooves, rolling wagons and carriage wheels.

When Ian finally drew rein, it was before a line of similar houses fronting on a rather narrow side street that was quieter than those they'd passed through earlier. "This be it, lad," he said. "Give a tap to the door. 'Tis likely that your father will be out just now, but I'm sure he's left orders for our welcome."

They dismounted and, with only a moment's hesitation, Jamie did as he was bid. The door was opened at once by a stern-faced old man who eyed him coolly for a moment, then broke into a wide smile. "Master Jamie?" he inquired.

"Carlin?" Jamie asked, dimly remembering the man from a long ago time when his father had made a visit to the north country.

-   The next hour passed almost without his notice. Servants swarmed about at Carlin's ordering. The horses were taken around to the stabling area in the rear. The travelers' meager belongings were brought in and unpacked in the large room that they would be sharing for the time being. Food was hastily prepared and served. Then, at Jamie's request, a bath was prepared for him.

"You're getting mighty fancy," Ian observed as he watched Jamie drying himself with one of the warm towels.

"This is no hovel," Jamie answered tersely. He felt a little foolish now himself, but he couldn't help thinking that it was important for him to appear well dressed and confident at this first meeting with his father after so long a time. "I'm sure my father wouldn't appreciate the stains of travel and the sweat of my horse."

Ian laughed. "Are you saying that I should do the same?" he asked.

Jamie blushed a little, then shrugged. "You know his tastes better than I," he observed.

Ian sighed. "Could be you're right," he said. "Fergus has long since left the days of horses and heather. Goes about in a carriage mostly, calling here and there, talking to people, saying the words Mr. Walpole wants said."

"I'll go down and order more water for you," Jamie offered, pulling on his best suit of clothing and smoothing the tangles from his hair and beard. The young man that looked back at him from the mirror was almost a stranger, he realized. The long ride had changed him, lightening his dark gold hair and darkening his skin so that his grey eyes looked lighter than usual—or was it just that his anxiety about the coming meeting made him look older? He couldn't be sure.

He'd just reached the bottom of the handsome front staircase when Carlin opened the front door and a tall, familiar figure entered the well-lit hall. Jamie stopped. His confidence left him. Then he swallowed his fear and moved forward as easily as he could on knees that were suddenly stiff. "Father," he said.

"Jamie!" There was no mistaking the warmth and the smile that lit his father's rather stern features. For a moment, all was well. It was like the many visits in Scotland when Jamie had tried to get to know the stranger who'd left him to serve the English. His father's hug was strong and full of welcome. In a moment they were both seated in the formal sitting room of the town house while Carlin poured glasses of wine.

"A toast to your new life here," Fergus said, his blue eyes glowing. "May you find London as rewarding as I have."

"I look forward to learning about this city," Jamie said, meaning it.

"Then you've not been frightened off by the size?" His father's eyes were questioning.

"Ian assures me that it's no harder to learn about than the Highlands, though I'm not sure I'll ever grow used to the crowds. I've never seen so many people, not on the biggest market days of all."

His father's chuckle was warm. "If I have my way, a great number of those people will soon be looking up to you and calling you by name."

"What do you mean?" Jamie asked, almost choking on his first sip of wine.

"I have a fine, handsome son. I can see no reason to hide him away," his father said with a smile that seemed somehow veiled. "Now that you're finally here, I have plans for you."

"What sort of plans, sir?" Jamie asked.

His father rose instead of answering. "Where is that worthless Ian?" he demanded. "Did he turn and ride away after dropping you on my doorstep?"

"Now would I do that, Captain? Without a decent meal or a night on a bed that doesn't squirm with a life of its own?" Ian asked from the doorway.

The men greeted each other with an affection that surprised Jamie, though he knew that it shouldn't. They were old friends and his father's changed status couldn't erase all the memories that Ian had shared with him.

"You've done a fine job, my old friend," Fergus said, settling himself once again as Ian poured himself a glass of wine. "I have a son to be proud of."

Jamie stirred, embarrassed to be discussed this way. "You mentioned the plans you have for me . . . father?" He hesitated slightly over the final word, still finding it difficult to say.

"Don't look so serious," Fergus said. "They're pleasant enough. To begin with, there will be a number of social occasions when I will introduce you to the men of the court . . . and to some of the women, too. There are many people you must know before you can be of any value to our group."

There were other questions Jamie wanted to ask, but before he could frame them, his father asked Ian about the estates in the north. The two older men talked through the evening meal, which was served somewhat informally. Jamie was not excluded from the conversation, but he felt no part of it either. He was glad when his father suggested they retire early since they would be expected at a gathering the next evening.

"You'll need all your senses about you, my son," he said. "There are many people to meet and you must learn to recognize them all and to know which are of the opposition."

He was gone before Jamie could ask for more details; and, when he questioned Ian later, he had little to say that helped. "Your father serves Mr. Walpole, his Majesty's First Servant," Ian said. "There are those who do not care for the policies of Walpole and who would like to bring him down and put a man of their own choosing in his place."

"But how can I help my father in that?" Jamie asked. "I know nothing of such things. They are the concern of Englishmen, not a Scotsman."

"Your father is no Englishman," Ian reminded him coolly.

Jamie subsided, unsure of the answer to that, for his father seemed very different from the men of the McDonald Clan he'd known. He suddenly longed for the peaceful confusion of his Uncle Liam's home.

"Think of it as a battle," Ian said, "for that's what it is, though they fight with words and promises and intrigues instead of with proper swords and other weapons. Your father will teach you the ways, Jamie, if you give him time. Just don't press him. Let him tell you his plans in his own time, when he thinks you are ready. Listen and do as he bids you and you'll find your way. Were we in a new part of the Highlands, you'd follow the man who knew the land, would you not? This is no different. Here your father is the man who knows the land. We must both follow him carefully."

With those words in his mind, sleep came slowly to Jamie; but when he woke he found that everything seemed a little clearer because of Ian's advice. London was far less disturbing viewed as another part of the Highlands, and his father was less awesome as a strange chieftain bound to guide them.

One day blended quickly into another as he moved about the city with his father—listening and watching, noting the landmarks and the people with almost equal care. There were new clothes and new friends. They met daily with men whose names had been taught by the old man who'd seen to Jamie's education. And in the evenings, there were balls and parties given in the finest homes and clubs of the city.

Weeks passed. He began doing a few errands on his own—delivering messages to friends of his father, moving about the city taking care of things that his father said could be trusted to no one else. It was a not unpleasant life, but as he began to know the people and the city better, he also began to wonder if this was all his father had planned for him.

"You must be extra careful tonight," his father said as they stood in the sitting room of the house one evening about a month after his arrival in London. They were both carefully masked and dressed in frontier costumes of buckskin leggings and fringed shirts.

"What is so special about this ball?" Jamie asked, adjusting his shirt a bit, feeling rather pleased at his rugged appearance and glad that his father hadn't chosen something more dandified.

"I want you to pay special attention to one of the young ladies, Amelia Starburough. You remember her, do you not? You were introduced at the theater."

Jamie considered for a moment, then smiled. "A pretty girl with pale hair and dark eyes. She was dressed in a pink gown and looked like a little apple blossom."

His father smiled. "So she made an impression," he said. "I'm glad of that. I only hope you did as well."

"What do you mean?"

"Her family is well placed at court. Under ordinary circumstances, I doubt that your suit would be considered at all. But Amelia is a younger daughter—a month or so older than you, I believe—and with three older sisters already well wed . . ."

Jamie just blinked at his father. "What do you mean, my suit?" he asked, hardly recognizing his own strained voice.

"I've talked with her father. Her dowry, along with the inheritance your mother left you, is enough to assure your beginning to make your fortune here. Her name alone will help you in court. Her father can be a powerful ally and it is said that she is his pet, so it would be wise for you to make sure that she's responsive to you."

"But . . ." Jamie shook his head. "I've no desire to marry," he said at last.

"You are nearing eighteen and this is an opportunity that won't come again," his father said. "Why do you think I've trotted you out at every ball I could get invited to? There are plenty of eligible young men in this city and not many young girls with the blood and the family connections Miss Starburough boasts, let alone her dowry. I hardly dared hope that we would be so lucky."

Jamie felt his mouth drop open, but he was too stunned to close it. "You mean you've been showing me off at all those parties like some kind of stallion to be put to stud for your benefit?"

His father's laugh was slightly cold, but the blue eyes that regarded him didn't waver. "I wouldn't have put it so crudely, but I suppose in the end that is about right. Things are changing now, lad. I think our hold is secure with Walpole. Still, with him one is never sure. The opposition is growing stronger with the increasing talk of war. There's the future to be considered and Starburough is set in the court with or without our Mr. Walpole."

"And that's why you brought me here?" Jamie still fought belief.

"I brought you here because a son's place is at his father's side."

"I won't go through with it," Jamie said, stiffening his spine. "I'll not marry some simpering little girl because it will get me a better position at court. When I marry, it will be a girl of my own choosing and . . ."

His father's hand caught him across the mouth, stopping the

words. "You'll do as you're bid," his father said. "And you'll begin tonight by making that girl care for you, do you understand?"

Jamie stared into the cold blue eyes, his fury rising. But something made him control his anger. It was the memory of Amelia Starburough's pale shoulders as they'd looked against the delicately shaded gown. He remembered, too, the dark eyes that had looked up at him through thick lashes and the way her rather sensuous lips had smiled at him.

"She's not a punishment, lad," his father said as though he were reading his mind. "You said yourself that she was beautiful, did you not?"

Jamie nodded, his face still stinging from the blow.

"Then treat her well. You'll have to marry, and soon. It is the way of things here. She at least has beauty to offer as well as the other attributes. She's not the only girl I could have chosen for you. But the others would leave a man cold and be suited only for bearing the children you'll need to have."

Jamie opened his mouth to protest, then closed it again, remembering the girls his father must mean. He'd paid so little attention really, concentrating on learning about the men he'd been introduced to, trying to sort out the relationships and positions as his father explained them—the girls he'd noted only casually, never dreaming...

"The club we're going to is a private one and I think it will afford you a chance to take her walking in the gardens away from the chaperones. Use that chance to make her remember you when her father mentions your suit. If she will agree without trouble, you can, perhaps, have a long engagement if you wish."

Jamie nodded, still wanting to protest, but knowing now that he really had very little choice in this. He thought briefly of Edwina and her warm embrace. Then the face of Amelia Starburough filled his mind. There had been something about her...

Chapter 5

ELENA WOKE LATE, having slept poorly. Her heart was heavy with guilt and sorrow for what had happened the night before. She'd made a stupid mistake, she realized—saying too much and knowing too little; but Celeste had behaved foolishly, too, running off that way. Better to be alone in the safety of the *hacienda*, than in the night.

As she washed and dressed, she decided that she would go to Celeste immediately to try once more to talk to her—to find a way to help. However, she'd scarcely finished arranging her hair when Dona Isabella came into the room, her face dark with anger.

"Where were you last night?" she demanded without preamble.

"What do you mean?" Elena asked, hating the hot glow of blood she felt rising in her cheeks.

"This was found on the grounds this morning," Dona Isabella said, brandishing the shawl Elena had given Celeste the night before. "It was caught in the thorns of a bush—where you no doubt left it."

For a moment Elena was overcome with guilt. Then she controlled it and reached for another of the rolls that Margo had sent up for her to eat as she dressed. "I probably lost it there several days ago," she said as calmly as she could manage. "Or did I have it yesterday when I went down to talk with my mother? Perhaps one of the servants had it. I never can remember which of my shawls I've worn."

Dona Isabella opened her mouth, but her dark eyes veered from Elena's gaze first and she closed it without speaking. It was obvious that she didn't believe Elena, but that she also didn't have any proof that she was lying. "Have you eaten?" Elena asked as pleasantly as she could manage. "Margo sent so many of these rolls and they are delicious."

Dona Isabella accepted a cup of chocolate from the tray, but shook her head at the proffered rolls. "I think you should go to your mother as soon as you finish eating," she said quietly, her eyes on the view of the vine-covered hills that was visible from Elena's window.

"Is something wrong?" Elena asked, instantly alerted by the woman's tone. "Has something happened?"

Dona Isabella sighed. "It seems that Celeste has disappeared," she said. "It has caused a flurry, though I understood that the girl was to be leaving in a matter of days, anyway. Your mother seems quite distraught; perhaps you can calm her."

Elena released the handle of her cup. Her fingers had suddenly grown numb. "Celeste?" she managed to croak.

Dona Isabella's eyes narrowed as she studied her. "Is there something wrong, Elena?" she asked. "Do you know something about the girl's whereabouts?"

"I know nothing," Elena protested. Then she realized that she'd spoken too quickly, for the curiosity in the older woman's eyes changed to speculation. "You saw how upset she was yesterday, crying that way and . . ." Elena let it trail off. "I'll go to mother at once," she said.

Dona Isabella shook her head. "I don't understand all the fuss over a mere *companera*, and one that has misbehaved at that. In my household such creatures were thrown out, not offered proper marriages and the bonus of an escape to a new land; but perhaps that part of it comes from someone else."

"What do you mean?" Elena asked, aware that her *duenna* seemed to be thinking of other things all of a sudden.

The dark eyes touched her reflectively; then Dona Isabella

nodded slightly. "You are old enough to be told, I think," she said. "Celeste is with child. She claims, of course, that she was a virgin taken by force by a gentleman, but I suspect that it was a more common story."

"You don't believe her?" Elena was shocked.

"It has been my experience that girls of her type get exactly what they ask for, my dear. She is a pretty little thing and I don't doubt that there was a man of substance involved. The fact that there will be money for her husband-to-be makes that clear. However, I want you to be more careful of your own actions from now on."

"What do you mean?"

"Only that Hernan's coming here will mean that there will be many men coming and going on the various business ventures that he is concerned with. Not all of them deserve the title of gentleman and you are a young lady for all your lack of training and proper control."

"I really don't understand . . ." Elena began, disturbed by the way Dona Isabella was staring at her.

Dona Isabella seemed to shake herself and a false smile lifted the corners of her thin-lipped mouth. "It is not necessary for you to understand," she said firmly. "Only to listen to me and obey. Now you go and see if you can comfort your mother. We'll talk again."

Elena hesitated, wanting to ask more; but Dona Isabella was already on her feet and out the door before she could frame a question. Elena swallowed the last of her chocolate before following her *duenna* from the room. She went down the corridor and tapped at the door of her mother's private sitting room. One of the Spanish maids opened the door with a look of relief.

"I'm glad you've come, *Senorita*," she said in soft Spanish. "My lady is very upset this morning. Perhaps you can help her."

"Elena, is that you?"

Elena hurried to her mother, who was lying on a velvet lounge. "Right here, mother," she said. "Is something wrong?"

"Did you see Celeste after we talked yesterday afternoon?" her mother asked, her face pale in the golden light of morning.

Elena chewed lightly at her lip, not wanting to lie, but afraid to tell all the truth. "What's happened?" she asked instead of answering, unable to make up her mind.

"I didn't want to tell you, but I suppose now that she's run away everyone will have to know. The silly girl is going to have a baby. I couldn't keep her on as your *companera*, of course, but I did what I could. I even arranged for her to marry that miller's son she was always talking about. They are to have a new life in New Spain. I thought she'd be happy enough once the child was born and..." Two tears rolled down her mother's cheeks, startling Elena more than the words did. "Nadine will never forgive me."

"Did she go away with Juan?" Elena asked hopefully, her mind haunted by the agony she'd heard in Celeste's voice last night.

Her mother shook her head. Then her eyes narrowed. "You knew, didn't you?"

Elena sighed. "I overheard some conversations after I left you yesterday," she admitted. Then she added, "I don't think Celeste wanted to marry Juan... not this way."

"But where will she go? What can she do? She has nothing, she'll starve to death on her own in this land. Without money there's no way she can get back to her family in France, if that's what she was planning. She..." Her mother let it trail off, then looked up at Elena. "You didn't help her, did you?" she demanded. "Give her some jewelry or something to buy her passage?"

"She never asked me," Elena said, feeling even worse at the thought. "Is that what she wants to do?"

Her mother sighed. "I don't know what she wants and I doubt that she does. She would be better off with Juan giving the child a name, but now I suppose... When she's found, perhaps I will send her back to her family. Let them take care of her, share her shame..."

"Will she be found?" Elena remembered the bitter pain in her friend's face.

"Of course." Her mother looked up at her quickly. "Are you sure you know nothing of this, Elena?"

"I don't know where she is," Elena said. "I didn't know she was going to run away. I knew she was unhappy. I tried to talk to her yesterday after I found out, but I couldn't seem to help her."

Her mother studied her for a moment. Then she asked, "You didn't by any chance find out who is the father of the child, did you? I've questioned the servants, but they never seem to tell me what I want to know."

Elena shook her head. "Just that he was a gentleman and that Celeste was forced."

Her mother closed her eyes. "You shouldn't know such things," she said. "You are still just a child."

"Celeste is no more than a few months older than I," Elena reminded her.

"Celeste is only a *companera*, that makes a difference."

"Yes, mother," Elena said, but in her mind she didn't believe it. Celeste's tears had been real and so had her anguish. She'd come for help and instead . . . Suddenly a thought crossed her mind.

There was a place in the groves, a deep, hidden place that was not far from the *hacienda*, but still so private . . . She'd gone there often after her father's death. Many times Celeste had come with her to offer what comfort she could.

"Did you want me to stay with you, mother?" Elena asked, suddenly on fire to leave.

Her mother sighed. "No, I don't think so. I may go back to my bed. This has upset me so that I can't face the day, I'm afraid. If Celeste is found, please send her to me at once."

Elena nodded, then slipped quickly out into the corridor where she paused, unsure of her next move. Dona Isabella would be waiting downstairs, she was sure, embroidery in hand, her face stern and unbending. And Celeste . . . She thought again of the small bower near the stream which watered a good part of the orange grove. Had Celeste fled there? Could she be nestled there in the long grass trying to decide what to do, where to run?

It seemed almost a sure thing and she couldn't ignore it. If Celeste had run away to avoid marriage to Juan . . . If she truly wanted to go back to France . . . Her decision made, Elena looked quickly up and down the corridor. A maid moved between the rooms at the far end, but there was no one else in sight.

Her step was light and quick as she hurried to the rear stairs and made her way to the kitchen. She gave Margo a smile as she let herself out into the bright sunlight which flooded the rear courtyard. There were few servants about, but she soon found a groom and ordered her mare saddled. She was mounted and on her way before she had time to change her mind.

The heady scent of the blooming orange groves was almost tangible as she rode through the narrow corridors made by the thick foliage. She could hear the distant shouts of the men who had, no doubt, been ordered out to search for Celeste; but she paid little attention, somehow sure that no one would have come this way.

The ride was almost too short, and she had no difficulty finding the small glade where a few gnarled old trees rose tall and spare above the shorter bulk of the orange trees. Here the stream had eaten a passage between the rocky walls of an outcropping. Leaving her horse tethered to a nearby tree, Elena made her way carefully along the rocky edge of the stream and into the little tree-shaded nook beyond the small barricade.

For a moment she was sick with disappointment, for her eyes were on the grass that carpeted the ground beneath the single old tree that sheltered her little hideaway. Then a slight stirring above made her raise her eyes . . . and a scream twisted in her throat. She had found Celeste.

Even as her senses warned her to look away, she saw the purple face, the distorted features, the protruding eyes and tongue, the unnatural angle of Celeste's head as she dangled from the end of a leather strap. The world seemed to tilt around her. She heard screams reverberating off the rocky walls. Were they Celeste's cries? Celeste needed her! She caught her breath—and the shrieking stopped. She realized, belatedly, that her own raw, torn throat had made the sounds.

Sick and weak, she glanced once again at the slightly swaying figure hanging from the same branch where she and Celeste had once sat surveying the orange groves and the distant mountains, talking shyly of love and dreams. Knowing she couldn't help her friend, she fled back to where her mare waited, scrambled aboard the sidesaddle, and galloped away from the terrible scene.

When Elena finally tightened the reins, the mare's shoulders were wet and she slowed easily. They'd left the groves far behind and were now in the hills where only flocks of sheep moved, watched over by their faithful dogs and the herdsmen. Her eyes burned with the tears that had flowed steadily since she had seen Celeste. She was too weary to do more than turn the mare back toward the *hacienda*.

For a long time she thought of nothing but what she'd seen—the horror and sadness of it; but as she neared the *hacienda*, her own position began to enter her mind. She'd ridden off without thinking, sure that she could find Celeste and bring her back; but now . . . A glance at the blazing sun told her that she'd missed the midday meal—a fact that would have alerted the entire household to her disappearance. It was, she thought grimly, entirely likely that the men now searched for her as well as for Celeste.

The stableyard seemed to prove her thoughts, for it was even more empty than it had been when she left. A few wary chickens pecked in the dust, too lazy to do more than squawk their irritation at the mare when she stepped too near them. Cautiously, Elena rode right into the stable and slid off the horse in the welcome dimness.

No stableboy rushed forward to take the mare. Elena, conscious of her father's training and her own love of the mare, realized that she couldn't leave her in her exhausted, hard-ridden condition. Aching with her own weariness, she unsaddled the tired beast. Seeing that the final slow miles had cooled her enough, she allowed her to drink before she used the water and a cloth to wash away the worst of the sweat stains. She filled her manger with sweet-scented hay, then carried her sidesaddle back to the small room in the rear of the stable where it was kept.

She was just stepping out of the room when she heard the sound of many hooves, and voices calling. Frightened, she shrank back into the shadows, not sure what she should do. Several men came in with snorting horses.

"'Twas the ugliest thing I've ever seen," a man said and she recognized Carlos, the head stableman's voice. "The poor creature made a bad job of it. Her fall didn't break her neck and she struggled long and hard. There were marks on the tree, and her hands were all torn from trying to pull herself back up before she died."

A sob wrenched at Elena, but she was too spent even to cry any more.

"I don't know why she did it." It was Hernan, her stepfather, speaking. "Things were arranged. She would have had a good enough life with Juan, and there was money for the care of her child. This will upset the Senora terribly."

"And Senorita Elena," Carlos said, his tone strangely cold.

"Did you say that it was screaming that brought you to the place where you found the girl?" Hernan asked.

"Si, Senor."

"But the girl had been dead for hours."

"There were tracks, Senor," Carlos said. "A horse was tethered near the place and a small footprint..."

"You think the Senorita was there?" Hernan sounded concerned.

"When the... when her father died, the Senorita went often to the area and sometimes Celeste went with her." Carlos sounded rather cold, though completely respectful.

"Are you saying that Elena found the girl first?" Hernan swore, his tone so ugly that Elena moved even further back into the shadows. "She must be found," he went on, "and quickly. Her mother will need her once I tell her about that blasted *companera*."

"Her horse is here, Senor," Carlos said, his voice coming closer.

"Perhaps the Senorita is already in the house," Hernan said. "In any case, I'd best go in and give them the news." There was a sound of movement. Then it stopped; and in a moment, Hernan continued. "This is an unfortunate thing," he said, his tone showing no regret. "It shouldn't have happened, but it was the girl's choice. I would like that made clear to everyone. She was given a chance for a good future; what she did was a sign of her own weakness, nothing else."

"Si, Senor," Carlos said, his tone so proper that only Elena, who'd known him through all the years of her growing up, sensed the suppressed fury beneath it.

"You will tell Juan." It was an order.

"He already knows, Senor," Carlos said. "He was among those who are bringing her body back here."

There was another moment of silence, then the sound of retreating footsteps. Elena leaned against the wall of the small room, suddenly weak and so sick she gagged a little. So cold, so unfeeling... Celeste had been driven to this final horror and all he'd said was that she'd made a choice...

"You can come out now, Senorita Elena," Carlos said softly. "The Senor is in the house out of sight. It would be best, I think, for you to slip in the back and go to your rooms. He is right—your lady mother will need you, I think."

Elena slipped out, conscious of the pity in the weathered face. "I..."

"It was an evil thing done to her," Carlos said, "but none of your doing. Juan would have cared for her and even come to

love her, given the chance. She was wrong to do what she did."
He reached out and to her surprise, touched her sun-reddened
cheek lightly. "Your father would have wept for her in anger, for
he worshipped life and was proud to have survived many
dangers himself. It is wrong to die that way."

"She was so frightened and sad," Elena whispered.

"She should have fought for life and for her child's life. To die
is not evil, but to surrender life . . . That is a sin. Remember that
and be strong, little Elena. Now go quickly before the others
come. You don't want to see more of this ugliness."

Elena hesitated only a moment more, sensing that there was
something behind the man's words, but unable to see what it
could be. Still shaken and unsure of herself, she left the stable,
ran across the courtyard and slipped into the house. The kitchen
was empty. She made it all the way to her rooms without seeing
anyone. Even Dona Isabella seemed to be occupied somewhere
else, for which Elena was very grateful.

Throwing herself on her bed, she sobbed out her sorrow once
more. Then, drained of everything but the aching memories of
what she'd seen, she got up, washed and changed from her
stained and horse-scented gown. Feeling strangely detached, she
left her sanctuary and went down the corridor to the knot of
servants outside her mother's rooms.

Chapter 6

THE NEXT FEW days passed slowly, a nightmare unfolding painfully. Elena spent much of her time with her mother—trying to comfort her, and at the same time wondering at the way Celeste's death had affected her. It seemed strange that her mother should mourn so; she'd been willing to let the girl go with Juan, yet now...

Her own grief was deep. Too often, when she slept, she saw Celeste as she'd seen her last—her young prettiness distorted and defiled by her ugly death. Such nightmares left her so shaken that she even welcomed Dona Isabella's comforting arms in the darkness.

To her surprise, no one mentioned her riding off—or even asked where she'd been that morning. Even Dona Isabella seemed content to ignore what had happened and to try to take up life where they'd left off—she never mentioned Celeste again.

A week passed, and then another. Life seemed to be moving at much the same pace as it had before Celeste's death. Everyone seemed to have almost forgotten Celeste—everyone except Elena. Even her mother was up and smiling again, laughing with

Hernan, gaily planning for the soon-to-come trip to Mallorca.

How could it be? Elena asked herself. Celeste had been a person, and now she was gone—buried, like some favored pet, at the edge of the grove, denied even a final resting place near the church she'd attended in life. Elena found her eyes drawn too often to the distant tree tops—to the particular tree where Celeste had died—and her heart ached.

Could she have stopped her that night? She asked herself the question a thousand times. Had her words been the final push that had driven Celeste to do such a horrible thing? She knew that she could never be sure and that the fact would haunt her forever. That, and the question her mother would asked—now, suddenly, she longed to know the identity of the man who'd hurt Celeste and driven her to her death. Such thoughts kept her from truly enjoying the preparations for the trip to Mallorca, though she longed more than ever for the day of departure. Once she was away from the estate...from the still too recent memories...

As the time grew nearer, however, her mother's attitude began to change. More and more she asked Elena to come to her room in the afternoons instead of going to the *jardin* to walk and enjoy the fresh air and sunshine. She slept late and retired immediately after they finished *eena*. There was no more talk of entertaining guests or going to any of the nearby *haciendas*.

Three days before they were due to leave, Elena settled herself in a chair beside her mother's bed, a book in her lap, ready to read to her mother—as she did so often these days. However, before she could find the place where she'd left off the day before, her mother sat up to face her.

"You're very eager about this trip, aren't you?" she asked.

Elena nodded. "I feel like I have to get away from here for a while," she admitted. "Ever since Celeste..."

Her mother's quick movement stopped her words. "I can understand that," she said. "I, too, had thought that going somewhere else, leaving all the reminders..."

"It *will* be fun, won't it?" Elena asked. "I mean, going somewhere else—meeting new people."

"I think it is very important for you, dear," her mother said. "Much more important to you than to me. Your father and I spent quite a bit of time in the company of Spanish families before we moved here, so I know quite well what their lives are like. You, however, have had no chance. I think you must go if you are to fulfill the plans that Hernan has made for you."

"Plans?" Elena sensed something behind her mother's words. "What do you mean?"

"You know that he wants you to be treated as his daughter— to take a proper place in the local society."

Elena swallowed a sigh. "*That*," she said dismissively.

"Don't cast it aside, Elena," her mother said. "If you wish to marry properly—have a home of your own—it is essential that you be accepted. We had thought, your father and I, that we would make the journey back to France when you were a little older—perhaps seek there for a proper husband for you, but now..."

"I don't want to think about marriage," Elena said, thinking of Celeste. "I just..."

"You'll soon be seventeen," her mother reminded her. "At that age, I was already engaged to your father. You have to think of the future, and I believe that the trip to Mallorca will be very important to you. You might even meet someone suitable there."

"So what is so important?" Elena asked, still disturbed by her mother's tone. "We're going to Mallorca, aren't we?"

Her mother sighed. "I'm afraid that I won't be able to go."

"What?" Elena stood up, dropping the book to the floor with a crash that she didn't even notice. "You aren't going, but..."

"I've been feeling ill lately, you know that. Your... Hernan brought a physician here to examine me this morning and it is his opinion that I must stay here. I cannot make the trip with you and Hernan."

"But I...I don't want to go without you," Elena protested, fear touching her as she noted her mother's pallor. "It wouldn't be..." She sought for a word that would disguise the fact that she simply didn't want to be alone with her stepfather.

"Dona Isabella will be with you, so it will be quite proper, I'm sure. Hernan himself suggested it. He said that you'd have a good time with his cousin's children."

"But if you are ill..." Elena protested.

Her mother lay back and sighed again. "I'm not ill, Elena," she said. "It's not proper for discussion, but I suppose you must be told. I am to have a child and since you are the only one I managed to carry while your father was alive, the physician feels that I must spend as much time as possible lying down."

For a moment the room seemed to tip and whirl about her,

then slowly the shock receded and she was able to catch her breath again. "A child?" she gasped, her thoughts touched by memories of Celeste.

Her mother smiled. "I know that you are still very innocent, my child," she said, "but surely you are not too surprised. I am a new bride, after all. What could be more natural than for me to wish to give my new husband a child?"

Elena saw her mother's pleading eyes, and she tried desperately to force herself to say the proper thing. "I... I'm very happy for you," she said at last. "I'm just... surprised, that's all. I never really thought..."

Her mother's fingers were warm on her arm. "Now do sit down, Elena, and compose yourself. We shall have to talk about this journey of yours, since I won't be going with you."

Elena did as she was bid. But as she listened to her mother's words, she could feel the last of her pleasure at the idea of going to Mallorca slipping away. Dona Isabella and Hernan were still strangers to her and the idea of traveling with them to the home of other strangers and staying there...

For the first time, she wondered if—in some way—this had been Celeste's feeling. It was as though everything in her world had changed in the past year. All her dreams and plans had been wiped away and new and frightening plans were being made for her—plans in which it seemed she would have no choice at all.

Still, when the three days passed she joined Dona Isabella in the carriage which was to carry them to the boat which would take them to Mallorca. In spite of her doubts and fears, she felt a surge of excitement as they left the *hacienda* behind and began to travel beside the river, which would eventually lead them to the Mediterranean Sea.

The trip was exciting—in spite of Dona Isabella's constant talk of being a proper lady, and Hernan's distant coolness. It was only after they reached Mallorca that her worst fears were realized. Teresa Valdez—small and slim and very pretty, with dark hair and dark eyes, which were always modestly downcast—seemed the epitome of everything Dona Isabella had urged her to become. For three days Elena hated her for it. On the fourth day, however, things began to change.

Elena had been placed under the care of Teresa's aged *duenna*, Carmella, so that Dona Isabella would be free to visit her friends and family. On this morning, Teresa and Elena had left Carmella dozing on a bench as they walked slowly about the extensive *jardin*. When they were out of earshot, Teresa halted and gave Elena a long, studied look. "Do you really like this?" she asked.

"Your home is lovely," Elena said, sensing that the other girl meant something else, but afraid to say more, since she still felt very much the stranger in the large *hacienda* with its multitude of servants.

"You aren't bored?" Teresa asked, her eyes taking on a new life. "Wouldn't you like to escape for a while?"

Elena hesitated, then decided to be honest. If this were a test that Dona Isabella had planned to check her behavior, failing it could do no real harm. After three days here, being sent back to the mainland would be a treat; she longed for home. "My father used to take me riding with him," she said. "I spent very little time embroidering or making polite conversation. That's why my handwork always looks as though chickens had pecked over it."

Teresa laughed and tossed her dark hair, which had somehow escaped the neat binding placed on it. "I'm afraid I can't offer you a horse to ride, but if we're very careful, we might be able to slip away and take the pony cart into town for a few hours. Would you like that?"

"I'd love it," Elena admitted, her heartbeat quickening, "but what about Dona Carmella. She would never..."

Teresa's giggle was light. "We'll fetch her a bottle of wine from the kitchen as a gift. After the noon meal, you must plead a terrible headache and go to your room. I'll come for you as soon as it's safe, and we can slip away while everyone is resting. Dona Carmella will sleep till I wake her to dress for *cena*."

Elena swallowed hard. "You mean it?" she asked.

Teresa nodded. "My friend Estrellita and I did it several times before her parents forced her to marry Jorge and move across the island. It's exciting to go about the markets without a *duenna* always at your heels. I'll bring peasant clothes for us. Then we can pass unnoticed in the crowd on the docks."

"Dona Isabella..." Elena began, fighting her own growing excitement.

"They are expecting callers in the late afternoon. My mother told me so this morning. So they won't be looking for us at all." Teresa's eyes narrowed. "You're not afraid, are you?" she asked.

"Of course not," Elena said. "I can hardly wait."

For a moment, her hazel eyes met Teresa's brown ones. Then the smaller girl reached out and gave her new friend's fingers a quick squeeze. "I'm glad you came, Elena," she said softly. "I've been very lonely since Estrellita moved away. The *hacienda* is so big and there are no girls my age at any of the nearer places."

"I know how you feel," Elena said. "I've never had a chance to make friends with anyone my age except the *companera* my parents brought from France and she . . . she killed herself just a few weeks before we left." The words came out in a rush, surprising her. She'd promised herself to forget Celeste while she was here, and now . . .

"How awful," Teresa said. "Why would she do such a thing? Was she punished for something?

Elena hesitated. Then slowly, carefully, she told Teresa the whole story—or as much of it as she knew. Teresa's eyes grew wide at the mention of the rape and the child. When Elena finished, she nodded. "I would do the same," she said. "No one should have to bear such dishonor."

"It is a sin to take a life, even your own," Elena reminded her.

"But there should be forgiveness in such horrible circumstances," Teresa went on piously. "She was the victim of an evil man. He should be condemned, not her. She must have been shamed by it."

"If I knew who it was, I would find a way to avenge her," Elena said firmly. It was a thought that came into her mind more frequently now as her own sense of guilt at having failed Celeste began to ease a little.

"That would be exciting," Teresa agreed, "but how could you find out? The girl is gone."

"I think the cook knows," Elena said. "When I get back, I'll make her tell me."

Teresa nodded, obviously impressed, and Elena felt stronger in her resolve, though she had a feeling that forcing Margo to do anything might be more difficult than it sounded. Still, there had to be a way. Celeste had been her friend—even though she was only a *companera*—and she deserved to be avenged after all that had happened to her.

Fascinating though that idea was, the afternoon's adventure seemed still more promising and Elena was glad to be caught up in the plotting with Teresa. In some ways it made her feel better just to know that Teresa wasn't the perfect young lady she'd been told to expect; but, more important, it was exciting to be going somewhere and doing something after three days of sitting quietly about the *hacienda*.

Everything went just as Teresa had planned. Dona Carmella sipped at the wine daintily; but by the time they'd finished the light meal, the bottle was nearly empty and the elderly woman was nodding in her chair. Elena began to complain of her head at once and was casually dismissed by a wave of the *duenna*'s hand. She left Teresa solicitiously offering to assist her *duenna* to her room to lie down.

Heart pounding, Elena went to the small, but attractive room that opened off the same sitting room area that Teresa's did. She tried to lie down, but anticipation was pulsing through her. She couldn't rest more than a moment before getting up and going to stand at the window. Beyond it, the windmills turned rather lazily in the wind coming from the sea; and the silvery leaves of the olive trees were like old storm clouds billowing and rolling in every direction.

As she watched, activity about the *hacienda* slackened as everyone prepared for the afternoon resting period and, almost before she knew it, her door opened and Teresa slipped inside—a Teresa she scarcely recognized. A full skirt swirled about her ankles, and a rather low-cut peasant blouse bared her pale shoulders. Her long black hair was totally free, falling in shining waves to her waist. Except for the fairness of her skin and the delicacy of her features, she could have been a peasant girl.

"Here," Teresa said, thrusting a skirt and blouse at Elena, "hurry and change. We have to harness the pony yet and we want to be well on our way before anyone starts stirring."

Elena did as she was bid and was shocked at the girl she saw reflected in her small mirror. Her own hair was paler than Teresa's—the color of cherrywood, brown in the dimness of her room, but full of auburn highlights when the sun touched it—and her eyes were a glowing green now as they sparkled with excitement. The blouse did strange things to her rounding figure, making her look older and more mature. The top curves of her bosom were white against the darker cloth.

They tiptoed through the house in bare feet. Then they donned the light sandals Teresa had brought, crossed the courtyard, and slipped into the silent stable. It took only a few moments to harness the fat pony to the small cart. Almost before she knew it, Elena found herself bouncing along the rutted road which wound through the groves and led into the small port town where she'd arrived what seemed a lifetime ago.

As she drove, Teresa talked of the other trips she'd made with Estrellita. There had been only three, but when she talked of the things they'd seen and the people they'd talked to in the streets, it sounded so exciting that Elena could hardly keep from urging the pony into a gallop. "We'll go to the waterfront this time," Teresa said. "I've never been really close to the little shops that line the area and I've always wanted to see them. My father says it's no place for a proper girl—but he says that about any place I want to go."

"It looked very interesting when we landed," Elena agreed, remembering how hopeful she'd been at first—and how disappointed she was after she met Teresa. She giggled. "I'd never dream you were the same girl I met the day we arrived," she said, eyeing her companion.

"Neither would I," Teresa said. "You looked like a sheep following cousin Isabella. Every time she said anything to you, you jumped as if she'd poked you."

Elena blushed. "She kept telling me that I must be careful not to disgrace my stepfather by acting like a wild foreigner."

"You were born in Spain, weren't you?" Teresa asked.

Elena nodded.

"Then how can you be a foreigner?"

Elena shrugged. "That's just what Dona Isabella calls me whenever I do anything that she doesn't approve of."

Teresa giggled. "Then we're both being wild foreigners," she said. "Cousin Isabella would never approve of this."

The town was stirring from its afternoon slumbers as they drove in. Once the pony was safely tethered in a protected area, they set out on foot, mingling with the crowd. They had only a few coins each, but it was fun to wander in and out of the stalls that lined the streets. Elena felt very much like a peasant girl— haggling with one woman over the price of a bit of lace that she had no desire to buy. However, the challenge soon faded as cries of "ship at the dock" led them in the direction of the waterfront.

Here the streets were narrower and the crowds thicker, which made walking more difficult. When Teresa suggested a short cut through a rather narrow alleyway, Elena was glad to agree. "You can see the ship from here," Teresa said, pointing down the dim alley. "See? There are people getting off the ship already."

They hurried out of the throng into the relative quiet of the alley, picking their way carefully—the ground was foul with litter from the close-hanging buildings. They'd gone about halfway when a door opened and a man stepped out in front of them. Elena hesitated as he loomed up between her and the end of the alley.

"Well, well, well, what have we here?" he asked, clutching at her arm. "And what might you be doing in my alley?"

"Let go of me," Elena said, jerking back. But the fingers only tightened. She caught a strong scent of spirits on the man's breath as he moved closer to her.

"Oh, no, not till I've had a good look," he said, grabbing a handful of her hair and forcing her head up to face him.

"Stop it! Let me go!" Terror made the words almost a scream. Elena was dimly aware of Teresa shouting something and swinging what looked like a broom handle at the man. For a moment she was free of his grip as he turned and swung a powerful hand at Teresa, sending her rolling into the building on the other side, where she quivered once, then lay still.

Shock held her. Before she could recover, the man's hands reached out and grabbed at her shoulder, tearing the blouse away so that it fell, leaving her heaving bosom bare. "Just what I thought," the man laughed. "A fair beauty just wandering along looking for me." His dirty fingers touched her pale flesh and Elena began to scream.

Chapter 7

THE CLUB WAS a surprise to Jamie. On the outside it appeared much like the other buildings on the street—a bit larger, perhaps, but no more brightly lit or imposing. Still, all the carriages ahead of them seemed to stop at the same door and the passengers alighting from them were mostly in costume, too. In the quick flares of light that showed each time the door was opened, many of the guests appeared quite elaborately masked.

"There is much that goes on here that is spoken about nowhere else," his father said, claiming Jamie's attention. "That is a rule we all abide by and I'll expect you to respect it. Is that understood?"

Jamie nodded, wondering what his father was getting at. "You've already told me not to talk about what I see and hear," he reminded his father. "Why would I think tonight any different?"

His father's smile was thin and humorless. "Because you may see things tonight that you have never seen before and . . . There is much that goes on in the court circles that I don't approve of, Jamie, but I've learned my place well. Your own behavior is your responsibility and I'll expect you to remain a gentleman. But what *others* do . . ." Again he let it trail off. "We'll talk about it tomorrow, if you feel we must. But it is best to regard what happens beyond that door as existing only there and not even think of it once you leave."

Jamie would have liked to ask questions, but before he could, they were pulling up at the door. In a moment they stood and were scrutinized by unseen eyes behind a small peek hole carved in the heavy wood. His father said nothing. After a moment, the door opened and they were admitted by an immense man in livery. He bowed, called them by name and waved them along the hall, closing and bolting the door behind them, though Jamie knew that there were more carriages already pulling into position at the door.

His father hesitated for a moment, then turned away from a handsome staircase that rose at the end of the elegant entry. "A drink in the salon first," he said. "Then perhaps a bit of gambling would be in order."

Jamie followed him, noting the handsomely costumed crowd that moved lazily about the huge, softly-lit salon. Several people he recognized in spite of their masks, and only a few who were without masks were total strangers. Still, except for the carefully guarded entrance, it appeared to be much like the other parties he'd attended with his father. His thoughts turned more to what he'd been told his mission would be here tonight.

A quick survey of the crowd showed that none of the dainty ladies had the long pale golden hair he remembered so clearly from his meeting with Amelia Starburough. Still, he studied the women and girls with more interest now, wondering which others his father had considered. It was a strange and rather unpleasant feeling to realize that someone else was making such an important decision for him . . . and that he was really nearly powerless to fight it.

The drinks were quickly served and his father was soon in deep conversation with a gentleman in the costume of a Harlequin. Jamie listened for a short while. Then he moved away, drawn by the distant sound of feminine laughter. Just because his father had made plans for his future didn't mean he had to accept them, he told himself. Perhaps he would find someone else tonight—someone he could really care about—and together . . . He thought of Edwina with a pang of sorrow.

He would have to send word somehow, he told himself. Perhaps Ian could take a note to her when he returned north.

"McDonald?" the male voice was smooth and Jamie recognized it as belonging to a young man he'd met at an earlier party. Turning, he was met by cool green eyes. "I thought it was you in buckskin," Daniel Hempstead murmured with a smile.

"Well, hello. Sorry I didn't notice you before," Jamie said. "How have you been?"

They exchanged pleasantries for a moment; then Daniel sighed and set down his glass. "Feel like trying your luck a bit?" he asked.

"Why not?" Jamie said, aware that his father considered Hempstead a proper acquaintance, had even urged him to make friends with the young man. "Is your wife ...?" He gestured at a group of young women who were gathered just across the room, realizing that he couldn't remember Lady Hempstead at all.

Daniel laughed. "Surely you don't think she'd come here," he said. "She might happen to see her father. That would cause an explosion, sure enough."

"Sorry, I didn't realize ..." Jamie said, feeling young and awkward—and hating it.

"Your first visit, isn't it?" Daniel asked, his expression softening slightly. "Well, enjoy it. That's what this club is for ... enjoyment."

"Everyone seems to be having a good time," Jamie agreed, adding his empty glass to the group on the ornate sideboard. He followed Daniel through the crowd and across the large entry to the staircase. A glance over his shoulder told him that his father had noted his leaving, so he went up the stairs in good conscience.

They passed several gaming rooms without even slowing. Then Daniel tapped lightly on a closed door. "Special game," he said with a wolfish grin. "Better stakes, I think."

The door was opened and Jamie was whisked into a very dimly lit room. It was small and quite warm. No one seemed to notice as they edged close to a small table where a slender brunette was drawing cards.

"One more chance, Jennifer," a man called from across the table. "You top my cards or you're mine for an hour."

The girl giggled, touched a card, hesitated—then moved to another card. She was lovely, Jamie thought. Her cheeks were glowing; her blue eyes were sparkling in the light which shone directly over the table. Finally she selected the card and turned it over. The young man groaned.

"Want to wager again?" the girl asked, her reddened lips curving into a teasing smile.

"Oh, come along," a vaguely familiar female voice said, "let someone else try a hand."

Jamie looked to his left and recognized the delicate form of Amelia Starburough. Tonight she wore a draped Roman gown of pale blue. It clung lovingly to her surprisingly ripe form and left her upper arms and throat shimmering in the light. Her dark eyes ranged over the crowd—then seemed to settle on him.

"How about you, Jamie McDonald?" she said, her eyes challenging. "Will you wager against me?"

Jamie gulped slightly, but before he could say anything, he was being propelled to the edge of the table by Daniel's strong hands. "Of course he will," Daniel said. "Isn't she worth a wager, my friend? A hundred pounds against an hour of her time."

Again Jamie tried to speak, but the general hubbub gave him no chance. An old man picked up the cards, shuffled them expertly, then swirled them once again on the pale cloth of the table. Amelia made no move to touch them. Instead, she languidly smoothed her upswept hair.

"What do you say, Jamie McDonald?" she asked. "Is that your wager? Or do you think the price is too high?"

"Your marker will be sufficient, sir," the dealer said softly, offering him paper and pen.

"Done," Jamie said, suddenly pleased that it might cost his father a hundred pounds. He'd been ordered to impress this girl, so how could he refuse? He signed the paper with a flourish, then looked across at Amelia. "What do I do to gain an hour of your time?" he asked.

"We draw five cards," Amelia said, "one at a time, alternating. If I have the higher total, I win your money. If you have the higher total, you have me for an hour . . . wherever you choose." The final words were spoken more softly and Jamie felt the surge of desire that they were meant to rouse.

"May Lady Luck be with me tonight," he said. "Draw away."

Amelia shook her head. "I prefer that you go first," she said, her sharp little tongue flicking at her lips in anticipation. "I want to know what I must draw."

Jamie bowed his head slightly and chose a first card. "Ten points," the dealer said. "A good beginning."

Amelia laughed and drew. "And ten for me," she said, smoothing her hair again with a graceful hand.

Jamie drew a five and then an eight. Amelia managed a three and another ten. His fourth card was a nine, hers an eight. His hands began to sweat a little as she leaned forward, her gown dipping so that he could see the swelling curves of her breasts. An hour with her... anywhere. He thought of the garden his father had mentioned and his hand shook a little as he made his final draw.

"Another ten," the dealer announced. "A total of forty-two points. Miss Starburough will need a joker to win."

A whisper of sound went through the small crowd. Amelia reached out, lifted a card—then dropped it back. "I surrender to Lady Luck, Mr. McDonald," she said, lowering her head. She looked at him through the fringe of her eyelashes. "I am yours for an hour."

Nervous giggles came from the three or four young women who stood among the predominantly male crowd. Several of the men pounded him on the back and Daniel leaned close. "Take her to the garden," he advised in a whisper. "That is the usual way."

Jamie took Amelia's arm. "You'll have to show me the way to the garden," he said softly. "This is my first visit here."

"But not your last, I'll wager," Amelia said, handing him the torn up bits of his marker. She pressed his arm tight against her side and he could feel her heart beating beneath it.

"If you can guarantee that I'll always have such luck," he said.

Her laugh was his reward, and in a moment they were out a second door. Amelia guided him along a narrow balcony and down some stairs into the dimness of the gardens, which, he assumed, were carefully secluded and enclosed by the high brick wall he'd noted once when he passed this way with a message from his father.

The gardens were discreetly lit by small, low, shaded candles which marked only the crossing of paths. As they walked, Jamie heard an occasional giggle from the shadows, but he saw no one at all. Should he lead her off the path? he asked himself. Did he dare to steal a kiss now that they were alone? Had the girl on his arm been Edwina, he would not have hesitated, but Amelia was a lady and...

"Shall we sit for a few moments?" Amelia asked, breaking into his thoughts. "There is a bench in a little bower just off the path here, I'm sure." She guided him easily off the path and across a small area of grass into a shadowed bower. The scents of flowers filled his nose. He could barely make out the pale outline of the bench that nestled in the concealed spot.

"Isn't this better than walking?" Amelia asked when they were settled on the bench.

Jamie smiled at her. "You seem to know this garden well," he said, acutely self-conscious. He was not able to think of a bit of the small talk his father seemed to find so easy.

"I've walked here before," Amelia said, her tone suddenly cool. "The gardens are most appealing in the daylight when the flowers are visible."

Jamie felt the glow of a flush in his face, realizing that he had—once again—said the wrong thing. Yet how could he apologize? Instead of speaking, he took her hand and raised it to his lips. "I'm honored to have so lovely a guide on my first visit," he said.

"That's sweet," Amelia answered, her voice warming. "I'm only happy that you won and could bring me here. I've wanted a chance to get to know you better. Did you know that our fathers are talking about a match between us?"

Jamie stiffened slightly, shocked that she should mention it and also more than a little intrigued by the way she seemed to have moved closer to him. He could feel the warmth of her body against his side and, almost without thinking, he slipped an arm around her shoulders. She snuggled even closer.

"Would you like that, Jamie?" she asked.

"I...I wouldn't mind at all," Jamie managed, forgetting entirely what he'd said to his father earlier. "I think I'd like it."

Amelia looked at him. Her lips parted slightly, and her dark eyes were mysterious pools in the fair oval of her face. In a moment Jamie found himself kissing her. Her lips moved under his, parting, yielding in a way that sent his pulse racing even more. For just a moment he considered pulling away her flimsy gown and...

He forced himself to release her, straighten his shoulders and move away from her warmth. "My apologies, Miss Starburough," he stammered. "I was carried away by the moment and my own good luck at being here with you."

"As was I," Amelia said. "And please call me Amelia, Jamie. If we are to be betrothed..." She moved closer to him again, looking up through the fans of her eyelashes. "Perhaps it isn't even wrong for us to get a bit better acquainted out here. Once the word is out officially, we'll be watched so closely, but now..."

Her movements were suggestive and he could feel the hardness of her breasts through his buckskin shirt. Had she been a tavern wench like Rosie, he'd have had no doubt about what she wanted, but Amelia was a lady and... He drew away again. "I think perhaps we should walk some more," he said. His voice was a little rough with desire.

"Oh, come now, Jamie," Amelia said, her arms slipping around his neck, her lips tantalizingly near his. "You don't really want to go walking again so soon, do you? You have a whole hour of my time out here. If we go back too soon, the others will wonder."

For a moment he almost surrendered to the temptation. Then the stern warnings he'd heard on Sunday in the kirk—and his uncle's firm counselings—rang in his ears. He reached up and gently removed her arms, getting to his feet. "I think we'd better be careful," he said as firmly as he could. "No matter what our fathers decide, we are not wed yet."

For several seconds she sat still looking up at him, her mouth sulky, her eyes strangely fixed, then she rose with a sigh. "I had no idea that Scots were so shy," she said, her tone derisive. "Well, if I must, I must."

Jamie opened his mouth to ask her what she meant, but before he could find the words, her hand shot out and he felt sharp agony as her fingernails dug into his cheek. Half in shock, he stepped back, swearing.

"Help! No, you must not! Please don't!" Amelia shook her head wildly. Her fair hair cascaded to her shoulders which were suddenly bare as she pulled her dress forward and down, leaving only the thin material of her undergarment covering the proud thrust of her breasts. She tore even that as she continued to scream.

Footsteps sounded on the stones of the path and before he could turn away, she threw herself at him, going limp, so that he instinctively caught her to keep her from falling. Almost at once a lantern nearly blinded him and two men came into the bower.

"Father," Amelia whimpered, pulling herself away from him and stumbling into the arms of an older man. "Oh, thanks be to God that you came in time."

Jamie opened his mouth, but no words came out. He saw only the outraged expressions on the faces of Amelia's father and Daniel Hempstead. "You brute," Daniel said, his tone ugly. "If I had known what sort of man you were, I would never have allowed..."

"Young man, you deserve to die for this," Mr. Starburough snarled. "My poor little girl...She's no tavern wench to be brutalized this way. I'll have you horsewhipped. I'll..."

Amelia moved away from her father, looking infinitely desirable in the glow of moonlight, for she'd done nothing to cover herself. "No, father," she sobbed. "Please, I came here with him...I...Perhaps he misunderstood."

Her father glared at her for a moment. "Cover yourself, child," he snapped. Then he turned back to Jamie. "What have you to say for yourself?" he demanded.

"I'll challenge him," Daniel said before Jamie could answer. "I'll defend your honor, Amelia. I'll teach this upstart that we don't allow decent ladies to be treated this way."

"Now, I don't..." Mr. Starburough began, but Amelia was ahead of him.

"Oh, please, no. Perhaps it is foolish, but I...I still care for him. All men are beasts at times, and perhaps...Please, father, if we could just become engaged this night, then if there is talk...No matter what happens, my reputation is soiled. No decent man would make an offer for my hand now, and..." She seemed to dissolve in a flood of tears, while Jamie continued to look at her without a word, unable to make any sense out of what was happening.

For a moment he wondered if he was losing his mind. Had he, in a moment of passion, torn her gown? Could he have dreamed that stranger who scratched his face and pulled at her own gown, screaming and tearing her clothing while he watched open-mouthed?

"Are you sure this is what you want, Amelia?" her father asked. "We could keep it quiet, I'm sure. No one here would speak, and..."

"Please, father." Her gown was miraculously back in place now and only her disheveled hair remained as a reminder. "The trees in this park have ears and people would laugh and whisper..."

Mr. Starburough sighed, then looked at Daniel. For a moment no one spoke. Then he nodded. He turned to Jamie. "You get away from here," he snarled. "I won't have you near my daughter till the ceremony has taken place, is that clear? And if you speak to anyone of this..."

Jamie swallowed hard, his senses still reeling. "But...I..." he began.

Daniel stepped between him and Mr. Starburough. "Be glad the poor girl is so willing to forgive," he hissed angrily. "I'll show you out. Then perhaps your father and Mr. Starburough can talk in one of the private rooms here."

"Thank you, Daniel," Mr. Starburough said. "Will you make the arrangements? Then I'd be very grateful if you would summon my carriage for Amelia. I'm sure she will wish to go home at once."

"I will see her safely to your door, sir," Daniel said, bowing to Amelia. He took Jamie's arm and half led, half dragged him out of the bower and along the path, leading him toward a rear gate which gave access to the street where coaches and carriages were parked awaiting their owners.

"Daniel, I..." Jamie began, but Daniel shook his head.

"A man gets carried away," Daniel said with a knowing grin. "Amelia is a very tempting woman, I know. Just be grateful that she is also in love with you. Her father could do you a great deal of damage if she weren't so willing to forgive."

"But..."

"Go home now," Daniel said. "I'll see that your father makes the right arrangements; don't worry."

Jamie stood for a moment, watching the man's retreating back. Then he shrugged and moved off among the carriages, seeking the one that belonged to his father. After what had happened, he was suddenly very anxious to go back to his father's house and the uncomplicated company of Ian and the servants—he'd had enough of the Club and the Starburoughs.

Chapter 8

THE HOUSE, HOWEVER, was not quite as welcoming as he'd expected. Carlin admitted him and produced the drink he ordered, but Ian was nowhere about, having gone off to amuse himself for the evening. Jamie longed to go up, remove his costume and climb into bed, but he knew that he couldn't. Once his father talked to Mr. Starburough, he'd come home expecting to be told what had happened.

Jamie settled himself on a large couch and leaned back. And what would he tell him? Sitting here in the peaceful room with a blazing fire before him, what had happened seemed too unreal— more like a dream than truth. He felt a quick surge of desire at the memory of Amelia Starburough standing in the moonlight, bare to the waist and sobbing, when only a moment before she'd practically offered herself to him, and ...

Involuntarily, he raised his hand to his face, feeling the scratches that he'd cleaned so inadequately at the horse trough before he found the carriage. He shook his head. They proved that his memory of the scene was correct, but made it no more believable. Why had she picked him out of the crowd, teased him into the wager, and gone with him so willingly? And why, when he'd been trying to act like a gentleman, had she changed into a tiger?

There were no answers in the bottom of his glass and the strong spirits—which he'd rarely tasted before coming to London—had almost lulled him to sleep when a stir outside told him that his father had arrived. Uncertain and a little worried, he got to his feet; he wished now that he'd gone up and properly cared for his face. The scratches burned like a brand on his cheek. He knew that they would give credence to the story his father had been told.

"So you're here," his father said, his face dark and angry.

"Where else would I go?" Jamie asked, surprised by the words.

"Perhaps after a tavern wench, since your appetite seems to be turned that way."

"I..."

"Don't tell me about it," his father snapped, before Jamie could protest. "I've heard the story from Starburough." He shook his head. "For a man who has deflowered every wench his wife has employed, he seems mightily upset over what happened to his daughter."

"Nothing happened to his daughter," Jamie said. "I kissed her, nothing more."

"And she did that to you for one kiss?" His father's tone was derisive. "From your face, you'd have done better to keep your hands to yourself. You're very lucky the girl cares for you; you could have been called out for what you tried to do. Girls of Amelia Starburough's position are never treated that way, no matter how they might seem to ask for it."

"I know that, sir," Jamie said, trying hard to control his own feelings. "That's what I'm trying to tell you. I did nothing to the girl except kiss her. She seemed to expect more, but I..."

"My Lord, lad, don't lie about it. I heard the story. Starburough himself found you holding her, her gown mostly torn off. The girl was heard screaming by half the company, I think. You're just lucky that she finds you so appealing in spite of your unbridled ways."

Jamie opened his mouth to protest again, but something about his father's face stopped him. It was obvious that he wouldn't be believed, no matter what he said. That knowledge hurt him far more than the scratches that throbbed on his cheek.

His own father held him in contempt—considered him little better than an animal...

"Go to bed," his father said. "The engagement will be announced tomorrow evening. It will be a short engagement, I promise you. The sooner you two are wed, the less talk there will be. You have shamed me, but perhaps it can be salvaged if you behave yourself from now on. You will. Is that clear?"

Jamie nodded, humiliated, angry, and frustrated by his own inability to clear himself. It was wrong, he thought as he climbed the stairs slowly and wearily. Something had to be done. He would marry the girl, but first she would have to clear his name with his father, at least. To be thought of as no better than a drunken lecher in a tavern...

Jamie slept late and was relieved to find that his father had already gone when he finally rose and ate his morning meal. Ian was also absent, leaving him far too much time for his thoughts. The more he considered the events of the previous night, the more sure he was that he must speak with Amelia. If they could just talk, perhaps...

He dressed himself in his most correct attire and ordered his horse saddled and brought around. He would just pay a call, he decided. Correct or not, a man had the right to see his fiancee on the day their bethrothal was to be announced—and he had every intention of doing just that. Since Amelia had been the only other person in that bower, she was the only one who could tell him exactly what had happened and—more important—why.

The Starburough house was only slightly larger and more imposing than his father's, but there was a lovely little park across the street from it, which made it most desirable. Jamie rang after only a little hesitation, and was admitted at once. However, it was another young lady who joined him in the sitting room.

"Hello," she said, "I'm Penelope Starburough, Amelia's cousin."

Jamie bowed over her hand politely, noting that though she was pretty, she lacked her cousin's exceptional coloring—golden hair and dark eyes. Penelope had soft brown curls and wide blue eyes.

"Are you truly going to marry Amelia?" she asked with childlike candor, though Jamie guessed her to be close to sixteen.

"The engagement is to be announced today," Jamie said.

"That's why I wanted a few moments alone with her. There are a few things we didn't have time to discuss last night."

Penelope nodded. "It is so romantic. Amelia has promised that I can be a part of the wedding."

Jamie felt a prickling of impatience, but held it in check, aware that the girl would soon be a part of his family and that he was already in enough difficulty with the Starburoughs. He needed no more enemies. "Is your cousin receiving guests today?" he asked gently.

"Oh, I'm sorry, that's what I came down to tell you. She's in the park with her maid. She likes to take a bit of air at this time of day. I used to go with her, but now she says that she wants to be alone." Penelope sighed. "I'm sure you can have your conversation there, if you go now."

Jamie left with a feeling of relief. It would, he thought, be best to see Amelia away from the formidable Starburough home. The park—in sparkling sunlight—seemed an ideal place. He left his horse and began prowling up and down the pathways, seeking Amelia.

After nearly half an hour of walking, he slowed his pace and looked around. He had covered nearly all the paths and had seen no sign of Amelia. Should he turn back? he asked himself. Perhaps she'd already returned to her house and was even now awaiting his arrival and their conversation. He started back along the path. Then he stopped as a familiar burst of laughter reached his ears.

"You're terrible," Amelia Starburough said, her tone warm enough to send shivers of desire down his spine.

Jamie looked around. He spotted a narrow path that he hadn't explored. He moved along it slowly, halting behind a large bush. Beyond it he could see the honey gold of Amelia's hair as it fell over the folds of her bright green shawl. But more than that, he saw the bulk of a man sitting on the bench beside her. The man pulled her close, kissing her passionately.

For a moment Jamie considered moving in on them; but before he could, the man released her, laughing. Jamie went cold, recognizing him as Daniel Hempstead. "I don't believe you," Daniel was saying. "No man could resist you so easily."

"That icy Scot could. One kiss and I was sure he'd do all I wanted, but then he pulled back and started muttering like an old maid. Do you know I finally had to tear my own clothes? And the look on his face!" Her laughter was cruel.

"So long as it worked, I don't care how it was done," Daniel said. "Jamie's not a bad sort. He'll be good to you and to our child."

Amelia laughed. "He might even believe that it's his," she said. "if the marriage can be arranged quickly enough. I shall become pregnant on our wedding night and take to my bed soon after. I can always go to the country for the birth and stay there long enough to still the wagging tongues."

"Perhaps I can arrange to visit near your father's country place," Daniel said.

"But of course," Amelia answered, her arms going around him with a casualness that made Jamie's head spin. "My having a husband means only that we'll have to be more careful, my love; Jamie may prove a bit less blind than your obliging little wife."

"But we'll manage," Daniel said, growing hoarse with passion as his arms tightened and his lips found hers. "I'd never be able to live without you, my Amy. You're in my blood now."

Jamie stepped back, unable to watch any further. Rage pounded through him and he longed for his sword. Had he worn it, he would have stepped around the bushes and challenged Hempstead at that moment, but without it . . .

He leaned against a tree, the whole incredible scene moving through his mind like an ugly dream. It explained everything— her teasing, her sudden change of temper, even her attack and hysterical screams for help. She was no better than a whore, he thought bitterly—Daniel's whore, carrying his child.

Still shaking a little with rage, he left the area and crossed the small park to his waiting horse. He mounted and headed home. *This* he would tell his father. Then perhaps the whole thing could be put to rest. One thing was sure—he was *not* going to marry Miss Amelia Starburough; of that he was positive.

His father returned late in the afternoon with Ian at his side. His face was grim and weary as Jamie stepped out of the sitting room and confronted them both. "I have to speak with you, father," he said.

"Not now," Fergus said.

"I think there is something you must hear," Jamie insisted. "It has to do with what happened last night."

His father's face hardened a little, but he sighed and went into the sitting room. "I hope you have finally decided to be man enough to admit what you did," he said.

"I told you what I did," Jamie said evenly. "Today I went to talk to Amelia, to ask her to explain her behavior last night."

"You *what*?" His father looked outraged. "If you've undone all the good I've done today..."

"I didn't speak with her," Jamie said, frustrated by the turn the conversation was taking. He sensed sympathy from Ian, but his father was as implacable as always. "I saw her, but she didn't see me."

There was a moment of silence, then his father asked, "What is that supposed to mean?"

Jamie took a deep breath. "She was in a very compromising situation with Daniel Hempstead and they were talking."

"And, of course, you stood and listened like an upstairs maid," his father said, his tone cruel.

"Only long enough to learn that the lady is expecting Hempstead's child. Last night was all arranged so that I can give the bastard a name."

For a moment something flickered in his father's eyes and Jamie felt exalted. Then they hardened into ice-bound blue lakes. "I don't believe it," his father said. "You're still attempting to get out of this marriage because of that girl in the Highlands. Starburough would never be a party to such a thing—not against me."

"It's the truth," Jamie said. "They were even making plans to continue their affair after Amelia and I are wed."

His father swore and turned away.

"That's not going to happen," Jamie said coldly. "I won't marry her, father. I'll not be so shamed."

"You'll do as you're told," his father thundered.

"Perhaps there's an easy solution," Ian said. His tone was conciliatory, even as he gave Jamie a wink.

"You believe this tale?" Fergus asked.

Ian shrugged. "There's an easy way of proving it," he said.

"What do you mean?"

"If the girl is carrying a child, nature itself will give her away in a month or two."

"They are to be married by then," Fergus said. "I spoke with Starburough this morning and he says the girl wishes the wedding to be as soon as possible."

"For obvious reasons," Jamie put in coldly.

"Silence!" his father thundered. "This mess is your doing, not mine."

"It would be worse if the lad's telling the truth," Ian said. "Think of the laughing that would go on. People will certainly count the months, and if they are too few..."

Jamie held his breath, hating to have it done this way. He was angry at his father's distrust, and hurt by it. But he was still willing for anything to be done to keep him from the marriage.

"What are you suggesting?" his father asked Ian.

"Even today Mr. Walpole asked you to send your most trusted messenger to carry his words to a friendly agent on Mallorca, did he not? And what messenger would be more trustworthy than your own son?"

Fergus walked away from them to the window which looked out on the street. He stood there a long time. Then he sighed and turned back to them. "If you are lying and make Starburough my enemy, you'll regret it, lad," he said.

"I've not lied to you in any of this," Jamie said, feeling the blaze of anger in his face and with it the renewed stinging from the scratches. "I have no need to lie."

His father sighed. "The engagement will have to proceed as it is planned," he said, "but I'll see to arrangements for you. If you can be on a ship within the week, I think that I can make Mr. Starburough believe that the orders came directly from Walpole." His smile was without warmth. "Even he can't question that authority."

"And when her condition becomes obvious?"

"That will be his problem, not mine." Fergus set down his empty glass. "Now I must go up and change. This little situation will take some fine work and I've very little time to handle it." He glared at Jamie, then turned his angry eyes on Ian. "For the present, I think you had better accompany my son whenever he leaves the house. It appears that he is very much in need of a keeper to see that he doesn't involve himself in further difficulties."

"It will be my pleasure," Ian said politely.

They stood in silence till Fergus had disappeared up the stairs, then Ian turned to Jamie. "Suppose you tell me everything that happened," he said. "I've heard several versions so far and none of them sounded like you."

For a moment Jamie stood tense and angry, wishing that it had been his father who'd asked instead of Ian. But his father didn't trust him even that much. He didn't even want to hear his side of what had happened.

Ian listened without questions to the entire recital, then nodded. "From what I've heard in some of the less posh areas, I'm inclined to believe you. Her reputation isn't very good. She's done a very clever job of this and if she doesn't show herself carrying a child, you'll not be able to escape, no matter what you know. The Starburoughs are a proud family, and if they think you've dishonored her..."

"What am I to do?" Jamie asked.

"Perhaps our voyage to Mallorca will take longer than planned," Ian said. "Winds are always uncertain and there may be a return message to wait for..." His smile lifted Jamie's spirits more than anything had since the scene in the bower the night before. It was almost enough to ease the pain of his father's rejection and distrust.

Chapter 9

THE DAYS PASSED with surprising speed, but Jamie's dour mood didn't lift. He avoided his father whenever possible, content to spend the days with Ian. There was, in truth, much to be done to prepare for their journey.

Clothes ordered for his life in London were put away and lighter clothing prepared. Ian was dispatched to find someone to teach them both Spanish during the voyage and a slim, rather dandified man came several times to instruct Jamie in the culture of the Spanish people that he would be visiting.

"Is all this necessary?" Jamie complained to Ian several days before they were due to sail. "Surely if I'm just to carry a message to someone . . ."

"Have ye paid no mind to all of your father's words?" Ian asked. "'Tis more than just a message he's trusting you with and I'm sure you know it."

"He talks on and on about the danger of war and how the country needs peace, but I've heard that man Jenkins, too. What the Spaniards did to him was shameful. Our honor is at stake and the Spanish need a lesson."

Ian snorted, obviously unimpressed.

"It was an awful story," Jamie insisted. "You should have seen the poor man, wearing that heavy, out-sized wig to cover his ear. You know the story, don't you?"

"A part," Ian murmured.

"His ship was captured by the Spanish coast guard, who were little better than pirates, and searched for treasure. When they didn't find any, they began torturing the men."

Ian nodded. "I've heard of their skill," he said. "They've a fondness for making men into eunuchs."

Jamie winced at the thought. "In Jenkins' case, they threatened to scalp him as the red Indians of the colonies are known to do; but his hair was too short, so they cut off his ear instead."

Ian laughed. "Could be he preferred to lose his ear," he said. "At least he's still a man."

"He carries the ear with him," Jamie went on. "Even let me touch it when I bought him a tankard of ale. It made me want to take my sword and..." Jamie let it trail off for a moment, remembering only too clearly how he'd been impressed by the slightly drunken old sailor with his tales of trading in New Spain and the Caribbean.

"'Twas all a very long time ago," Ian said. "If there was to be a war with Spain, it would have been then. I've heard it said that Jenkins has two ears like anyone else; that it's all a tale to fill an ale tankard."

"And the man the Spaniards gelded like a beast, is he still a man?" Jamie demanded coldly.

"I'm sure your father takes no pleasure in hearing you talk like that," Ian said mildly.

"My father may believe as he likes," Jamie said coldly. "I'm sure he hasn't the slightest interest in what I think, since he'll not take my word above that of a girl who's no better than a whore."

Ian laughed. "So that's the burr beneath your saddle," he said. "You'll have to admit that your tale was an unlikely one. A prim little lady tearing off her clothes to trick the likes of you into marriage when her father could find any number of young gentlemen more than willing to make an offer for her hand."

"You believed me." Jamie stated it coldly, angrily, the pain of that betrayal of faith still hurting his pride.

"Aye—but then I've known you since you were too small to wipe your own nose."

"He's my father."

"And he'll believe you soon enough," Ian said, getting up. There was a trace of impatience in his voice. "Once the truth becomes obvious, he'll see the error of his ways and he'll trust your words as I do. He's risking much by sending you away like this. Starburough is in a positive lather about the postponement of the wedding."

"Do you think he knows?" Jamie asked, curiosity winning over his distaste for the whole discussion. He'd not seen Amelia since the day in the park, but he was vitally interested in what was going on, since his own future was very much involved.

Ian considered for a moment, then shook his head. "His talk was too strong. The man is no better than a beast himself, so I doubt that he could rage about purity so much if he knew the truth. 'Tis said his bastards are supported all about the countryside and even the older, uglier maids aren't safe in his house when he's had too much to drink."

Jamie shook his head. "Amelia is his proper child," he said. "Perhaps I should have taken what she was so ready to offer."

"It would have ended the same way," Ian said, "only you'd not have been able to slip away so easily. As it is Starburough can only complain of the taint to her reputation and, though he isn't happy, he can't really make too much trouble about delaying the wedding a month or two since your father has made it plain that you will return as soon as possible to marry her."

"Never," Jamie said coldly.

"That is our secret for now," Ian said. "Your father has finished the arrangements. We'll be traveling to join the *Fleet Lady* tomorrow in the company of a Mr. Corona. He's to be your instructor and mine, too, I suppose."

Jamie sighed. "What sort of person is he?" he asked without much interest. The journey held little promise for him except as a way to prove his truthfulness and avoid the trap that Amelia had so cleverly set for him.

"An old man. He worked as a scribe and translator for one of the big merchant firms. He's ready to retire and wants to go to Mallorca for the sun and because it was his home as a child. Says he's been saving for it most of his life. So when your father offered him free passage in return for his teaching services..."

"I suppose it will pass the time," Jamie said without enthusiasm.

Ian nodded. "You'll be glad of it, I suspect," he said. "I've made a few trips on the water, and the days can be endless."

Jamie scarcely responded. His thoughts turned again to the night that had trapped him into this journey. He'd been a flattered fool; but she'd looked so seductive, so challenging, he'd been unable to resist her. His cheeks flushed at the memory of her advances and his own cold withdrawal. Protecting her innocence—what a joke that had been. And still, as Ian had said, it was lucky, for if he'd taken her as he had Rosie...

Anger and frustration made him think longingly of a war with Spain. How much better to be on a mission against the ports of New Spain with their bulging hoards of gold. He pictured himself with sword in hand avenging poor, drunken Mr. Jenkins. He'd cut off more than their ears, he thought grimly, and there'd be no foolish talk of marriages if there was a war to be fought.

They sailed with the tide on a grey day—much to Jamie's relief, for he feared to the last that Amelia would find a way to keep him in London and force the marriage. The *Fleet Lady* had been a real surprise. A tall, three-masted ship, she was built more for speed than for carrying cargo. The three waist cannon that lined each of her sides and the bronze swivel gun on her stern castle proved that she was able to take care of herself, too. For the first time a little excitement began to banish Jamie's depression.

His pleasure was short-lived, however, for the moment they left protected waters, the ship's pitching began to make him regret all the hearty meals he could remember. Too sick to do more than wish for death, he settled in the cramped and musty-smelling cabin. There he stayed for three long, miserable days.

Ian came to him regularly with food and drink—all of which Jamie refused with moans of pain. Finally, on the third day of their voyage, he accepted a bit of broth and kept it down. Ian watched him and nodded. "You're over the worst of it now, my lad," he said. "Rest a bit and I'll bring you a more substantial meal. You'll be needing to get your strength back."

"It does seem better," Jamie agreed. "Were we in a storm or something?"

Ian smiled. "'Tis just the same, Jamie, but now you have your sealegs, so it won't bother you unless we run into a real storm."

Jamie shook his head, unable to believe his friend, but too weary to argue. Still, he forced a weak grin. "I was even beginning to think it would have been better to have stayed and married Amelia," he confessed.

"You weren't *that* sick," Ian said with an answering grin. "What you need is fresh air and some sunlight. You're pale as a girl. Once you've eaten, you'd best go on deck for your studying with Mr. Corona."

So the days of the voyage passed. Jamie, at first reluctant, soon caught the lilt of the Spanish language and began to enjoy the lessons. He quickly surpassed Ian in spite of the man's lessons while he was ill. By the time they'd passed into the Mediterranean and were approaching Mallorca, Jamie spoke at least a broken Spanish and could make himself understood quite well.

"Most of the homes that welcome you will also have a knowledge of French," Mr. Corona assured him, "so if your Spanish is not adequate..."

"My French will do much better, I think," Jamie said with a smile. He'd come to like the quiet little man. "But the Spanish will at least help in the inns and with servants."

The little man nodded. "The more languages a man knows, the richer he is," he said. "I was very lucky to have learned your language as a child. That gave me a chance to rise to an excellent post in your country. I can now retire in Mallorca's warm sun and enjoy my last years without worry."

"I would like to help that retirement," Jamie said, offering the man a small pouch of coins. "You have done me a good service by telling me far more about your country than the man my father asked to inform me, and I am grateful. If my mission is successful, you will be a part of the reason."

The little man muttered slightly, flustered by the words, but as Jamie left him, he knew that Mr. Corona had been pleased, too, and that the coins would be a help in the days ahead. Jamie went below to gather his belongings and to change into more formal clothing for their landing.

"You'd better leave that here on the ship," Ian counseled as Jamie picked up his sword.

"What do you mean?" Jamie asked. "This is a foreign port and the Spanish may well be our enemies, so..."

"You can't fight the entire island with one sword," Ian said, "so it would be best not to start the battle, don't you think?"

Jamie hesitated, aware that the words had merit, yet still half-wanting to find trouble. "But to go unarmed..."

"You have your dirk in your boot, do you not?" Ian asked. Jamie nodded.

"Then I think you'll be safer not offering a tempting target. And don't forget—a man who knows the language of the land has the advantage when he doesn't let others know of his knowledge."

"Meaning?"

"Only that you'll overhear a great deal more if no one knows that you understand what you are hearing." Ian grinned. "That is a principle I plan to put into action in the town's busiest tavern the moment I get off this ship, and I would advise you to do the same. I wager we'll learn a great deal more about the temper of Spaniards there than you will in their fine drawing rooms."

Jamie sighed. "You do as you like," he said. "I think I'll take a little walk first. It will be a treat to tread on something that isn't eternally shifting."

Ian laughed. "You'll never make a sailor, lad," he said. "And I'm grateful. It's not a life I'd choose for meself either."

They laughed easily together and when the ship finally was at the dock, they went ashore together. They enjoyed the sensation of solid ground beneath their feet. The air was rich with the much-missed scents of life and growth and civilization. As promised, Ian headed for the nearest tavern, and Jamie, after a glance inside, moved on along the street.

Conversation went on all around him, but he soon realized that he was understanding no more than a word or two, for the people spoke too quickly and their accents were often quite different than the precise tones of Mr. Corona. Sighing, Jamie relaxed, just enjoying the sights and sounds of the port, no longer caring what he might or might not overhear.

He'd just turned from one section of the waterfront to another when he heard a scream—a woman's voice, crying for help in French. He hesitated only a second as his ears placed the direction of the sounds. Then he headed for the alley way that opened off the street he'd been following.

It took his eyes a moment to adjust to the lack of light, but he quickly saw what was happening. One girl lay on the ground while the second, a tall wench with a cascade of brownish hair, fought with a huge lout of a fellow. He'd already torn her blouse away, revealing startlingly white and appealing breasts, and was now trying hard to pull her skirt away as well.

The girl was fighting like a tiger, though obviously

weakening. The man's face showed the marks of her nails, and his arm was welling blood from what looked suspiciously like the marks of teeth. "You there! Stop that at once!" Jamie shouted in his best Spanish.

For a moment the two struggled on. Then the man lifted his head, still holding the girl against him. "Go find your own wench," he snarled in street Spanish.

"This one has no desire for you," Jamie argued, well aware that he had no right to interfere, but also feeling the draw of the girl's surprisingly bright green eyes. "Let her go and find one that is willing."

The man's face twisted into even deeper ugliness, and Jamie sensed that he wasn't going to give in easily. The man began to swear in short, vicious breaths, using words that Jamie didn't recognize, though their meaning was clear. Slamming the girl against the wall, the man charged at him.

Jamie was gathered and ready. He stepped aside easily, slipping his dirk from his boot as he turned to face the man. A sudden kick in the shins kept the lout off balance and Jamie moved behind him to rest the blade of the dirk at his throat. "I said let her alone," he repeated coldly, moving the knife just enough to draw a single drop of blood.

"Yes, sir," the man whined, all the fight suddenly gone. "I didn't know she was yours. Came down my alley, practically offering herself at my door, and..."

"Get out," Jamie ordered, withdrawing his dirk enough to allow the man to move away.

"Yes, sir. Yes, sir. She's all yours, and good riddance, too." The man scuttled away, his vast size seeming reduced by what had happened.

Jamie waited till he disappeared beyond the end of the alley. Then he slipped his dirk back into place. He turned to the girl then, only to find her bending over the second girl, shaking her.

"Teresa, Teresa, wake up, please," she was sobbing, tears running down her cheeks. "Oh, please, Teresa."

"Take it easy, Senorita," Jamie said, noting again her pale skin and, of course, the loveliness of her half-naked body.

The girl looked up, and her eyes grew wide with terror as she tried ineffectually to cover herself with the remnants of her blouse. "Oh, please, sir, I... I'm not what he said. We were just going to the docks to watch the ships and he..."

"Are you French?" he asked, realizing that she was still speaking that language, not Spanish. As he spoke he slipped off his cloak and settled it lightly around her shoulders. "I won't hurt you," he added. "What happened to her?"

"I think she hit her head. She was trying to help me and he hit her, and..." Fresh tears streaked the girl's cheeks. "Teresa. Teresa."

The girl moaned and stirred, then suddenly sat up, her dark eyes full of terror. "Elena?" she screamed.

"It's all right," Elena said, reaching out a soothing hand. "I'm right here."

"The man...?" The frightened eyes rested on Jamie.

"He's gone, Senorita," Jamie said, realizing that this girl was no peasant either, despite her poor clothing. "You are quite safe now. How do you feel?"

"Elena, he didn't...?" The girl turned to her friend.

"He tore my blouse beyond repair, that's all," Elena assured her, speaking flawless Spanish now that her friend was awake. "This gentleman heard my calls for help and frightened him away."

"This is no place for you two," Jamie said, his patience wearing a little thin now that the danger was past. "If you are feeling better, Senorita, perhaps I can see you both safely to your home."

Silence fell over the alley way, and Jamie could clearly hear the sounds from the streets on both ends and even a stirring in the shadows where a rat or other small creature scuttled. The girls exchanged glances. Then Elena helped Teresa to her feet.

"You are most kind, sir," Teresa said, "but that won't be necessary. If my friend can just keep your cloak until we reach my father's house, we will be glad to send one of the servants back with it. We are most grateful for what you did, but..."

Anger flooded up in Jamie's mind. "Of all the..." he began. Then, trapped by his inadequate Spanish, he switched to French, sure that Elena at least would understand him. "You two aren't safe in the streets. Haven't you learned anything by what just happened? If I hadn't come along that man would have..." He stopped, aware of the burning red in the fairer girl's cheeks, Elena's cheeks. He noted the way it extended over the creamy flesh of her shoulders to the bit of her stomach that he could see as she clutched the cloak about her.

"It would only cause you trouble, Senor," Teresa said. "We have a pony and cart that we'll be safe enough in, I'm sure, and we'll go right home."

Jamie glared at them both, realizing at once that they were afraid to have him escort them, yet not sure why. "Let me at least see you to that cart and safely out of town," he said stubbornly. "Elena is scarcely well dressed in that cloak."

Again there was an exchange of glances. Then Teresa nodded grudgingly. "I don't wish to be rude," she said. "but it would be wrong for you to take us home, please believe that."

"Oh, I believe it," Jamie said. He remembered what Mr. Corona had told him of the custom of *duennas* watching over young ladies of marriageable age. "Your parents don't know about this, do they?"

Both girls looked miserable. Then Elena shook her head. "It would be better if they never find out," she said softly. "If you would be so kind. Where should I send the cloak?"

"Have it delivered to the *Fleet Lady*," Jamie said, smiling at them both. They reminded him of Edwina and his girl cousins. "Now where is the cart? I'll go along with you till you're safely out of town; and I'll say nothing about this if you'll promise me that you'll never do it again."

For a moment Teresa looked rebellious, then her dark eyes dropped. "I don't think I would want to," she said softly. "It was so awful, and if you hadn't come . . ." She was still shivering a little when they left the dimness of the alley and stepped out into the late afternoon sun.

Jamie escorted them through the streets, then followed the pony cart till it was well on its way along a road out of town. As he watched them go, he sighed, wishing that he'd asked their full names or found out where the fairer one lived. Elena, he thought, tasting her name—Elena, with the cherrywood hair and the eyes that changed from flashing green to a soft and warm hazel when they met his.

"Perhaps," he observed to a patiently standing donkey, "the Spanish are more interesting than I thought." He headed back toward the docks with a light step, eager to tell Ian about his adventures and to find out what his friend had learned in the tavern. There were, he remembered belatedly, still some arrangements to be made. He must get in touch with Esteban Valdez as soon as possible if he was to deliver the messages his father had entrusted to him.

Chapter 10

IN SPITE OF their fears, Elena and Teresa reached the *hacienda* in safety and were able to slip back to their *salas* without being seen. Only then, when she was completely alone, did Elena take off the cloak and look at herself in the mirror that adorned one wall of her room. What she saw brought the color of flame to her face and breast.

She thought of the tall, golden-bearded young man. He'd seen her this way—seen her as no man had since she was a child in her father's arms. For a moment she was only ashamed. Then slowly she studied her swelling figure, and, in spite of her shyness, she wondered what he had thought. Had he found her attractive?

"Elena?" Teresa's voice forced such thoughts away and Elena hurriedly pulled on fresh underclothing as her friend entered. "I'd better send one of the servants with the cloak," she said. "We don't want anyone seeing it and asking questions."

"I wonder if we'll ever see him again," Elena said thoughtfully as she bound her hair up again and smoothed down the skirt of her gown.

"I doubt it," Teresa said. "He is a foreigner, probably just in port for a day or so. Such persons are rarely invited to our *hacienda* unless they have an introduction from someone." Teresa picked up the cloak, then turned back, her dark eyes quizzical. "He was handsome, wasn't he?" she said.

"Very," Elena agreed. "And he did save me, Teresa. It was so awful. If he hadn't come that man would have . . . I would have been like my poor friend Celeste."

Teresa shuddered. "And I, too, no doubt," she said. "I think perhaps I won't make such trips any more. Dona Carmella is dull, but at least with her I would have been safe."

Elena nodded. At the same time, she thought of the stormy grey eyes that had looked at her so strangely. Though she'd been terrified, now that she was safe . . . If they hadn't gone, she would never have even seen the handsome, golden-bearded stranger, and she had a strange feeling that she would have been sorry not to have known him even for those few terrible moments.

"I'll go get rid of this," Teresa said of the cloak. "Then I think we should go wake Dona Carmella. It must appear that nothing has changed, and that we've been resting later than usual, you know."

Elena nodded, touching the cloak once more before she let Teresa take it. How she wished that she'd asked his name instead of being so careful not to tell her own. Even a memory should have a name. She thought of calling after Teresa and having her ask the servant to make inquiries—then shook her head. She must forget him, she told herself. It would be best if she forgot the whole incident . . . and the sooner the better.

For the rest of the day and the next morning, she managed fairly well, though the man's face had haunted her dreams through the night. Several times she woke, shaking with fear as she relived the horrible moments in the alley way; but each time he came to her rescue, and she stood again with his cloudy eyes on her body and heard his hesitant Spanish and excellent French as he offered comfort.

It was late morning, nearly time for the noon meal to be served. Elena sat with Teresa on the paved area just beyond the main *sala*, enjoying the still cool air and the sweet scents of the surrounding *jardins*. Dona Carmella dozed on a bench near them, but seemed completely uninterested in the progress of their needlework, which pleased Elena, for hers showed no sign of improving.

There was a flurry of sound from inside the *hacienda*, but neither girl paid any attention. Maria and Dona Isabella had left earlier to visit old *amigas* and Elena had seen little of her stepfather or Teresa's father except at the evening meal. However, in a moment there were voices in the house and Elena straightened as she heard Esteban Valdez say, "I would like you to meet my daughter and our guest, Senor McDonald. They will entertain you for a few moments, while I put these papers away."

Elena turned, her best shy smile already in place, her head down so that she had to look at him through the thick forest of her eyelashes. When she did, her heart seemed to stop beating and she heard no more of the introductions. It was him! The man from the docks now stood on the paving stones, bowing politely, greeting them as though he'd never seen them before.

Esteban remained for several moments, making polite conversation. Then he excused himself, carrying with him a packet that he seemed to have received from the young gentleman who—Elena now knew—was called Senor McDonald. She felt his eyes on her and knew that she must be glowing as scarlet as any of the flowers that grew in the *jardin*.

Teresa seemed in better condition, for she rose. "Would you care to stroll a little, Senor McDonald?" she asked. "I'm sure my *duenna* will not mind so long as we stay where she can see us."

"I should like that very much," he said.

Elena moved with them, still too numb to speak. Teresa waited till they were well out of Dona Carmella's hearing, then stopped. "Thank you for not saying anything," she said. "When I saw that it was you . . ."

His laugh was easy and the grey eyes seemed to warm as they turned to Elena. "You were no more surprised than I, Senoritas," he said. "I never dreamed that I'd had the honor of saving such carefully guarded flowers."

Teresa's smile faded. "We did a foolish thing," she said. "One we will not repeat."

Elena tossed her head, slightly angered by his tone. "We only wished to wander in the shops and to see the ships arriving at the docks. We had no idea . . ."

Jamie looked around and nodded. "I'm pleased to have saved you, and I thank you for returning my cloak so promptly."

They strolled some more. Teresa asked him questions while Elena could only watch him and feel the pulse beating in her throat whenever his arm lightly touched hers. She alternately blushed at the memory of all he'd seen and chafed at her own

shyness. She longed to attract his attention away from Teresa—
to hold his eyes and his thoughts for even a moment.

Esteban returned with Hernan and ended the pleasant
moments by claiming all Jamie's attention. Elena poked at her
embroidery, pretending to watch her stitches, but instead her
mind was busy listening to the men's talk. Jamie was some sort
of courier, she learned, bringing messages from men in Britain.
There was talk of war, of New Spain, of trade and ships, and of a
man called Walpole.

Hernan, strangely enough, seemed more interested in Jamie
himself than in the messages he'd brought. He asked him a great
deal about his family, his connections, even his plans for the
future. To this Elena listened avidly, trying to picture the world
Jamie was describing. She'd read a little of Britain and her father
had told her what he knew, but still...

"Will you be remaining in Mallorca long?" Hernan asked
casually as more wine was poured.

"Perhaps," Jamie said. "My mission was to deliver the papers
to Senor Valdez. Now that I've accomplished that, I think I
should like to see a little of your land, perhaps even travel in
Spain, if that can be arranged."

"I'm sure it can," Hernan said, smiling warmly. "In fact, I
would be honored if you would consider a visit to my *hacienda*.
We will be returning in two or three weeks and I know that my
dear wife would enjoy the distraction of a guest. She was sad to
miss this journey, and a diversion..."

Elena's heartbeat quickened as she felt the grey eyes touch
her face. She heard him accept the invitation. She tried to
picture what it would be like if Jamie came to the estate. If it had
been her father making the offer... She pictured herself riding
out with him, showing him about the vast lands; but with
Hernan... Still, if he came, there would be the long evening
meals and perhaps strolls in the *jardin*, and...

"I would be honored to visit you," Jamie said. "You've been
so very kind to me."

There was much more conversation. In the end, Jamie left
only after promising to return for the *cena*. Teresa led Elena up
the stairs for the afternoon rest with a teasing smile. "I hope you
like Senor Jamie McDonald," she said.

"He is very charming," Elena said cautiously.

"So it seems," Teresa said with a giggle. "At least your
stepfather seemed to find him so."

"What do you mean?"

"I think he is planning a match for you," Teresa said.

"What?" Elena stopped in the middle of the corridor to stare at the other girl. "I don't ... You mean..."

"There is no other reason for him to wish to invite a stranger to visit. You must know by now that he thinks little of foreigners. My father has made some welcome here, but I've heard them talking, and Cousin Hernan is not fond of people from other lands."

"My mother came from France," Elena said, trying to think as her mind whirled halfway between fear and excitement.

Teresa merely shrugged. "Perhaps I'm wrong, but I don't think so. I have two older sisters, and I remember well the questions that were asked when their prospective husbands came to call."

"But he is British," Elena protested. "From so far away."

"Then you must refuse to go along," Teresa said. "Pretend that you hate him. Perhaps you can have a terrible quarrel with him before you leave here. I'm sure Cousin Hernan wouldn't force the match if you truly dislike him. Or Jamie might decline the invitation himself, if you don't get along." She tossed her head and her dark eyes were suddenly quite wise. "There are many ways to get what you want, Elena," she said. "I know I shall make sure that I choose my own husband, though of course my father will believe that he has done it."

Elena sighed, feeling her inadequacies once again. "But if Don Hernan has already made up his mind..." she began.

"Perhaps he is just thinking about it," Teresa said, "but I suspect we will be seeing a great deal of Senor Jamie for the next few weeks. I'll even wager that he'll be invited to the big *fiesta* next week."

"*Fiesta*?" Elena paused at the door of her room. "I didn't know there was to be a *fiesta*."

Teresa rolled her dark eyes heavenward. "I am an idiot," she said. "It was to be a surprise for you and for Cousin Hernan and Cousin Isabella. You must not tell them, and *do* pretend to be surprised when you're told about it, or I shall be in trouble. It's to welcome you here and to give Cousin Hernan and Cousin Isabella a chance to see more of their old *amigos*. There will be fifty or sixty guests, gypsy dancers, a show of horsemanship in the afternoon, and music, a great feast, and ... It'll be marvelous, you'll see."

Elena lay on her bed, but sleep didn't come. Her mind was too full of what Teresa had said. Sometimes she believed her. Other times, she was sure that she must be mistaken; but mostly she just thought of Jamie McDonald, remembering everything he'd said and done in their two meetings. What did she feel? she asked herself. What would she do if Teresa were correct? How did she really feel about him?

The next few days seemed to prove that Teresa's guess was correct. Jamie McDonald was a frequent guest—sometimes alone, sometimes with an older man he introduced as his friend and companion, Ian Turner. She and Jamie were together often—always well chaperoned, of course, but still allowed to stroll or sit in the *jardin* and visit. Every moment they spent together became precious to Elena.

She tried to obey all the advice she received from Teresa, from Dona Carmella, and even from Dona Isabella, who seemed interested, too; but mostly she just listened to Jamie, and wished that she dared ask him the things that really interested her. She wanted to know about his life, what he planned to do. Would he be content to be his father's courier, or did he long to return to the Highlands that he sometimes discussed so lovingly?

And what did he think of her? Did he mean the compliments he inevitably paid her, or was he merely being polite? Did he ever remember those moments in the alley when she'd stood before him half-naked? Did his heart leap when he saw her, as hers did when he was shown into the *casa*?

The day of the *fiesta* dawned clear and lovely. The *casa* had been decorated for a full day—the party was no longer a secret. Even as she rose to drink her morning chocolate and eat the rolls the maid brought, Elena could smell the scents of a dozen different foods being cooked in preparation for the feast. From her window she could see the curling smoke that rose from the fires in the gypsy camp beyond a row of trees. She stood at the window, staring across the trees, almost afraid of this day.

Tonight, perhaps during the *fiesta*, she would have a chance to be alone with Jamie, she was sure. She remembered only too well the excitement and confusion that had reigned at the *fiesta* Hernan had arranged at their *hacienda*. She and Celeste had been alone and unsupervised much of the time.

The thought of Celeste saddened her and she turned from the window. Was that part of the reason she was so willing to consider marriage to a foreigner? she asked herself. Was it because she felt there was nothing for her at the *hacienda* with Celeste dead? She didn't think so, but still, how could she be sure? Perhaps tonight something would happen, something that would end her doubts. She sighed and returned to her morning meal.

Guests began arriving early, having come from distant parts of the island. There were many people to enjoy the cold buffet that was served outside at noon; and the *casa* didn't settle into its usual somnolent state afterward, for there were still many comings and goings. No one seemed much inclined to sleep away the hot hours of the afternoon.

Elena moved about the house and grounds with Teresa, watching everything and everyone, doing her best to imitate Teresa's attitude and actions; but always watching for Jamie's arrival. When he came, however, she was in the *jardin* and she didn't know he was there till a hand touched her shoulder.

"Will you walk with me for a while, Elena?" he asked, his voice low, sending shivers down her spine.

"Oh, Jamie, I didn't know that you were here," she breathed, looking up into his clear grey eyes and seeing something there that she hadn't noticed before. There was a challenge to his gaze.

"Where is the lovely Teresa?" he asked, his tone slightly mocking.

"Greeting some old friends, I believe," Elena said, fighting a quick twinge of jealousy. "If you wanted to see her..."

"You mean we are to be alone?" Again his tone was mocking, and she smarted under it.

"My *duenna* is over there," Elena said with a wave of her hand.

"I'm sorry," Jamie said, "I'm just not used to your customs. In the Highlands a lad and his girl could walk or ride together without being watched so closely. Do you ride?"

"My father took me everywhere with him," Elena said, as he tucked her hand beneath his arm and led her down one of the little paths that wound between the flowers and shrubs of the carefully tended *jardin*. "I didn't have a *duenna* until my mother remarried."

"You managed to evade her once," Jamie said, his eyes caressing her in a way that made her face burn with the memory. "I'm sorry," he said again. "I don't seem to be able to say anything well today."

Elena said nothing, sensing that something was troubling

him, but afraid to ask what it might be. Finally, after several minutes of silent strolling, Jamie stopped by a bench. "Shall we sit here for a while?" he asked.

"I'd like that," Elena said, noting that the late afternoon sun was well shielded from the bench by an old tree and that the area was rather secluded. "Perhaps then you'll tell me what troubles you today."

They sat in silence for a while. Then Jamie squirmed. "Your father called on me yesterday," he said.

"My stepfather?" Elena was startled. "But what...? Why?"

"He didn't talk to you first?" Jamie looked surprised.

Elena shook her head. "He never speaks to me except for politeness," she said. Then she was instantly ashamed. "He's kind, of course, but Spanish fathers... It is just different between us than it was when my real father was alive."

Jamie caressed his carefully trimmed beard, his eyes no longer on her, but focused on some distant corner of the *jardin.* When he finally spoke, he might have been talking to a tree. "He came to tell me that he has settled a large dowry on you. I think that he would like us to marry."

Elena opened her mouth, but no words came as she looked up at him. For several seconds, he evaded her gaze, then slowly his eyes came down to hers. He plainly expected her to say something, but she couldn't speak. After several minutes, he drew her gently into his arms and his lips found hers. The world seemed to tilt around her and, in one breathless second, she knew that there was no longer a question of her feelings. She was in love!

Chapter 11

THE NEXT FEW hours were the happiest she'd known. Her response seemed to have been enough to satisfy Jamie's questions, for he smiled at her and held her gently afterward. "Would you be afraid to go to England with me?" he asked after a while.

"No, I'm not afraid," Elena said. "But what of your family? Will they be angry if you bring home a foreign wife?"

"There is only my father," Jamie said, "and he'll be pleased, I'm sure." He brushed her lips lightly again. "Now, let us walk some more before someone decides we're hiding from them and makes trouble."

The evening flew by. No one seemed to care that she spent most of her time with Jamie. Even Dona Isabella smiled benignly in her direction as Jamie took her arm and guided her from one scene of the festivities to another.

Hernan's pleasure seemed to lead him on a new course, Elena noted. He was a different person to her—laughing and drinking, putting his arm about her shoulders and calling her his little girl. He seemed so pleased, that she tried to overlook the strong

liquor scent that hung about him when he hugged her for the
fourth time before he went to watch the gypsy dancers, who were
entertaining the late crowd in the *jardin*.

"I must be leaving," Jamie said. "I have some urgent business
to take care of tomorrow morning, and if I am going to visit your
family in Spain . . ." His fingers caressed her cheek. "Besides, it's
growing very late and I'm sure your *duenna* will soon be sending
you inside. You're far too lovely a young lady to be wandering
around in the darkness."

"She won't need to send me inside," Elena said. "When you
leave, I'll go willingly."

His pleased laugh told her she'd said the right thing and his
gentle kiss left her glowing as she made her way back toward the
crowd around the well-lit dancing platform. She would find
Teresa and tell her the news, she thought. Then perhaps they
could go upstairs together and talk about this wonderful,
heavenly evening.

As she neared the crowd, however, she saw that one of the
gypsy girls had just finished her dance and was leaving the
platform, while another jumped up, her fingers snapping, her
full skirt swirling high about her legs. To her surprise, her
stepfather detached himself from the crowd and moved after the
first girl, stumbling a little in the rough grass when he left the
path.

Elena frowned. He'd had too much to drink, that was
evident; but what should she do? She looked around for
someone to help her, but the faces she could see were mostly
unfamiliar.

She looked after her stepfather again and saw that he'd
stopped the dancer, and was apparently talking to her. Perhaps
he would be all right, she thought; the dancer would send him
back to the crowd in the *jardin* and . . . But two men seemed to
materialize in the glow of the gypsy campfires. Her stepfather
turned away from the girl to go toward the groves instead of
coming back to the *jardin*.

Elena watched him for a moment, hoping that he'd turn, but
he didn't. Remembering that the land beyond the groves was
broken by deep ravines and other traps for the unwary, she
sighed and left the protective glow of the lantern and torch-lit
jardin to hurry after her stepfather.

The pulsing beat of the gypsy music quickly faded as she left
the *jardin* and made her way across the rougher ground. She

reached the grove of olive trees, where she paused, not sure exactly which way Hernan had gone after he'd entered that shadowy world. She heard a crashing in the brush off to her left, and a muffled curse. Sure that it would be him, she turned that way. She tripped on a root as she fought her way between the smaller trees.

It was much darker here in the grove than she'd expected. The ground, uneven from the windmill-fed irrigation system, caught at her feet, making her passage nearly as noisy as her stepfather's. Elena tried to call out to him—to ask him to wait for her—but she couldn't catch her breath. She stumbled around the gnarled trunk of one of the older trees—and strong hands caught at her.

"So you *did* like the sound of my offer," Hernan chortled, pulling her to him for a rough kiss that frightened her. "I thought it was just the young bucks coming up that changed your mind. Well, I'll pay you well in gold, little gypsy."

"No," Elena gasped, terrified. "No, you ..."

His hands were tearing at her, bringing back too clearly the awful moments in the alley way before Jamie had come ... She tried to scream, knowing that the trees would muffle her voice, but still hoping that someone ... that ...

"Blast you, stop that! You'll bring them after us again." Her stepfather's hand caught her hard across the mouth and sent her reeling back into a hard tree branch. For a moment the darkness was lit with stars of pain. Then she lost consciousness.

She was being buried alive. Her face was covered with cloth and a heavy weight was dropping on her. She screamed as a terrible pain ripped through her loins. At once a hand clamped over her mouth through the fabric of what she now realized must be her own skirt. She couldn't breathe. She fought desperately, trying to move away from the agony, trying to kick, to stop this monstrous violation of her body. But he was like a huge animal, pinning her, helpless, to the hard earth. The darkness returned and she welcomed it.

The cloth lifted from her face and the weight was gone from her body as she once again surfaced. He was bending over her, blotting out the faint light of the stars and the infant moon. "Well, now, let's see your face, little filly," he said. His voice was still thick, and his breath was sickening as it blew in her face.

"Don't touch me," Elena sobbed, the horror filling her mind. "Get away from me."

"But I haven't paid you yet, my little gypsy," Hernan said. "Surely you'll want my gold now, won't you?" His hand came out and touched her cheek.

Elena screamed and tried to scramble away from him, but he caught her easily and dragged her out from under the sheltering olive tree into the faint light that spilled between the boughs. He was still breathing heavily. Then suddenly he stopped.

"Elena!" The word was as filled with horror as his face was. "My God, I thought you were the gypsy wench!"

"Get away from me." Elena tried to crawl back under the tree, but her legs scarcely seemed to move. "You're an animal. You didn't care who I was, or what I was."

He swore, then ran a hand through his disheveled hair. His expression changed, hardening. "Be quiet," he ordered. "I have to think. What am I to do with you?"

"Haven't you already done enough?" Tears of pain and rage flowed over her cheeks. "When they find out..."

"You'll tell no one." His voice was like an icy hand on her spine, cold and emotionless. "Do you want everyone to know? What of your beloved foreign suitor? Do you think he'll still have you, if he finds out you're not a virgin? You'll be silent, like that cursed *campanera* of yours, or..."

"You!" Elena choked on the word. Sickness burned in her throat. "*You* were the one. You did this to her, too, and then sold her to Juan so that he'd take her away. You killed her as surely as if you took that strap and..." Rage won over her pain and she struggled to her feet, wavering and dizzy, but burning with her hatred. "I'll make you pay for it! I'll..."

A sudden blow sent her reeling back to the ground. "You'll do nothing," he snarled, looking around. He picked up a large rock. "You'll be found here in the morning, a victim of the gypsies. Everyone knows what they are. They lured you here, raped you and then killed you..." He laughed, his face a mask of evil. "It'll be much easier than marrying you off. I'll be so heartbroken to lose my lovely stepdaughter, but perhaps I'll have a son soon—and then I won't care at all, will I?"

The rock crashed down, blotting out the evil face and ending the pain that still pulsed between her thighs. She neither saw nor heard him as he stood over her, laughing softly, cruelly. Then he dropped the rock and made his way back into the trees, no longer staggering from all he'd drunk through the long day of the *fiesta*.

* * *

Elena woke slowly, aware first of movement—rhythmic and somehow relaxing. She sighed and moved, then whimpered with pain as the various parts of her body throbbed to life, too.

"Lie still, little one," a soft voice said. "The bleeding has stopped, but we must not start it again. You are quite safe here."

Elena opened her eyes and realized that she was lying on a bed in what appeared to be some sort of wagon. A dark-skinned, dark-eyed old gypsy woman sat beside her smiling widely as she offered her a mug of water.

"Drink this, it will make you feel better," she said.

"Where am I?" Elena croaked after the slightly bitter-tasting liquid eased her dry throat and cracked lips. "What happened?"

"You don't remember?" The dark eyes narrowed. "The grove of olive trees... the man..."

For a moment they were just words, then Elena remembered and the horror of it twisted inside her. "He meant to kill me," she cried and her head throbbed in painful agreement. "He raped me and he wanted me dead so that you... that your people would be blamed."

The old woman nodded. "Miguel heard him speaking to you and he summoned me when they found you were still alive. It was not safe to leave you there, so we brought you with us when we left at dawn yesterday."

"Yesterday?" The odd brew seemed to have eased the agony that had plagued her and she was able to think a little more clearly now. "I've been here since yesterday?"

The old woman nodded. "For a time I didn't know whether you would wake, but now you will be all right, I think. Just rest quietly for a day or so. There was far too much blood; you need time and good food to make you strong again."

Elena closed her eyes. She remembered what he'd done; and she saw Celeste's face as it had been the last night she'd been alive. For the first time she could understand the shame and suffering she must have felt—and she understood, too, why Celeste had refused to tell Juan the name of her ravisher. Her own stepfather... He was no better than the back alley scum she and Teresa had met on their trip to the docks, no better at all. She shuddered.

The woman brought her broth to drink, then insisted that she sleep. It was evening before she was fully aware of her surroundings again. This time when she tried to sit up, the woman helped her, wrapping a blanket lightly around her shoulders before she brought her a pan of savory stew and a large chunk of bread.

Once she'd eaten, Elena began to feel much better; but with her returning strength came questions. "Where are you taking me?" she asked.

The woman shrugged. "We simply travel," she said. "There are other *fiestas* to dance for; and we go to the markets to tell fortunes and trade horses with the local people."

"But what about me? There must be people looking for me."

The old woman smiled bitterly. "And for us," she said, "if that man has his way."

"You must leave me somewhere," Elena said. "You won't be safe with me here."

"Where?" The dark eyes were mocking. "Do you have family on Mallorca? Friends?"

"The Valdez family . . ." Elena began, then let it trail off. How could she return to them? she asked herself. How could she go before all of them and accuse Hernan of . . . of what he had done to her? And what of her mother?

Scenes from long ago filled her mind. It was six or seven years ago. She'd been too young to realize what was wrong with her mother—why she spent so much of her time lying down. She realized now that her mother had been pregnant. Her mother had been lying on a lounge in the *jardin*, watching her ride her pony around, when suddenly Elena had decided to try jumping the little horse over a low pile of wood.

The pony, unused to jumping, had shied at the last moment, sending her crashing into the wood pile. She'd been scratched and bruised, but the physician summoned for her had spent most of his time at her mother's bedside, barely able to save her life when she lost the child she'd been carrying.

Elena sighed, well aware that the shock of hearing about Hernan would be a far worse blow and might even kill her. But what could she do? If she went back, what might Hernan do to her? How long before he found another rock, or perhaps caught her alone on the deck of the coaster ship they would take back to Spain. The possibilities were endlessly horrible.

Jamie's face filled her mind and her heart raced at the memory of his kisses and tender words. He would take her away. If they insisted on marrying before they left Mallorca . . . The golden dream faded as quickly as it had come. She couldn't do that to him, she realized. To marry him now would be worse than lying, for he believed that she was pure and innocent, and . . .

If she told him the truth? She remembered the sound of Juan's voice—the coldness and the doubt. She would never be able to bear that, she decided. Better that he should believe her dead or missing than despise her for what had happened.

"You are a member of the Valdez family?" The old woman's eyes were bright with curiosity.

Elena swallowed hard. "My stepfather, the man who did this to me, is Hernan Valdez."

The gypsy nodded slowly. "And you would go back there?"

Elena considered it for a moment, then shook her head. "I never want to see him again."

"Sleep now," the old woman said. "Tomorrow we will talk again. You are safe here with us for now."

The old woman left and Elena lay back, tired from her thoughts and fears. She would have to do something, she realized, but what? Where could she go? And how? She had nothing, no money, her clothes had been torn, her jewelry was not worth much and . . .

She closed her eyes and thought of her mother and her father: the happy days they'd shared at the *hacienda*, all the dreams and plans, and . . . France. The idea slipped into her mind and warmed her like a ray of sun on a cold damp morning. If she could go to France, to her father's people, they would help and care for her, she was sure.

All the stories of France and the people there filled her mind with pictures full of promise. She dozed off feeling much better. There was hope, a future. All she needed was a plan . . .

In the morning she woke before anyone was stirring. The old woman snored loudly on the narrow couch that ran down the opposite wall of the wagon. Elena smiled at her warmly, suddenly aware that if not for her kindness, she would have died in that grove of olive trees.

She would need money, she decided, and quite a lot of it—enough to pay the gypsies for their care, and plenty more for the journey she would be taking to France. She smiled coldly now, her mind functioning better. Hernan Valdez had the money and he owed it to her—her dowry, she thought bitterly. He'd stolen her innocence and destroyed her dream of a proper marriage with Jamie, so let him pay; but how . . . ?

Before the gypsies had broken camp, she'd formed a plan, but she waited to speak of it, wanting time to think it over again, to make sure that there was no danger in it—no way it could help Hernan and put her or her new friends in any jeopardy. It seemed almost foolproof.

She would write a note to Hernan and ask the gypsies to deliver it. In the note she would tell him only that she was alive and safe and that she was willing to leave Mallorca and Spain without seeing her mother or telling her what he'd done—for a price. If he would give her the money she needed to travel to her father's people in France and to repay those who'd helped her after his attack, she would leave him in peace. Otherwise, she would tell everyone—accuse him of her ravishing, and of the rape and suicide of Celeste. He would, she was sure, agree to her terms.

By the time the gypsies stopped and made camp outside a small village, Elena was feeling almost like herself again. She got up, washed in the tepid water the old woman had left her and, after a moment's hesitation, donned the gypsy blouse and full skirt the woman had supplied. The tangles combed out of her hair, she opened the rear door of the wagon and stepped out into the late afternoon sun, feeling a little like a child released from lessons after a difficult day. In spite of what had happened, it was good to be alive and to have another plan to follow.

Chapter 12

JAMIE RODE THE borrowed gelding slowly, weary from two days in the saddle and fast losing hope of ever seeing Elena again. He'd checked three gypsy camps already and found nothing but hot-eyed wenches and their cold-faced men. They all pretended not to understand his halting Spanish and he could almost feel the steel of their knives as he moved through their camps, looking into the squalid wagons that were their homes.

He shook his head again, unable to believe it. How could they have carried her off? What had she been doing away from the well-lit *casa* or crowded *jardin*? Surely what had so nearly happened to her at the docks should have taught her something, but . . .

It was late afternoon when he rode into another gypsy camp. As before, the men were cold-eyed. He noted that their hands often touched their sashed waists where he suspected a knife might be concealed. That alone made him very glad that Ian was following him, sitting quietly on his horse while Jamie asked the questions.

No one knew anything, of course. They denied being at the

hacienda of the Valdez family and seemed quite indifferent to his questions about a Spanish girl. However, when he mentioned the idea of searching their wagons, he sensed a sudden change of attitude. His pulse quickened. Could there be something here after all? he asked himself. He'd begun to doubt, to lose hope, but if Elena was here...

Before he could press his demands, the small door on the rear of one of the wagons opened and a girl stepped out into the sun. For a moment he didn't really notice her, except to be surprised at the reddish glow of her hair in the sun and the hesitant way she seemed to move, almost as though she were blinded by the brightness of the day.

"Where is Tia Rosa?" she asked one of the young gypsy men and the sound of her voice brought his eyes back to her in shock. There was no mistaking the tall, ripening form or the wide hazel eyes that suddenly met his. He had found Elena!

For what seemed a long time, she just looked at him. He could see a parade of emotions passing over her pale face. Then, suddenly, her eyes began to glow. "Jamie!" she cried, half-falling down the rickety steps of the wagon and racing to throw herself into his arms. "Thanks be to God that you've come!"

Instinct brought his arms around her and he felt a quick surge of desire as she clung to him, but he hurriedly forced it back, remembering only too well how he'd responded to Amelia Starburough. Gently, but firmly, he disengaged himself from her arms and stepped back. "What are you doing here?" he demanded, looking around, noting that the members of the gypsy band were now all watching him.

"They saved my life," Elena said. "They've been taking care of me since..."

As he watched, he saw the joy drain from her face and the green glow fade from her eyes, leaving them lovely, but sad. She moved away from him. "How did you find me?" she asked.

"Everyone has been searching for you since dawn of the day after the *fiesta*. Your stepfather sent men after me, to the ship; they thought that you might have slipped away with me, or..."

"Him?" Her lip curled in a way that made her almost ugly. "I'll wager he was searching for me and frantically, too."

"What are you saying?" Jamie asked. "Everyone has been searching. We decided that you must have been stolen away by the gypsies, since they were gone, too." He looked around the camp. "Is that what happened, Elena?" He switched to French. "We can protect you if you're afraid. We'll get you away from them."

"Afraid?" Elena looked around. "They saved my life." Another thought seemed to cross her mind. "*They* must be protected, Jamie. Say you found me alone, wandering in the countryside or something."

"What?"

"Please, where are the others? Where is my stepfather? He isn't with you, is he?"

Jamie shook his head, more confused than ever. He could see the darkness of a bruise on the side of her head and there were more marks along the side of her jaw, but she seemed all right except for the things she was saying. "He's with another party searching the other side of the island," he said, and was surprised at the way his words seemed to soothe her.

"Come along, I'll take you back to the *hacienda*," he said. "They'll be so happy to see that you're safe and well. We all feared you were dead."

For a moment she seemed about to agree, then she stepped away from him. "I cannot go back there," she said. Her voice was soft, but firm.

"Are you saying you want to stay here . . . with them?" Jamie waved a hand at the gathering throng of men, several of whom he could see eyeing her with interest. "What are they to you?" he asked, suddenly suspicious.

"I told you, they saved my life; they've taken care of me since . . ." Her eyes fled his and her skin darkened in a flush that seemed guilty.

"And you want to stay with them?" Jamie asked, his temper rising. To think that he'd loved this girl, even considered marrying her against what he knew would be his father's wishes. Was she no different than Amelia Starburough? Were they all like that? Pure and sweet on the outside and full of evil guile within?

"No, of course not. If you could find me, he could, too. My being here is a danger to them, but I . . . Would you help me, Jamie? Please, can I trust you not to betray me?"

"Betray you to whom? Help you what? I've spent nearly three days looking for you, and now you act as though you didn't want to be found. If you don't tell me what is going on, I'll ride away and you can stay with your cursed friends." Jamie spoke with the anger of frustration and he felt better when he saw her wince from the words.

"I will tell you . . . everything, if you will promise not to take me back to the *hacienda*," she said, her eyes down, her shoulders slightly bowed.

Jamie opened his mouth to refuse to make such a promise, then glanced questioningly at Ian, wondering if his old friend had made more of this than he had. Ian nodded slightly, his expression unreadable. Jamie sighed. "All right, I swear not to return you to the *hacienda* unless you wish it," he said. "Now tell me."

"I think we would do better to take her out of here first," Ian said softly in English. "I don't like the look of yon man."

Jamie followed the older man's gaze and saw the burly gypsy watching them. His eyes were on Elena covetously, and his hand rested on his belt in a way that gave the impression he wouldn't mind fighting to keep the girl.

"Can you ride?" he asked Elena in French.

She nodded. "I must thank Tia Rosa," she said. "She took care of me and . . ."

"Go, child, and find peace," a low voice said, and an old woman stepped out of the shadows between Elena and the burly gypsy.

"But I want to reward you," Elena began.

"Tell no one that you were with us. That will be reward enough," the old woman said.

Elena started to protest, but Jamie had waited long enough. He vaulted to the back of his horse, then bent down to lift her up in front of him. She cried out in pain or fear, but he paid no attention, riding out of the camp before the men could do anything. He didn't draw rein till they were well away from the gypsies.

"What were you so afraid of?" Elena demanded when he dumped her rather roughly on the ground, then slid down to stand beside her.

"One of your male friends back there didn't seem too eager to let you go. Perhaps he thought to keep you for himself."

"I saw none of the men," Elena said. "I made no friends among them. Tia Rosa kept me in her wagon since that night. She said I had to stay there till . . ." The flush returned. "Till it was safe for me to be on my feet again."

"I saw the way they looked at you," Jamie said. "The way you're dressed. If it hadn't been for your hair, you'd look just like one of their wenches."

"Stop it," Ian said quietly. "Sit down, Senorita Flambeau. Tell us how you came to be in that gypsy wagon, and why you don't want to go back to the Valdez *hacienda*."

"Couldn't you just trust me ... help me?" Elena asked. "I would rather just send a message to my stepfather. You could bring me the reply, and ..."

Jamie shook his head, controlling his temper only with an effort. She looked so young and frightened now that he longed to agree, to hold her in his arms and protect her, or ... He pushed the thoughts away, reminding himself that he was a gentleman, not one of the gypsy men to take any wench he saw without a thought. "I'll not take another step with you without knowing what happened after I left the *fiesta*, Elena," he said. "You owe me that, you know. We were to be wed when we said goodnight, then at dawn I learn that you're gone and no one knows where."

The girl closed her eyes and sank down on the grassy slope, looking both weak and weary. "I ... I was attacked that night, left for dead. The gypsies found me and took me with them. I am afraid to go back to the *hacienda* because it would only happen again."

Jamie stared at her, willing her to lift her head, to meet his gaze. Her skin blazed with the same rosy blush he'd seen before and he felt another throb of desire. "Who attacked you?" he demanded. "How could such a thing happen in that crowd?"

Elena moved, seemed to cower a little; he saw her tongue come out and lick her lips. "I ... I don't know who it was," she said. "I left the *jardin* for a moment. I thought I saw someone I knew in the grove, and I followed him. The person knocked me down and covered my face ... He hit me with a rock and left me for dead afterward. The gypsies were to be blamed."

She was lying. The knowledge was like a knife in his belly. "How do you know it wasn't one of the gypsies, if you didn't see his face?" he demanded, fury rising like poison.

For a moment she looked stricken, then relieved. "His clothing. I felt the fine fabric. No gypsy would have been dressed that way."

"Are you saying that someone at your ... at the *fiesta* ..." Jamie couldn't find the words.

Two tears welled out from under the fan of dark lashes on her pale cheeks and ran, untouched, down to her chin. "He forced himself on me. He struck me when I screamed..." Her voice broke and her head dropped into her hands as her whole body shook with sobs.

Jamie started to reach out, but then he saw Amelia's mocking face before him. She'd sobbed, too; and cried rape when he'd refused to touch her, when she was already carrying the child of another man. How could he trust this girl? How could he believe her tears? He got up and walked away, leaving Ian to comfort her.

Only when she was quiet did he return to ask, "What about your stepfather? If you tell him what has happened, he'll protect you."

The eyes, green again and hard now in spite of the red rims left from her tears, met his. "And if he doesn't believe me any more than you do? He doesn't care for me, you know. He only offered me in marriage to you because he was sure you'd take me far away from Spain."

"You said you wanted to send him a message," Jamie reminded her, confused by the words. Hernan Valdez had been a charming host, and nothing he'd said or done...

"I will ask for my dowry, or at least a part of it. That's all."

"What?"

"To buy my passage to France, to my father's people there. That is all I want now."

"And what of your mother?" Jamie asked, totally lost.

"I would write her and explain somehow. I can't tell her the truth. It might kill her. She... she is to have a child, and she... she has had difficulties in the past. She nearly died when she saw me fall from a horse some years ago. It would be worse for her now, I think."

Jamie just looked at her, noting that her skin was darkening with shame again. Could anyone appear so shy and innocent and not be? he asked himself. But her eyes weren't innocent: they were cold and hard, and yet demanding. "Will you help me?" she asked.

"What did you plan to do while you were with the gypsies?" Jamie asked instead of answering.

"Just what I've told you. I was going to ask one of them to deliver the note to my stepfather and to bring his answer."

Jamie laughed. "A gypsy bring you money? That would be

strange indeed. From the look of the men in that camp, they would have taken you and the money, too. Perhaps that was why they helped you in the first place: to sell you back to your stepfather for a ransom."

"They would have been very surprised if they'd asked for one," Elena said, her tone bitter. "Tia Rosa would have helped me. She took care of me after..."

"This is getting us nowhere," Jamie said, not wanting her to refer to what had happened, not wanting to think of any man touching her lovely body, forcing himself upon her and..."We can't stay here. It will be dark before long, and I'm still not quite sure your gypsy friends will part with you so easily."

"You promised not to take me back to the *hacienda*," Elena reminded him, and he saw genuine fear in her eyes. "Please, if you don't believe me, leave me here. I'd rather die in this harsh land than go back there."

"Or take your chances with the gypsies?" Jamie asked, then hated himself when he saw the words cutting her down. He knew she'd lied about the rape in the grove. However, she wasn't lying about her fear of the *hacienda*, or of someone who lived there. Also, in spite of his doubts about her story, he didn't really think that the gypsies had touched her... not yet.

"I can't leave you here," he said coldly.

"Where will you take me?" Elena asked, not moving.

Jamie looked to Ian for a suggestion.

"Perhaps a room over one of the taverns," the older man suggested. "Dressed as she is, if she covers her hair and keeps her eyes down, she'll look like just another gypsy wench brought in for pleasure."

Jamie watched the blush rise in Elena's face and asked himself once again if he was a fool. "Come along," he said, reaching out to her.

She stepped away from him. "You'll carry my message to my stepfather without telling him where I am?" she asked.

"Blast it," he swore. "I can't do that. The man has treated me decently. I can't be a part of your scheme to get money from him."

"Then how will I get to France?" Elena asked.

Jamie grabbed her arm roughly and half-dragged her to the waiting gelding. "We'll talk about it later," he said. "Right now I want to get you back to town before dark. Obviously you're not safe anywhere alone."

He lifted her more gently this time, but he didn't miss the way she winced in pain as he settled her before him, nor did he fail to note that she wore nothing beneath her skirt and blouse. What had happened to her dress, her petticoats, the proper underclothing she must have been wearing at the *fiesta*? What was true in her words and what was not? And who had the man been?

They made the ride in silence, reaching the now-familiar port just as afternoon turned to night. Jamie let Ian choose the tavern and make the arrangements, then he carried the exhausted girl up the narrow stairs to one of the small, musty-smelling rooms. She hardly stirred when he laid her, none too gently, on the narrow bed. Her skirt was pulled up, and he moved to ease it down to cover the milky skin of her leg. She shuddered at his touch and he saw terror in her eyes when they met his.

"I'll not touch you," he said.

Her eyes closed and she looked near death.

"You need some food," Ian said, "and a bit of something to perk you up. I'll fetch it for you, and then I think it would be wise for us to ride out to the *hacienda* and let them know we've returned from the search."

Jamie turned to speak, but Elena sat up. "You'll not tell them where I am?" She was shaking with fright. "You'll not let them find me!"

Jamie and Ian exchanged glances, but Ian offered him no answers. It was clearly being left to him, Jamie realized. "I'll say nothing," he said at last, aware that the girl would run if he didn't promise her. Sick and ill as she appeared, she would run until someone else found her and . . . He pushed the thoughts away. "Get the food," he said to Ian.

Chapter 13

ELENA SLID THE chair into place as Jamie had shown her, wedging the back beneath the knob of the door so that it couldn't be opened, even if someone else was given a key. There were sounds from outside the door and from the tavern below— frightening sounds—but she was too tired to care.

The food had helped a great deal, bringing back her strength and her will to live, but the conversation hadn't been too rewarding. Jamie didn't believe her; it was in his eyes every time he looked at her, and she couldn't honestly blame him. She had lied, to protect Jamie as well as herself. If he knew, if he went in search of Hernan to avenge her ... She had no doubt that Jamie would die just as she would. She shuddered as she remembered her stepfather when she'd last seen him in the grove, then pushed the memory away, unwilling to suffer her stepfather's touch even in retrospect.

Would Jamie give her away? She didn't really think so. Whether he believed her or not, he had given his word, and she had a feeling he was honorable. But if he continued to refuse to help her get the money necessary for her escape from here ...

103

A pounding on the door brought her mind back to the moment. A man called loudly and drunkenly for Stellita. Elena cowered against the wall, suddenly feeling how alone and vulnerable she was with Ian and Jamie gone. The chair quivered a little, but held firm till the man gave up and staggered on to pound on the next door. It was opened and she heard female giggles through the none-too-thick walls. Her stomach lurched a little, but she swallowed hard and lay down, her hands over her ears. It was going to be a very long night.

The sound of knocking roused her from a deep sleep, and for a moment she just lay still, not sure where she was. Then her memory returned. "Go away," she shouted, thinking it must be still another of the drunken men who'd wakened her through the night.

"Let me in, Elena," Jamie called, and her heart lifted in spite of the way he'd treated her.

She ran her fingers through her sleep-tousled hair and hurried to obey, wishing mightily that she'd had a chance to wash and change into something more suitable than the stained and wrinkled gypsy costume Tia Rosa had given her. "I . . . I thought you were another of the men from downstairs," she explained lamely when she opened the door.

"Did you have a bad night, Senorita?" Ian asked kindly as he followed Jamie into the room. He carried a small box, and when he opened it Elena saw that there was food inside. Elena ate greedily as she described the night. "It was horrible," she finished.

"Perhaps you would have preferred the gypsy camp," Jamie said.

"I had only Tia Rosa's snoring to put up with there," Elena snapped, then blushed. "I'm sorry. I'm really very grateful to you for hiding me here and bringing me food. I'll repay you when I get the money from my stepfather, but till then . . ."

Jamie shook his head. "You'll have no money from him," he said quietly.

"What do you mean?" Elena asked.

"Your gypsy friends have been busy." His smile was not kind.

"I don't understand," Elena said, shaking her head. "What are you talking about?"

"While we were talking to your stepfather and his cousin, a messenger arrived from a rocky area of the island. They brought your clothes and said that someone reported seeing you fall from a cliff into the sea. The story is that you were stolen by the gypsies, raped, then set free. It is assumed that in your terror and shame you threw yourself off the cliffs."

"Like Celeste!" Elena gasped, reliving it for a moment, sick with all that had happened first to her friend and now to her. "Did he believe it?" she demanded, her fury pulsing back at the memory of what had happened to Celeste, what she'd been driven to.

"Who?" Jamie looked confused.

"*Him*. My stepfather. Did he believe the story?"

"He was grief-stricken, and his sister—your *duenna*—was terribly upset. She blamed herself, said that she should have watched over you more carefully, should have realized that with your upbringing you might be inclined to do something foolish."

"They are talking of returning to Spain tomorrow," Ian added. "Your stepfather is most concerned about breaking the news to your mother."

Elena shook her head. "I must do something," she said, her mind racing. "I have to get the money and leave here."

There was a long silence, then Jamie cleared his throat. "You won't allow me to tell them the truth?" he asked.

"Never." Elena stiffened her shoulders. "I'll find another way to get to France. Perhaps I could work for a family. I speak both French and Spanish, and I have had a very good education. My father taught me far more than most girls are allowed to learn, and..."

"That won't be necessary," Jamie said softly. "I'll see that you get to France."

"I can't ask you..." Elena began, then stopped when she met his eyes.

"And I can't abandon you here," Jamie said with a sigh. "How long do you think you would last in this place? You wouldn't get half a mile in that garb before some man carried you off. Didn't you learn anything the day you came to town without a *duenna*?"

Elena felt the red rising in her face. "That was foolish, but now I have no choice."

"You can listen to me," Jamie said. "It will be difficult, but I think I have a way to get you safely away from this place without anyone being the wiser."

Elena started to protest further, then let the words die in her throat. She had no choice, she realized. Though she hated the idea of inflicting herself further on Jamie, the only alternative was the street—and her brief taste of that with Teresa had been more than enough. Lowering her eyes so that he wouldn't see how it hurt her to accept his help, she said only, "What would you suggest?"

"I've spoken with the Captain of the *Fleet Lady*, and he tells me that he has business along the French coast, so you will be able to travel with us on our return journey."

"But I have no money," Elena protested.

"You'll not be booking passage," Jamie said. "The Captain has heard the details of the disappearance of a young lady of quality, so he would never anger the Spanish by helping us spirit you away from here."

"But you..." A wave of his hand silenced her questions before she could put them into words.

"He would not, however, question my bringing along a cabin boy," Jamie said, then smiled unpleasantly. "Of course, you'll have to cut your hair and dress in boy's clothing. And we'll have to do something about your skin. No peasant lad of this island could have skin like yours."

"A cabin boy?" Elena couldn't go on. The implications brought the same flush to her skin as before, and she wanted to cry out in protest, but she was too shocked and ashamed. Suddenly she understood why Celeste had taken the strap and gone to the grove to die. It was obvious that Jamie thought her no better than a tavern wench.

"Don't look like that," Jamie said. "I'm not your fine gypsy friend. Ian has booked the small cabin next to mine. We'll have to be careful, but we'll manage it so you can sleep in there, though the others on the ship must never find out."

"I didn't..." Elena began, relieved and ashamed at the same time. "It's just that..."

"Where is your father's family, Senorita?" Ian asked, changing the subject and easing the situation.

"Le Mans, I believe," Elena said. "I've never been there, of course, but my father had a painting of the villa where he grew up, and it was very lovely. I'm sure I would recognize it. It is just a little outside Le Mans."

"And we are to stop at La Rochelle," Jamie said, nodding. "That will not be too bad, I don't think. We can see you overland to your relatives, and I'll still be able to return to England before my father has apoplexy."

"I'm sorry to cause you so much trouble," Elena said, meaning it. "You really have no reason to do this for me. The promises made between us were from another time. I don't expect..." The pain of what she felt choked her, and in that moment she realized the horrible truth. What had happened in the grove, the awfulness of it, hadn't changed one thing—she still loved Jamie McDonald.

"We had better get started with our preparations," Jamie said, seeming to ignore her words. "The *Fleet Lady* sails tonight."

"*Tonight?*" Elena gasped.

"You can still change your mind," Jamie said, his eyes holding hers and forcing her to meet his gaze. "I can ride out to the *hacienda* and tell them it is all a mistake, that you are very much alive." He paused, then added, "You wouldn't have to tell them too much. Say you fell and hit your head and don't remember what happened. You have the bruise to prove it."

For a moment she hesitated, wanting the safety of familiar faces, the chance to go home and be with her mother; then she remembered the voice from the grove, the touch of his hands, the pig-grunting sounds and the pain... To go back would be to face him, and she knew she couldn't do that. Even to be in the same room with him would be too much. She would either kill him or herself.

"I can't go back," she said quietly. "Not now."

"So be it," Jamie said with a shrug. "We'll get some scissors to cut your hair, then see about the stain and boy's clothing."

Elena held the scissors for several minutes after they left her. Her hair was long and heavy, reaching nearly to her waist and waving softly when it was unbound. The small bit of mirror showed only half her face, and even that rather dimly.

For a moment she weakened, thought of Teresa and her family. If she told them what had happened to her... Then she remembered the closeness between Hernan and Esteban. Would they believe her? Teresa might, but the rest... Closing her eyes, she held her hair steady and began hacking it off just below her ears. By the time Jamie tapped on the door again, it was a thick, wavy pile about her feet, and her head was covered with waves and curls.

"She'll never pass for a boy," Jamie said, stopping just inside the door. "She's too tall, and—" His eyes rested on the swell of her bosom.

"That's why the clothes are big," Ian said. "And the hat will help. Tuck most of the hair up under it. She'll have to keep out of sight till we're well away from here, but after that . . ." His smile was cynical. "Let the crew and the Captain speculate a bit, Jamie. A gentleman of quality might take a gypsy wench along for his comfort on a sea trip, might he not? All you'll see is a bit of envy, so long as they don't guess her identity and you don't admit to having anything but a cabin boy."

"I suppose you're right," Jamie said, but Elena could see the doubts in his face. He didn't want to take her, that much was obvious.

For a moment she considered releasing him from the whole thing, but deep down she knew he wouldn't leave her here alone. And there was nothing else she could do. Ian, having looked over her hair-cut, nodded, then picked up the scissors. "I'll return these and see to the moving of my belongings. We don't want the good Captain to doubt your story."

"But the stain . . ." Jamie began. Ian was already out the door.

"I'll do it," Elena said, looking dubiously at the container of liquid. "My face and my hands, and . . ."

"You'd better put it all over," Jamie said. "The less people even guess at your gender, the safer you'll be—no matter what Ian says. Besides," he continued, and his lips twisted slightly, "if too many of them guess about you, they may decide they'd like me to share your favors."

Elena winced, fighting tears. "How dare you!" she cried then let it trail off, her own position making it clear how he might dare even more insults.

"I'm sorry," he said, looking properly contrite. "I was just trying to make your understand the whole situation. It isn't going to be an easy journey, Elena, and I can't honestly promise to get you to your family safely."

"If I stay here, I won't be safe at all," she said, head down now, not wanting him to see how he'd hurt her.

"I could give you some money. I don't have a great deal, but you could buy passage to your home."

She shook her head firmly, stopping his words. "Your kindness is my only hope. I'll try not to be a burden to you."

Jamie shrugged. "Let's put the stain on," he said. "I want to take you on board during the afternoon when most of this town is asleep. You'll be safer in my cabin than you are here."

Elena looked down at the blouse and skirt, then over at the shirt and trousers Ian had laid on the bed. "Shall I change?" she asked uneasily.

"And get stain on those? Of course not." Jamie glared at her. "Take off your clothes and wrap that bed-cloth around you. We'll have to do your back and your legs and."

Elena stiffened, red blazing in her face. "I can't," she began, furious at the suggestion. She saw anger rising in Jamie's face, too; then it subsided and he sighed.

"Elena, we're going to be sharing a cabin for a voyage. Whether you sleep there or not, you'll have to spend most of your time in my company, so you'll have to get used to it. I can't step outside here. I'll turn my back if you're still so shy. Now get out of your clothes and let's get this blasted stain on you so I can see if you'll pass for a boy in those clothes."

He turned his back, standing stiff and angry and glaring—she was sure—at the wall. She hesitated for a moment, remembering two things: his tenderness in the *jardin* and the later agony she'd suffered in the grove. It had happened to her, she realized sorrowfully. She had no innocence to shield her now; she was, perhaps, only a little better than the tavern wenches who, she assumed, sold themselves in the rooms along this hallway.

Closing her eyes and shivering slightly, even though the room was warm, she slipped out of the gypsy clothes and carefully wrapped herself in the thin cloth from the bed. "All right," she said, her voice reflecting her fears. "You can turn around."

"I'll start with your back," he said, his tone so devoid of emotion she was almost frightened. "I want to see how it goes on before we do your face or your legs, since they will show more."

Elena said nothing, too terrified and too ashamed. How could she bear it? she asked herself, then pushed the idea away. She would bear it, that was all. She would take whatever came and get home to France, to her father's people. Once she was there, they would love and care for her and make everything right once more. Till then she would just survive; that was all that mattered.

His touch was light and gentle in spite of his coldness, and as he worked the strange liquid into her skin she heard his breathing change. She sensed that he wanted her. It frightened her at first, but as he continued to change her pale skin to dark with the stain, she began to find the sensation pleasurable, too.

He could pretend to hate her now, but it wasn't all gone, there was still some feeling, some desire at least. For both of them.

The thoughts shamed her. She was glad the stain hid the blushes she could not control, and gladder still when he said he'd leave the rest for her to do, once he'd dyed the skin of her face. His touch was still gentle, and his hand shook a little as he smoothed the dye over her throat and down her shoulders. Then he stepped back.

"I'll go down for a bit of ale while you finish," he said. "Just stuff your gypsy clothes under the bed and come down when you're ready to go. It will be better if no one sees me fetch a lad from a room where I left a wench."

Elena nodded. "I won't be long," she said. "And thank you, Jamie."

"Best you call me Senor from now on," he said, turning his back. "And speak as little as possible. You don't sound like a boy."

"*Si*, Senor," Elena said, anger deepening her voice. How could he be so cruel? she asked herself. Why must he make her feel so unclean? Memories of the grunting animal in the grove filled her mind and she shuddered, realizing that she was dirty now, ruined by his touch for any decent man. Despair swept over her once again, and she didn't even see Jamie leave the room for her eyes were glazed with tears.

It was only later, when she dried her tears on the bed cloth that she remembered the stain and hurried to the mirror. It was unchanged by her crying. She studied herself for a moment, shocked. She looked like a rather dirty, dark-skinned boy. Too pretty, perhaps, with her curling hair and wide eyes, but—with the hat and if she kept her eyes down and her shoulders hunched forward to cover her bosom—she might yet be convincing.

Yes, it might work, she thought. It would *have* to work! She returned to the bed and quickly spread the rest of the stain on her thighs and breast, then put a wide band of it around her waist and hips, working till no more white skin was visible to her. Only then did she pull on the well-worn shirt and trousers Jamie and Ian had brought.

The trousers had to be tied at her slender waist, and even so felt strange and tight against her legs. The shirt hung loose and free as Ian had promised, hiding well the feminine swell of her figure. She walked the length of the room several times, trying to adjust to movement without skirt or petticoats, then she put on the hat—tucking as much of her hair up under it as she could. She was a stranger to herself when she looked in the mirror and stepped out into the hall. She was frightened, not sure just yet what would happen to her now.

Chapter 14

THE JOURNEY BEGAN badly for Elena. The cabin was small and dark and oppressively hot, just as the day had been. Everything had been so still in the streets on the way to the ship, and even the sweating men who were finishing the loading of the ship seemed strangely quiet when they went aboard.

There was so little wind, even in the evening, that the ship scarcely seemed to move. And when Elena peered out the dirty porthole, she could see that the land mass of Mallorca was still close by, even though they had been rocking in the water for some time. It seemed to be holding them, and Elena turned away fearfully.

Ian arrived with a tray of food. "We'll be dining with the Captain tonight," he said, "but eat hearty, you may need it later."

"What do you mean?" Elena asked, instantly fearful.

"The Captain is predicting a blow after this heat, says it could start before dawn." Ian set the tray down on the small table that was fastened to one wall of the cabin. "I hope you're a good sailor," he added as he went out.

The food was unappealing, but Elena ate stolidly, not thinking of meals past or future, not even allowing herself to think of what might lay ahead tonight or tomorrow. She was away from Mallorca, on her way to France and her father's family. That was enough. Just to know she would never see Hernan Valdez again gave her a bit of peace.

The storm struck even before the Captain had expected it. Ian and Jamie had just come to the cabin—a little flushed from wine—when the ship suddenly bucked and began to creak and strain as the wind filled sails that had been hanging slack only moments before. They could hear the shouts from above, the sounds of running feet on the decks as the Captain's orders were put into action.

"Perhaps we should make the exchange of cabins now," Ian said. "It sounds as though everyone must be on deck at the moment."

"Do what you like," Jamie said, "but that's where I'm going. One of the men I talked to told me it was staying in the cabin that made me so sick coming out. This time I'll stay on deck, storm or no storm." His eyes turned briefly and impersonally to her. "You can sleep here tonight, if you like," he said. "I won't be back."

Ian opened his mouth, and for a moment Elena thought he was going to protest, but in the end he merely shrugged and followed Jamie out—leaving her alone once more. At first she was relieved to be alone, but as the noise increased and the ship began to roll and stagger, she longed for company.

There was no standing on the heaving floor, and the heavy meal she'd eaten soon left her. Ill and terrified, she took refuge in one of the small sleeping bunks that were set in the wall of the ship itself. There she hung on, gritting her teeth and trying not to scream at the worst of the pitching, but moaning when she heard crashes from above.

Were they sinking? Had she escaped death at her stepfather's hands only to die here in the sea? By the time she finally lapsed into uneasy sleep, she was too sick to care whether the ship made it or not. What seemed only a moment later, the door of the cabin burst open and Ian came in, shouting "Up, you lazy boy, and help me with your master!"

For a moment Elena only blinked at him, dazzled by the light of the lantern he carried. Then she saw the two sailors carrying Jamie, placing him cautiously in the other bunk. Pulling her shirt around her, she slipped from the bunk and crossed the room, aware of the stares of the rough men but unable to do anything to cover her tumbled hair.

"You'd best get back on deck," Ian said coldly to the men. "We'll care for him now. Thank you for your help."

Elena glanced for the first time at Jamie and barely controlled a scream. His head was gashed and blood was oozing sluggishly from the wound. His clothes were sodden with saltwater or rain and he looked half-dead, so pale and still was he. "What . . . what *happened*?" she gasped when the door closed behind the sailors.

"The cursed wind tore some of the rigging loose, and with it a piece of wood. It came down and hit him, near knocked him into the sea. I had the devil's own time keeping him on the deck till I could summon help. They've lost a man or two already and a good bit of sail."

"Are we going to sink?" Elena asked, picking up a cloth and cleaning the area around the wound.

"Not if the Captain can help it. I'll help get him out of his wet things, then you'll have to watch over him while I go back on deck. I'm no sailor, but the Captain needs everyone's help this night."

Elena nodded, too sick to even blush as she helped Ian peel the soaked clothing off Jamie's inert body, then wrapped him in the rough blankets from both the bunks. "If he wakes, there's a bit of spirits in that chest," Ian said, indicating the small trunk in the corner of the room. "Give him some to help with the warming, but only if he's able to swallow on his own. He'll choke on it if he isn't."

Elena nodded. "I'll take care of him," she said.

The night was endless. Jamie didn't wake; he scarcely moaned or responded to the continued pitching and rolling of the ship. Elena stayed at his side, her own violent seasickness fading as she began to fear more and more for Jamie's life. Still, she was so tired that—when the ship's pitching lessened a little— she fell asleep at her post; her head beside his, her low stool against the side of the bunk. She was still there when the door opened much later.

"How is he?" Ian asked, startling her so that she squeaked slightly in fear before she remembered where she was and who he was. "Has he awakened yet?"

Elena looked at Jamie and shook her head. "He's not moved," she said sadly.

Ian bent over Jamie, holding the lantern closer than she had, gently removing the bandage Elena had made so he could see the wound. He sighed and shook his head. "There's naught to be done for him," he said. "Not till he chooses to wake." His eyes turned to her. "And what about you?"

Elena shrugged. "I'm all right," she said. "I was sick at first, but now . . . What of the storm and the ship?"

Ian sank down on the stool she'd vacated and she could see he was terribly weary. "The storm ended several hours ago, thanks be. We have damage, but the Captain seems to think we can continue on and make our own repairs. We'll not be going back to Mallorca, if that's what you fear."

Elena stood up straighter, responding to his tone. "I hadn't thought of that," she said coldly. "Only of going to the bottom."

Ian's face softened. "Well, you can go sleep in my cabin now, if you like. I'll watch over Jamie."

She started to move away, then—seeing his face in the light of the lantern—shook her head. "It's you who needs the rest," she said. "I can watch over him just as well now as I did last night, and you're just beyond the wall, are you not?"

Ian nodded.

"I'll pound on it if I need you," she said. "Go and rest. You can watch over him when you've had some sleep."

So that day passed as did the next. Jamie roused only slightly, drinking some broth Ian brought, muttering a little, crying out, then lapsing back into stillness. Elena stayed in the cabin with him, changing his coverings, washing the wound, keeping him covered when he began to sweat and tried to throw off the covers, then even lying beside him when he began to shiver with the chills that marked the ebb and flow of his fever.

She was lying there, sleeping, when a hand caressed her cheek. Startled, she opened her eyes to see that Jamie's eyes were open, too. "What are you doing here?" he asked, his voice a little hoarse, but completely natural. His hand slid down her neck to touch her shoulder, then moved more intimately to her breast.

Elena tried to pull away, but his other arm slipped around her and he held her easily, laughing softly. "Let me go," she protested. "I . . . You've been ill of a fever."

"And you've been taking care of me," he said, his lips finding hers before she could say more. His kiss was like it had been in the *jardin* that night, what seemed a lifetime ago. He continued to touch her, to caress her, till she stopped her struggling.

"You've taken good care of me," he said as her shirt somehow slipped away from her, and he began kissing her soft skin. "I had such dreams of you, Elena. Pretty, soft, Elena. You must be cold out there without a blanket."

She tried once more to pull away, but her body was strangely disobedient. Her mind was fluttering with fear, with memories of terror in the olive grove, but somehow she moved closer to him, not away. "You can't," she whispered.

"Were they all dreams, little Elena?" he asked. "Or were you here in my arms, kissing me, wanting me as much as I've been wanting you?"

His lips moved over hers again; his touch, so gentle, soothed the fears her mind kept trying to produce. Only at the last moment, when her foggy mind finally realized what was happening, did she try to fight, to push him away, but he only laughed at her and held her easily with the weight of his naked body. His lips covered her screams as he claimed her.

The struggle was brief, and the pain she feared didn't come. Only afterward, when he lay slack and sleeping beside her, did the hurt begin. And it was in her heart, not her body. Shame burned through her as she slid from his bunk and pulled on her clothes with shaking hands. She glared at him, hating him and loving him at the same time.

"Like a tavern wench," she whispered, tears running down her face. "I was there, so he just reached out and took me."

There was no response from Jamie, beyond a slight snore and a restless moving about the bunk. Elena crossed to the small basin of water that Ian had brought earlier and, with shaking hands, she pulled her clothing off again and washed herself, scrubbing her body till even the stain was a little lighter. But the feel of his hands, his body, didn't fade, and she dressed again with a heavy heart.

"You look poorly," Ian said when he came in later. "Want a few minutes on deck, some fresh air? I can sit with him for a while."

Elena nodded, picking up her hat and hastily tucking as much of her hair under it as she could. It seemed a thousand years since she'd seen more of the sky than the porthole permitted, smelled air that wasn't scented by mold or the odors of illness. Besides, she wanted to escape, to be away from Jamie and the room and the memory of what had happened to her there.

She strolled about the deck slowly. It was late in the day, near dusk. There were few members of the crew to be seen, and no one even tried to approach her. She had time to do plenty of thinking, none of it pleasant. She was leaning on the rail, staring down at the sea, at the furling white of the wake and wondering what it would be like to drown, when a hand touched her shoulder.

"You are wanted by your master, pretty boy," the sailor said, laughing crudely to show the stumps of his broken teeth. "Perhaps he needs someone to..."

Elena fled from the words—not sure what they meant, but aware from the tone that they were evil. However, when she reached the cabin door, she stopped. How could she go in? What if Jamie was awake and wanting her again?

"I thought I heard you." Ian opened the door and half-pulled her inside. "Where have you been? He's awake and hungry for real food. Now stay with him and I'll go get something from that creature that claims he's a cook."

Before she could speak she found herself alone with Jamie. He was, she was surprised to see, sitting on the bunk, partly dressed. Feeling shy and ashamed, she stayed near the door, eyes downcast after a first quick glimpse.

"Ian tells me I owe you a great deal, Elena," Jamie said quietly. "He just told me what happened. I can't believe it has been three days since the storm."

Something about his tone brought her head up and she met his gaze briefly. He was smiling, looking young and pale. "You're feeling better then?" she asked, not sure she could believe the innocent look on his face.

"A little weak, but I suppose that's to be expected. And my head hurts, too. It must have been quite a blow."

"You had a fever," Elena said, watching him closely, searching for some sign that he was taunting her; playing some game by not admitting what had happened before she went up on deck.

"And dreams," Jamie said, standing up, wavering a little, then settling back against the bunk. "Is my shirt somewhere about?" he asked.

"I'll get you one," Elena said, going to the chest and getting a clean shirt for him. When she was closer to him, she looked into his eyes and saw nothing of what she feared—or *hoped*—would be there. Her knees felt a little weak as she realized that he didn't remember.

"I hope I wasn't too difficult a patient," Jamie went on,

pulling his shirt into place. "When I decided to help you get to France, I certainly didn't mean for you to spend the entire voyage taking care of me."

"I didn't mind," Elena said. "But I'm glad you're well now." She turned away, then feeling his eyes, glanced back. His expression was unreadable. Was he remembering a dream? Did he think that perhaps it *could* have happened? Her skin felt hot at the memory, and she prayed he would never know.

"How are you now?" he asked. "Do you feel more comfortable now we're well away from Mallorca?"

"I'm all right," Elena said, but deep down she wondered if she would ever be. How could she endure the voyage, the nearness of Jamie, without letting him know her feelings? And Jamie? Would he someday remember and claim her again? She shuddered at the thought, but she couldn't be sure whether fear or anticipation sent the chill down her spine.

Perhaps, she thought bitterly, she truly was no better than a tavern wench or harlot. Decent ladies never felt as she had, never yielded themselves so willingly, not till they were safely wed—and only then so that heirs could be born. They didn't, as she did now, long for kisses, for their lovers' warm embrace.

"Ian says you've not left my side since the storm," Jamie went on, his tone strangely probing.

"We agreed that the less I was seen the better," Elena reminded him, without looking up.

"I probably owe you my life," he said quietly.

"Then we shall be equal, won't we?" Elena said, looking up at last, bracing herself, keeping all she felt carefully hidden. "You saved me by getting me away from Mallorca. And now I've helped you through this."

"You're not sorry about leaving?" Jamie's eyes searched her face. "There's still time for you to land in Spain and go to your mother."

"I would have been happy to go to the bottom of the sea," Elena said, "rather than return to *him*."

"You hate your stepfather so?" Jamie sounded surprised. "But why?" There was a long silence, during which she dared not face him. Finally he spoke again. "That night at the *fiesta*, the man . . . are you *sure* you didn't see his face, Elena?"

Elena closed her eyes, seeing Hernan's face all too clearly as it had been, twisted and ugly, full of hate and the remnants of desire. She shuddered. "Does it matter now?" she asked. "When I reach France, I want only to forget it all."

"You *do* know!" There was triumph in his tone.

Elena turned away, unable to face his eyes.

"That's what you were lying about." His first excitement had faded and his tone was quizzical.

"I'm tired. May I go to Ian's cabin and rest?" she asked, not looking back at him.

"Of course." All emotion was now drained from his voice. "You must be weary after sitting up with me so long."

Elena sensed disappointment in the words, but she said nothing. She slipped out the door and into the nearby one as quickly and silently as possible. Once inside she leaned against the door, fighting the weakening sobs that brought tears to her eyes.

She would stay here, she decided, and avoid Jamie as much as she could for the rest of their journey. Away from him she could be strong and wise. It was only when those grey eyes were on her that she lost her will to resist, that she wanted to sob out the whole story and be comforted and loved.

She forced the thought away, reminding herself that she'd been saved from her own weakness once. Jamie had no memory of her yielding, and it must remain that way. For her own sake, she must never weaken again; must never let him know how easily she could be claimed. If there was ever to be even a chance of his love for her returning, it would have to begin by her regaining his respect. She sighed and closed her eyes, wondering if God would ever grant such a wish.

Chapter 15

FOR A FEW days things went smoothly enough. Elena managed to avoid spending any time alone with Jamie. The hours were long and empty for her. She stayed carefully out of sight in Ian's small, airless cabin, emerging only for meals and for an occasional short stroll about the deck.

It was the time on deck that meant the most to her; smelling the fresh scent of the salt air and gradually sensing her own freedom. She had escaped, she realized with elation. She was free of Hernan Valdez and his evil forever. She would soon be in France, the land her mother and father had talked of so often.

She closed her mind to thoughts of what might happen once she arrived there. She knew so little of the family that awaited her; only that they were her father's people and that there was no one else. Feeling a little frightened, she turned her face to the wind and let it dry the tears of loneliness that had risen unbidden at the thoughts of her parents. It was only a little longer, she told herself, only a few more days till they would reach the port of La Rochelle. Then she would be in her new homeland.

Suddenly a prickling in her shoulders warned her that she was not alone, and she turned to see the first officer of the ship—Mr. Peters—watching her from a short distance away. Fear rose at once, for she was only too aware that the wind had molded her thin shirt to her breasts, and she knew that the wind-dried tears could well have left their marks on her cheeks, too.

Not knowing what else to do, she hunched her shoulders against his eyes and scurried for the sanctuary of Ian's cabin, fighting a fresh sense of despair. Had he seen too much? Would he guess her identity? And worse, what would he do about it? She crouched on the tumbled bunk, painfully aware of her vulnerability should she be discovered.

An hour inched by, then another. The world began to dim a little beyond the tiny porthole, and her fears ebbed. Perhaps Mr. Peters had seen less than she imagined, she told herself. It might well be that he only saw a young boy crying with homesickness at being taken so far from his island home.

The reassuring thoughts revived her body, and she became aware of her gnawing hunger. It would soon be time for Ian or Jamie to bring her the bowl of stew and the hard tack that formed most meals on the ship. Feeling grimy, she poured a small amount of her water supply into the bowl on the little table and carefully removed her stained and dirty clothing, intending at least to be clean beneath it.

The water was cool and refreshing and she washed vigorously, well aware that the stain could be allowed to fade quickly now—since she would soon be a young lady again, and in need of the popular pale milky skin she'd once had.

She'd nearly finished her ablutions when a slight sound brought her mind away from the water and her own glowing skin. Startled, she turned in time to see the door of her cabin inching open. "No," she gasped. "Please, wait!"

Her voice sounded high and frightened in her own ears, but she was powerless to control its timbre as the space widened enough for the First Officer to slip inside. He closed the door firmly behind himself. "So I was right," he said, smiling widely.

Elena felt his hot dark eyes on her naked flesh and shrank away from them, trying frantically to think, even as she reached for her boy's garments and tried to hold them in front of her to screen away his searching eyes. "Get out of here," she ordered with all the authority she could manage. "Get out of my cabin!"

His laugh was hard. "*Your* cabin, slut?" he asked. "Don't you mean your *master's* cabin? Or do you belong to his man?" His grin widened and his tongue slid over his lips in clear anticipation. "Share you, do they? All the trip, coming down here while the rest of us work and dream..."

"Get out of here," Elena repeated, terror almost closing her throat. She longed to scream, but a deeper fear held her silent— for she realized that anyone summoned might share the man's views.

"Time for them to share a bit more," Mr. Peters said, taking a step toward her and looming like a giant in the small cabin. He was blocking her way to the door quite effectively. "No reason they should be the only ones to enjoy a lovely little girl like you, my pretty. I'll not tell the Captain, if you behave."

"Stay away from me," Elena cried, backing away from him, still grasping the shirt and pants over her swelling breasts and naked loins.

"You want to be put ashore, slut?" Mr. Peters demanded, one big hand snaking out at her. "The Captain of this ship would have no understanding of what your masters are doing, and no pity for the likes of you. If he finds out, he'll sail into the first friendly port and put you in some house where you can serve the needs of all the sailors. Is *that* what you want?"

Elena gasped at the threat and dodged behind the table, her attention half on his words and half on the door—wondering if she could somehow get him to round the table so that she'd have a chance to reach it before...

He lunged suddenly, grabbing her clothing and snatching it from her, leaving her body open to his ravishing eyes. "But you're too young and pretty for that," he said, his lips loose and nearly drooling as he stared at her. "Used to a gentleman's ways, are you? Well, could be I can teach you more of pleasure than he did. I've not whored in a thousand ports for nothing."

Shivering in terror, Elena plunged for the door, but she was too slow. The hot hands caught at her, one clutching her arm while the other sought her breast, squeezing it till she cried out in pain. His lips covered her mouth at once, hot and wet.

She tried to fight him, but he was very strong and held her easily. His mouth left a slimy trail over her throat and moved down to her breasts as he held her body tight against his own. Screams welled in her throat, but she fought silently, choking on her own teror and the knowledge that any sailor summoned by her screams would merely hold her and wait his turn.

Jamie! she thought. *Ian!* But they'd been on deck, too, when she came down. She dimly remembered seeing them with their heads together as they leaned on the rail on the far side of the deck. She doubted they'd even known she was out on the deck, and they certainly wouldn't have seen her come down or noted Mr. Peters following her.

She struggled harder, suddenly aware that she was being forced backward toward the bunk, and that Peters—panting now like the winded beast her stepfather had been, was pulling at his own clothing with eager hands. Desperately, she tore at his throat with her teeth, tasting the hot saltiness of blood even as he released his hold, cursing viciously.

His hand caught her face, slamming her back against the hard wood of the ship. She began to fall, too dizzy to stay on her feet or run. Still cursing, the blood dripping freely from his throat, Peters' big hands caught at her and threw her into the bunk. He followed, shutting out the dim light of the cabin, and his hands were brutal as they tried to open her body to him.

Suddenly the weight of him was jerked away from her and he fell swearing furiously to the floor of the cabin. Elena froze, feeling as the rabbit must as it faces the implacable jaws of the wolf. She couldn't move, couldn't even breathe in the depths of her terror.

"Cover yourself," Jamie ordered, his voice like a bucket of cold water washing over her.

For a moment she only looked up at him, uncomprehending. Then, slowly, she felt the contempt of his eyes and saw herself as she must appear to him. Racked with shame, she squirmed beneath the thin blanket that covered her bunk. "Thanks be to God that you came," she breathed.

"Who do you think you are?" Mr. Peters demanded, scrambling clumsily to his feet and straightening his clothing. "How dare you lay your hands on me, McDonald? Just because I want my share of the goods you've been enjoying on this voyage..."

"Get out of this cabin before I go to your Captain," Jamie said, his voice heavy with menace.

For a moment Peters withdrew a little, then Elena felt his eyes on her again and she shuddered. She could still feel his hands tearing at her, and her own powerless terror as she'd tried to protect herself and been unable to do more than slow him down.

"You'll not go to the Captain," Peters said. "Not if you value this wench as much as you seem to."

"What's that supposed to mean?" Jamie asked. Elena could

hear a wavering in his tone.

"The Captain is a man of high moral principles," Peters said; his tone had changed now, too, and was no longer so defensive. "If he knows you had a wench down here, he'd dump her at the first friendly port."

"I don't believe that," Jamie said, but without confidence. "The girl is mine. Why..."

"He's done it before," Peters said. "One word from me and this sweet little thing will be in some waterfront dive for sale to any dirty sailor who fancies her." He leered at her, plainly enjoying himself now. "And there will likely be plenty of them for a while, for she is a likely wench."

"Get out," Jamie ordered again, and Elena could see the blood rising to pulse in his face. His eyes were now the cold grey of hard steel. "Get out before I kill you for what you were attempting."

"I'll go to the Captain," Peters said, but then his tone turned wheedling. "I don't ask for much: just a little longer with her, then your secret is safe with me. What will it hurt? She'll still be yours. I won't come often. It's been a long voyage, and there was little in Mallorca..."

Jamie's fist stopped the words and Peters fell back against the side of the ship, nearly dropping to the floor from the force of the blow. "You tell the Captain about her and I'll tell him you discovered her identity when you came in here looking to steal from me," Jamie said, his voice low but menacing. "What do you think he'll say to that—especially when he finds a bit of my gold in your pockets or in your belongings?"

"But..." Peters' face darkened with rage. "You can't..."

"Think not?" Jamie's face was harder and colder than she'd ever seen it. "You think the loss of this wench will mean as much to me as the loss of your officer's papers will mean to you? I've plenty of money to buy more wenches, and to make sure no one else offers you a place on a ship. What do *you* have?"

The silence was so thick in the small cabin that Elena was suddenly conscious of the slight sounds of the creaking of the rigging that came from above. Peters continued to glare at Jamie for a moment, then his gaze shifted to Elena. She clutched the blanket even tighter, though she knew he couldn't see beneath it.

"Keep the wench," he said at last, spitting viciously in her direction. "But be sure she doesn't go flaunting herself about the deck again, if you don't want the rest of the men sniffing about.

There are many who'd not mind losing their posts on this ship for the touch of that fine silky flesh."

"Just get out and keep your mouth shut if you know what's good for you," Jamie said. "If I catch you near her again, I won't hesitate to go to the Captain with my protests—and you'll be the loser."

Peters hesitated a moment longer, glaring impartially at her and at Jamie, then he turned and left the room without a word. Elena lay still, too spent and weak with relief to even move as the silence spread out between them. Only when she'd caught her breath did she turn to look at Jamie. "Thanks be to God that you came when you did," she gasped. "I ..." The words she'd been about to speak died before the coldness of his gaze.

"How many times?" he asked, his voice choked and thick. "How often will I have to fight off the men you flaunt yourself before? I should have known better, that first afternoon when I found you in the alley. Perhaps you aren't worth the trouble."

"But I ..."

He didn't wait for her to go on; without another word, he turned on his heel and followed Peters out the door of the cabin, slamming it hard behind him. Elena started to follow him, but the moment the cooler air of the cabin touched her hot, naked skin, she sank back.

What could she say? What words could she use to convince him she'd done nothing to attract Peters, that she was innocent. Tears welled up as she realized bitterly that she could never again lay claim to that word. The agony of the grove had forcibly ended her innocence. And the other time ...

She felt warmth in her face as her thoughts filled with memories of the moments in Jamie's bunk, when he'd caressed and loved her. She could claim no innocence when her traitorous body still throbbed with desire at the memory. How could she explain to him the terror she felt at one man's touch, when she still longed for his arms and his lips with all the passion of a tavern wench.

Tears washed the feel of Peters' mouth from her face and, after a while, she rose and washed the itch of his hands from her body before pulling on the boy's clothes that now seemed to offer such feeble protection. She was in control of herself when Ian brought her food; she even managed to thank him before tears of total despair rose again to salt the dinner she could not eat.

Whatever dreams or hopes she'd cherished where Jamie was concerned now faded behind the leering face and grasping hands of the ship's First Officer. She would simply endure now, till they reached France and she could say farewell to Jamie and thank him for his rescue.

She must grow up, she told her aching heart. She was no longer a girl with dreams and hopes; she was a woman with pain and a future that loomed both frightening and insecure ahead of her. Once she left the ship, she knew her life could never be the same. Once she was ashore, she would never see or hear of Jamie McDonald again.

Chapter 16

JAMIE LEFT IAN's cabin still shaken. His murderous rage at
the ship's First Officer had eased a little, but hot on the heels of it
had come a feeling he liked even less. Desire for Elena blazed in
his loins with the aching pain of torture. Never had he wanted
anyone the way he wanted her.

He closed his eyes against it, then wished that he hadn't, for
he could still see her as she'd been when he pulled that animal off
her. Only as he slowly remembered the blankly staring green
eyes did his need for her ease a little. No matter how lushly
inviting her swelling breasts and satiny thighs, her face had still
been frozen in terror. He swallowed hard.

"What is it, lad?" Ian asked, breaking into his thoughts.

"The First Officer knows about Elena," he said numbly, his
desire ebbing slowly, painfully.

"Will he go to the Captain?" Ian asked, then his face changed
as he surmised what Jamie had not told him. "Elena?"

"Her virtue, or whatever you'd call it now, is still intact. I
stopped him before..." A shudder racked his body as he
remembered the scene he'd found when he entered the cabin,

drawn by sounds he couldn't identify. A flailing, clawing hand and one naked leg had been all that was visible of Elena and Peters.

"Will he go to the Captain?" Ian pressed, looking both concerned and relieved.

"I threatened to accuse the man of theft, and to use my father's position to keep him from ever serving on another ship if he opened his mouth," Jamie explained wearily. "There's only another day or two of the journey. I think he'll keep his peace that long."

"We'll have to guard her every minute till we're ashore," Ian warned.

"You'll have to guard her," Jamie said, turning away from the questions in his friend's eyes.

"Why do you hate her so?" Ian asked. "What's she done, besides nurse you lovingly when you might have died without her attention? Do you think any of this is her choice?"

"She could have gone back to her family," Jamie protested, unwilling to admit—even to himself—that it was his own overwhelming desire for her that made him want to keep his distance. He remembered only too well his pulsating dream of passion; it had haunted him, waking and sleeping, since his fever had broken. He could scarcely look at her without remembering her willing body, the yielding hunger that seemed to match his own until the final moment when she'd become so afraid.

"You know that's a falsehood, lad," Ian said, interrupting his thoughts. "She dared not go back."

"Why not? Do the Spaniards allow their women to be raped without avenging them? Do they cast them out?"

"And if the ravisher is a family member?" Ian asked. "A man her stepfather has cause to care for or believe? A woman can be falsely accused by a man, you know—especially one as young and frightened as Elena."

"I'm sure she knows who did it to her. She could have named the animal who . . ." Jamie choked on the words.

"Of course she could have." Ian seemed unmoved.

"But she lied," Jamie began, looking at his friend for the first time.

"And you've blamed her for that, haven't you?" Ian's face was old and hard in the dim light of the ship's corridor. "Blamed her for saving your life."

"What do you mean by that?" Jamie asked, angry and confused at the same time.

"What would you have done if she'd named the man? Challenged him?"

"That would have been the honorable thing," Jamie said, feeling a flush rising to his face. "It would have been her father's right, but if he was so unwilling...After all, I was going to marry her before..."

"And if you killed a Spanish Don, what do you think the rest of his family would do to you, my fine young buck?"

"But if he..."

"If she had reason to doubt that her stepfather would believe her in her battered condition, what makes you think your words would mean more to the man?"

Jamie wanted to protest, but the wisdom of Ian's words was too obvious. He swallowed hard. "Do you really think that's why she lied?" he asked after several minutes.

"That, and her own shame over what happened and the way you treated her when you found her in the gypsy camp."

"You saw the way that big gypsy was looking at her," Jamie began in his own defense.

"Not so differently than the way you were looking, as I recall," Ian said. Then his eyes narrowed. "Is it because of what happened at the Club, Jamie? Do you mistrust everyone because of that Starburough wench?"

Jamie squirmed beneath his stare. "She was a proper lady, according to my father, but I heard her in the park with her lover, heard what she planned for our life together. I'd never have been able to accept a child of hers without questioning who its father might be."

"Not all harlots walk the streets, Jamie," Ian said. "That's why I didn't doubt your words. But don't judge Elena by those lights. Do you think Amelia Starburough would have cared for you the way Elena did? She needs your comfort now, not your suspicions."

"I cannot be near her," Jamie said.

"Then I'll go to her," Ian said, and Jamie sensed disappointment in the man's tone. He turned away, fled to the cool air of the deck and paced it till the agony of his desire completely faded into weariness. Only when he was totally spent did he go back to the cabin to find the quiet, downcast Elena.

"Has Ian explained to you that we will stay with you day and night till we reach La Rochelle?" he asked, keeping his tone neutral only with difficulty.

She nodded, not lifting her eyes, which seemed fixed on her hands as they twisted in her lap.

"We will be docking at La Rochelle day after tomorrow," he went on. "We have to make some plans."

"Is it far from there to Le Mans?" Elena asked, her tone betraying none of the enthusiasm he'd expected to hear.

"Quite a distance," Jamie said. "We'll be about a week on the road, I expect, if I can obtain a suitable conveyance quickly."

"We?" There was something strained in the small word.

"I shall take you to your family," Jamie said, regretting now the plans he and Ian had made.

"But I thought . . . You've brought me to France, and I know you must be anxious to return to your home. The *Fleet Lady* . . . will she wait for you so long?"

Jamie shook his head. "The harbour at La Rochelle is too shallow for the ship to anchor at the dock. It will lie off-shore for several hours, then go on to England." He lifted a hand to stop her protests, meeting the wide hazel eyes for just a moment before they were veiled again by her long, dark lashes. "Ian will return to London with the ship and explain to my father that I've been delayed. I'll take a coaster back myself, when I've seen you safely to your family."

"Ian won't be with us?"

He was conscious of a change in her tone. He sensed fear—and something else—in the words. If he hadn't been so sure of her fear of him, he would have thought it was excitement.

"I can take care of you well enough," he said, anger touching him as he felt an answering flare of response to the very idea of being alone with her. "It would be too disturbing for my father if the ship returned without either of us. Besides, I'm not sure Peters can be trusted. If he went to my father and told him about you . . ." Jamie let it trail off, feeling a glow of guilty satisfaction in the way she shuddered at the mere mention of the First Officer's name.

"Perhaps you could just lend me enough money to hire someone to drive me to Le Mans," she began.

He laughed bitterly. "Have you learned nothing from what has happened to you?" he asked, angry at her now. "A young girl alone in the French countryside with some lout of a driver! How long do you think you'd be safe from him? Or is it me you fear, even after all these days? Do you think I will treat you as Peters did?"

Her curls trembled wildly as she shook her head at him, but she didn't lift her eyes from the floor. Anger spurred him further. *What did she think?* he asked himself. *What did she expect of him?*

"You'll be safe enough," he said coldly. "I've no intention of touching you. I leave that for your Spanish friends and the likes of Peters. I am a gentleman." Angry and shamed by the memories of his desire, he rose and fled from the cabin.

He heard her begin to sob, but he didn't look back. She would never know how he felt, he told himself angrily. He'd take her to her people and leave her, forget forever the wide, innocent eyes and soft appealing lips that melted so sweetly under his. He remembered the lushness of her body, and the familiar aching struck him again. He pounded a fist against the heavy timber of the ship, hating himself for the weakness, and resolved to see no more of her till they were ashore in La Rochelle.

Ian landed with them, making arrangements to ride out to the ship with the last load of goods to be transferred that evening, then set about making arrangements for Jamie and Elena. Leaving Elena in a room at the best *hotellerie* to be found, he went out to buy a good, second-hand traveling gown and a second, more informal gown—along with the necessary petticoats and other undergarments, a sturdy cloak, and shoes. These he placed in the battered case he had purchased, then he hired a rough cart and a nag to pull it.

Jamie went with him from shop to shop, watching his mentor's handling of the matters, then they returned to the *hotellerie* and Elena. She was pathetically delighted with the clothing. "May I change now?" she asked, combing at her tangled hair.

Jamie opened his mouth to give his permission, but before he could speak, Ian shook his head. "You'll be safer if you remain a boy till you're closer to Le Mans. When you stop for your last night, Jamie can sell the cart and horse or trade them for something more suitable for a lady. Then you can change into your better things. It would be improper for a man and woman to travel together, and besides, the cart I found is hardly suitable for a lady of quality. It will be safer, for no highwayman will be interested in a man and boy on such a poor conveyance."

Her bright features seemed to wilt like flowers in the heat. "You must realize how much trouble it would be if anyone discovers you're a woman," Jamie said quickly. "Remember how Peters behaved.":

Her crestfallen look rewarded the reference, and Jamie was properly ashamed of himself.

"I'll have to leave you now," Ian said, interrupting Jamie's thoughts. "I'll tell your father to expect you in a bit more than two weeks." His face softened. "Be strong, Elena," he said, reaching out to touch the rough waves of her cherrywood hair. "Go to your family with pride. Wipe all this from your mind and they will accept you easily."

Too soon he was gone, and they were alone in the room of the *hotellerie*. Jamie watched Elena, sensing her immediate withdrawal from him though she'd not moved at all. It angered him and he rose at once. "I'll be going down to the public rooms," he said. "Do you want anything special for supper?"

Elena shook her head, not looking up.

"I'll send it up in a little while," he promised, then changed his mind. "*I'll* bring it up," he said, giving her the key. "You keep the door locked till you hear my voice. Is that understood?"

A nod was his only answer, and he left her feeling both angry and frustrated. He had a tankard of ale, then ordered a plate of food for himself and another to take up to Elena. It galled him to be running errands this way, but there was no help for it. There was no way Elena could appear to be a servant boy when she ate: her manners were too dainty and well-bred.

Once the food was delivered, he settled down to his own plate and tried to banish her from his thoughts. There were serving wenches here, pretty French girls as willing and flirtatious as the girl Rosie had been—how long ago had it been? He smiled a little as he recalled his first wild night, and looked again at the girls moving about the room.

Viewed more closely, their prettiness seemed to fade or coarsen, and he remembered the things he'd been told about such wenches and the trouble they could bring to a man. He ordered more ale to wash down his dinner. He knew he wasn't contrasting the girls with Rosie's warm charms, and he was shamed by the realization. It was Elena he wanted, there was no denying it. He wondered, sickly, how he would bear the days...and nights...ahead.

Ale brought him sleep the first night ashore, and again the second, and the pain it left in his head made him silent and short-tempered during the days as they drove through the French countryside. Elena soon learned not to even speak to him as they rode along, and he was relieved by her silence.

By the third afternoon, however, his whole body rebelled against the idea of still another night of lonely drinking in the *hotellerie* public rooms. In spite of his bad temper, he was too aware of Elena. Each bounce of the wagon on the rutted road was reflected in the movement of her full breasts, and he was only too well acquainted with the sweet scent of her warm skin. Her full pink lips pouted at him, and the sooty lashes lay heavy against her golden cheeks, hiding the flashing green eyes whenever he looked at her.

"What will you do?" he asked, almost against his will.

"What do you mean?" she asked, plainly startled by the question.

"Will you stay with your father's people?" he asked.

"Have I a choice?" she asked. "If they will take me in, I must stay with them. I have nowhere else to go."

The words stung him, reminding him that he had been willing to offer her another place once, that he'd offered her his own home in London or—if his father rejected her—his uncle's lands in Scotland. "Why would they not take you in?" he asked, shortly. "You are still their kinswoman, no matter what has been done to you."

"They must never know about it," Elena interrupted, her voice hard. "You agreed that we . . ."

He lifted a hand to stop her. "I'll not give you away," he said quietly.

"What will you do?" she asked, apparently reassured by his tone and his words.

"Return to my father," he said, thinking at once of Amelia Starburough. "Deliver my messages and make my peace with him."

"There is trouble between you?" Elena asked, and he felt her eyes on him.

"Nothing to trouble you," he said quickly, slapping the reins on the bony haunches of the horse. "We'll stop a little earlier tonight," he said. "There are no towns after the one ahead for quite a distance, so we must stay there if you wish a bed to sleep in."

Elena sighed. "It matters little to me where I sleep," she said wearily.

Anger touched him, then remorse. She had had even less joy on this journey than he had, he realized bleakly. It wasn't her fault that the mere sight of her filled him with desire, yet he'd punished her for it ever since they left the ship.

"Perhaps tonight we could do something a little different," he suggested. "Would you enjoy a proper meal in the room? Surely such a thing would be possible for a price, and we could have at least one meal together."

Her eyes brightened in a way that made his senses leap. "Could I even put on one of the dresses?" she asked timidly.

"I see no reason why not," he said, both pleased and disturbed by the turn of the conversation. "We'll have to be careful no one else sees you, but that's not so difficult."

The arrangements were surprisingly easy to make. Jamie rented the best rooms in the *hotellerie* and ordered the finest meal and wine they offered. The table was quickly set up in the larger room while Elena stayed hidden in the small curtained alcove that opened off the big room.

Once everything was in place, he dismissed the saucy little dark-eyed maid and opened the wine himself. "You can come out now, Elena," he said, pouring the wine.

The girl who greeted him was a shock. Except for her short hair—still attractive in its fall of waves and curls—and the faint remains of the stain that still darkened her flawless skin, she looked little different from the girl he'd fallen in love with in Mallorca. When he looked at her, he longed to pull her into his arms and kiss her as he had in the garden that last evening. The stirrings of his body shamed him and he tried hard to stem the tide of memory, concentrating on the wine though his fingers felt suddenly numb as sticks.

"Do I look all right?" she asked, her tone anxious as she whirled before him, her lovely figure clearly outlined in the severely cut gown.

"Dinner will be getting cold," he said gracelessly, dropping into the nearest chair without the slightest courtesy.

Her whole body seemed to shrink accusingly as she slumped into the chair opposite him. "You look lovely," he said, hating himself for the unintended cruelty his shame had produced. "As beautiful as you did in Mallorca."

Her eyes lifted and he could see the sheen of tears in them.

She tried to speak but no words came, and he lifted his wine in a quick attempt to cover the moment. "A toast to your future," he said. "To your new life! May it bring you all the happiness you deserve."

Flame rose in her face, but she didn't turn away. After a moment, she picked up her wine and sipped it, too. Jamie filled the silence, talking almost aimlessly of his life in Scotland, his uncle's family, and finally—rather shyly—his introduction to London and his first few days in his father's house. Never had he talked so much.

As he spoke, he could see that Elena was relaxing. He poured the wine lavishly, drinking more himself than he should have and pressing it on her till she was giggling at his stories and eating without her usual shyness. He ate almost nothing, his appetite gone as he looked at her and felt the swelling desire returning.

She was so beautiful, so young and vulnerable, her green eyes flashing, her soft body swelling beneath the severe brown gown. He rose abruptly, nearly upsetting his plate. "Shall I get more wine?" he asked, looking down at her.

"I think I've had enough," she said, giggling. "More than I've ever had in my life. I'm not even sure I can stand up." She slid back her chair and tried to rise; her skirts tangled about her feet and she would have fallen had his arms not been there to welcome her.

"Elena," he whispered, holding her close. "My darling Elena."

His fingers tangled in her hair, then slipped down to tilt her face up to him. He looked into the depths of her green eyes and saw the warmth there, the love . . . Then they were closed and his lips found hers. For a moment it was as it had been in the garden when they pledged their love and he held her close. The dream rose around him and his hands moved to caress the warmth of her body as her lips opened under his. For what seemed an eternity she clung to him, her body responsive and seeming as hungry as his own. Then suddenly she jerked away.

"No. Please Jamie, *no!*" The words were sobbed, more in pain than fear.

He moved after her, reaching out, sick with his need for her, with the memories that refused to fade. "Elena," he murmured, catching her and pulling her back against him. "You want me too, I *know* you do."

For a moment she seemed to yield. Her body molded willingly to the heat of his, her lips open and her eyes closed in a kind of eager surrender. Then, as he fumbled with the fastenings of her gown, she stiffened and the panting breaths turned to sobs. "*No!*" she cried, pushing at him, then lifted her hands to scratch at his face when he refused to release her. "I'm no tavern wench," she sobbed. "Leave me alone."

For a few seconds he couldn't let her go. They struggled, then his desire turned to anger. All the love, the longing, the nights of torment on the ship and in the *hotellerie* since their landing swept over him and he slapped her, knocking her back against the bed.

Her tears stopped, and for a moment she seemed not to breathe as she lay there. Her green eyes blazed as they met his. "Are you no better than he was?" she asked, her voice cold and hard now. "Is this why you sent Ian back? Why you drove the First Officer away? Did you mean all along to keep me just for yourself, at least until you could deliver me to my family?"

Hot protests rose to his lips, but he couldn't speak them as he watched the print of his hand rise red on her pale cheek. She was still the most desirable woman he'd ever seen, the more so now with her lips swollen from his kisses and her heaving bosom straining the fabric of her gown. For a moment he longed to offer her marriage, honor, anything to make her his forever— then shock at the idea reached him.

She was no innocent maiden to be revered and married now. He had no words to clarify his confusion, and the frustration fueled his anger at her and at himself.

"Get into the alcove," he snarled. "I mean to have a woman tonight. If it isn't to be you, no doubt one of the serving wenches will be glad of my attentions."

Her gasp was ample salve for his pain, and he watched contemptuously as she scuttled away from him and disappeared behind the curtain. He went to the door and let himself out, taking the key and locking it firmly behind him.

Once down in the public rooms, his fury wavered and he almost went back to apologize. Then a woman laughed mockingly—so like Amelia had—and his anger returned.

Elena had flaunted herself at him, he told himself, led him on and then turned cold. Perhaps she meant to trap him, drive him so wild he'd offer marriage even to such as she. Anger rekindled his desire, and he quickly selected the youngest of the wenches and offered her a coin to accompany him to his room.

Once there she complied without shyness, stripping off her gown to show him a well-rounded body still unblemished. Yet even as he eased his aching need with her, he was aware of Elena just beyond the curtains and his shame robbed him of all pleasure. He felt only relief when he slapped the wench's round bottom and sent her back to the public rooms. He sank into sleep without hearing a sound from beyond the curtain, and his dreams were haunted with accusing green eyes.

Chapter 17

ELENA EMERGED IN her boy's clothing when he summoned her for breakfast. She said nothing, refusing even to look at him. He was relieved to see that his slap had faded from her face, but her very downcast silence made it clear that what he'd done later had left a deeper mark than any blow could.

They rode through the day in silence and spent the night the same way. Though he longed to escape her accusing presence, he found himself unable to leave her for more than a few moments at a time. He couldn't even escape to the public rooms to drown his guilt in the ale that flowed so freely there.

Things remained that way till their final night on the road. As they sat at their silent meal, which Jamie had brought to their room, he cleared his throat. "Tomorrow we will reach Le Mans," he said. "I've sold the cart and rented a small carriage and driver to take us there. It better befits a lady."

Elena nodded, still not speaking.

"You *must* speak to me, Elena," he said, aware it was his fault she still hadn't, "if we are to appear normal to your family." He took a deep breath. "I beg you to forgive me," he said. "I behaved as evilly as the witch I'm betrothed to, and I..."

"The *what*?" Elena's head was up and her hazel eyes were wide with shock.

Jamie swallowed hard, realizing what he'd said. "I mean..."

"You are *betrothed*?" The words were spoken so softly he sensed, rather than heard, the question.

"My father insisted on it," he said. "I care nothing for the girl."

"You were betrothed to her even while you courted *me*, while you agreed to marry *me*?" There was still doubt and accusation in her voice.

"She was an evil woman. I left London so that it could be proved. When I return she won't be waiting for me." Jamie felt the heat in his face and knew he could never confess what had happened to him, how he'd been trapped like a rabbit.

"And if she is?"

"I'll never marry her."

"And if you'd brought me with you, what would your father have said?"

Jamie shrugged. "Does it matter?" he asked.

Elena turned away and took her traveling dress from the small case, hanging it up so that the worst of the wrinkles would drop out during the night. Jamie watched her with sad eyes, wishing he could find the words to make her understand how he felt. Then he shook his head, realizing bitterly that he had very little idea how he felt about Elena. He knew only that he would be glad when he could deliver her finally and safely into the hands of her family. Only then could he begin the process of forgetting her.

He was surprised to find that thought painful. It confused him so that he left her for the first time since the night he'd brought the serving wench to his bed. The public room was hot and noisy, and the smoke made his head ache even more than the ale. Finally he went out and strolled through the streets of the small town, listening to the sounds of it and longing suddenly for the peaceful world of Scotland.

Elena would have fit in so well there, he thought wryly. If his father had been too angry over the marriage, they could have left London and returned to the north. He forced the thoughts away, reminding himself coldly that the Elena he'd pledged his love to no longer existed. The stranger he'd brought from Mallorca was just an unfortunate girl. He was to deliver her to her family, and there their acquaintance would end.

Such thoughts brought him little pleasure and, feeling older and unsatisfied, he returned to the *hotellerie* and the stuffy room where Elena already slept. Staring down at her in the light of the flickering candle, he ached to touch her, to hold her and caress her and reassure her that it was going to be all right. Neither of them could know what they would find when they reached Le Mans—and the villa that Elena had seen only in her father's water-color painting.

Things worked out better than he'd dared hope. Pierre Flambeau, an elderly gentleman, made Elena welcome at once, though Jamie sensed that his daughter-in-law Hermione was a little less pleased. Still, the story they had concocted during the final hours of their carriage ride was readily accepted, and Elena was properly hugged and welcomed into the handsome villa.

Jamie was greeted courteously, too, and quickly invited to spend the night or as long as he might wish as their guest. When he mentioned his intention to rent a horse and ride on to Cherbourg, they were quite adamant about insisting he release the rented carriage and take one of their horses for the ride.

"We've agents in Cherbourg," Pierre assured him. "Just leave the horse with the DuVals. They can find a berth on a coaster for you, too, I'm sure."

"That's not really necessary," Jamie assured him, a little embarrassed by the older man's concern. "I mean, I don't want to cause any trouble."

"But you've been so kind to our *petite* Elena," Hermione said. "Whatever would she have done without you to escort her?" Her eyelids fluttered and Jamie had a sickening feeling the old woman was flirting with him.

"I told you, Madame, that I only met your niece on the final leg of her journey, when Mrs. Renneau fell and she and her husband had to leave the group. I scarcely know Mademoiselle Flambeau. I simply offered to see she reached her destination safely, since a young lady wouldn't be safe traveling alone even for half a day."

"Ah, too true," Hermione said, looking rather disappointed. "I am truly surprised that her parents allowed her to make such a journey without them."

"My mother is unable to travel," Elena said quickly, her

flushed cheeks telling Jamie she'd understood the implications of her aunt's words. "She is in a delicate condition at the moment, and of course my stepfather couldn't leave her."

"If they'd written, I could have at least met you in La Rochelle," Raul said, his lazy smile irritating Jamie as he noted that the sleepy-looking eyes were avidly admiring his cousin Elena. "Would have saved Monsieur McDonald the long trip."

"I had some business to take care of," Jamie said coolly, "otherwise I shouldn't have been with the group and able to help Mademoiselle Flambeau."

"Well, whatever the reason, I'm delighted to have you here, *cherie*," Pierre said. "Your father was a fine young man, almost like another son to me, and I was very sorry when he chose to go to Spain to seek his fortune. Especially when my own son was killed. I asked them to come back, but of course he had his *hacienda* and a family." He smiled and closed his eyes. "I cannot believe that he is dead."

The fourth member of the family smiled then, her blue eyes on Jamie. "It must have been so exciting," Angelique said. "I do wish you'd stay longer, Monsieur McDonald. You must have so many tales to tell."

Jamie forced an answering smile for politeness' sake. The girl was a lovely blonde, but there was a coldness about her that showed even when she was being flirtatious—as she was now. He glanced at Elena and saw she was now talking animatedly to her great-uncle. She looked happy enough, he thought; perhaps it would be better to go on now, rather than to wait for the evening meal, the visiting afterward, and tomorrow's farewells.

"I'm afraid I really cannot stay at all," Jamie said, getting to his feet. "I've just realized the date and I must start at once for Cherbourg. There are things in London that..." A glimpse of Elena's face stopped him. She looked suddenly pale and terrified. He closed his mind against her, realizing now that he dared not stay.

A flurry of polite protests answered his decision, but in the end Raul led the way to the stable area. As they stood together, waiting for a horse to be saddled, Raul smiled, his eyes questioning. "It must have been a pleasant journey with my pretty cousin for company," he said. "It will be difficult to ride on without her."

"Pardon?" Jamie said, catching the implications but pretending not to understand. "Your cousin is indeed a very lovely young lady, but I'm afraid I had no chance to become acquainted with her on the voyage. I spoke a few times with the gentleman, Monsieur Renneau, but today was the first time I had an opportunity to exchange words with Mademoiselle Flambeau."

"Oh, of course, I had forgotten." Raul looked disappointed, and Jamie had to conceal a smile as he wondered what the young Frenchman would think if he knew the truth. How Raul would have behaved on a voyage such as he'd just made!

"I thank you for your kindness and the use of the horse," Jamie said earnestly. "I'll make sure he's in good shape when I reach Cherbourg."

Raul shrugged, taking the reins from the groom and holding the horse for Jamie to mount. "Oh, by the way," he said as Jamie settled into the saddle. "What of Elena's luggage? She brought so little."

Jamie swallowed hard, cursing himself for a fool to have forgotten such a thing. "It was to be shipped separately. She sailed from Mallorca, but her main luggage was to be sent from her home. I suppose it will be along later."

Raul nodded, but Jamie sensed that he hadn't been completely believed. He reined the horse around slowly, thanking the young man again but still wishing he could change his mind again. He had a feeling that Elena might still need him; that she might not yet have found the haven she'd hoped for.

He looked back several times before concentrating his thoughts on the route to the *hotellerie* he'd been told he should reach about dusk. There was no sense in his remaining, he told himself. He could do no more for her. She was with her family; the rest was up to her. He would now forget ever having known Elena de Vere Flambeau.

And so he could, through most of the days as he rode, but at night . . . The tavern wench he took into his bed became Elena—soft and sweet and shy as she'd been in his dream—and he was almost angry with the girl when she laughed and spoiled the illusion.

Cursed dream, he told himself. So real. *Too* real. He saw her again as she'd been that night in the *hotellerie*, felt her response in his arms, then endured the rejection and relived his own shameful revenge. How many women would it take to banish the feel of her silky skin? he asked himself. How long before he stopped feeling the trembling of her lips, stopped seeing the green, green fire of her eyes as she answered his desire with her own?

Jamie rode for the coast as though she were pursuing him, and he was a little ashamed of the leg-weary condition of his mount when he turned him over to the DuVals. It was a relief to find himself aboard the ugly, dirty coaster. To evade his memories, he rode the entire time on the deck, seeking with his eyes the green English coast where he hoped to forever erase from his mind the sun-burned soil of Mallorca.

A public carriage met the coaster when it landed, and he had enough money left to buy a seat into London—though not much more, having left a fair amount of his dwindling funds with Elena as insurance for her future. He rode through the darkening streets of London with a mingled feeling of excitement at going home, and a growing uneasiness about his welcome.

Everything had seemed fine enough when he'd parted with Ian in La Rochelle, but now... What had Ian told his father? And more important, what had his father had to say? Now that the truth about Amelia was obvious, was his father in a more forgiving mood? Or would he still be angry about the long delay in Mallorca and the detour to France?

Jamie sighed, wishing he'd taken time to ask Ian what he was going to tell his father. If his father was waiting for him and... He was relieved when Carlin opened the door for him and said, "Master Jamie, your father will be most disappointed that he is out tonight and not here to welcome you home."

"No more disappointed than I am," Jamie lied. "And what of Ian? Is he with my father, too?"

"Not a chance," Ian said, coming up behind the old servant. "I'm here to await the prodigal's return."

"How is my father?" Jamie asked as he and Ian went into the parlour and waited while Carlin fixed them something to drink.

"Most anxious to see you, of course," Ian said. "He was disturbed when I came home alone, but he could understand why you might feel you should escort an injured young man to his home. After all, an accident at sea can be very dangerous and a young man of good family is always a wise acquaintance."

Jamie nodded. "My duty as a Christian," he said, trying not to grin.

"And how did the young lad make the journey?" Ian asked, his eyes on Carlin. "Was he well when he joined his family?"

"I believe so. I didn't even stay the night, since I knew how things would be here. Still, it went well, I think. They were glad enough to see him."

Ian looked relieved, but before he could say anything more there was the sound of a carriage out in front and Carlin left them to admit the master of the house. Jamie sipped his whisky and looked down at his travel-stained clothing, wishing he'd gone straight upstairs. He suddenly felt unready to face his father. It was, however, much too late to escape.

"So you're back," his father said, his eyes cold. "I was beginning to think you were too much of a coward to show yourself."

"Ian told you where I was," Jamie said, feeling younger than his eighteen years and hating himself for it.

"Aye, he told me a tale. But it wasn't the real one, was it?" His father's ice-blue eyes probed at him.

"I don't understand," Jamie said, fearful thoughts swirling in his head. What had his father heard? Had Peters left the *Fleet Lady*, perhaps talked of what he'd seen in Ian's cabin? He'd not thought the man such a fool, but he knew from his own experience what madness could come from lust.

"I mean your long stay was meant to avoid your responsibilities here. Any way you could think of to make me a laughing stock and to shame me in the court circles. Or did you manage to forget you were to come home quickly to marry Amelia Starburough?"

"I should think by now her condition would make it plain that someone should have married her more months ago than I've been in London," Jamie said, relaxing a little. "Or haven't you seen my dear intended since our betrothal was announced?"

"Of course I've seen her," Fergus said, frowning more ferociously than ever. "She was in the country for a few days several weeks ago, but she was in attendance last night."

"What?"

"Her waist could be spanned by my two hands, you lying coward," Fergus bellowed, rising to his full height and towering over Jamie in his chair. "I don't know why you won't accept your responsibilities, or why you made up that preposterous tale about her and Daniel Hempstead. But I do know it *was* a lie. And there will be *no* more fiddling about. We'll go to Mr. Starburough tomorrow and begin the plans for the wedding, if he'll still accept your suit after the way you've behaved."

Jamie opened his mouth, but no words came out. His father's stern features gave not an inch and his eyes were so full of accusation Jamie couldn't speak.

"I would suggest you go up and get some rest," his father said coldly. "You look as though you've been on the road for months, and not in a gentlemanly manner." With that Fergus turned on his heel and left the room, his footfall heavy on the stairs as he climbed them.

Jamie turned to Ian. "But..." he began.

Ian lifted a hand. "I still believe you, lad," he said, "but there's not a thing I can do for you. The plans are made and the lady is waiting for you. If you'd come home with a bride..." He shrugged. "The scandal would have been ugly, but there would have been no question. As it stands now, you'll just have to do as he says and marry the wench. Once she's yours perhaps you can beat some of the devilment out of her. I know no other way."

Jamie swallowed hard, thinking of Elena. For a moment he could see her before him, soft and warm and loving as she'd been in those first golden moments in Mallorca. She'd wanted him then, he knew. He forced the memories away, trying to be cold. She might not be quite as beautiful as Amelia Starburough, but when a man took her in his arms there'd be no wondering who'd held her the hour before. He closed his eyes, remembering what it had been like in his too-real dream, wanting her as he'd never wanted any woman before. Even what had happened to her the night of the *fiesta* seemed unimportant now and he cursed himself for a fool.

"Go to bed," Ian advised. "Perhaps tomorrow it won't seem so bad. He'll forgive you once the wedding is over, never fear. He's just been hard put to keep Mr. Starburough from suspecting what a scalawag you are, and he resents it."

"Starburough should look at the harlot under his roof," Jamie said bitterly. "That's all she is, Ian, I swear to you. I've told you the truth about her, what she did—and what I heard her and Daniel saying."

"My believing you does no good," Ian said. "Best accept her. There's ways to handle such a one once she's your wife. Send her to the Highlands. They'll keep her chaste enough for you to be sure whose seed she carries."

Jamie sighed and nodded, aware that he would have to do as ordered whether he wanted to or not. "Just so long as I don't strangle her before the ceremony can be held," he said coldly.

"That's the biggest danger to my father's fine plans."

Ian followed him up the stairs, still laughing a little, though Jamie knew his old friend shared his sense of despair. There was nothing to be done, no escape. He pictured Amelia's face in his mind, and saw her lips twisting in a mocking smile.

Chapter 18

FOR TWO DAYS Jamie stayed out of his father's way, keeping mostly to his rooms, pleading weariness, but mostly nursing his anger at the trap he'd come racing home to. Finally, on the second night, he had wearied of staring at four walls. Aware that his father had gone out much earlier, he set out on his own, heading for one of the lesser clubs where his father's name would grant him admission.

Once there, he began to drink, thinking all the time of Daniel and Amelia. There had to be a way, he told himself. He'd heard their plans, heard them laughing at him. She'd admitted to being with child and yet ... He was on his third or fourth drink when the mocking dark eyes faded and another face entered his mind. Green-hazel eyes regarded him accusingly, while short, tousled red-brown curls tumbled about darkened cheeks.

"May I buy you another?" a male voice asked, interrupting his thoughts. "You look as though you need one and I, frankly, have had more than enough of my own company tonight."

Jamie looked up and found himself smiling in spite of his misery. The young man looked to be close to his age, but there all resemblance ended. Percy Chatworth, as he introduced himself, was short and stocky, with red hair above a square, freckled face and the lightest blue eyes Jamie had ever seen. They were, at the moment, filled with a kind of loneliness that instantly touched a chord in his own mind.

"My company may not be much of an improvement," Jamie said honestly, "but I'd welcome the distraction."

"You look rather like a man who's drinking to forget something," Percy said, settling himself near Jamie.

Jamie nodded. "Doesn't seem to work, though. At least not so far."

Percy looked as sad as his humorous features would permit, nodding. "I've been trying for a week," he said, "and the only time I'm successful is when I wake up in the morning. Then I feel so wretched I can't even remember my name."

Jamie laughed. "You must have something pretty awful to forget," he observed.

"The biggest mistake of my life," the redhead said. "And I did it myself, by my own choice. My friends tried to warn me, but I wouldn't listen. Now I can't face any of them."

"What did you do?" Jamie asked, too intrigued to be polite.

"I bought a commission in the Navy. I'm to serve under Vice-Admiral Vernon." Percy lifted his glass and drained it, then choked a little.

"That doesn't sound so bad," Jamie said. "I've met quite a few men in the court who are attached to the Royal Navy, and they seem quite happy and successful."

"Do they get sick rowing out to the ship?" Percy asked, his light eyes bleak. "A friend of my father's took me out to his ship the day after I received my commission. I was so sick I saw nothing but the rail I was hanging over. The cursed ship was at *anchor* and I was sick. What will it be like if—*when*—we're at war with Spain? I thought to stay in London and serve the Navy, but now I think I won't live a week after we sail. I'll never be twenty-one."

Jamie laughed in spite of his own depression.

Percy glared. "I can see you're no different from the rest," he said, picking up his glass and starting to rise. "Well, I'm happy to have lifted your gloom anyway. It's too much to hope that anyone would understand."

"Wait, wait." Jamie caught his arm and held him back. "I *do* understand. I just made my first sea voyage and I was sick as a dog, believe me. But it doesn't last, Percy. You want to die for a while, then all of a sudden it's over and you don't get sick again. At least *I* didn't, not even when we were in a storm coming back."

"How sick were you?" Percy asked, his expression guarded, but with a new light of hope in his eyes.

"I couldn't even drink water," Jamie said, remembering with pain.

"And you were all right later?"

Jamie nodded. "My friend who was traveling with me says it happens to most travelers, but that everyone survives."

"That deserves another round," Percy said, looking much improved.

"My treat," Jamie agreed, feeling better in spite of himself. He'd had little chance to meet anyone near his own age since he'd left the Highlands, and he liked Percy at once. "When do you sail?" he asked.

Percy shrugged. "I haven't asked for sure. I don't think I really want to know. There's to be a fine gathering in a week—all the officers and their guests are honoring the Vice-Admiral in the evening—so I suppose we'll be told then." Percy hesitated, then asked rather shyly, "Would you like to be my guest?"

"I don't know," Jamie began, aware that his father had been trying to arrange an evening with the Starburoughs.

"Have you met the Vice-Admiral or that man Jenkins—the one who had his ear cut off by the Spaniards?" Percy asked. "He's to be there, I think, and there will be plenty to eat and drink. A hearty meal for the condemned." His laughter sounded almost genuine.

"I think I'd like to go," Jamie said, warming to the idea. "If there is to be war with Spain, I have some private interest in it."

Percy's quick interest kept the conversation going, and Jamie found himself describing the Spanish way of life on Mallorca in great detail. The liquor flowed steadily and, as he drank more and more, other things came out as well. He told Percy about Amelia and, even later, about Elena, describing her beauty and the evil that had befallen her—though he spoke not at all of his desire for her or of Peters' attack. They left the club very late, barely able to stagger, holding each other up till they reached their carriages for the ride home through the sleeping streets of London.

Jamie lay against the cushions of the carriage, dizzy and

slightly ill. He found himself wishing he'd met Percy before, or that Percy wasn't leaving so soon. With a friend like Percy life would have been almost bearable, he decided. Percy understood. They were going to meet tomorrow night and try to find a way to solve his problem.

Jamie chuckled drunkenly. Solve Amelia, that was some problem. Maybe he should have taken what was offered that night in the garden. If he was to be trussed and delivered as a ravisher, why not claim at least the small pleasure it might offer?

Elena slipped unbidden into his mind, and for a long moment he was back in his shipboard bunk with her beside him, reliving the haunting dream that somehow refused to fade as any normal dream might. Then the other memories came, and she was pushing him away, shaming him with his own behavior.

Jamie spent the next evenings with Percy, discovering a side of London life he hadn't known before. Percy seemed to know an amazing number of people, and all of them welcomed the redhead with what appeared to be genuine affection. There were always girls—and plenty to eat and drink. Time grew hazy with the drinking and, too often, large bits of it seemed to disappear; but Jamie never worried. His coin purse was always there when he looked for it in the morning and, once his head grew smaller, he felt well enough to face the next night's revelry.

Nearly a week passed in that fashion. Then he made the mistake of going downstairs a little earlier than usual and found his father waiting for him. "So you *do* still live here," his father said coldly. "I was beginning to wonder."

"I've been making friends on my own," Jamie said defiantly.

"In every club in the city," Fergus growled. "Don't think I haven't been told."

"Are you having me watched?" Jamie demanded angrily.

"It's hardly necessary when you bear a name that is known in court circles. There are always plenty of people willing to watch a young man making a fool of himself."

"Just because I don't enjoy sitting around listening to a lot of stuffy old men expound on the merits of peaceful existence with Spain..." Jamie began.

"You'd rather listen to the hotheads shrieking for war, would you? I understood you were well treated by the Spanish on Mallorca. What changed your mind?"

"I don't ask a man his views before I drink with him," Jamie snapped. "I just enjoy being with my friends, nothing more."

"Your friends are all on the side against Walpole." His father spoke softly, and Jamie was surprised to detect a strange note of approval in his tone.

"They're my friends, nothing else."

"That's well and good, but tonight I think you should make an appearance in the other camp. There is an entertainment this evening, and I'm sure the Starburoughs will be in attendance. You've not even had the courtesy to call upon your bride-to-be since your return, so it would be wise for you to be there tonight."

"Call on *Amelia*?" Jamie glared at his father. "You've committed me to the marriage, father, and I'll honor the committtment. But that's all. I know what that 'lady' truly is, and I'll treat her just as she has treated me."

His father's face darkened, and for a moment Jamie thought he might strike him—as he had the night he'd first learned of the marriage plans. But before Fergus could react to his words, the tense stillness was broken by a rapping on the door. In a moment Carlin was showing Percy into the parlour. Jamie made the introductions, his voice shaking only slightly.

Percy smiled at him rather tentatively. "You haven't forgotten, have you?" he asked.

"Forgotten what?" Jamie asked.

"Tonight is the gathering for the Vice-Admiral," Percy said, looking nervously from Jamie to his father and back again. "I mentioned it the first night we met. You *are* still planning to be my guest, aren't you?"

Jamie's smile was only partly for Percy, for it was mostly relief that he wouldn't be forced to see Amelia yet. "Of course I haven't forgotten," he said. "I was just unsure of the hour we were expected. Let me get my cloak and I'll be ready."

Fergus moved abruptly—fury plain in the blazing blue eyes as they stabbed at Jamie—but his voice was pleasant as he ordered Carlin to offer Jamie's guest a drink and began asking Percy a few questions. His politeness and hospitality were shaming, and Jamie swallowed his pride enough to say, "If you see Miss Starburough tonight, father, please offer her my compliments and tell her I shall call in a day or two."

His father's eyes were expressionless as they turned his way, but he nodded. "I'm sure she will be pleased to hear that," Fergus said, his tone heavy with irony. "It is difficult for proper wedding plans to be made without the consent and advice of the groom."

Only when they were outside in Percy's carriage did Jamie slump down, his smile of confidence dropping away. Percy sighed. "I stepped into a family quarrel, didn't I?" he asked. "I'm sorry. I should have reminded you about tonight before this."

"And I should have remembered," Jamie admitted. "But I'm grateful for the rescue anyway. Anything to escape that blonde witch for another night."

"I'm sure the evening ahead won't be that bad," Percy said with a chuckle. "I hear there are to be a number of interesting people in attendance. I'm almost looking forward to getting to know some of the men I'll be serving with."

Jamie smiled, putting aside his own depressing thoughts. "I'm sure it will be a fine evening," he said firmly. "And I thank you for inviting me to share it with you. I think, perhaps, I'm just a bit envious. At this moment I'd gladly change places with you. Seasickness seems mild beside the illness I'm going to get when I marry the fair Amelia." He laughed without humor.

"I only wish we could trade," Percy said, laughing, too. "I think you'd make a much better man to serve our country than I will. I honestly feel sorry for the men I'll be commanding. They will, no doubt, know a great deal more about ships and the sea than *I* do."

"I should hope so," Jamie teased. "But you'll learn. By the time you come home, loaded with plunder and tales of all your adventures, you'll be a regular sea-dog, and I'll still be tied up doing my father's errands and keeping watch over my wife's virtue."

The thought was so depressing it cast a pall over the first hour of the party, but as the company began to warm with the drinking and they were escorted to tables heavy-laden with food, Jamie felt his spirits rising. He'd had another chance to see and touch the paper-thin ear that Jenkins carried with him, and he'd listened to the old man talking of the horrors of Spanish torture. Now he spotted Percy waving across the room and hurried to take a seat beside him.

"I want you to meet Reggie Hinton," Percy said, indicating a slender, dark man beside him. "He's to be ship's surgeon for the voyage."

"Ship's surgeon," Jamie said. "How are you at treating seasickness, Reggie?"

The dark man smiled, and his intense features became instantly warmer. "I've assured Percy that I won't let him die," he said. "Beyond that, I don't know. We didn't get many cases when I was taking my training—on dry land."

Percy laughed easily, obviously having had enough to drink to drown his fears. "We have here a compatriot in suffering, Jamie," he said, indicating Reggie. "A fine surgeon, top of the group, cast out just before he was to receive his certification for a mere infraction of the rules."

"Percy," Reggie said, his expression very uncomfortable. "I don't think . . ."

Percy shook his head. "You can trust our Jamie," he said. "He's got troubles of his own. Besides, he might be able to help you: his father is a big man. *Very* big."

"I . . ." Jamie began, but there was no stopping Percy.

"Got caught with a corpse, he did," Percy said, shaking his head. "Did you know that's what they do, Jamie? They steal corpses and cut them up. That's how they learn to be surgeons." Percy chuckled. "Bet it will seem strange to cut on something that fights back now, won't it, Reggie?"

Jamie swallowed hard, then asked, "If that's how you learn to be a surgeon, why did you get into trouble for having a corpse?"

"You're not supposed to get caught taking them," Reggie said. "Everybody does it. I mean, you have to if you're going to learn, but you're not supposed to get caught. The richer students hire it done, but the rest of us . . ." He shrugged. "I went once too often to the death bed of a poor soul. Now I can't get into practice as I planned; no one will accept me."

"So you decided to join the expedition," Jamie said, nodding. "By the time you come back maybe it will all be forgotten."

"I was lucky," Reggie said, digging into the gigantic platter of food before him. "If I'd had the money to buy a commission, I wouldn't have needed to join the Navy. A bribe in the right place would have gotten me out of the body-stealing charge."

"You didn't buy your commission?" Jamie felt a nudge of curiosity about the slender man. "But how . . . ?"

"One of the court fellows—Hempstead, I think his name is—found me and asked me to attend a friend of his. Took me clear out to the country to handle it." Reggie shook his head. "Young girl, short-on with child, and I guess she'd tried to get rid of it herself. Anyway, she'd botched the job and was near dying. I had to do what I could."

"Did you save her?" Percy asked, his eyes bright.

Jamie said nothing. He was chewing a bit of roast, but could neither swallow nor spit it out. A young girl in the country—and Hempstead. He had no doubt the man was Daniel, and the girl could only be Amelia.

"I saved the girl all right," Reggie went on, "but she'll never bear a child now. 'Tis a shame, too, for she was very young and it would have been her first child."

"Was the girl a blonde? Very pretty, with dark eyes?" Jamie asked, his voice sounding strange and distant even in his own ears.

Reggie shrugged. "I didn't see her face; they were careful about that. But she was fair. Actually, I couldn't even tell you where I was taken. My guess is that the girl is unmarried, which would explain the secrecy."

"How long ago was this?" Jamie asked, no longer even pretending to eat.

"Close on a month, near as I recall. Long enough for Hempstead to make the arrangements for my commission." Reggie's smile was cold. "I'm truly a fine surgeon, and I want to serve the people who need me. If they won't allow me to do it here, then I'll take care of our soldiers and sailors. Perhaps they're more deserving, anyway."

"Hear, hear," Percy said, calling for more drinks. "A toast to our fighting future," he said.

Jamie drank and ate with them, but a part of his mind was still staggering under the weight of what he'd heard. He had no doubt that the woman in question was Amelia and that Daniel Hempstead had arranged for Reggie to treat her; that explained everything. Everything except the most important thing—how he could make his father understand, convince him that he couldn't be tied to a not only unfaithful wife, but one who would be barren as well.

The harder he thought about the problem, the quicker he emptied his glass and the less he was able to eat. By the time the speeches began, he was so numb he scarcely heard the first speakers. However, as they went on, he became absorbed.

One after another toasts were offered to the Crown, to England, to Britain, to the Empire, to the war that would avenge the maiming of poor Jenkins. On and on it went till even the Vice-Admiral himself rose to call on all present to support him, to make the war a rousing victory. *That was it!* Suddenly Jamie found himself on his feet, pushing his way through the crowd till he was in front of Vernon himself.

"I wish to join in that effort," he said, keeping his voice steady with the same effort he had concentrated on his feet and legs. "I wish to pledge my sword, my heart, and even my life to the service of this mighty venture. I wish to take a commission and serve Britain against the Spanish."

Miraculously, papers appeared and he heard himself promising again, then signing papers giving his small inheritance from his mother to buy his commission. He was immediately surrounded by people, Percy and Reggie among them. Everyone was pounding him on the back and cheering while others were hurrying forward to sign the papers, too.

A weight seemed to lift from his heart, and he laughed and drank and ate with new appetite, thinking of nothing beyond the night. Only when, near dawn, Percy helped him from the carriage and delivered him to the waiting Carlin, did Jamie begin to wonder what he'd done.

"Your father is in the parlour," Carlin said. "He's been waiting for hours."

Jamie squared his shoulders and held up his head as he walked in and halted before his father. "Father, I have something to tell you," he began, his voice slightly shaky.

"I've already been told," Fergus said. "Sit down before you fall down. Of all the asinine, unforgivable, ridiculous..." He seemed to run out of words. "If you had set out to ruin me, you could hardly have chosen a more effective means. Starburough will never forgive this."

Jamie just looked at him. "What difference does it make?" he asked, feeling as stupid and thickheaded as his father seemed to think he was. "I've done nothing to stop this travesty of a marriage."

For a moment his father just stared at him. "Dear God, you don't even know, do you?" he asked.

Jamie could only shake his head.

"You sail from Spithead in two and a half days, you little fool. How am I to explain that to Starburough? What is he to think?"

Jamie stared at his father for a moment, then smiled and said, "I'm sure you'll find the words. You always have words. You could defend the harlot, perhaps now you may even find something to say about your own son." On that note he turned, nearly fell, righted himself, and went up to bed with all the dignity he could muster.

Chapter 19

THE FIRST GLIMPSES of the house in Le Mans made her heart leap with joy, for it matched perfectly the painting she'd stared at so often while her mother and father talked of what life had been like in France. It would be home, she told herself. She'd belong here as she hadn't belonged in Spain after her father's death.

The old man who came down to greet them after she'd sent a servant in to announce their arrival looked a little like her father might have in another twenty years. Tall, still straight and proud, Pierre Flambeau was the *grandpere* she'd never known and always longed for. The others, the rather stern-faced Hermione and her two children were less familiar, but with her great-uncle's arm about her shoulders, Elena didn't really care.

The greetings and explanations went better than she'd dared hope. Jamie was perfect in his casualness and, though her heart ached, she was grateful to him. She dared not show her feelings, she knew, and if he had been attentive or even reasonably friendly . . . She pushed thoughts of the past away and smiled at the delicate blonde Angelique, who appeared to be close to her own age.

The questions about Spain came rather quickly, taking her mind from Jamie and from her hoped-for friendship with her cousin. She answered as truthfully as she could, trying hard to remember where she was forced to lie. A message about her visit had been sent, she said, but when there'd been no reply she'd merely blamed the dangers of the sea and time and distance and come ahead.

Everything was fine, her mother was happily remarried and expecting a child, she explained. However, it had been her father's wish that she return to the land of his birth for a time, and since he was no longer alive to bring her and the Renneaus were making the voyage to this very area . . . She let it trail off, leaving much unsaid, trying to make it all sound simple and everyday.

Her great-uncle Pierre seemed quite willing to accept it, but even after Jamie beat his unseemly retreat the women had doubts in their eyes. Elena swallowed a sigh, promising herself that she would win them over, make them love and accept her. Still, it seemed a gigantic task, and she was glad when Hermione suggested that she must be tired after her long journey and should be shown to a proper room to rest before time for the evening meal.

"I would be so grateful," Elena said. "I realize my visit must be an imposition, but I had no idea that *ma mere's* message had never reached you. I do hope you'll forgive me."

"But we are delighted to have you," Hermione assured her. "I'm only sorry that your fine escort couldn't stay with us also."

Elena winced slightly. "I fear I took him a bit out of his way, and he was in a great hurry to return to England. I believe he said he had a fiancée awaiting him." The words were like a knife in her breast, but she forced herself to sound casual.

There was a moment of silence, then her aunt nodded. "It is fortunate that he was able to come with you at all."

"If he hadn't, I would have been forced to remain with the Renneaus till I could send a message to you," Elena managed, smiling most demurely. Though she longed to hate Jamie for the lies he'd told her and the contempt he'd showed for her after she'd rejected his advances, his riding away had left her feeling far lonelier than she'd ever been before. "I'm glad to be able to spare you such a burden."

"I'm sure my brother would have been delighted to bring you

here," Angelique said, her tone making it plain that she suspected he wished for more than that.

"You are too kind," Elena said, hoping they wouldn't hear the sarcasm she couldn't quite control.

"But you are our family," Hermione said. "I've heard so much about your father, it is a great pleasure to finally meet you." She opened the door to an airy suite of rooms. "I only hope you will be comfortable here," she said.

"It will be heaven," Elena said, meaning it. After the dirty *hotelleries* and the crowded ship's cabins, the rooms looked larger than the entire *hacienda*. The thought of actually being alone in them was marvelous.

"If you'd like a bath, I could ask one of the maids..." Hermione said, then she frowned. "And what of your luggage? I see your little case has been unpacked, but surely you had trunks!"

Elena opened her mouth to deny the fact, then realized she couldn't. "Of course," she said, "but I left from Mallorca and my belongings were to be sent from Spain. My maid will be bringing them. I'm afraid I will have very little till then. Several of my gowns were ripped beyond repair in the storm, and I didn't take time to try to replace them once we reached La Rochelle. I was hoping that when I reached here..."

"I'm sure some of Renée's old things would fit her," Angelique said, her dark blue eyes faintly mocking. "She was my *institutrice* till I finished with my studies last year. She married rather above her station and—thanks to her husband's money—had a new wardrobe made. She left everything behind. Shall I bring them down from the attic?"

Sensing the snub, Elena longed to refuse, but—realizing that there would be no trunks arriving from Spain—she swallowed her pride. "Perhaps, if it wouldn't be too much trouble. They will give me some variety while I wait for my trunks. Of course, I'll want to have some new things made." She looked at Angelique's dress critically. "You do have a competent seamstress, I presume?"

Angelique glared at her for a moment, then left to dispatch one of the maids to the attic. Hermione remained only long enough to mention the hour of the evening meal and the fact that it would be informal, then she left, too. Elena sank down on the nearest chair, fighting tears. Though nothing had been said, she knew instinctively that she'd made a very bad beginning.

The days that followed seemed to bear out her first impression. Pierre was kind, but there was no softening in either Hermione or Angelique. They were polite but distant. And there were questions, always little questions waiting to trip her up. Had she written her mother of her safe arrival? When did she think her maid would arrive with her belongings? Was she betrothed to someone in Spain? What were her plans for the future?

Though no one asked outright, Elena knew that the last questions were meant to find out the intended duration of her stay, and she winced each time she was forced to evade them. She'd hoped so desperately that she'd find someone here to confide in, but—as the days became weeks—there was no one in the family that she could talk to.

Pierre was kind, but his interests lay only in the extent of the estates and in hearing stories about her father; she couldn't even consider telling him what had happened in the olive grove. The two women . . . she could only too easily envision their pretended horror, and at the same time the way they would treat her. She'd heard them gossiping often enough to know they would have no sympathy for her. And if they knew of the manner of her journey from Mallorca, and her days and nights with Jamie . . .

Raul was another hazard. He pretended to treat her as another sister, but his caresses were not brotherly. She sensed his desire to corner her alone, and thus she trusted him no more than she had Mr. Peters after his attack on the ship. For the first time since that afternoon near the docks, she longed for the protection of a *duenna*.

Her days and nights were haunted by memories. She saw Jamie too often in her dreams: always she clung to him, surrendered to his touch. Only when she was awake did she remember the horror of the night in the *hotellerie*.

Tears burned her eyes each time she relived her moments of weakness, knew again her longing and the agony she'd felt when she fought her way free of his embrace, rejected the momentary joy he offered as she attempted to force him to respect her once again.

A bitter mistake, she'd learned as she sat silent and sick in the alcove. Her hands over her ears hadn't been able to shut out the love-making sounds of Jamie and the tavern wench, and her fury wasn't enough to totally overcome her longing to take the girl's place in his arms.

What had she become, to feel so wanton? she asked herself. What kind of creature had emerged from the hell of the grove and the ecstacy of that one brief interlude on the ship? Not even the pain of Peters' attack and Jamie's cruelty had been able to destroy her love for him.

Among the entire household, there was only one friendly face—that of the middle-aged maid, Sylvie, who had been assigned to care for her. She was a cheerful woman who did much to banish some of the emptiness Elena felt. Under her guidance, Elena managed to trim and brighten the wardrobe of drab gowns Angelique had sent to her rooms. And it was to Sylvie that she turned when the second month of her stay at the villa passed and she knew that something was seriously wrong.

Once she'd told Sylvie what troubled her, the older woman studied her carefully. "There has been a man, hasn't there?" the maid asked. "Was it him who sent you here with no luggage and only a few gold coins."

Elena gasped, blushing. "No," she protested. "I ran away from him, Sylvie. I . . ." The whole story burst from her, pouring out in a rush of tears as she described the night of the fiesta and the horror of the olive grove.

"*Men!*" Sylvie spat, showing no surprise. "Your own stepfather! They should all be locked away, or allowed only the company of the kind of women who don't care for their virtue."

"But that was so long ago," Elena said, spent now from her weeping. "I came here to forget, but I've felt so ill and now . . ."

"Now you're to bear a child," Sylvie said quietly.

"A child?" Elena gasped, blinking in disbelief. She began to protest at once. "But I *can't*. I'm not married, Sylvie. I just *can't!*"

Sylvie rolled her eyes up, but after a moment she began to explain patiently but firmly all the things Elena's mother had never told her. Sick at heart, Elena listened and realized that Sylvie spoke the truth.

"Just like Celeste," she whispered. "Dear God, shall I do what she did? Shall I kill myself rather than bear the shame?"

"Don't speak foolishly," Sylvie said, crossing herself devoutly. "A child is a gift from *le bon Dieu* and has no way of knowing how he was conceived."

"But what am I to do?" Elena asked, knowing even as she did so that the servant would have no answers for her. "How can I tell Hermione and my great-uncle?"

Sylvie shrugged, then eyed her slender waist. "In a month or two they will know, whether you speak or not," she said quietly. "It would be best to tell them before that, I think."

Elena nodded, acknowledging the truth of the woman's words. "Thank you, Sylvie," she said softly. "I needed to know."

The older woman shook her head and sighed. "'Tis wrong to keep young girls in such ignorance," she said. "It didn't protect you, and now you're far from your mother and the care you should have."

Elena watched the round woman bustle out, then settled herself on her bed. A child? She gagged a little at the memory of that night in the grove, then another thought slipped into her mind, of another night; but this one much different. What if the child were Jamie's? she asked herself.

For a moment hope flared in her heart. If they could be married . . . She could send him a message somehow, and once he knew . . . The pictures of happiness faded almost before they were full-blown in her mind. How could she tell him? Expect him to believe her when he plainly didn't even remember those magical moments in his cramped bunk?

Besides, she thought bitterly, there was the contempt he'd felt for her since Peters' attack. She swallowed hard, remembering again the way he'd left her and taken a tavern wench. And, of course, there was the fiancée he'd so conveniently forgotten to mention till their final days together. By now he would no doubt have married her in spite of his unexplained reluctance.

So there was no one, she thought bitterly, suddenly envying Celeste in spite of the pain she knew her friend had been suffering. At least she'd had someone. She'd had a chance at a new life with a man she'd loved and who had once loved her— and might have again, if he'd been given a chance. Tears burned in her eyes, but she blinked them back. There was no time for tears now; she had to think, to plan. Somewhere she had to find the courage to tell Uncle Pierre the truth of what had brought her to France so precipitously.

The day passed, and another, and another, and still the answer hadn't come. Each day she rose with the resolve to tell him, and each day things seemed to go wrong. There just wasn't an opportunity, or he was in a bad humor, or they were interrupted, or . . . In truth, the words just wouldn't come—for she knew she couldn't bear to see his eyes lose the warmth they now turned toward her. He was her only family, and to lose him would be the final emptiness.

So the days passed and she went to bed in failure each night. Her skirts began to grow tight, and at last, aware that her time was running out, she rose one grey and threatening morning knowing that she must do it today—no matter what. She dressed carefully, sipping daintily at the chocolate Sylvie brought her, but not touching the rolls. She'd just finished dressing her hair when a young maid came to the door.

"You are wanted down in the *petit salon*, Mademoiselle," she said.

"Who is it?" Elena asked, not too startled, for her great-uncle often summoned her to talk to him whenever he had a free hour.

"The family is gathered, Mademoiselle," the maid said. "There was a rider at dawn."

"A rider?" A thousand hopes and fears flooded her mind. Had Hernan found her? Or was it Jamie, his memory magically restored and his love for her once more strong?

The maid shrugged. "They said only that you were to hurry, Mademoiselle."

"Tell them..." Elena began, then gave it up. "I'll go right now," she said, dismissing the girl and going down the graceful stairway herself. Whatever it was, she knew she would have to face it sooner or later, so she might as well get it over with now.

"Sit down," her uncle said when she entered the room. His face was unfamiliarly cold and hard.

Elena glanced around quickly, noting that Hermione looked pleased, as did Angelique. Raul—his narrow features were unreadable, though she felt his eyes caressing her almost openly. Had they found out? she asked herself, looking to see if Sylvie might be lurking somewhere in the shadowed corners of the room. There was no one she could see, only the family gathered and all looking at her.

"Is something wrong?" she asked, her voice betraying her nervousness with a squeak.

"You've been with us nearly two months, *cherie*," Hermione began, a fake smile twisting her thin lips but not touching the coldness of her eyes. "We'd expected by now that you would have heard from your *mere*, or that your trunks would have arrived."

Elena nodded, both relieved and apprehensive. "I had expected them also," she began, but she was given no chance to go on.

"You have written to your dear *mere*, have you not?"

Hermione asked, as she had several times before.

"But of course," Elena said. "I've told you how I miss her and how worried I've been." That at least was the truth, though the carefully written letters had all been torn up instead of being dispatched, since Elena knew all correspondence was given to Hernan when it arrived at the *hacienda*.

"It is amazing how your letters and your belongings seem to go astray when the ones I write go to their destination without any difficulty," Hermione said, the smile still there, though the eyes now glowed with something very like triumph. "But I'm sure there is a good reason for that, isn't there, Celeste?"

"Celeste?" Elena looked at her aunt, then at the other faces turned her way. Only one pair of eyes showed compassion—and that only briefly—for her great-uncle turned away and moved to the window, plainly wanting no part of what was happening.

"When I thought over your strange arrival, I wrote to your *mere*, fearing that there was more to the story, that you might even have run away," Hermione said with elaborate patience. "I received my answer today."

"You wrote to *ma mere*?" Elena gasped. "But how is she? What did she say?"

"Such touching interest," Hermione said. "You seem quite at home in the role of Elena de Vere Flambeau, but I suppose that is not surprising since you shared her life for a number of years. That, however, is about to cease, for we will not tolerate your charade for another night, Celeste. It is over. This letter tells it all."

"What does it say?" Elena demanded, scarcely conscious of what the woman was saying. "What has happened to *ma mere*?"

"Your employer is ill, but expected to keep the child she is carrying," Hermione said. "No thanks to you, of course."

"What do you mean?" Relief swept through Elena, then apprehension followed as the full realization of what was being said reached her. "What are you talking about? Why do you keep calling me Celeste? Celeste is dead. She hanged herself in the orange grove rather than bear the child of the beast who raped her." Elena choked, longing to name her stepfather but still unable to tell the whole story while she was facing the unfriendly faces.

"How awful," Angelique gasped, but her eyes were bright with interest.

"Lies!" Hermione snorted. "Like all those you've told us

while you lived like a daughter of this house. You can't deny this. Your stepfather writes clearly of the death of Elena Flambeau in a fall on the island of Mallorca. He even says it was that tragedy that has made his wife a near invalid."

"But I'm not dead," Elena protested. "I just let him believe that so that he wouldn't try to find me and kill me."

Hermione returned to the letter. "He writes, 'I can think of no one who might have come to you with such a claim except the *companera* of my stepdaughter, a girl called Celeste. She was most disturbed over Elena's tragic death and disappeared soon after.' Then he describes you perfectly, Celeste."

Elena opened her mouth to protest, to scream that her stepfather was a liar, that he wrote those things only to further cover what he'd done to her, and to poor Celeste before her. But the glaring, accusing eyes killed the words in her throat. "It's not true," she said. "He is lying. *I* am Elena. *I am!*"

"You'll leave here today," Hermione said. "You may take the clothing if you like, and I'm sure one of the servants will drive you into Le Mans. From there you may do as you like, but don't you ever come here again or let us hear that you are claiming to be Elena Flambeau. If you do, you'll face a court for your crimes against us. Is that clear?"

"But . . ."

"Any more from you and I'll make trouble for you now," Hermione said. "I'd like to keep the family name out of this, but if you insist, perhaps a French *geole* would be more to your taste."

Elena closed her eyes, then opened them to cast one last longing glance at the back of her great-uncle. He hadn't moved from the window, and she knew from the way he stood that he wouldn't oppose Hermione's decree. There was nothing she could do, no way she could make them understand now. It was too late for the truth. Hernan had done his work only too well.

"I'll go," she said, knowing she had no choice.

They said nothing as she left the room. No one came as she packed the few belongings she'd taken for her own into the case Jamie had bought her. Numb with pain and fear, she took out the few coins that remained of the horde Jamie had given her. A tap on the door interrupted her as she hid the purse in her cloak.

"Elena . . . Celeste?" It was Raul.

"Have you come to throw me out?" Elena asked, her heart too heavy to care.

"I'm sorry about what happened," he said, "but what else can you expect? It was a foolish thing to do. You should have known that *ma mere* would write sooner or later. You came so strangely, and with only the Englishman as a companion. The family is not so trusting."

Elena shook her head, unable to answer at once. The sympathy in his voice seemed more painful than the coldness she'd encountered in the others. "I am *not* Celeste," she said wearily, not really thinking he would believe her. "Celeste died before we went to Mallorca."

Raul shrugged, obviously not believing her but not arguing either. "You've nowhere to go, so let me take care of you," he said, reaching out to touch her shoulder. "I have room in town, a small place where you can stay and be safe."

For a moment she flinched from his touch, then the kindness of his offer reached her. "You mean it?" she asked. "You'll let me stay there till I decide what I'm going to do?"

His smile was warm and kind. "Would I let a pretty girl like you wander alone on the streets of Le Mans?" he asked. "You'd hardly be safe there."

"I'd be so grateful," Elena admitted.

"So I hoped," he said softly, then he looked around. "Have you packed everything?" he asked in a more normal tone.

Elena nodded. "I've few belongings," she admitted.

"We'll remedy that, too," Raul said, taking the case. "But in the meantime, I think we'd better get away from here before *mere* gets impatient and calls in the authorities. She claims to be angry at you, but I suspect she is most angry at herself for being so easily taken in. After all, she did introduce you to quite a number of our friends." He laughed unkindly.

"I've fooled no one," Elena said bitterly, hopelessly. "My stepfather is a liar and worse. He killed Celeste as surely as if he'd plunged a knife into her heart, and he would have done the same to me if I'd remained in Mallorca. That letter is a lie, *another* lie, another attempt to destroy me."

Hard hands caught at her arms, forcing her to turn and face him. "You'll have to stop that," Raul said roughly. "I can't help you if you continue to make those claims. It's one thing to defy the family a little bit, but in this . . . Even *grand-pere* will not be tolerant enough to accept my keeping you if you continue to pretend to be my cousin. Is that clear?"

Elena blinked at him for a moment, aware of the pain of his

grip and of another pain, too. She wanted to continue the argument, to force him to realize that she *was* Elena, but she sensed the hopelessness of any words. She had no proof, no one to vouch for her identity.

"I will be Celeste," she said quietly, obediently.

His smile was quick and his grip became a caress. "You'll not regret it," he promised with a lingering gaze that touched her entire body. "You'll soon find that life in my town rooms can be far more exciting than living in this drab old villa. We'll have plenty of good times, you'll see." He picked up the case he'd dropped when she'd called herself Elena. "Now let's be on our way before *mere* comes along and insists on sending you off with one of the servants instead of me."

Elena followed him down the stairs without looking back. She was afraid of many things, but for the moment, he seemed to offer help—and she could only accept it with gratitude.

Chapter 20

THE SMALL CARRIAGE was waiting in the stable yard. Raul assisted her into it without comment, and in a moment they were out of the area of the villa and on their way along the road that Elena recognized from her arrival with Jamie. She swallowed hard at the memory. She'd come with such hopes, and now this!

"Don't be sad," Raul said. "Tomorrow we'll see about having some new gowns made for you and perhaps some jewelry. Your eyes cry out for the echoing fire of emeralds, I think."

"Oh, but..." she began, but he gave her no chance to talk as he pointed out the houses along the road, naming the owners and making up terrible stories about each one. Though some of the things he said made her blush, she also found herself responding to his high spirits, and before they reached the outskirts of Le Mans she was laughing along with him.

The streets were busy with people and Elena was pleased when Raul suggested that they go to the *hotellerie* and eat before going to his rooms. In spite of his kindness and offer of protection, she was beginning to feel a little shy about all he'd offered. If he'd believed that she was, indeed, his cousin and in need of his protection while she proved her identity, it would have been understandable; but now... During the drive, she'd had a chance to think and, in spite of his consideration, she could think of no reason why Raul Flambeau would want to help her.

The *hotellerie* he chose was a rather elegant one, and the food and wine were far better than she'd expected after her journey with Jamie through the French countryside. The proprietor seemed to know Raul and came by their table several times to make sure the food and wine were to his taste.

Elena ate hungrily, having had nothing but her chocolate in the morning, a precaution she'd found most helpful in controlling her easily disturbed stomach. Raul seemed pleased with her appetite and was generous with the wine in spite of her protests. Under its influence she relaxed a little, even considered telling Raul the whole story since he was being so kind.

Raul, however, gave her little chance to tell him anything. The wine seemed to have effected his tongue, for he talked without ceasing, describing his life in Paris before he'd been summoned home to Le Mans to take over a part of the control of the estate. The tales were wild and frequently naughty, but Elena pretended to believe them, though she seriously doubted that such things happened in proper society.

"Would you like to go there with me?" Raul asked as the serving girl cleared away their empty plates and brought a second bottle of wine on Raul's orders.

"To Paris?" Elena gasped, her eyes widening at the idea. "I never thought..."

"You would be much admired there," Raul said, "once I've outfitted you properly. You could help me in my meetings, I think. A smile, a proper word to some of the gentlemen I entertain..." He laughed easily. "A smile from you could melt the hardest heart and make my persuasion so much easier."

"I'd be delighted to help you," Elena said, pleased at the idea. "I'm sure I could arrange whatever entertainments you need. Before my father died I was already learning about the management of the servants and the proprieties of a lady."

Raul nodded. "No one would ever believe that you are anything but a lady, Celeste, that's what makes it so fascinating. I'll be proud to have you at my side and there will be plenty who'll wish to steal you away once they've seen you in the proper light."

Elena winced at the name, but kept her peace, reasoning that his insistence on using it might be for her own protection, since his *mere* had been so emphatic about her promise to prosecute Elena if she continued to claim her own identity. "I would be pleased to act as your hostess," she said. "I only hope that it won't cause you trouble with our—with *your*—family."

Raul laughed. "Let me handle them," he said. "I've dealt with them before. It would please *ma mere* if I would live forever at the villa and seek no life for myself until she can arrange a suitable marriage for me; but *grand-pere* understands that a man must have more than the simpering promises of a new bride."

"You are to marry soon?" Elena asked, surprised, since she'd heard nothing of it before.

"Negotiations are under way with half the families of the area," Raul said with a sigh, "and not a prize to be had among them. You'll put them all to shame, I'm sure. And make it far easier for me to accept whichever one *grand-pere* selects for me."

Elena frowned a little at that, not sure exactly what he meant. She started to ask more questions, but before she could find the proper words, he was off on another subject.

"We'll go to Paris next month," he said. "There is something that I must see to there and I know there will be parties, lots and lots of parties where I can show you off. You will be a prize to be displayed with jewels and satin and I'll be the envy of everyone. No one in the court will have a girl to match your beauty, I'm sure of it."

Elena sipped her wine, picturing the gowns, the lavish parties that Raul had been describing to her. It sounded marvelous, the kind of life she'd once dreamed of. Then she sighed, well aware that she couldn't hope to share it, not this year. In a month even new gowns wouldn't be able to hide her thickening waist. She'd gained only a little now, just enough to make the slightly too-small gowns she'd been given too tight, but in a month or two . . .

"You are tired, *ma cherie*," Raul said, his dark eyes instantly concerned. "I talk on and on and don't even realize that you've had an evil time being found out so suddenly and then ordered out that way. Come, come, I'll take you to my rooms and leave you to rest for a while. I must return to the villa and pretend not to know where you are."

"I *am* tired," Elena agreed, aware she would have to tell Raul the truth, but unable to face it yet.

"Rest well then, for I'll be back as soon as I can escape the lecturing. Tonight will be our night, *ma cherie*."

He summoned the proprietor and settled their account with a flourish, then took her arm and escorted her out of the *hotellerie* with ceremony. The drive was a fairly short one, and the street where he stopped the carriage was a quiet, prosperous one. The building's *concierge* emerged at once to carry her small case up a single flight of stairs and to murmur pleasantly as Raul unlocked the door to the rooms that she was to occupy.

Elena looked around curiously. The first room was not large, but it was well furnished and seemed clean and tidy, though the air was stuffy—as though the room hadn't been used for a time. Soft divans and chairs were well arranged and the drapes on the single window were of luxurious velvet. The second room was dominated by the ornately carved and luxuriously appointed bed, but there was also a dainty carved dressing table and plenty of cupboards and drawers for a wardrobe many times the size of hers.

"Think you will be happy here?" Raul asked, caressing her shoulders with his strong fingers.

"It's lovely," Elena said, "but..."

"Then I must leave you to rest and put away your things," Raul said with seeming regret. "You will probably find some gowns and other things in the cupboards and drawers and you're welcome to them. They may even fit, though I think Babette was shorter than you are."

Elena opened her mouth to ask about Babette, but before she could speak, his lips were on hers. She was too startled to protest, and he held her only briefly before stepping back with obvious reluctance. "It will be far too long till tonight," he said with a sigh, "but I must go before *ma mere* begins to suspect." He touched her cheek with one finger. "Till tonight, my lovely Celeste."

He was gone before she could speak. Elena looked around again, vaguely disturbed by his words and his actions. The rooms were almost too opulent, oppressively cloying. She hurried to open the window in the *petit salon*, sniffing the fresh air eagerly. It carried the scent of flowers and seemed to help.

Elena spent an hour exploring the rooms fully, carefully. There were clothes in the drawers and cupboards, and when she tried them on she found that they were exactly what she would need in a month or two, for the waists were several inches larger than her own—and the fact that they were several inches too short posed no problem. Even her poor needlework was equal to that small effort.

Most disturbing to her was her discovery that there was no provision for food preparation, and only a small area where some wine was stored. Was she to live here alone without even a maid? she wondered. And if so, how was she to eat? She ventured to the door they'd entered and looked out into the hall, wondering if there might be some sort of communal cooking facilities shared by what appeared to be other rooms like those she occupied.

Before she'd taken more than a few steps into the hall, the door across the way opened and a slender young girl stepped out. Elena smiled and greeted her at once, happy to see that she would have someone close by to talk to while Raul was away.

"Do you live here?" she asked when the girl responded to her greeting with a shy smile.

The girl nodded. "For two weeks now," she said. "My cousin, Madame duFol, offered me a place to stay till I assume the post she has arranged for me." The girl drew herself up proudly. "I am to be an *institutrice* to two young children."

"How nice for you," Elena said, well aware that the post of governess was something she might have had to consider for herself if Raul hadn't made his kind offer of protection and help. "I've just moved in and I was wondering about the building. My name is . . . Celeste de Vere." She swallowed hard at the lie, but accepted the necessity.

"Yvonne la Fleur," the girl said, "and I'm so happy to meet you. It has been very lonely. My cousin has an interest in a small *hotellerie* and she spends all her days there watching over the employees and buying their supplies, so I've been alone here."

"We shall have to keep each other company," Elena said. "I'm sure my cousin will have little time to visit me, though he has been very kind."

They walked about the building and Yvonne showed her the small rear garden area where they could sit on rough benches and enjoy the flowers that bloomed there. Once they were seated, Elena said, "You must be very pleased to have found a post so soon after coming to Le Mans from your family's home."

To her surprise, Yvonne shook her dark head at once.

"You do not wish to work for the family?" Elena said.

"They are most kind," Yvonne said, "and the children are

sweet, but..." She broke off. "I must not discuss it," she said.

"I'm sorry," Elena said quickly. "I didn't mean to pry, Yvonne."

The girl's face clouded and Elena was startled to see tears in the dark eyes. In spite of the fact that she suspected Yvonne was no more than a year younger than she, she felt much older and wiser. "I didn't mean that," Yvonne said. "You weren't prying, it's just that I've made so many mistakes, Celeste, and now... I just can't talk about it."

"How soon do you take your post?" Elena asked, wanting to help but respecting the girl's reluctance to discuss whatever was troubling her.

"In about a month," Yvonne said. "Only one more wonderful, golden month."

"You sound as though you think the world will end then," Elena teased, remembering how often she'd felt that way in the more innocent years of her life.

"Mine will," Yvonne said with a sigh. "Once I leave here, it will all be over for me."

"Oh, now really," Elena began, but before she could go on, a shout from a window intruded and Yvonne leaped to her feet.

"That's my cousin," she said. "I have to go in now, but I'll see you tomorrow, won't I? I've really enjoyed talking with you."

"We'll have lots of time together," Elena assured her happily. Though she didn't know what exactly Raul expected of her here in Le Mans, she was sure it wouldn't demand too much of her time.

She stayed in the garden for another hour, resting and thinking little about anything, just listening to the birds that nested in the small trees and enjoying the touch of the sun on her shoulders. Only the thought of the coming night got her to her feet as the shadows lengthened. With no place for food, she would have to do something, she realized. There were shops along the next street, Yvonne had told her, and after a little thought she got a coin from her small horde and set out to buy bread and cheese to sustain her till she had a chance to discuss the problem with Raul.

The walk was refreshing and she enjoyed the crowded, noisy market street. In some ways it reminded her a little of the day she and Teresa had gone into the little port of Mallorca, the day she'd met Jamie. Mostly, however, she just enjoyed her freedom, the sense of taking care of herself, thinking for herself once again. She'd been too long dependent on people who cared nothing for her, she told herself, envying Yvonne even though she knew the girl was unhappy about her future.

Once the baby was born she would take action, she thought serenely. If Raul would just help her through that time, then she would try to find a post of her own. She was well educated; far better, she was sure, than Yvonne and even with a child of her own to care for... It would be difficult, of course, but there were not many choices and she longed to be able to hold up her head again and to keep her own name.

The crusty loaf of bread and the small wedge of cheese cost more than she had anticipated, and that dampened her independent spirit a little as she made her way back through the quieter streets. The scents of cooking evening meals flowed through open windows along the street and she felt a twinge of loneliness as she saw families settling themselves to eat together.

When she reached the building again, Elena noticed a horse tied out in front, but she paid no attention to it, going up the stairway with only a casual wave to the old man who served as *concierge* for the building. She unlocked the door clumsily, nearly dropping her purchases as she stepped inside.

"Where have you been?" Raul demanded angrily.

Elena blinked in the light of the lamps that he'd lighted, realizing that he'd also closed the drape over the window, shutting out the evening breeze. "To buy food," she said, surprised at his tone. "I assumed that you would be dining with the family, but I..."

Raul took the loaf and cheese from her hands and set them on the table, his scowl fading. "You shouldn't have wasted the effort," he said. "I will make the same arrangements for you that I made for Babette. You can take all your meals at the *hotellerie* at the end of the street. It's clean and decent and you'll be left in peace there once it's known that you belong to me."

"That's very kind, but..." Elena began, then let it trail off as her mind began to register fully what he had said. "How long did Babette live here?" she asked, suddenly very curious about the woman whose belongings she'd found. "And why did she leave her clothes here?"

"Why so curious?" Raul asked, his expression teasing now. "Aren't you going to eat your bread and cheese?"

"Will you share it with me?" Elena asked, uncomfortable, but not sure what to do about it. For the first time she was struck by how little she really knew about Raul. He was her cousin, but she'd seen little of him during her stay at the villa.

"I've eaten," he said, "but I'll see about some wine."

He disappeared into the small storage room she'd explored and returned with wine, exquisite wine glasses, and a knife for her to use on the bread and cheese. Once the wine was poured, his good temper seemed to return.

"Babette was with me for three years," he said. "She's back with her own people now, nearer to Paris. She took what she wished with her, what she left is only a tiny bit of what I gave her during our time together, so you can expect much, much more. You are far more beautiful, Celeste, and I'm sure you'll be far more valuable with my friends. Babette was always a country maid at heart, and it often showed at the wrong time."

"Was she a relative, too?" Elena asked, washing down a large bite of bread and cheese with the wine.

"A *relative*?" He looked at her for a moment, frowning with confusion, then laughed heartily. "My dear child, Babette was my mistress, nothing more."

The food in her mouth turned sour and she could neither swallow nor spit it out as the words sunk fully into her mind. Her eyes glanced slowly over the room and in her mind she saw the room beyond it, the huge bed with all its obscene implications.

His laughter died into silence and the dark eyes narrowed. "What have you been thinking, little Celeste?" he asked. "Did you think I brought you here just because I was sorry for you?"

Fear made her swallow and she nearly choked on the food, barely managing to get it down at last. "I am your *cousin*," she gasped, tears filling her eyes from the horror of her realization. "I thought you would help me because I am your cousin."

His face hardened. "Don't start the lies again," he said coldly. "We all know who you are and what you are. I'm giving you an opportunity to make something better of yourself. As my mistress you'll be respected and appreciated. I'll make few demands on you beyond our relationship. A few of my friends might wish to share your favors in Paris, but here you will be my property alone. And if you please me, I can be very generous, *ma cherie*—very generous indeed." He had risen as he spoke, and to her horror he came toward her and reached out to stroke her face, to brush his fingers along her cheeks.

"No," she gasped, knocking over the chair in her fever to escape his touch. "You must not. I am your cousin. I am Elena

Flambeau in spite of what that animal in Spain has written. He killed Celeste and he tried to kill me, too!"

His slap stopped the words before she could go on.

"Stop that, Celeste!" he snarled. "I've no wish to hurt you. That's not the way I enjoy my women, but I won't tolerate this continued pretense. You *are* Celeste, and you are going to be my mistress unless you prefer to find your living in the streets.

Protests clogged her throat, but something in his face kept her from speaking. He reached out for her, tried to pull her close. "The first time will show you, *ma cherie*," he said with a chuckle. "I'll show you what our life will be like and you'll not be so anxious to deny me again."

His hand stole down to caress her breast, and the terror overwhelmed her. She struck at him with a strength she'd not realized she possessed, and when he momentarily slackened his hold on her she fled from him, racing out the door and down the stairs into the night.

Chapter 21

"WAKE UP, LAD. You can't be sleeping this day away." Ian's hand was rough on his shoulder, forcing Jamie's dreams of a yielding, willing Elena into the background.

"Go away," Jamie moaned, his head aching as the first rays of the sun touched his eyes. "I need to sleep."

"Then you'll have to do it on horseback," Ian said, his hands shaking him again. "You've got to try on this uniform, then we'll be on our way or you'll not reach Spithead in time to go aboard your ship."

"Spithead," Jamie said miserably, then turned over, doing his best to focus his mind in spite of the whisky-induced throb between his temples. "*What* uniform?"

Ian laughed. "Thanks to your father, I've spent the early hours well. I found a uniform that looks as though it will do with only minor alterations, and I've purchased material for several more. It's likely that the ship will carry a good tailor, what with so many last-minute commissions being sold."

Jamie closed his eyes for a moment, remembering only too

clearly the party and his own speech about God and Country and serving the King. His head rattled with the pain of the memories. "Must we go now?" he asked.

"It may take us two days," Ian said.

"You're going with me?"

"I'll see you safe aboard your vessel," Ian said, then grinned. "'Tis your father's wish," he added.

"Has he forgiven me?" Jamie asked, remembering the bitter scene on his return.

"He will," Ian said. "Already he's beginning to think of the good that can come from what you did."

"*What* good?" Jamie asked, struggling to his feet and washing in the hot water Ian had brought for him. "Last night he seemed sure that I'd ruined his life."

"Last night he was thinking only of Starburough," Ian said. "This will surely anger the man."

Jamie sighed. "Let the bitch find another master."

"You still believe what you heard?" Ian asked. "She's shown no proof of it, I've seen her myself."

"Last night I met the man who took care of the proof," Jamie said bitterly. "It seems my charming bride-to-be found a way to rid herself of her problem. Reggie, the ship's surgeon, cared for her afterward. It's his opinion that she'll never bear a child, so she's not only a harlot, she's barren as well."

Ian gasped. "You're *sure* of this?" he asked, moving about the room, packing for Jamie as they talked.

"As sure as I can be," Jamie admitted. "Reggie didn't see the woman's face, but he was taken to her by Daniel Hempstead, and Daniel wouldn't be willing to pay what he did for anyone else, I'm sure."

"Hempstead paid the man?" Ian's glance told Jamie that he was convinced.

"Bought him his commission in the Royal Navy," Jamie said. "Clever bastard, wouldn't you say? Pays the man off and gets him neatly out of the country at the same time. Daniel is resourceful, if nothing else."

Ian nodded. "You'll be well out of it," he said.

"Not to hear my father tell it," Jamie reminded him bitterly.

"I'll tell him what you've said when the time is ripe," Ian assured him. "Besides, he'll be keeping an eye on the girl himself, I'm sure, and she's likely to reveal herself while you're safely at sea. Once he sees the truth, he'll have no trouble freeing you from the alliance."

Jamie nodded, then wished he hadn't. "Remind me never to drink again," he groaned plaintively.

Ian laughed. "I've a powder for your head, then—after you've tried on your uniform—I'll have some food brought up."

"I couldn't eat anything," Jamie protested, accepting the mug Ian offered and swallowing the bitter liquid he'd just mixed in it.

"You can't ride on an empty stomach," Ian said. "Now put this on."

The uniform was a pleasant surprise. It fit quite well, and as he surveyed himself in the mirror Jamie couldn't help feeling a thrill of excitement. He was, after all, going off to fight the Spanish. He would be on a ship taking Elena's revenge against the people who had so badly mistreated her.

"Fits well, doesn't it?" Ian asked.

"I don't know how you did it," Jamie admitted.

Ian shrugged. "The man makes uniforms for most of the younger men who buy commissions. This was ordered by a fellow who met with an accident and who won't be sailing for at least another six months. You're just fortunate that he wasn't short and fat."

Jamie laughed, the evil-tasting mixture having soothed the worst of his head pains and settled the turmoil in his belly. "I'm fortunate to have someone to get these things for me," he admitted. "I'm grateful, Ian."

"Your father's orders," Ian reminded him. "Said he couldn't have you going off like some late-comer. Wants you to be a proper officer for the Crown." He laughed. "Also, it would be best to be on time. They might sail without you, if we don't get moving. I'll send your food up and you can eat while the horses are being saddled."

"What about my father?" Jamie asked reluctantly. He wasn't sure whether he wanted to see him or not, but he felt he had to ask.

"He was summoned to the court early this morning, and I doubt he'll be able to come back to say his farewell before we must be off," Ian said. "But he did leave this for me to give you." He handed him a money pouch that clinked heavily. "He said the commission would have taken all your mother left you, so this is to see you through till your ship claims its first prize."

"You'll have to thank him for me," Jamie said, both relieved and disturbed by his father's gift. He would, he thought sadly, have liked to talk to his father now that he was leaving, but there simply wasn't time. It might be several years before he returned and . . . He pushed the thoughts away and took off the uniform, changing quickly into his riding clothes.

It was late the second day when they reached the anchorage and Jamie finally saw the eight ships that were to comprise the fleet. It seemed forever before he was rowed out to the *Buford* and welcomed aboard by Percy and Reggie.

Percy, though slightly pale, embraced him warmly. "I was beginning to worry," he admitted.

"We were afraid you wouldn't make it," Reggie said. "Glad you're aboard. We arranged for you to share our quarters."

"I had quite a bit to do before I could leave London," Jamie admitted. "And for some reason I wasn't feeling too well the morning after the banquet."

Percy laughed heartily. "I thought I was going to die," he said. "But after a couple of miles on that damned horse, I was afraid I was going to live to suffer."

"How've you been since?" Jamie asked.

"Don't ask," Percy said. "I prefer not to even *think* of tomorrow. How did your father take the news?"

Jamie shrugged. "He wasn't happy, but he didn't try to stop me."

Reggie laughed. "After your speech, no one could have. You're responsible for more than a dozen new officers on the various ships. If we have a rough passage, you may have to hide yourself from them."

"Don't even say that," Percy said, paling once more and moving closer to the slop basin Jamie had noted when he came in.

"The sooner we sail, the better for him," Reggie said with compassion. "Might as well get it over with before he worries himself into a watery grave."

Percy shuddered and looked at the basin again.

"You'll laugh one day," Jamie assured him, but Percy remained unconvinced.

They set sail with the tide on July 24th, but the quick passage was not to be. Violent winds rose, forcing them back into Plymouth out of the channel between the mainland and the Isle of Wight. The days dragged by as the winds raged and teased them. Percy took to his bunk, sick and miserable from the battering, as they tried the channel each day and each day were forced back to their anchorage. The winds plagued them till

August 3, 1739, when they were at last able to escape the harbour
at Spithead and move on their way.

Fortunately, once the winds shifted their tack, Percy
recovered and was able to accept the broth that Reggie had been
bringing him for days. He regained his strength quickly, and by
the time they left the *Lenox*, the *Elizabeth*, and the *Kent* to
cruise off Cape Ortugal on the northwestern coast of Spain, he
was almost back to his normal, rollicking self again.

They prowled the decks together, speculating on the
possibility of finding a Spanish vessel on their passage across the
Atlantic. With their remaining five-ship fleet, they were sure
they would capture such a prize, but none appeared on the
empty horizon. After a long succession of fair winds and
reasonable seas, they reached English Harbour on the island of
Antigua on September 29th. Here they set their anchor to await
information about the Spanish, and to rest and resupply the five
ships who'd made the crossing together.

The harbour was impressive. A winding entrance channel
protected it from any marauding Spanish ships, and the heights
surrounding it offered several well-armed forts as added
deterrent. Stone quays abounded, and there were facilities for all
manner of repairs and ship building. Sturdy brick buildings had
grown along the waterfront area, and behind them the hill rose
green with brush and trees.

The very sight of land was a tonic to them all, and once they
were offered leave to go ashore the men streamed off the ship as
though it were on fire. "Where to first?" Jamie asked, looking at
the bright, seething scene of the docks.

"A tavern," Percy said with a grin. "Then there must be
women on this island somewhere, and I've a *great* need!"

Reggie's laugh was easy. "I'd advise you to take a little care
with that, my friends," he said. "'Tis a busy port we're visiting,
and the ladies who serve it may offer more than a few lice and a
warm and willing body."

"Oh, please, not another of your lectures," Percy protested.

"You've not seen what I have," Reggie said. "One hour's
release is not worth long weeks of discomfort. You'd be wise to
listen to me for once."

"And what would you have us do?" Jamie asked, caught
between the two as usual.

"Drink and look about a bit. See where the men go, mind the
wenches they go with, and then beware of them. There may be

officers from the other ships who've been to this anchorage before—and they may be willing to share a fact or two over a bottle. There are some families here, I'd judge, and perhaps a bit of more polite society."

"I wasn't exactly thinking of spending my time drinking tea and smiling," Percy said sourly, his freckled face reddening a little. "Of course, you surgeons may feel differently about the ladies, but..." His words were stopped by a light—but firm—blow to his sturdy midsection.

"I've been as long without a woman as you," Reggie said. "I'm only saying I'd wait one more night if I could guarantee the next one I set myself to wouldn't be my last, if you understand me."

Jamie sighed. "I think he's right, Percy," he admitted. "My uncle warned me often enough of the dangers, and in a port like this, with so many ships sailing in and out..."

"Then let's find a tavern. Maybe we can wash away the taste of the sea and try to forget the rest," Percy said with a good-natured growl. "I'll let you two be my conscience for tonight, but beyond that I make no promises."

Laughing and joking, they wandered along the street till the raucous sounds of men drinking and arguing drew them toward a small building. In a moment they were happily absorbed into the smoky, liquor-scented interior, commandeering a table and ordering the first of many rounds they were to drink to their coming victories.

It was near nightfall when they returned to the ship, staggering a little on legs unaccustomed to surfaces that didn't move beneath them, and singing merrily of the women they still longed to conquer. Only when they reached the deck of the *Buford* were they stilled by the appearance of one of the sailors.

"The Vice-Admiral wishes to see you, sirs," he said to them with a slightly alarmed look. "He sent someone to find you nearly an hour past."

"*Us?*" Jamie gulped, his head clearing slightly at the words. "But we saw no one."

"He asked for you specifically, sirs," the sailor said, "and I'm sure he is still waiting to speak with you."

Jamie swallowed hard, aware his appearance was disordered and his mind likewise well-fogged with drink. A glance at his two companions told him they were in no better shape.

"Please tell the Vice-Admiral we are back aboard, and we will be with him in a moment," Jamie said with as much steadiness as he could manage, suppressing an urge to giggle.

The young sailor left them and Jamie led the way to the cabin the three of them shared. Once there, he lit a candle and peered at himself in the small mirror they had secured to the bulkhead.

"What do you think he wants?" Percy asked, sounding far more sober than he had a few moments before.

Jamie shrugged. "It could be something simple," he said. "But who knows?"

"We've done nothing to shame him tonight," Reggie said, then added with a grin, "Thanks be."

Jamie and Percy nodded, brushing at their rumpled clothing and smoothing their hair after washing quickly in the basin. "I guess we won't know till we report to him," Jamie said, feeling a bit more in command of himself now.

"We may be happier not knowing," Percy said, but his grin was confident.

The Vice-Admiral was seated and his eyes were appraising as they stood before him.

"May I offer our apologies, sir," Jamie said after an awkward silence. "We didn't learn of your summons till we returned to the ship. We came at once."

An eyebrow lifted. "From the nearest tavern, by the look of you," Vernon said without emotion.

Jamie swallowed hard. "Yes, sir."

The Vice-Admiral sighed. "A time-honored tradition," he said, his countenance softening just a little, "but not one to be over-indulged. Tomorrow you will stay out of such places, and in the evening you will accompany me to the Rathbone residence. We have been invited to take the evening meal with them."

"We have, sir?" Percy spoke up, looking surprised. "Would that be a Mr. Jedidiah Rathbone, sir?"

"It would." Vernon frowned. "You know him?"

"He was a guest in our house once, many years ago," Percy said. "He had some business with my uncle. I was too young to do more than meet him, but I have heard of him since."

Vernon nodded. "Then I'm sure he will be very pleased that I've included you in his invitation to bring several of my young officers with me." Here another slight smile touched his lips. "He has, I believe, two marriageable daughters, and you three are the most presentable of my bachelor officers."

Jamie stiffened a bit, remembering his father's tactics on such matters and resenting the way the Vice-Admiral seemed to be echoing them. Then he forced himself to relax. Vernon was his commander, nothing more, he reminded himself. He could go, enjoy the time he spent with the Rathbone girls, then simply walk away.

"We would be honored, sir," Percy said, filling the silence before Jamie realized it had become awkward.

The Vice-Admiral said nothing for a moment. Then, as Jamie was trying to think of something proper to say that would allow them to escape the Admiral's sobering presence, he cleared his throat. "I would like you to remain for a moment, McDonald," he said. "You two are dismissed."

Jamie stood as Reggie and Percy filed out, leaving him alone with the Vice-Admiral. The silence grew in the room, making him more and more uncomfortable. In spite of himself, he found his mind ranging back over the voyage, seeking something he might have done or said that would have led to his being singled out for this private conference. There were small things, some that might have been favorable—others that were not—but none of them seemed remarkable now.

"I suspect you've wondered about your assignment for the days ahead," the Vice-Admiral said, ending the suspense.

"I have been curious, sir," Jamie admitted. Reggie, of course, had come aboard the *Buford* aware that he would be her surgeon, and Percy had been given command over the young boys who served as powder monkeys and supplied the cannon from the powder magazine that lay deep in the bowels of the ship—carefully protected below the waterline. Only Jamie had been left without a formal assignment throughout the voyage.

"I've heard you're good with weapons, so you'll be given charge of a company of marine sharpshooters. They will be the best shots, as determined by testing tomorrow, and you'll have the duty of training them while we're here in port."

"Training them for what, sir?" Jamie asked, wishing he didn't have to appear so uninformed before the old man. However, they'd had no encounters with the Spanish on their trip across the Atlantic, and he knew little about sea battles beyond what he'd heard from old sailors when they began to tell tall tales.

"Your men will be expected to take up positions there in the rigging and on the masts. From that height, they will be able to fire down upon the ships we may engage, or in the forts we will have to capture to take those port cities the Spanish prize so highly."

Jamie nodded, curbing a desire to swallow hard and shake his head. Like the others, he'd tried climbing the rigging during their passage, and he'd found it a terrifying experience. Above deck the ship's pitching and rolling was even more pronounced, and he'd been hard put to keep his hold with both hands. The thought of firing a musket from that position filled him with dread. The sailors, who climbed with ease and clung to the rope like monkeys, might have managed it, but the marines would find the task herculean.

"We will be in port for some time," the Vice-Admiral went on, "and I would advise you to begin drilling your men soon. They will need time to master the climbing before they'll be able to handle a musket without falling into the sea."

"I'll begin tomorrow," Jamie said without much hope.

"Wait another day," Vernon said, shaking his head. "You three weren't the only ones seeking the taverns. You'll drown good men if you force them into the rigging tomorrow. Besides, we may be a day or two determining the best shots."

"Yes, sir," Jamie said, privately realizing he'd probably drown a number of them anyway, no matter how long he waited.

"We are to be at Rathbone's by six-thirty," Vernon said. "Please inform your friends. And be ready in full uniform, of course."

"Yes, sir." Jamie sprang to life, aware that the words were dismissal. "And thank you, sir, for my assignment. I'll do my best to have the men ready to serve you."

"See that they are," Vernon said, turning his attention back to some papers that rested on a table beside him.

Jamie hurried out, then stopped, surprised to find Reggie and Percy waiting for him.

"What was it?" Percy asked, "Something we did?"

Jamie smiled wryly. "Something *I* did, I think," he said. "I've finally been given my assignment."

"Something special, I'll wager," Percy said. "Keeping you waiting this long, it figures to be."

"Want to trade?" Jamie teased, interrupting him.

Percy's eyes narrowed. "That bad?" he asked.

"I'm to have charge of a company of marine sharpshooters, the best of the men we've brought with us."

"That doesn't sound so bad," Reggie said.

"I'm to train them to shoot at the enemy from the rigging," Jamie said.

There was a long silence, then Reggie sighed. "I can see why he waited till we were at anchor," he said. "Those marines are no more sailors than we are. I'll wager a good share of them were never on a ship before this one."

"I don't know if they'll be able to do it," Percy said. "When I was up there, it was all I could do to hold on and not fall into the sea. If I'd had a musket, I would just have dropped it."

Jamie nodded, then said, "Well, we might as well try our bunks. The Vice-Admiral wants us in full uniform and ready to be proper gentlemen by six-thirty tomorrow night."

"*That* I'm looking forward to," Percy said, "even if the girls look like my favorite hunter, they'll at least be there to dance with and talk to, and who knows what else?"

Jamie frowned at his friend. "You'd better be careful," he said. "If you seduce one of them, you may have to answer to the Vice-Admiral."

Percy frowned. "Proper young ladies like that? Why, Jamie, that you should even *think* such a thing about me! If we weren't friends, I'd be forced to challenge you."

They laughed together and Jamie felt the weight of his worries about his assignment slipping from his shoulders. Tomorrow night's party would come before he had to face his marines, and it held far greater promise for pleasure.

Chapter 22

HAVING SPENT THE early part of the day exploring the near area of the island and standing on the high ridge staring out at the beautiful and everchanging blues and greens of the lapping sea, Jamie and the others were clear-eyed and ready when the Vice-Admiral came on deck to meet them.

"I have hired a carriage," he said. "It will be a pleasant drive: the house is only a short distance and the evening is mild."

They commanded great notice as they moved through the crowded waterfront area and beyond it to the quieter streets where the better houses of the area were built. Jamie was aware of envious eyes following them and felt a swift rush of pleasure. For whatever reason, they were going to a party—and it would, in many ways, be like being back in London.

Or on Mallorca? The thought came unbidden to his mind as the soft breezes from the sea caressed his face. He saw Elena in his mind with vivid clarity: not the troubled, angry, wounded creature he'd taken from the island to France, but the young girl he'd strolled with in the gardens of the Valdez *hacienda*.

The picture shamed him, for he felt again his love for her.

Had what happened changed her so much? he asked himself. All that he'd been told said yes—that she was degraded, no longer acceptable as a bride since she had no innocence to offer him— but could he really accept that? The idea was disturbing, for he knew that nothing that had happened, not even his own shameful behavior in the *hotellerie* on their journey, had changed the simple fact that he still cared very deeply for her. His need to know that she was safe and happy was fierce, sometimes overpowering.

"You'd better change your expression," a voice hissed his his ear, snapping him back to the present. "If the Vice-Admiral looks at you now he'll send you back to the ship." Reggie was grinning at him, but Jamie sensed that the warning was sincere.

"I was thinking about something else," Jamie confessed, looking around.

They drew up in front of the large house that had been pointed out as belonging to the Rathbone family, and in a moment they were inside being greeted by a tall, hawk-faced man and his small, round wife Amanda. Two young men flanked their father and were introduced, then it was several minutes before the guests were led into the drawing room where the rest of the family waited.

Jamie was aware that there were several people in the room, but his eyes were drawn at once to only one. She was perched like a butterfly on the edge of a chair, her golden head held high. Wide violet eyes surveying the room calmly touched him, then Percy and Reggie, then slowly came back to meet his with the delicacy of a caress.

The girl rose at a summons from her father and approached them with dignity. Her every movement had the fluid grace of a prowling cat. She was introduced as Rebecca, the eldest of Rathbone's three daughters.

Her gown was a shade of violet just a little darker than her eyes. It was well cut, leaving her creamy shoulders bare and emphasizing the swelling ripeness of her figure. Yet there was more than that, Jamie realized, unable to take his eyes away from her. The golden hair, the unusual eyes, her pretty features and stunning figure—though powerfully attractive—were still not what held him. It was a glow that seemed to come from within, a glow of sensuality that made a mockery of her downcast eyes and shyly whispered greeting. It was like stepping from shadows into blazing sunlight—but in this case, the heat was centered in his loins.

A second daughter was introduced to them, then a younger boy and girl; but Jamie scarcely noticed them. Even when Rebecca moved out of his view for a moment he was conscious of her presence, and as soon as he could he turned to her, drawn like a moth toward the flame of her appeal. He was not, however, alone, for Percy and Reggie were with him, obviously drawn by the same current.

The evening moved sluggishly. The middle daughter, Sarah—or Sally, as she was called—played for them on the spinet while the younger children sang, but Jamie was only slightly aware of it. His eyes were drawn ceaselessly to Rebecca, and when she smiled at him the entire party disappeared.

At dinner Jamie ate mechanically, tasted nothing, chewing and swallowing automatically as he watched Rebecca across the table. Jealousy flowed through him as she tilted her golden head toward Percy, then filled the air with the silvery sound of laughter.

"Is this the first time you've been away from England, Mr. McDonald?" a feminine voice inquired from his side, forcing him to turn his gaze for a moment. He was surprised to see that Sally was seated on his right.

"Not really," he said. "I was in Mallorca and made a brief journey in France before I joined this expedition."

"But you're not like the others," the girl said, smiling up at him. She had the same golden hair, and her features were similar to her older sister's, but her eyes were a soft, unremarkable blue. In spite of her prettiness, she seemed ordinary compared to Rebecca. "You speak differently."

"I was raised in the Scottish Highlands," Jamie admitted, longing to turn back to the torment of watching Rebecca and Percy, but forced by politeness to continue the intrusive conversation.

"Oh, do tell me about it," Sally said. "I've never been allowed to make the journey to Britain but I do so want to. We were all to go next year, but now Papa says the trouble with Spain will make the journey too dangerous. We shall have to stay here forever."

Jamie smiled at her, thinking of his cousins in the Highlands. Sally seemed younger than her seventeen years, like a little sister. His eyes left her for a moment and wavered toward Rebecca. To his surprise, she met his gaze, her eyes almost beckoning in their sensuous warmth.

"She'll just lead you on," Sally said from beside him. "Every man on the island is mad about her, but she doesn't really love anyone. It's all a game for her."

"But she's so *beautiful*." The words were forced from him by the pain of his infatuation.

"You're different," Sally went on, and he forced himself to meet her clear, bright eyes. "Don't let her trap you, too."

"Such . . ." he began, only to be interrupted by the end of the meal. The girls were led away by their mother, much to his regret, and he was left to listen to Rathbone and the Vice-Admiral discuss the possibilities of the coming attacks against Spanish holdings. He was relieved when commotion at the front of the house announced the arrival of more guests, and there was the sound of music from a distant room.

"I've arranged for some dancing," Mr. Rathbone said, "and invited most of the local families. We are not too many, I fear, but we try to maintain a proper life here, as we would if we had remained in England."

"We are delighted to be allowed to share in it," the Vice-Admiral said quickly. "On the seas one longs for such amenities, and so few ports have them to offer."

"Shall we join the ladies, then?" Mr. Rathbone asked, ending for Jamie the torment of waiting.

Doors on the far side of the entry hall had been opened to show a large ballroom which was already filling with people. There were, of course, far more men than women, but Jamie had no difficulty locating Rebecca in the crowd. By fast footwork he managed to be at her side when the musicians struck the first tune.

At first it was enough just to hold her as they swirled about the room, but by the time she'd granted him a second and finally a third dance, he longed to have her alone for a moment. To his surprise, she gave him an opening just as the music ended. "It has grown so warm in here," she said, touching her pale forehead delicately. "Do you think we could step outside for a moment?"

"A wonderful idea," Jamie said. He took her arm possessively, feeling the heat of it against his side, and led her through the doors that opened onto the garden.

There were other couples moving about the shadowed area, but Rebecca knew the paths well, and in a moment they emerged from a tree-shaded path into a small open area where there was an empty bench. For just a heartbeat, Jamie remembered another garden and another lovely blonde, but then he pushed the thoughts away. Rebecca was nothing like Amelia Starburough, he was sure.

As if to prove his opinion, Rebecca began asking him questions about himself and his family in the politest of terms, her eyes downcast and shy now that they were alone. He spoke freely of his brief time at court and the mission he'd been sent on to Mallorca; but he didn't mention either Amelia or Elena, though he felt a pang at the memory of the green-eyed girl he had come so close to marrying.

"You will be here for a few weeks," Rebecca said, "and then you will sail away and forget all about us."

"I'll never forget you," Jamie said fervently. "And we will come back, I'm sure. English Harbour is ..."

"Such promises," Rebecca interrupted him, her soft lips pouting in the moonlight. "They've been made before, but not kept. I suppose I should dance only with the men of the shipyards or the sons of my father's associates here, but they talk only of life here, and ..."

She looked up at him, her lips slightly parted, inviting. Jamie hesitated only a moment, then bent to kiss her, drawing her gently to him, half expecting her to pull away. Rebecca, however, seemed quite willing, her lips answering his tantalizingly. He tightened his embrace and she immediately stiffened in his arms.

"Jamie, dear, *please!*" She pulled away from him, fanning herself lightly with a dainty, perfume-scented scrap of cloth. "You move so quickly, and I find myself overwhelmed."

"I meant no disrespect," Jamie assured her. "It is just that you are so lovely here in the moonlight. Rebecca, please, you must let me call on you again. Tomorrow afternoon perhaps, or in the evening. Perhaps we could take a drive if there are carriages to be hired."

Rebecca's face was instantly touched with sorrow. "Tomorrow I cannot," she said, "but perhaps the next afternoon? My father would never allow me to leave the house in the evening, but a drive in the afternoon would be lovely. Our island is beautiful, and there are many places I could show you."

"I shall come for you at two," Jamie said, his heart pounding with excitement at the prospect.

"There is only one thing," Rebecca said, her slender hand touching his arm in appeal.

"Anything," Jamie said, his head spinning with the scent of her perfume and the excitement of knowing she would let him see her again.

"You must tell no one I've agreed to see you," Rebecca said. "Please promise me you won't."

"I vow it," Jamie said. "But why?"

"I seldom go with anyone from the ships, and if it is known that I've agreed to see you the others will only be encouraged to try again." Her sigh moved him deeply.

"Your secret is safe with me," Jamie said. Then, lifting her hand and pressing it to his lips, he touched her delicate, slightly salt-tasting palm with the tip of his tongue. Her violet eyes widened a little at the sensation, but her fingers remained in his hand for several minutes.

"You're a naughty lad," she whispered, drawing her hand away slowly, letting her fingers caress his cheeks. "But so exciting!"

He kissed her again before she insisted they return to the ballroom before they were missed. She was the answer, he thought, watching her swirl away from him as she was claimed by another of the young men who seemed to throng about her every moment. She would make him forget Elena's blazing eyes and ripe body; she would banish forever the shame and pain and love he'd felt for the abused—but still proud—French girl.

"Did you kiss her?" The question startled him so that he nearly dropped the glass of wine he'd taken from one of the servants. Feeling a flush of red rising in his neck, he turned to face Sally.

"Is this our dance, Miss Rathbone?" he asked coldly.

"I thought you were going to call me Sally," she replied, her eyes impudent and teasing. "And of course you kissed her. No one walks in the garden with Rebecca without kissing her."

"Why are you so interested in what your sister does?" Jamie asked, holding his temper with determination. "It's really quite unseemly for you to say such things."

Sally shrugged, her green gown revealing a body as flawless as her sister's. "When I was younger, I used to follow her around and spy," she admitted without a trace of shame. "I know all her tricks." In parody, she opened her eyes wider and formed her lips into a delicate pout. "But you move so quickly, I'm quite overwhelmed," she mimicked, her tone catching an emphasis so perfect that for a moment he thought she must have been listening while he was in the garden with Rebecca.

Sally's laughter was tinged with sadness. "I wasn't watching you," she said. "I was dancing with your handsome surgeon friend, but Rebecca never changes her pattern. She'll allow you to kiss her and hold her, but..."

"Stop it," Jamie said harshly, his temper finally escaping his control. "You're behaving like a spoiled child and it doesn't become you. Your sister is a beautiful young woman and her behavior should be none of your concern. You must have suitors of your own, and they should keep you too busy to spy on her."

Sally's saucy face seemed to crumple and the pale skin darkened to a furious red. They were near the doors to the garden, and in a moment she broke from him and fled out the door, her eyes full of tears. Jamie glanced around quickly, fearful that someone had seen her face and would interpret it to mean something far different; but no one seemed to be looking his way. He moved out of the well-lit room into the cool night air.

Feeling a little guilty over his words, he looked around for Sally, but she had vanished completely. She'd deserved it, he told himself as he moved away from the door and leaned against a tree trunk. Saying such things about Rebecca, trying to poison his mind against her sister—it was scandalous!

The thought of Rebecca brought her face back into his mind, banishing everything else, and he smiled at the night. She'd agreed to see him again, he reminded himself, nothing was more important than that. Rebecca liked him and wanted to see him again—hope that she could care for him took precedence over Sally's childishness.

The rest of the evening passed rather swiftly for him. Rebecca allowed him only one more dance, but when he said goodnight, her eyes were a kiss and her lips breathed a promise as she whispered, "Day after tomorrow." The magic of it carried him back through the night till they neared the quay where the *Buford* was anchored. Only then was he forced to remember that there was a day to get through before he saw her again, and that he was to spend that day training his first command.

The rigging looked less substantial than ever in the moonlight and the slight rocking of the ship reminded him of the difficulties that he and his sharpshooters would have to overcome. Regretfully, he forced the glowing image of Rebecca

Rathbone from his mind and followed his friends onto the deck, where they said their goodnights and thanked the Vice-Admiral for having included them in his evening.

Vernon smiled at them all. "It is pleasant to have gentlemen to accompany me," he said, "and to know they will bring me no disgrace."

It wasn't till after the Vice-Admiral had disappeared into his large cabin that Reggie laughed. "I think you two have just been given a warning," he said.

"Us? What do you mean?" Percy asked.

"I've been rejected as too poor for the Rathbone daughters," Reggie said without rancor, "but you two seem to be in the running. I think our good commander was just letting you know your intentions had better be honorable!"

Percy laughed. "As if gentlemen could have anything but honorable intentions," he said archly, "especially where such lovely young ladies are involved."

Jamie joined in, but without too much enthusiasm, remembering only too clearly how Rebecca had seemed to enjoy dancing and flirting with Percy almost as much as she had with him.

"If you two romantics are interested, I did learn something of the side of life here," Reggie went on. "It seems there are clean ladies to be had for a price only a bit of a drive from here. The eldest son, Jonathan, told me of the place. From what he says, I'd say it might be worth spending a bit of money to ease the long night ahead."

Percy made a few inquiries as they leaned on the ship's rail, but Jamie said nothing—his eyes going once more to the rigging. By the time they retired to their cabin, his mind was full of half-formed plans and ideas.

He rose early in spite of a restless night and climbed the rigging himself as soon as he'd had a bit of the bread and fruit the ship's cook offered to early risers. The ship rocked rhythmically even at the quay and, once he'd chosen his position, he found himself having to hold on with at least one hand. He moved onto the mast and locked his legs around it. In that position both his hands were free for firing, but if the ship were moving under full sail or recoiling from the force of fired cannons it would not be so easy.

Jamie shook his head and climbed slowly back to the deck. There were few people to ask advice of, so he left the ship.

Wandering first through the cluster of the town, he then climbed into the brushy hillside, seeking a spot where he could rest and think.

The bright tropical sun was already heating up when he found a shaded patch of grass and settled on it. Below him the ship lay at anchor, along with the others of their small fleet. He could see the marines being formed up and marched off somewhere. He watched them go with worried eyes, aware that soon some of them would be in his charge—and that what he did now might well determine whether they were to survive the battles that lay ahead.

It took him only a short time to devise a solution, and he hurried down the hillside much more swiftly than he'd climbed it. A visit to the ship's smithy ended Jamie's morning, and by afternoon he had a short length of rope with two small but sturdy hooks attached, one at each end. Carrying that, he climbed the rigging once again and selected a position in the lines. Then he wrapped his small rope about his body, clipping the hooks to the taut lines of the rigging. By leaning into this improvised belt and making sure that his feet were firm in the rigging, he had both hands free to handle a musket.

Relieved and pleased with his own inventiveness, he ordered the smithy to prepare more of the rope belts, then he went to inquire of the Vice-Admiral as to how many men he would be commanding.

Before nightfall he'd assembled his men, told them what would be expected of them. Then he demonstrated the rope device himself, promising them that by morning they would be testing its usefulness themselves. That accomplished, he wearily settled himself with Reggie and Percy, pleased with himself and full of plans for tomorrow afternoon and his drive with the lovely Rebecca.

With his mind full of Rebecca, he refused to join Percy and Reggie when they left the ship to seek a tavern. Only as he slipped into sleep did the golden haired beauty begin to change. The violet eyes changed to green and the hair became tangled cherrywood curls and waves. Murmuring the remembered name to himself, he buried his face in the rough blanket, willing her to let him forget the shameful way he'd treated her—and the love that still ached in him when he least expected it.

"Elena," he whispered to the night. "Why did you curse me with such love, Elena?"

The night offered no answers.

Chapter 23

ELENA RAN NEARLY a block from the building before she slowed enough to look back. To her surprise the street behind her was empty of all but an old man and two small boys, none of whom seemed even aware of her existence. Still panting from her fear and the effort of running, she reached a corner and took shelter there in a shadowed doorway, trying to decide what to do next.

The streets seemed different now than they had earlier when she'd returned with her bread and cheese. Night was falling; but more important than that was her fear, she realized. Before she'd believed herself safe and protected. Now suddenly she realized she had no protection, and the world had become a hostile place.

Where could she go? she asked herself, acutely aware that the air was cooling and that she had not even a shawl to protect her from the night wind. Nor any money, she realized. Her small horde of coins was still in the rooms that Raul had brought her to, carefully hidden among her belongings and thus totally out of reach.

She looked back along the street fearfully, but the horse still stood tied at the post and no familiar figure moved along the deserted way. Elena closed her eyes, reliving the day. Suddenly she understood all the small things that had troubled her and realized that, except for her own foolish innocence, she should not have been so surprised.

Her gratitude to him made her blush even in the darkness, and another face filled her thoughts. Jamie would have offered her such care, she thought sadly. Even though he'd ill-treated her at the end, shamed her with the wench from the tavern, his kindness had always shone through. But he knew who she was, she reminded herself coldly—or who she had been.

The brutal fact rested heavily on her mind as she looked around again and, seeing the light spilling from the door of a small *hotellerie*, began to move toward it. As Elena Flambeau she'd had some slight protection and acceptance. Now, stripped of her identity by Hernan Valdez's lies, she had nothing and no one to turn to. As Celeste she would have to find work and a place to stay—and do it quickly, for the night was upon her and she feared the streets even more than she feared Raul.

A small man met her at the door of the *hotellerie*, his eyes cold. "What do you want?" he asked.

"I . . . I can cook and serve the tables in return for a place to sleep," Elena said, trying to sound confident and strong though her knees were shaking under his glare.

His eyes went over her quickly but thoroughly. "If it were up to me, you'd be welcome in my tavern and in my bed," he said, licking his lips, "but my wife would have none of you. Be on your way, lovely, before she comes after you with a broom."

"But I'm not . . ." Elena began, but was given no chance to finish the words.

"No decent woman prowls the street seeking a bed," the man said. "Be off before I call the watch and have you given a bed in the *geole*. Time behind bars will teach you your place."

More frightened than before, Elena moved on, leaving the lighted doorway and making her way along the dim street. She wandered more slowly, looking back often, keeping her head down. Twice more she approached the lighted *hotelleries* and once ventured to a *cabaret*, but each time men came out to greet her and their avid eyes turned her away in terror.

Soon she became aware of footsteps behind her. Fearing Raul, she looked back, but the shape pursuing her was small and female. Hopefully, Elena slowed a little, allowing the woman to catch up with her.

"Girl," the woman called, her voice betraying the fact that she was old. "Come here, girl."

Elena hesitated a moment, for the woman had stopped beneath one of the rare street lamps. Then she gained control over her fear and approached her. "What is it?" she asked.

The old woman's eyes fastened on her face at once, looking at her with such care that Elena had to fight an impulse to turn away or cover her face with her hands. "What are you doing on the streets alone?" the woman asked.

"I had nowhere to go," Elena said, disturbed by the woman's gaze, yet desperate enough to beg for help from anyone now that the hour was growing late.

"Nowhere to go, is it?" The crone was smiling, but without warmth. "Well, perhaps we can take care of that."

The final words were spoken more loudly than the first, and suddenly Elena saw a movement in the shadows beside her. Before she could do anything, strong, hard hands were grasping her arms.

"She's a pretty one, Ma," a male voice rumbled. "Can I have her?"

"Don't be foolish," the crone said. "She'll not be for the likes of you till we've collected from a couple of gentlemen. Likely as she is, they'll pay a pretty penny for her favors."

"Ah, Ma..." the huge man whined. "I saw her first!"

Elena's mind cleared and she began to struggle. "Let me go," she cried, finding her arms held so tightly she couldn't break free. "You have no business holding me here. Let go of me or I'll scream."

"A husband has every right to take his wayward wife home," the crone said, her lips curling in a smile so evil it made Elena cringe. "Or perhaps you'll attract a customer with your noise and I can deliver you right away."

"No," Elena screamed. "No!"

It was a nightmare. The old woman ordered her hulking son to drag Elena along the street to a well-lit *cabaret*. Elena tried to fight, but the animal who had captured her only laughed as she tried to bite and scratch and kick at him. He held her as easily as she might have held an angry kitten. They were nearly to the *cabaret* when the old woman lifted her head and signed for the man to stop.

"Could be we'll do better here," she said. "Yonder comes a man with the price for one so young and fair."

Elena redoubled her efforts, but this time the coarse man was unamused. "Be still," he ordered, twisting her arm around till she feared it would snap. Whimpering a little with the pain, she looked up as the old woman called out to the rider, urging him to view the fine young maid who could be his—for a price.

"Let her go!" Raul's voice was low and controlled, but somehow more deadly than a shout. Elena felt the fingers loosening their hold on her wrist.

"You've no right," the woman cried. "I found her, she's mine to sell."

Raul swore at her, using words that made Elena's face burn in shame. He rode forward till his horse nearly trod on her, then ordered the cowering hulk to lift her up behind him. Elena offered no resistance, holding on to him as tightly as she could as he turned his horse and spurred him into a canter.

"Well, dear Celeste. Are you ready to go back with me?" he asked. "Or do you prefer the streets?"

Sobs of weariness and relief shook her, and she could only lean her head against his back. She had no fight left. What had happened to her would happen again, she realized. She had no one, nothing to protect her now, no one except the man who had come for her and was taking her back to his rooms.

"How did you find me?" she asked, hoping to avoid answering him as he slowed the horse in front of the building she'd fled from a deceptively short while ago.

"I asked at the *hotelleries* and *cabarets*. There are not many tarts on the streets with your youth and beauty, Celeste. And by morning, I assure you, you would have little of either left. I won't hold you against your will, though. If you wish to leave me again, go; I won't follow you or bring you back a second time. You're not a child, so you must make the choice yourself. Which is it to be?"

Sick to her very soul and suddenly fully understanding why Celeste had gone into the grove with the strap, Elena slid down from the horse and waited for him. Her fingers touched her stomach, cradling the tiny life within her. Had she been sure that it was Hernan's seed, she would not have hesitated to kill herself—no matter if her soul was eternally condemned, for no hell could be worse than what she saw ahead of her—but if the child was Jamie's, if she could keep even a part of him to love . . .

"Say it, Celeste," Raul said, standing beside her.

"I will stay with you," Elena said, not lifting her eyes from the ground. "I will be your mistress."

His hands were gentle as he led her inside and up the stairway. "Come along and let me wash the touch of that creature from you," he said. "We'll drink some wine, and when you're feeling better we'll see what else we can find to do."

Elena controlled a shudder and nodded her agreement. No more tears, she told herself firmly, no more running away. She drank the wine till it clouded her mind, and when Raul carried her to the bed she closed her eyes and pretended the hands that caressed her belonged to Jamie. He was kind and gentle, and sometimes—thanks to the wine—she could almost believe and respond as if the man who held her and claimed her compliant body was Jamie.

Afterward, when he was gone and she was alone in the rooms, the tears came, but without violence. She would never be clean again, she thought sadly. But she and her baby would survive. Before she slept, she had made peace with herself.

The next day dawned cloudy and, remembering Raul's words, she went to the nearby *hotellerie* for chocolate and fresh rolls. Then she strolled about the neighborhood again, seeing it in a new way, accepting it as she was now trying to accept her new role. When she returned, she found Yvonne sitting on the front stoop of the building, her eyes red from crying.

"Oh, Celeste," the girl cried, jumping to her feet. "I'm so glad to see you! I tapped on your door before, and when you weren't there I was afraid you weren't going to be here any longer."

"What's wrong?" Elena asked, thinking wryly how near she had come to not being here—to not really being *any*where— today. "Has something happened?"

Yvonne sighed, then led the way through the building to the sheltered rear garden and the bench. "I just talked to my cousin and—Oh, Celeste, everything is so *wrong*!"

"Perhaps if you tell me about it," Elena suggested gently, "together we might be able to think of something."

For a moment she saw hope stirring in the girl's eyes, then it died. "I'm afraid there's nothing anyone can do," she said. "But if you have some time..."

Elena smiled bitterly. "It seems I will have plenty of time," she said. "My cousin will be away for several days, and I have little to do but lengthen some gowns."

"I'll help you with that later, if you like," Yvonne said.

"Thank you," Elena agreed. "Now. Tell me what has upset you so."

Yvonne leaned back against the sheltering tree. "My family is a good one, but the years have been less than kind and the land—too much has been sold off. What remains doesn't always provide enough for us. The last few years have not been easy."

Elena nodded. "It can be cruel."

"We were all educated together," Yvonne went on. "My father even insisted we girls learn to read and write. Then my cousin, the one I live with here, came out to the farm and said some friends of hers in Le Mans were looking for an *institutrice* to take care of their children, and that they were willing to pay quite well in advance for the right girl." Yvonne stopped and swallowed hard.

"It was an opportunity for you," Elena said, filling the silence.

"I was willing," Yvonne said quickly. "I wanted to come. My father asked both my sister and me, but she was afraid, so I offered." Her face clouded. "I was eager to live in town and learn a few things about this way of life. I even came early to stay with my cousin so I wouldn't have to stay on at the farm till the time came for me to take my post."

She stopped, and Elena waited several minutes before asking, "And now you want to return to the farm? Is that what troubles you, Yvonne?"

The girl started a little, then shook her head. "I could be very happy here," she said, "and if the family were going to live here, perhaps... I could work for them for a year or two, until my family's debts are paid. But now they've decided to leave France and go to the new world, to some wild island. I'll *never* see Frederick again!" She burst into tears.

"Frederick?" Elena blinked at her, then smiled gently at the bowed figure, fully understanding for the first time. "You've met someone," she said.

"He's so wonderful," Yvonne said. "He's a soldier, a sergeant, and so brave and strong. He's Swiss, and that makes it all the worse. My father doesn't approve of him, refuses to even *meet* him." Her eyes met Elena's. "He wants to marry me, Celeste. He has only another six months before he can go home and buy the small farm near his family's holdings. He wants to take me with him, and—oh, I want *so* much to go with him."

Elena slipped an arm around the girl, understanding only too well her suffering. To love someone and be unable to marry him!

Her mind was filled with Jamie's face, then she pushed the memory away.

After last night there was no hope for that dream. Even if the child she carried beneath her heart was truly his, Jamie would have no use for her now she'd become the mistress of Raul Flambeau. What had happened in the grove had been ugly and horrible, but she'd had no choice about it. What she was today was of her own choosing.

"Perhaps your sister could take your post," Elena suggested, forcing herself to think of Yvonne's problems and not her own.

Yvonne lifted her head, but only to shake it. "She is only fifteen, too young for the journey," she said. "Once they heard that, my parents refused even to consider such a thing. She would die; she was afraid to come this far from home."

"What does your sergeant say?" Elena asked.

"That he loves me, and that he will find a way," Yvonne said. "But how can he, Celeste? He will not marry me without honor, he has said that often enough." Her smile was sad. "He is older— past thirty—and very proper, but so gentle and kind and when he kisses me." For a moment her eyes brightened, then dimmed with fresh tears. "I'll never see him again," she sobbed.

"What do you mean 'without honor'?" Elena asked.

Yvonne stared down at her hands, her fair skin coloring. "I offered to run away with him," she said. "I know it is shameful, but I love him so much."

"Perhaps he will wait for you," Elena suggested. "You would have to serve the family for a few years, but at the end of that time you could return to France and..."

"And then go to his country and seek him out?" Yvonne asked. "He is a handsome man, Celeste, and ready to marry. He loves me now, but in a year or two he might find some other girl and forget me, I know it. When I sail with the LaCroix family, it will be the end. I'll never see him again."

"Have you told your family how you feel?" Elena asked, wanting desperately to help the girl.

"They tell me there will be other men," Yvonne said bitterly. "Because I am only seventeen, they think I will forget." She sighed. "The money is gone already, paid for new stock and seed and to settle bills. They couldn't give it back even if they wanted to."

"Don't give up yet, Yvonne," Elena said. "I know it's hard to go on believing, but there must be a way."

"Yvonne, are you out there?" The woman's voice was harsh and demanding.

"I'm in the garden," Yvonne answered, quickly wiping at her eyes with the hem of her gown.

A stout woman came through from the street and looked around. Her eyes touched Yvonne, then settled on Elena with a force that was almost a slap. She strode forward in obvious anger. "What are you doing with this creature, Yvonne?" she demanded in a loud voice.

"This is Celeste," Yvonne said, looking confused. "She's staying in her cousin's rooms for a while, and . . ."

"Her *cousin!*" The thin lips curled. "Is that what you call him? How sweet! Get inside, Yvonne. I never want to see you speaking to this woman again, is that clear?"

Yvonne rose slowly, her eyes full of questions, protesting; but Madame duFol gave her no answers, just ordered her out of the garden. Only when the clear sound of her door slamming reached them did the woman turn back to Elena.

"How dare you associate with her, slut?" she snarled. "My cousin is a decent child, completely unaware of ugly women such as you, and I want her to stay that way. Is that clear?"

"I would not harm her," Elena protested. "She was crying, and . . ."

"Her childish romance is nothing to you. You stay away from her, understand? I don't care how rich and powerful your 'cousin' is, I can make trouble for you if you don't obey me, and believe that I will. I'm a decent woman and I don't like living in the same building with the likes of you anyway, so stay out of my way. Understand?"

Elena opened her mouth to protest, then closed it without speaking. There was no defense, she realized miserably. She was exactly what the woman called her. The fact that Raul truly was her cousin only made the whole thing worse, and the circumstances that had brought her to this situation would have no meaning to a woman like Madame duFol. Feeling far heavier than her pregnancy should have made her, she rose from the bench and left the garden without looking back.

She kept her head high and her sobs tightly controlled until she was inside the rooms and her door was locked, then she dropped on the nearest divan and sobbed into the pillow that cushioned it. Never had she felt more dirty and alone. She hugged her arms around herself, remembering that she wasn't truly alone—that she did have something, someone to live for.

Closing her eyes, she lifted her face and began to pray, asking nothing but that her child be protected from all the evil that touched her life. And that it be Jamie's seed, not that of the monster who'd forced himself on her in the grove. The prayers brought her peace in spite of her feeling of unworthiness, and she felt better as she went slowly into the bedroom to begin work on the gowns that were hanging there. It would be more difficult to do them alone, but she had no hope of finding any new friends now; Madame duFol had made it clear just how unwelcome she was in this building.

The lonely days moved by slowly. Raul came seldom, in spite of his talk of the wonderful times they would share, and Elena, in her loneliness, soon came to look forward to his visits. He was always full of tales about the people of the area, the balls he had been invited to, the girls his mother was constantly mentioning as future wives for him.

What came later she endured, hating herself for the fact that her body responded to his caresses. Raul was pleased and he brought her gifts, telling her how wonderful she was and promising that they would soon go to Paris.

Each time he spoke of the future, she tried to find the words to tell him about the baby, but he listened to little she said, preferring to kiss her and caress her. And in the end, she would simply close her eyes and conjure up Jamie's face, his arms and hands and the body she'd loved so briefly and yet still hungered for.

Though Yvonne no longer came near her, Elena often saw her entering and leaving the building. She even saw her with the sturdy soldier that she knew must be her Frederick. Her heart ached for them, for it was easy to see he loved her as much as she loved him.

A week passed, then another. The dresses were all hemmed, and the two rooms shone with the force of her constant cleaning and polishing. She'd seen nearly every street in Le Mans on her endless walks, and still the hours spread emptily ahead of her. She was sitting in the *petit salon* alone just before noon, wondering what she could do next, when a light tapping brought her to her door.

When she opened it, she was startled to find Yvonne standing on her doorstep. "Please, Celeste, may I come in?" Yvonne asked.

"Of course," Elena said, stepping aside, then closing the door quickly behind the girl. "But what of your cousin?"

"She's to be gone all day," Yvonne said, keeping her head down. "I've missed you so much! I don't care what she said, Celeste, but I don't believe her."

"Sit down, Yvonne," Elena said, seating herself opposite the girl. "Let me tell you how I came to be here, to be what I am, but first you must promise me to tell no one, no matter what."

"I promise, but . . ."

Elena silenced her with a look, then carefully began telling her of the real Celeste and the night on the island. She omitted little from the story, leaving out only what had happened between her and Jamie and the fact that she was carrying a child. When she finished, Yvonne was pale and silent.

"So you see," Elena said, "I *am* Raul's mistress. I had little choice in the matter, but I am what your cousin says I am. And she's right, you shouldn't be seen with me. You are a decent girl, and you must never let anyone have the slightest doubt about that. Do you understand?"

"But I *want* to see you, talk to you, be your friend."

"You are welcome here any time," Elena said. "I've missed you, too. Tell me, how does it go with the sergeant? Has he thought of a plan?"

Yvonne nodded, but her expression was no brighter. "He is willing, but I cannot bear it," she said.

"What is that?" Elena asked, feeling better than she had in days.

"He will hire himself to the army for another three years and use the money he's saved, the money for his farm, to buy my freedom from the LaCroixs."

"He loves you very much," Elena said, for nothing could be more obvious.

Yvonne nodded. "We shall be married, and I will stay with him unless he is sent somewhere to fight."

"Why are you so sad?" Elena asked. "Isn't that what you dreamed of, being his wife and not having to sail away to the new world?"

"The farm he's always dreamed of will be sold to someone else," Yvonne said. "It's sad, Celeste. He's wanted it ever since he was a boy, and he's told me about every little hill and the brook that waters it and the house that he wants to build for us and ... How will he feel when we go back to his home and he must find another farm to buy? How can I let him make that sacrifice?"

"What else can you do?"

"He has some time free, a leave coming in a few days. We could run away together. By the time we come back, the LaCroixs would have sailed. I'm a good seamstress, and I could find some work while he serves the rest of his time in the army. I could repay the money a little at a time, and ..."

Yvonne got to her feet and moved about the room restlessly, finally stopping at the window that looked down on the street in front of the building. "I'm going to ask my cousin to go to my family and ask them to return a part of the money, whatever they can. They'll be angry, but if I can earn the rest myself ..." She gasped. "She's coming!"

For a moment Elena didn't move, then she pushed the girl toward the door. "Go to the garden," she whispered. "She'll never know."

From her window she saw Madame duFol's sturdy figure approaching the house, then in the distance, she saw a rider and, recognizing the bay horse, she hurried to the mirror in the bedroom, anxious to tidy her hair, aware that it was too late to change into something more suitable than the loose-waisted gown she wore to free the the thickening waist that her other gowns were beginning to pinch painfully.

She would have to tell him soon, she told herself grimly; but not today. First she would make a few arrangements, like selling a little of the jewelry he'd given her and hiding the money so that she would never again be thrust out in the street as she had been that first night after she'd come to these rooms. She'd been a child then, but now she was a woman who would soon have a child of her own.

Her eyes were grim as she smiled at her image in the mirror. Today she would please Raul, make him so happy that he'd forgive her anything. He'd told her often enough that he adored her. Perhaps it would be enough. She hurried into the *petit salon* just as his key turned in the lock, but her smile faded as she caught sight of his expression. He had obviously not come seeking love.

Chapter 24

"BOLT THE DOOR," he ordered coldly, his eyes raking over her without any warmth or desire."

"What is it?" Elena asked, hastening to obey. She tried to think of something she might have done to anger him, but nothing came to her mind.

"Take off your gown," he ordered. "Take off all your clothes."

"But . . ." Elena stopped, shocked by the words. In spite of their intimacy, Raul had never treated her this way. His eyes told her there was nothing of passion in his request.

"Do as I say," he ordered, "or by all that's holy, I'll strip them from you myself."

Elena began slowly, with shaking hands, to do as he requested. Her loose gown fell about her feet, was quickly followed by her petticoats, and then, reluctantly, by the remainder of her underclothing. She shivered in spite of the warmth of the room, then drew herself up firmly, holding her hands at her sides, aware that she could not protect herself from his eyes and refusing to cower.

"It's true, isn't it?" he said, his eyes raking over her.

"What are you talking about?" Elena asked, her fright turning now to anger.

"You're carrying a child!"

His tone was so full of fury that her arms came unbidden to shield the tiny bulge she'd tried so hard to conceal with the new gowns. For a moment she thought to lie, to deny the fact, but her own intelligence admitted the futility of that. Even if she convinced him that he was wrong now, in a month or so he would know the truth. "What if I am?" she answered, tossing back her nearly shoulder-length mane of curls.

Raul said nothing, sinking down on one of the divans as though her words had struck him.

"May I dress now?" Elena asked, buoyed by her own anger.

He nodded, his face reflecting conflicting emotions.

Elena drew on her clothes quickly, both relieved and frightened now that he knew, then she frowned. "How did you know?" she asked.

His face twisted with a bitter smile. "The proprietor of the *hotellerie* told me. He seemed so sure that I'd had you somewhere else for a while, perhaps brought you from Paris because of your condition. It seems his eyes are better than mine."

Elena sighed. "I was going to tell you," she said, tired now as her own anger ebbed away.

"How long did you plan to wait?" he asked, his eyes freezing her. "Or were you hoping I would believe the child was mine?"

"I am not a fool, nor do I think you are one," Elena said. "I was in this condition when I came to your home, though I didn't know it myself." She blushed. "Thanks to my mother, I was told nothing of such things. A maid in your household explained it to me."

"The Englishman!" Raul was on his feet, pacing the room. "I thought he was too proper, even though I saw you looking at him with those cat eyes." He turned on her, and for a moment she thought he might strike her.

Anger stirred her, and with it the desire to protect Jamie. "I was raped by my stepfather, Hernan Valdez," she said coldly. "He tried to kill me afterward. That's why I fled Mallorca and came here, to seek help from my father's family. Whether you wish to believe it or not, I am Elena de Vere Flambeau. Celeste was my *companera*. She was raped by Hernan also, but she chose to kill herself. I had neither her courage nor her weakness, though sometimes I wish that I had."

He lifted a hand to slap her. "Don't start those lies again."

"They are not lies. If you wish proof, take me to Paris. I will go with you to Celeste's family and you can ask them if I am their daughter."

Raul opened his mouth, his face purpling with rage, his raised hand shaking, then he turned away and went to the window. Elena stayed where she was, seeing that his knuckles were white as he grasped the sill, obviously fighting his own fury as he digested her words.

"The letter," he said. "I saw the letter, read the description."

"The man raped me, Raul. He was drunk and thought I was a gypsy dancer. But when he discovered the truth he picked up a rock and hit me with it. He left me for dead. The gypsies saved my life by taking me away from the *hacienda*. Jamie and his man got me off the island and brought me here to save my life. Hernan had no idea where I was; I suppose he assumed the gypsies had kept me for themselves, and then your *mere* wrote him. What else could he do? How could he admit that I was alive?"

"I can't believe it." His voice was full of doubts.

"You don't *want* to believe it," Elena said.

"You let me bring you here, make love to you, my own *cousin*!" His guilt made him turn from her.

"I believe you made it clear to me what my choices were," Elena reminded him coldly.

He turned to her, his eyes cold and ugly. "No one must ever know," he said harshly. "It would kill *grand-pere* and *mere*. You would ruin everything for me. The scandal!"

"Then you believe me," Elena said.

His dark eyes touched her, then winced away. "I will never admit it, Celeste," he said, his voice hard. "If you speak of it to anyone, I will denounce you as a whore. Is that clear?"

For a moment fury pulsed through her. She longed to scream at him, to force him to . . . to what? she asked herself. He believed her—that was clear from his anger and his shame—but she also realized his determination not to admit his belief. She nodded, aware that she couldn't go back to the villa, anyway; there was no place for her there, no future for her child.

"What would you have me do?" she asked. "Go back to the

street and find that crone and her animal son? I am a Flambeau, whether you wish to acknowledge it or not."

"I just want you to go," Raul said. "Take the gifts I've given you. Take this." He drew a purse of coins from his belt. "I am on my way to Cherbourg on an errand for the family. I'll be gone for at least a week. Be gone when I return, and never try to contact me or any member of the family again."

"But..." Elena gasped.

"If you do, I'll finish what Hernan Valdez began," Raul said, his eyes cold. "There is too much at stake to let you destroy everything."

Elena shrank from his gaze, sick with fear, yet relieved, too. It was over. She was no longer trapped here, a prisoner to his whims, forced to submit to his touch to keep herself and her unborn child safe.

Raul looked around the room, then picked up his coat. "One week," he said threateningly, "and I want you out of Le Mans, away from anyone who might see you and tie you to me or my family. Is that clear?"

Elena nodded.

Raul left, closing the door softly behind him. Elena locked it after him. She was shaking with the aftermath of tension, but relief and fear of the future stirred inside her. Numbly, she carried the purse into the bedroom and spilled its contents onto the bed. Then she added her remaining horde, and also the jewelry, to it. Was it enough? she asked herself. Where would it take her? How long would it keep her and her baby safe? And when it was gone—then what?

For two days she stayed in the rooms, venturing out only for her meals at the *hotellerie*. She was aware of the proprietor's curious eyes, but she ignored them. She would have liked to move to that *hotellerie*, since it was small, cheap, and clean, but she knew she dared not stay in Le Mans. Where *could* she go? What place would welcome her?

She thought often of Jamie, wondering if she dared try to find him. If the child was his... But the spectre of his wife filled her thoughts. He would be wed now, she was sure, and that left her without hope. She looked around the small rooms, wondering how she would feel about such an arrangement if the man who came were Jamie and not Raul. It was a frightening thought, for her heart leaped with joy and shamed her.

It was late the second evening when a tapping on her door brought her out of her dreaming and worrying. Cautiously, she asked, "Who's there?"

"Please let me in, Celeste." Yvonne's voice was broken and full of pain.

Elena opened the door at once. "What is it?" she asked, shocked by the agonized look on the girl's usually pretty face. "What has happened?"

"They won't agree," Yvonne sobbed. "My cousin spoke with my father, and he refuses to consider *any*thing. He has forbidden me to see Frederick again. He won't even accept the idea of his buying my freedom from the LaCroixs. It's over! *Over!*" She dissolved into fresh tears on the divan.

Elena stroked the girl's tangled hair and patted her shoulders, feeling torn with frustration and anger at the unfeeling way Yvonne's plans had been destroyed. "Surely there's something," she said. "What does Frederick say?"

"I don't know," Yvonne sobbed. "I wasn't even allowed to see him or tell him. My cousin has gone to meet with him now."

"Perhaps he will come for you, take you away anyway," Elena suggested.

Yvonne lifted her head for a moment, then let it sink back in misery. "He would not do that. He's too honorable. He would buy my freedom, but if my father forbids it, he told me before that the agreement must be honored. I must sail in three days, and I'll never see him again. I'd rather be *dead*!"

"So soon . . ." Elena sank down on the divan beside Yvonne, an idea forming in her mind even as she absorbed the information. "When do you go to them?"

"Tomorrow morning," Yvonne said. "That's why I came up. I had to say *adieu* to you and tell you what happened."

"And when does your Frederick's leave begin?" Elena asked, paying no attention to the rest of the girl's words.

"It began yesterday."

Elena took the girl's hands, forcing her to lift her head to meet her eyes. "If I could suggest a way for your agreement to be fulfilled without your having to leave, do you think he would agree to it?" she asked.

"What?" Yvonne's eyes brightened, then clouded with doubt. "But *how*? What do you mean, Celeste?"

"I have to leave here, too," Elena said. "I was educated by my father as a son might have been, so I could take your place as an *institutrice* for the LaCroix children."

"But you are a ..." Yvonne stopped, and her face flushed. "I'm sorry," she said, dropping her eyes. "You've been so kind to me, and ..."

"I told you how I came to be here," Elena said quietly, absorbing the pain of the rebuff without allowing it to affect what she was thinking. "I have no desire to remain what I am. All I want to know is whether or not you think the LaCroixs would accept me."

Yvonne gnawed at her lip for a moment, then nodded. "You could tell them you are a cousin of mine," she said. "Madame LaCroix is kind. I told her once about Frederick, and she was most understanding. She would have accepted my sister if my parents had allowed it."

Elena looked around the room, her heart pounding with hope. It was a miracle, she told herself. A new chance for her and, in the process, a chance for Yvonne to claim the happiness that she and Jamie would never know. For a moment she enjoyed the feeling, but then her practical side returned.

"I must talk to your sergeant as soon as your cousin returns," she said. "He must approve of the plan, and you can't go to him. Where can I find him?"

Yvonne gave her the address and Elena nodded, hating the thought of the dark streets but aware that she dared not wait till morning for fear the man might be gone. "You go down to your own rooms," she said. "I'll watch for Madame duFol from here."

"How will I know what he says?" Yvonne asked.

Elena frowned for a moment, then picked up a bit of ribbon from the table. "When I come back, I'll tie this on my door if you are to go to him in the morning. Now tell me where I may find the LaCroixs, too, for I'll have to go to them in the morning before they can contact Madame duFol and destroy everything."

The plan, so hastily made, went far better than Elena had dared hope. She found the sergeant without difficulty and, once he realized she wasn't a street woman seeking business, he listened intently to her words. He was a big man, blocky and blonde, with stern features and gentle eyes.

"Why would you do this for Yvonne?" he asked when she'd finished. "What is your price?"

Elena bridled for a moment, angry at the intimation, then—realizing the question was a logical one—she relaxed a little. "I am nearly alone in the world," she said. "My distant relatives have arranged a marriage for me with a man I hate and fear. They will be coming for me in a week. This way they will never find me. You and Yvonne will be doing me a kindness by accepting my offer."

The shrewd grey eyes studied her for a moment, and Elena held herself firmly, aware that he might doubt her word. She willed herself to believe her own lies long enough for him to become convinced. Finally he nodded. "The contract will be kept? You understand that you will have to serve the family for more than a year without receiving any money?"

"I have a small sum of my own," Elena said, dropping her eyes demurely. "All that remains of my poor family's holdings."

Suddenly the stern features melted into a smile that lit the pale eyes and made him as handsome as Yvonne always described him. "We shall name our first daughter for you," he said, "and bless you always."

"Just get Yvonne away quickly and make her happy," Elena said. "She loves you very much."

The darkly tanned skin of his face darkened even more with a blush, and he nodded stiffly. "She will want for nothing," he assured her, rising. "Now, I will see you safely back to your rooms. The streets are not safe for decent women."

"Thank you," Elena said, her heart lifting at the words. Perhaps, once more, she *could* be a decent woman, she thought—once she was away from Le Mans on her way to the new world.

She spent the night packing her possessions in the case Jamie had given her. She heard a stir in the hall near dawn and opened her door to find Yvonne standing there. Without a word she kissed the younger girl and sent her on her way, grateful that she, at least, would have her dreams come true.

Later, when Madame duFol had departed, Elena asked the *concierge* to summon a public carriage for her and, with her belongings, she set off for the address Yvonne had given her. This was, she knew, the most dangerous part of her plan, the part most likely to go wrong. Still, knowing that she couldn't return to the rooms Raul paid for, she dismissed the carriage at the door of the well-kept and handsome house. With her case at her feet, she lifted the ornate knocker and let it drop.

Chapter 25

THE TRAINING WENT better than Jamie had dared hope. Though the men were fearful at first, he soon had them leaping into the lines with as much courage as the sailors, though with little of their cat-like grace. They quickly mastered the use of the lines and hooks, and with a little practice could load and fire their muskets without falling or dropping anything to the deck or the sea below.

When Vice-Admiral Vernon came on deck near noon, Jamie felt no shame to have him watching the men as he gave the order that sent them into the rigging. Vernon studied the maneuvers, then turned to Jamie. "Where did you get the ropes, and how do they work?" he asked.

"I had them made up, sir," Jamie said. "It seemed to me the only way a man could be secure in the rigging and have both hands free to use his musket."

"Very ingenious," Vernon said. "I will order them used by other sharp-shooters. It should greatly improve their accuracy."

"Thank you, sir," Jamie said. He waited till the Vice-Admiral left the deck, then signalled his men to return to the deck. He

dismissed them for the day after reminding them that they were
to report to him again the following morning for more practice
in the rigging.

Jamie ate his noon meal alone, then strolled along the
waterfront till he found a stable where he hired a small carriage
and a rather bony mare to draw it. Excitement filled him as he
drove to the Rathbone house to make his call on Rebecca.

To his surprise, she was waiting for him a little way from the
house and waved gaily as he stopped the mare. "Am I late?" he
asked nervously.

"Of course not," she said. "It was such a lovely day I couldn't
stay inside like a proper girl and just wait for you." Her long
lashes lowered demurely over violet eyes, then she tilted her
golden head to one side and stole a glance at him. "Do you
disapprove of me, Mr. McDonald?"

"Please call me Jamie," he said, "and how could I disapprove
of anyone so beautiful? Shall I drive you to the house to tell your
parents we're going for a drive?"

She seemed to consider for a moment, then tossed her golden
curls. "Let's just go," she said. "If I return now, that tiresome
Sally is liable to come out and ask to join us, and we don't want
that, do we?" Her hand slipped daintily to rest on his arm.

"Then we'll be on our way," he said, not moving a muscle. "I
don't want to share you or this afternoon with *any*one."

Her laughter sang in his ears and brought him into action.
She smiled up at him warmly as he helped her into the carriage.
"Where shall we go?" he asked as he turned the mare around.

"There is a cove on the far side of the ridge," Rebecca said.
"Few go there, but the water is so lovely."

It was a long drive, but Jamie was scarcely conscious of the
passage of time. Rebecca was captivating. A sensuality seemed
to radiate from her, giving an air of naughtiness to everything
she said—though he sensed that she was not always aware of it
herself.

Not that she was totally innocent of the effect she had on him,
for she was flirtatious and teasing, allowing him a few kisses yet
withdrawing from his embrace the moment he seemed about to
seek more. Once in the cove, she was even more confusing. One
moment she clung to him eagerly, answering his kisses; the next
she was outraged at his behavior, accusing him of taking
liberties because she'd trusted him enough to come without a
chaperone.

His head was spinning by the time she finally asked to be driven home. He longed to make love to her, yet the fact that she was a young lady of position and breeding kept him from simply pressing his advances beyond the limits she set for him. She angered him with her teasing, yet as they neared her father's land he found himself begging her to see him again, to allow him to call.

"Perhaps tomorrow evening," she suggested. "If you should come by just after we finish our evening meal, we might be allowed to stroll in the garden for a while. Would you like that?" Her sleepy eyes and pouting, half-open lips were an open invitation.

"I'll be there," he said, stopping the horse and gathering her in his arms.

Her kiss was passionate, yet she feigned fear when he released her. "I should say never again," she murmured. "How can I trust you alone in the dark garden? I'm just a poor little island girl, while you've been over so much of the world. You'll take my kisses, then sail away and forget me."

"I won't," Jamie said. "I could never forget you, Rebecca."

"Well, I . . ."

"You'd better get in the house," a familiar voice said, interrupting them. "Father has been home for half an hour, and he's furious that you weren't here to welcome him."

"Oh, I must go." Rebecca slipped from his embrace and was out of the carriage before he could move to assist her.

"I'll come with you and explain," Jamie said, trying to untangle himself to follow her.

"Oh, no, I can handle him better alone," Rebecca called, blowing him a kiss with one pale hand. "I'll see you tomorrow night."

Jamie watched her disappear around the flowering bushes that edged the drive and hid them from the house, then sighed and turned back to find Sally glaring at him. "I didn't know you were there," he stammered, remembering the passionate embrace Sally had found them engaged in.

"That was obvious," she said, "but then no one ever does notice me when she's around. She sees to that." She sighed. "I don't know why men are so stupid, but I should be used to it by now."

Anger and embarrassment brought heat to his face, and he was about to protest when she turned and melted into the bushes, leaving him alone. Sighing again, Jamie turned the weary mare around once more and drove back to the stable.

The next week passed in a haze. He saw Percy and Reggie, drilled his men, but with only a part of his mind working. It was like walking in his sleep or being continually sodden with wine, for nothing seemed quite real when he was away from Rebecca. She was a fever in his blood, raging out of control, exciting him, tormenting him, delighting him with her games.

He saw her nearly every day, sometimes for afternoon drives, sometimes for the intimate strolls through the darkened garden. Each time they met she seemed more desirable, and she allowed him to kiss her more freely, to touch more of her satiny skin. And yet each time his ardor grew, she would flee from him, regretfully.

Finally, half-mad with desire, he held her. "Let me speak to your father," he said hoarsely. "Let me ask for your hand. We could be married before the *Buford* sails, and then you'd know I'll come back to you."

"Married?" The wide violet eyes seemed to grow even wider. "You've never talked of marriage before," she said, no longer pushing him away as he caressed her hard-pointed breasts.

"What did you think I meant to do?" he asked. "I'm in love with you, Rebecca, surely you know that. But you've kept me from speaking to your parents."

"Only because I want to spend every moment with you," she said, her lips curving seductively. "You couldn't do this sitting with my parents, could you?"

"When can I talk to your father?" Jamie asked, kissing her pale skin.

"Perhaps tomorrow evening," she said.

"Why not tonight?" Jamie asked, a distant sound making him lift his head and look around the little cove. Trees and brush shielded the grassy clearing on all sides, except for the narrow spit of sand that gave access to the ever-restless sea that caressed it. There was no one to be seen, yet his neck hair prickled with the feeling of being watched.

"We are having guests for the evening," Rebecca said with a sigh. "He would have no time for talking." She smiled and lifted her arms to pull his mouth down on hers. "Let me prepare him," she whispered. "I don't want him to refuse you, dearest."

He caressed her more violently till she pushed him away and scrambled to her feet, daintily eluding his grasp as she rearranged her clothing and smoothed her disheveled hair. "Or perhaps I shall have to ask him to refuse you, *dearest*," she said, pouting at him. "You are so naughty, like a wild stallion, so strong and eager you frighten me. Perhaps you are too wild for me."

"I would never hurt you," Jamie said, controlling himself only with great effort. "You must believe that, my darling. It's just that you're so beautiful."

"Well, it's time we went back," Rebecca said, going to the shore to splash cool water on her pink-tinted cheeks. "I must be back early this afternoon to prepare for our guests. My father does depend on me to help him entertain."

Jamie returned to the ship in a state of high excitement. Though he'd said nothing to anyone about his visits with Rebecca, he was now too full of plans to keep quiet. He hurried down to the cabin, wanting to share the news with Reggie and Percy.

"Well, hello, stranger," Reggie said, looking up from some writing he was doing at the table. "What brings you back so early?"

"Where's Percy?" Jamie asked, after greeting Reggie. "I was hoping to talk to both of you."

Reggie shrugged. "I've seen little more of him than I've seen of you," he said. "What's on your mind?"

"Marriage," Jamie said, sinking down on his bunk. "I'm going to ask for the hand of the fair Rebecca. What do you think of that?"

"You, too?" Reggie laughed.

"What do you mean?" Jamie sat up so quickly he hit his head on the bulkhead of the ship.

Reggie sobered at once. "Haven't you seen the star-struck way our red-haired friend has been walking around?"

"Has he told you something?" Jamie asked, a mixture of anger and dread stirring inside him.

"Well, no, not outright, but I saw his face when we went to the Rathbone house with the Vice-Admiral. I just assumed he had marriage mischief on his mind."

"You must be mistaken," Jamie said. "I've been seeing Rebecca since then, and she's made no mention of Percy. Only today I told her I would speak to her father, and she was eager to accept."

Reggie shrugged. "I'm sorry," he said. "I must be mistaken.

Perhaps it was the other one, the younger girl that attracted him; though from what I saw it was you she was looking at. Not that you would have noticed."

"Sally is a child," Jamie said carelessly, "and she's jealous as a cat of her sister."

"Jealous, yes. But a child? I think not." Reggie shook his head. "She's as much a woman as the beautiful Rebecca, or perhaps more—for the right man."

"Then why are you here talking to me?" Jamie asked, sensing something in the dark man's tone.

"Because I'm not the right man. Besides, I've nothing to offer a bride yet. You and Percy have honored names and good families; I'll have to make my own name and build my fortune with my share of the prize we take."

"What do you think of Rebecca?" Jamie asked, not really interested in discussing Sally.

"I think you're in rather too much of a hurry to commit yourself to her," Reggie said. "Didn't you leave England to escape marriage? Why are you so eager to take a wife now? There will be other ports and other girls just as lovely."

"There is no one like Rebecca," Jamie said, angered by the casual words. "She is driving me mad. I must have her as my wife. If I don't claim her now, someone else will come along and take her from me."

Reggie sighed, glancing at the dimming scene beyond the porthole. "I'm afraid you'll have to suffer through this evening alone, unless Percy comes back," he said. "I've been invited to join some of the other officers at a private party."

"Go," Jamie said, moving restlessly about the cabin. He smiled ruefully. "I'm not going to be fit company for anyone tonight," he added.

Reggie laughed and hit his shoulder gently. "Good luck," he said as he let himself out of the cabin, leaving Jamie alone with his thoughts.

An hour crawled by and Jamie paced about the cabin. He longed to escape the ship, yet he was not drawn by the nearby taverns—or even by the promise of the wenches Reggie had told him about. His mind was too full of Rebecca to accept a substitute now. It was almost dark when a knock summoned him to the cabin door. A young sailor handed him a piece of paper. "A servant brought this for you, sir," he said.

"Thank you." Jamie gave him a small coin, then hurried to the lantern and read it.

"My darling," it began in clearly feminine script,
    "Meet me at the cove as the moon rises. I have a surprise for you."

It was signed by Rebecca.

Jamie left at once, rented a horse at the stable and pushed it mercilessly as he rode along the now-familiar trail. It wasn't till he neared the cove that the first flush of his excitement abated and a cooler turn of mind took over. He slowed the horse and left the trail, riding along in the shadows till he was close enough to tether the weary beast and go forward on foot. As he walked, he tried to understand why Rebecca had summoned him here, when she'd told him earlier that she would be entertaining her father's guests at the house.

Still, as he neared the cove, he saw the outline of a small carriage and, in the distance, he heard Rebecca's laughter. Heart leaping, he hurried forward, then slowed again as the man's laughter rumbled. It was oddly familiar laughter. Chilled, he moved forward more slowly, easing from shadow to shadow, passing the carriage, slipping into the brush that edged the small clearing where he'd spent so many delicious hours with Rebecca.

The moon had risen, and its light flooded the scene with a silvery glow, hiding nothing. Rebecca was there, a breath-taking vision as she danced about the grass with a white piece of cloth in her hands and flowers twined in her flowing golden hair. She wore nothing, and the cloth was only a slight shield as she draped it about her glowing body.

"Am I not a wood nymph, Percy?" she called. "Prettier than the ones in the book you showed me?"

"You're more beautiful than any nymph," Percy said, getting to his feet and following her. "But there is a time for dancing and a time for something even more pleasant, and I've had enough of your silly games."

She ran from him, laughing delightedly, eluding his fingers only by inches, teasing him with her ripeness, the promise she plainly offered him. Sickened, Jamie turned away, wincing at the sound of Percy's laughter and hearing him say, "Now I've got you, I don't mean to let you get away again, little nymph."

It was the same racking pain of betrayal he'd felt in the gardens of the Club, and the sounds behind him might have come from Amelia Starburough and Daniel Hempstead instead of Percy and Rebecca. Jamie had to stop and fight nausea before he reached his horse. He was still leaning against a tree when a slender form emerged from the woods. For a moment his heart leaped as he thought it was Rebecca, but then he recognized the slightly different features of Sally Rathbone.

"Now do you see why I warned you?" she asked. "Now do you see what kind of creature you've been simpering over like a schoolboy? She had no intention of letting you ask for her hand, or of accepting it. His family has far more money, you know. He's even in line for a title. His uncle is old and childless, and Percy is his favorite. How could *you* hope to compete with *that*?"

Jamie just stared at her, hardly comprehending the words at first, then suddenly he understood. "It was you, wasn't it?" he growled. "*You* sent me the note, not Rebecca!"

"You wouldn't listen," Sally said. "You never heard anything I said, so I had to let you see what she's really like. She could never love you, Jamie, not the way I do. She just laughs at all of you. Talks about the way you pant after her, how easily you can be controlled by just a look, a touch. She . . ."

Fury and pain rose and he slapped her, stopping the hateful, cruel words that were tearing the last shreds of his self-respect and manhood from him. She staggered back but didn't cringe away. Instead she moved closer to him, lifting her head. "Go ahead," she said, "hit me again if you think it will make you feel better." She shook back her hair, which hung loose and waving to her waist. "I know she hurt you, but I can make you forget her. I know I can."

Suddenly, without warning, she was in his arms, lifting her lips to his, pressing her warm, throbbing body against his. He tried to thrust her away, still burning with anger and shame at what she'd made him see and feel; but she clung only harder, forcing his head down to hers. Her lips were greedy, opening hungrily under his. And after a few moments, he found it easy to forget everything else.

She was so like Rebecca—her body as well-formed, her hair the same silky curtain. In the shadows of the trees, he couldn't see her eyes, he could only feel her eagerness. The pent up pain and passion fused within him and he tore at her clothing, freeing her body, not even aware of the moment when her passion fled and she tried to pull away. In his mind it was Rebecca he possessed on the grass, and it was only afterward—as she sobbed in his arms—that reality intruded, and with it a new sense of shame.

"Sally...dear God," he whispered. "I didn't *mean* to! I'm sorry if I hurt you."

She lifted her head from his chest, her eyes wide. "You were the first," she said proudly. "And you will be the only one—ever. I love you, Jamie McDonald, and now you belong to me."

Jamie looked down at her, protests forming in his mind, but he pressed them down. She spoke the truth, he realized, and her blood proved it. He swallowed hard. "I will go to your father tomorrow," he said quietly. "We will be married as soon as it can be arranged."

Her tears stopped. She smiled as she pulled his lips down to hers. "Teach me to love you," she whispered, clinging to him. "Teach me *now*!"

Chapter 26

THE NEXT FEW days passed in a haze. From the time Jamie escorted Sally back along the secret ridge trail she'd used to ride down to spy on Rebecca, till he met with her father and formally asked for her hand in marriage, he felt like a criminal. He said nothing to Reggie or Percy about what had happened. In fact, he found it hard even to look at Percy without seeing him as he'd been in the clearing by the cove.

His love for Rebecca blazed into hatred, yet he felt nothing for Sally when she came forward to welcome him at the house. Memories of what had happened between them shamed him, and when he kissed her cheek it was out of duty, not desire.

Their engagement was announced at a family party the second night after their meeting at the cove. Sally glowed as he arrived with Reggie and a rather quiet Percy. She took his arm with a smile of possession, yet his eyes were drawn to Rebecca. She smiled, too, but her eyes were mocking. Later, when they danced, she suggested they go out into the garden.

"Why, Jamie?" she asked, as they walked along one of the hidden paths she knew so well. "You were going to ask for my hand. Why did you change your mind?"

Jamie stopped and looked down at her, hating himself for the passion he still felt for her. "Perhaps I don't have Percy's taste for wood nymphs," he said, measuring the words slowly and coldly so that she would understand them fully.

Her gasp was his reward. For a moment he could see the shock in her eyes, then she covered it and smiled at him. "But I don't understand," she said. "What is a wood nymph?"

"A woman who lies and cheats and deserves only to be used and forgotten," Jamie said, removing her hand from his arm and turning back to the house without her. In a moment he found Sally standing near the open doors. The fear in her face touched him, and he took her hand at once.

"You are lovely tonight," he said. "By far the loveliest girl on this island. I'm glad that we can marry so soon, for I shall find it hard to wait."

Her blue eyes met his and she laughed. "Ride to the cove tonight and you won't have to," she whispered, running her fingers slowly along the smooth skin at the side of his neck beneath her ear.

"No," he said, taking a deep breath. "I've dishonored your father enough. We'll wait the three days, like a proper couple."

"Our time together will be so brief," Sally said. "It's said that you'll be sailing soon."

Jamie nodded. "We shall," he said, "and we won't be returning to English Harbour for a long time, I fear. The talk is that Port Royal in Jamaica will be our next port."

"Then I shall go there and wait for you," Sally said quite calmly. "I have an aunt who lives there, and my father has ships that carry trade that way frequently. By the time you come into port, I shall have found a house for us and everything."

"But the seas are too dangerous," Jamie began, frightened by her words. He'd secretly welcomed the news that he wouldn't be returning to English Harbour too soon. He realized that he had to do his duty to Sally, and he meant to keep his vows. Eventually he would take her to England and his father, but just now he could not help his distant feelings. "Your father would never allow it."

"A wife's place is at her husband's side," Sally said, "and I intend to be with you, my love, wherever you go."

Jamie forced a smile, then led her back inside to the dancing. He tried to lose himself in the gala party, drinking more than he should and laughing too loudly at the lecherous jokes about his very short engagement. Only when it grew late did he find himself alone with Rebecca again. She smiled up at him teasingly.

"It's not too late, you know," she said. "You can still have me instead of that child. Tell my father it was a mistake. I'll make him change his mind. We could be married in three days, and then I'd be yours, Jamie—only yours."

Jamie stiffened, hating himself for the flare of excitement the words brought him. "Until the next full moon?" he asked, forcing a smile. "Or until another ship comes into harbour with someone you like?"

Her violet eyes darkened to near purple-black with fury. "You can't treat me this way," she snarled.

"I'm treating you the way you've behaved," Jamie said, keeping his voice low with an effort. "You may be fine for a tumble in the moonlight, but for a wife a man expects a little more."

Her fingers curled and Jamie tensed, ready to stop her if she tried to claw him, but after a moment she seemed to relax. Her eyes were mocking as they met his. "We'll see about that," she said sweetly. "We'll see about that, Jamie McDonald."

Though he expected her to cause more trouble, the few days between the announcement of his engagement and the wedding itself passed peacefully. The strain he felt toward Percy eased a little, especially when Jamie realized that Percy's congratulations came without reserve or relief. It was plain that he'd known as little about Jamie's meeting with Rebecca as Jamie had known about his before he received the note from Sally.

The marriage ceremony itself passed in a blur, as did the feast following it. Jamie remembered little beyond the toast the Vice-Admiral offered—saying he was standing in for Jamie's father—and the teasing comments of his friends. Percy and Reggie offered plenty of advice, most of which made his ears burn. Still, he preferred the confusion of the guests to the hours later when he was alone with his bride.

Sally's love was an accusation; her passionate eagerness worse for him than coldness would have been. Though he liked her and wanted to make her happy, the thought of spending the rest of his days with a woman he didn't love or even truly desire was dreadful. He could only be grateful that her lack of experience protected her from guessing how little joy their lovemaking brought him.

Since they were forced to stay in the Rathbone house for the brief interlude of their marriage, Rebecca was a constant presence, and her smiles—while never reaching her incredible eyes—were like furtive caresses. Jamie was almost glad to spend a part of each day drilling his men.

He watched Percy curiously. The redhead continued to call at the house, escorting Rebecca on drives and to the few social occasions that took place in the settlement, but he said nothing about calling on her father. He seemed content with things as they were, though Rebecca showed signs of restlessness.

The *Hampton Court* sailed in, bringing more men and Commodore Brown to share their adventures. Jamie grew tense as he watched the work on that ship, aware that the order to sail would be coming soon. Yet the days went by. His men needed little more training, having become nearly as proficient with their muskets from the rigging as they were on solid ground.

Jamie had just dismissed them one noon when Reggie came onto the deck. "Have you heard the news?" he asked.

"What news?" Jamie asked, his eyes still on the youngest member of his command as he left the ship in the wake of the older men.

"We sail tomorrow," Reggie said. "The stores are nearly loaded. The men worked all yesterday afternoon while you were off with your young bride. The decision has been made, now the *Hampton Court* is here. We're going to do it!"

"Do what?" Jamie asked, hating his innocent role. When he'd shared the cabin on the ship, he'd known everything that was going on, but now he felt left out, ignorant.

"Take Porto Bello, of course." Reggie frowned at him. "Has marriage addled your brains completely? That was one of the main reasons for our coming. That's where the Spanish outfit their smaller ships; you know, the *guarda-costas*. Once we've crippled them, we'll be able to do more about all the gold being shipped back to Spain." He grinned wolfishly. "Remember, I have a fortune to build."

"What sort of port is it?" Jamie asked, smiling in answer. "I've an interest in building a fortune, too, now that I've a wife. In case you've forgotten, I left a fiancée in England, and I may be disowned when I return with a wife."

Reggie laughed. "From what you told me of the 'lady', she's not likely to be waiting for you." He sobered. "I've not heard much about the port itself, but someone has told the Vice-Admiral that the governor is very lax in his fortifications. It's said he depends mostly on the vessels he outfits to protect him. Besides, it is far to the west where the land begins to close on the sea. Probably the Spanish don't believe we will go so far to attack them."

"It will be a pleasure to surpise them," Jamie said, his mind leaving the present and ranging back to Mallorca and Hernan Valdez. He remembered only too well the fear Elena had displayed. A man so distrusted by his own stepdaughter that she feared he would believe another man's story before he would believe her own. Jamie frowned. What other man? he asked himself, as he had on so many other occasions during the voyage to France and since. Hernan's brother Esteban seemed the only person Jamie could think of, yet he found it hard to believe Esteban Valdez would touch a child like Elena, especially when she had been so close to his own daughter.

"I say, come back, Jamie," Reggie said loudly, breaking into his thoughts. "Battle won't be that bad, you know."

Jamie forced a smile. "I was thinking of the past, not the future," he said. "This talk of the Spanish takes me back aways."

"What do you know of them?" Reggie asked, his eyes bright with curiosity.

"I told you that I was on Mallorca and met a girl there," Jamie said.

"*Another* discarded fiancée?" Reggie asked lightly.

Jamie shook his head. "The girl was raped by someone. She wouldn't tell me who, but she refused to be taken back to her family when I found her. She was afraid of her stepfather." The whole scene washed through his mind painfully.

"Perhaps she had good reason for not going to him," Reggie said, his dark eyes probing.

"What do you mean?" Jamie asked.

"He could have been the one who did it," Reggie said calmly.

"Her own stepfather?" Jamie gasped.

"Had he raised her as his own from childhood?" Reggie asked.

Jamie shook his head. "He only married her mother a short time before," he said, "but still, it couldn't have been him."

"Was the mother close to the girl?"

"I think so, but she wasn't with them on Mallorca. She was expecting a child, I believe, and remained in Spain while Elena came to the island with her stepfather and his sister."

"Did the girl return to her mother?"

"No," Jamie said, frowning in the bright sunlight. "That always seemed strange to me. I mean, I offered to take her back to the family *hacienda*, but she refused that, too. She insisted on going to her late father's family in France. She wouldn't even send word to them that she was alive when her stepfather was given reason to believe that she was dead."

"Sounds like it must have been him," Reggie said.

"But he was her *father*," Jamie protested, seeing the logic of the words and hating himself for not having understood it far sooner.

"It's not uncommon," Reggie said. "Especially where the daughter is older and the mother is away. It would depend on the man, of course. Was he older or younger?"

Rage boiled up in Jamie as he pictured the handsome, worldly Hernan Valdez—so charming, so interested in furthering a match between his stepdaughter and an Englishman. If he'd known, if he'd even guessed enough to confront the man... His hand itched for the hilt of his sword and the clean release of combat.

"What is all this to you?" Reggie asked, and Jamie became aware of his intense scrutiny. "Was the girl more than an acquaintance?"

Elena filled his mind with a thousand images, and the pain the memory brought told him his blazing infatuation with Rebecca had done nothing to help him forget her. "She is the reason I want to kill the Spaniards," Jamie said heavily. "I only wish we were going to invade Spain itself so I could kill the miserable bastard who ruined her." Jamie stopped, aware of the shock on his friend's face.

"What became of the girl?" Reggie asked.

Jamie turned away from him, moving to the rail of the ship to stare at the mottled blue-green waters of the harbour. "She is safe with her father's family in France," he said. "Far from his reach, at least."

"You left her there?" Reggie sounded surprised.

Jamie sighed. "What else could I do?" he asked. "My father

would never have accepted her if she came without dowry or family connections. And besides, after the rape she was no longer a virgin to be wed properly."

Reggie sighed. "I wonder how many proper brides bring a true gift of innocence to their marriage beds. Not nearly so many as their husbands believe, I'm sure. I've heard far too many tales to see its importance. A wife who brings love and compassion and true fidelity has more to offer. Do you love your Sally less now than you did the first time you touched her?"

"Sally?" For a moment Jamie just blinked at Reggie, then he felt the rising of blood in his face, for he knew the question had betrayed the fact that he'd honestly forgotten that he was wed. His thoughts had been only of Elena. "A man doesn't think of his wife that way," he said quickly. "Besides, I know I was the first—the *only*—man to touch her."

Reggie shrugged. "And so tomorrow we sail," he said. "And who knows what lies ahead for any of us?"

"And I must be getting back home," Jamie said, collecting himself firmly. "I want to be the one to tell Sally. She's sure to be upset."

Reggie nodded, but Jamie was aware of the curiosity in the man's eyes as he left him. Jamie made his way across the ship and returned to the quay where his horse waited to take him to the house. In spite of his words, he moved slowly and held the beast to a walk as his thoughts fled back to Elena again.

Had she been waiting at the house for him, he thought bitterly, he would have spurred the poor horse into a full gallop and raced to spend every moment at her side. He hated himself for the weakness that fact betrayed and, because of it, his last night with Sally was the sweetest they'd shared. As he held her he vowed silently that she must never suffer for his own flawed character—or the love he could not banish from his heart.

Chapter 27

A MAID OPENED the door for Elena, her eyes touching first her face, then the case at her feet. "I am the new *institutrice*, come to see Madame LaCroix," Elena said as firmly as she could, not wanting to betray her doubts and fears to anyone.

The maid escorted her into a small room, leaving her there with her belongings. Elena stood quietly, looking around at the attractive room with its worn but good-quality furnishings, wondering about the woman she would have to face. She hadn't long to wait.

The woman who stepped through the door was dainty and quite attractive, with dark hair and deep blue eyes that regarded Elena questioningly. She seemed no more than five or six years older than Elena, and when she spoke her voice was without anger.

"I was expecting Yvonne," she said. "I spoke with Madame duFol yesterday, and she told me her cousin would be coming to me this morning."

Elena swallowed hard, then forced a slight smile. "I am another cousin of Yvonne's," she said. "I have recently lost my

husband. I was well-educated by my family, and when I came to
Le Mans and told Madame duFol and Yvonne of my trouble
they seemed to feel you would have no objection to my accepting
the post instead of Yvonne."

The carefully shaped eyebrows knit together in a frown.
"Without warning?" Madame LaCroix asked. Then her
expression altered slightly. "It is the man, is it not?" she asked.
"Yvonne has run away with him."

For a moment Elena hesitated, then she took a deep breath
and nodded. "She loves him deeply, Madame," she said. "And
he loves her. He was willing to spend his savings to buy her
freedom from this agreement, but her family refused to accept
the match even so."

"Are you truly a cousin of the family?" Madame LaCroix
asked, her expression showing no sign of shock or anger.

Elena shook her head. "But I am an *institutrice*, Madame,"
she said, "and I suspect a much better educated one than
Yvonne."

"You understand that you will not be paid till you've served
us for a year?" the woman asked.

Elena nodded, her knees weak with relief. "I wish only to
leave Le Mans and my sad memories behind, Madame," she
said. "In return I will teach your children languages, art,
mathematics, the geography of the world, and music—besides
reading and writing."

"What is your name?" Madame LaCroix asked.

"Elena. Elena de Vere," Elena said. Then, after a moment of
hesitation, she asked, "You will accept me then?"

"You will have to speak with my husband," Mimi LaCroix
said, "but if you've represented yourself honestly and he has no
reservations, you will be welcome to sail with us."

"Thank you, Madame," Elena said.

"If you will wait here, I will tell my husband." Mimi left her
and Elena sank down on the nearest chair, her knees suddenly
too weak to support her. So far she'd been safe. There'd been no
questions she couldn't answer, but there was still the interview
ahead.

It went well in spite of her fears. Andre LaCroix was a small
man, wiry and lean, quick-moving and quick-thinking. He
asked so many questions about her education that her head was
swimming by the time he asked, "Do you know anything about
the island of St. Domingue?"

Elena frowned. "It is an island in the new world, is it not?"

Andre nodded. "That is where we will be going. Your education has been more than adequate, and if my wife accepts you I will have no quarrel. We shall be far away from formal teaching for the children, so it will be good to have someone of your training to see to Josette and Serge."

"Thank you, sir," Elena said.

"My wife will wish to speak to you again," Andre LaCroix said, leaving the room.

Mimi LaCroix came in a few moments later and waved Elena into a chair. "There are still a few things to be discussed," she said. "You spoke of a husband?"

Elena nodded, casting her eyes down so that she would not have to meet Mimi's gaze. "He was ill for several months and unable to work. I couldn't manage and care for him, so we lost everything but what I've brought with me."

"Then you've had no experience as an *institutrice*?"

"No, Madame, I have not," Elena admitted. "I was married only a short time, but . . ."

"You are very young."

"I will love your children and care for them as though they were my own," Elena said, fear making her voice rise a little. Though she doubted that Yvonne could be found now that she and her sergeant had had several hours to leave Le Mans, she was well aware that she couldn't allow Madame duFol to know she'd come to Madame LaCroix. Once Madame LaCroix knew where she'd spent the last few weeks, she would be thrown out of this house like the garbage Madame duFol had chosen to liken her to.

Mimi LaCroix studied her face for several minutes, and it took all of Elena's control to keep herself still and meet the probing eyes. It was only by reminding herself of what she had once been, of the girl who'd been raised in Spain with love and care, that she could overcome her own shame at what she'd become at Raul's hands.

Mimi rose with a sigh. "I'll have the maid show you to your room," she said. "We have only a few days to finish packing everything, and I've so many things to see to." She shook her head. "I'll come for you in time for our midday meal; you'll meet Serge and Josette then. In the afternoon perhaps you could spend some time with them. There's no use starting lessons, but it would be best for you to get to know them before we leave."

It was a difficult and wearying day, but long before she surrendered herself to the comfort of her narrow bed Elena knew she'd found her answer. Josette, who was just seven, and Serge, four, were good children, bright and eager to learn, and the LaCroixs were more than kind. The only thing that haunted her was her still-concealed pregnancy.

Thanks to her altered gowns, she was quite sure she could hide her condition for the few remaining weeks before they sailed, but once it became obvious she would be at her employers' mercy. She cringed at the thought of what Mimi LaCroix would have to say. She would deserve her fury and contempt, and Elena hated herself for the necessity of deception.

The next few days passed quickly in a whirl of packing and preparations, and Elena was delighted when they were finally ready to leave Le Mans and the ever-present danger of a visit from Madame duFol. She took her place in the carriage with Serge, Josette, and Mimi, while Andre climbed to the seat of a second wagon which carried all their possessions. They rode out of Le Mans in the bright dawn of the day.

As they rode along Mimi leaned back and smiled, looking younger than she had before. "I've been very uneasy about making such a long journey with the children," she said. "And who knows what lies on that island, what kind of world it will be?"

"It is frightening," Elena agreed.

"It will be wonderful to have you with us, Elena, to have someone to talk to, another woman." Her eyes were warm with friendship. "I would like for us to be friends, Elena. From just these past few days I can see that you're much more than just an *institutrice*, and I hope someday you'll feel free to tell me more about what brought you to my doorstep in place of Yvonne."

Elena stiffened a little, frightened by her own desire to confide in Mimi, but then the older woman changed the subject to the days ahead and she could settle back. Still, her heart ached at what she was doing. Guilt made her feel worse than before.

The days on the road tormented her conscience, for she was with the LaCroixs constantly. Mimi was unfailingly kind, and Andre was unfailingly considerate of her. As for Serge and Josette, she loved them as the brother and sister she'd never had. The lie that she was living swelled between them, and Elena knew as they neared the port city and their sailing day that she couldn't go through with it.

The last evening, when they stopped at a *hotellerie*, she called Mimi aside and said, "Could I have a private word with you after the children are asleep, Madame?"

"I thought you were going to call me Mimi," the older woman said, smiling lightly. Then she sobered. "Is something wrong, Elena?"

"It's a private matter," Elena said, her heart aching at the thought that she might lose Mimi's friendship once the truth was out. "Just something that I want you to know before we go aboard the ship tomorrow night."

Mimi sighed, then said, "Come to my room once the children are asleep. Andre will be off talking to some men till late, I'm sure. He has so many questions about St. Domingue, and so few people we know have been there."

"Thank you," Elena said, fleeing before she could change her mind about her confession.

The hours of eating dinner with the children and seeing them safely to bed passed all too swiftly, and she was haunted by the knowledge that she might never see them again, that they might never again kiss her goodnight. Her steps were slow as she walked along the hall and tapped on the next door. Mimi opened it at once, inviting her in.

"Sit down, Elena, and tell me what the trouble is," Mimi said, her eyes full of concern.

Elena dropped on a stool, tears stinging in her eyes, but no words came.

"What is wrong, Elena?" Mimi asked after several silent minutes had passed.

"I am," Elena said. "I love you all so much, and yet I can't go on with you like this."

"What are you saying?" Mimi demanded, frowning. "What has happened? Why can't you go with us?"

"Because I've been living a lie. I mean, what you believe about me isn't the whole truth. There's something else."

"Are you saying you lied to me?" Mimi asked, her face stern. "Are you not Elena de Vere? I didn't talk to Madame duFol, but I assumed you had told me the truth. Perhaps you'be better tell me the whole story, Elena."

For a moment Elena wanted to flee, to take back her need to clear her conscience, but then she met Mimi's gaze and knew she couldn't. There was much she couldn't tell the woman, but her pregnancy could not be kept from her. She had a right to know that now, before they sailed.

Elena closed her eyes so that she wouldn't have to see Mimi's face. "I am carrying a child," she said softly.

For a moment there was no sound and, fearfully, she peered from under her eyelashes to see what Mimi might be doing. To her surprise, the woman was smiling widely. "But that is wonderful news," she said. "Why should I be angry?"

Elena opened her mouth, but no words came out. As she watched, Mimi's smile faded and something seemed to change in her eyes. "There was no husband, was there?" she asked softly.

Miserable, Elena shook her head.

"And the man? The father of the child?"

"He has no idea," Elena said. "It was an accident, a twist of fate, and now he is far away and can do nothing to help me."

"Your family?"

Elena swallowed hard, wanting to tell as much of the truth as she could while still concealing what Raul had done to her. "My father's people threw me out, and I have no other family in France. My mother's people died in an epidemic a few years after my parents were married. My own parents are dead." She stopped and took a deep breath. "I know I should have told you before. I shouldn't have lied to you and I'm ashamed that I did, but I so wanted to help Yvonne." She paused again, then went on. "I will understand if you don't wish to have me with you."

Mimi sighed. "You will go with us," she said firmly. "I can't leave you here with no one. Who will care for you when the child comes? How will you live? What would you do?"

"You'll forgive me for not telling you sooner?" Elena asked, fresh tears spilling down her cheeks. "You won't send me away?"

"Pooh. You think I would be as heartless as your family and the man who did this to you? It's not your fault. You're a girl of good family, I could tell that the first day we talked." Her eyes regarded Elena shrewdly. "A much better family than poor Yvonne, I would say."

Elena dropped her eyes and nodded. "But what of your husband?" she asked.

"I will tell him once we are on the ship," Mimi said. "He may be a little angry at first, but he'll come around, you'll see." She patted Elena's shoulder, then grew serious again. "There is one thing. It might be well for you to go on claiming to be a widow, for the sake of your child. I'm glad you told me the truth, but I think even my husband will be happier to believe the child is legitimate. Men can be such fools about things like that."

Elena nodded, relieved. "I just hated living a lie," she said.

"It won't always seem a lie," Mimi said. "In time you'll believe it yourself, and then—once we reach St. Domingue— you can make a new life for yourself and your child. You are young and quite beautiful, and I've no doubt you will have plenty of suitors. We're all going to start a new life on the plantation, and I promise you it's going to be a happy one."

Elena smiled up at her gratefully, willing to believe that Mimi could make things right, willing to hope once more—even though her heart told her nothing could ever be right for her unless Jamie McDonald was a part of it. Then other memories touched her mind, reminding her of what she'd become, what Raul had made of her, and she knew nothing could make her clean again.

Whispering her thanks to Mimi, she went back to the room she shared with the children. As she stared down at their sleeping faces, she caressed her own body, wondering about the child she carried. What would he be like? And whose child was it? She shivered at the thought that she might bear the seed of a man like Hernan Valdez.

And if the child were Jamie's? She pushed the thought away, not wanting to think of him any longer. Let him have his proper wife and forget her, she thought. Somewhere out there she would find someone, too, and then she would try to begin again. She slipped out of her clothes and lay down, composing herself for sleep, aware that tomorrow would bring them to the coast and the ship that would take them all to St. Domingue.

Chapter 28

THE JOURNEY WAS more pleasant than Elena had dared hope. Where she had at first thought of herself purely as an employee of the LaCroix household, living so closely with Mimi made them *amies*, and by the time they neared their destination even the quiet Andre had begun to treat her a little like a younger sister.

He had been angry about the baby at first, but Mimi knew her husband well: by the time the ship anchored off the coast of St. Domingue, he had fully accepted her and the child she now so obviously carried. Best of all, he'd never questioned the story of her marriage, and his belief had made it seem real—even to Elena. He had, however, insisted on a small lie of his own.

Elena was to be introduced as a distant relative. The story would be that her husband had been killed in an accident and, with no one else to turn to, the LaCroixs had taken her in, bringing her to the new world with them in return for her acting as *institutrice* to Josette and Serge. This way she would have a better position in the household and could meet the prosperous *planteurs* of the island on equal terms, so that later she might make a good marriage.

"Where is the port?" Mimi asked, leaning on the rail in the hot tropical sun. "Why have we stopped here? Are we taking on supplies again?"

"We are waiting for our new servants to welcome us," Andre said with a rather tentative smile. "According to the Captain, the plantation lies beyond those first low hills. He picked up my uncle here several times and brought him back, too. He says our sails will have been sighted, and we can expect boats from shore any time."

"You mean we'll be leaving the ship here?" Mimi sounded less than pleased at the prospect. "But there's nothing here! How can you be sure that . . . ?"

"Do you think those come from nowhere?" Andre asked, pointing to several long boats putting out from what appeared to be a small inlet in the coast. Each boat was rowed strongly by a pair of black men, and they seemed to fairly skim over the silky sea.

"But we can't . . ." Mimi looked down the steep side of the ship. "How are we to get into them?" she asked. "And what of the children and Elena?"

"You'll have to climb down a rope ladder, I'm afraid," Andre said. "I'll go first, of course, and help you all I can, but there's no other way."

"Surely this God-forsaken land has seaports and roads," Mimi protested.

"The nearest port city is many miles from here, and the land between is wild. My uncle made the journey once and swore never to do it again. You and the children would be in grave danger. This is the safest way, and you'll manage just fine, I know."

Andre left them to speak to the Captain. Mimi turned to Elena. "What do you think?" she asked nervously.

Elena shrugged, aware that she wasn't really being consulted now any more than she had been before. "We must do as he says," she said. "The boats are coming for us."

"But what of your condition?"

Elena touched her now swollen belly. "I shall just have to be very careful," she said.

Mimi continued to look mutinous, but when the long boats were actually bumping gently against the side of the ship, there was little she could say or do. Andre was first over the side, climbing with evident ease down the rope net the Captain had ordered secured for them. One of the sailors followed with Serge, another with Jósette, then—too soon—it was Elena's turn.

She climbed over the rail clumsily, only too conscious of the men below and the billowing of her skirts in the slight breeze. Though her undergarments covered her to the knees, she hated the long, agonizing moments of feeling for each cross rope with her feet and easing herself down one hand-hold at a time. She was almost glad when strong hands lifted her off the rising and lowering net and settled her easily in the bottom of the boat. She turned to thank the man and was startled to see that he was a black-skinned giant.

"Thank you," she managed to murmur, thinking that the dark-skinned people she'd seen in Spain were pale beside such glowing blue-blackness.

White teeth gleamed and the dark eyes rolled a little as the man nodded, but he said nothing, turning instead to wait as Mimi began her protesting descent. Being fully a head taller than anyone in the boat, the man reached for her and plucked her from the side of the ship too, then climbed the net himself.

"Where's he going?" Elena asked without thinking.

"He'll help the sailors with all our baggage," Andre said. "He'll come ashore in the last of the boats, I imagine. He is called Gilles, and is the boss of all the fieldhands—though he is, of course, a slave himself."

The other black men in the boat rowed for shore while the second long boat was eased alongside the ship ready to be loaded with all the boxes and bales Elena had helped Mimi pack. Elena looked back at the ship sadly, thinking that their passage had been the happiest time she'd known since the days before her father was thrown from his horse.

Such thoughts were painful and she banished them to look ahead, wondering what they might find. The coast itself was beautiful, if only because it offered space and dry land after so many long weeks at sea. It was a wild scene, however. Trees and plants grew in a tangle, bright with flowers, but also menacing.

There was no welcoming sandy beach here, only the restless sea and rocks with the plants crowding behind them, reaching almost to the waterline. The boat, however, turned to follow the shore, then was maneuvered through a rather narrow inlet. For

a moment it was like being rowed into darkness and Elena could
see little, for the trees met overhead, blocking the sun. Then her
eyes adjusted and she saw that a half-dozen wagons were waiting
on a sandy stretch of what must be a river bank. There was no
fine carriage, but several young black boys came forward to help
haul the boat up on the sand, and in a few moments Elena found
herself sitting comfortably on the hard seat of a wagon—Mimi
beside her, and Josette and Serge in the box of the wagon with
the few belongings they'd brought with them in the first boat.

"I take ladies to house?" the elderly black driver asked in
rather poor French.

Andred frowned. "I don't think..." he began, looking
around. "How long will it take to unload the ship? I'd really like
to keep us together."

"Tante Derra say she fix tea for ladies," the man said. "Long
time to bring everything and load. Ladies get fever near river."

"Perhaps we should go on, dear," Mimi said, not looking at
all confident. "I'm sure it isn't far, and the children will be so
restless if they have to stay in the wagon."

"I take care," the driver said. "Not far to house. I come back
and help with loading."

For a moment Andre seemed undecided, but finally—much
to Elena's relief—he nodded. Though she tried to ignore her
pregnancy as much as she could, the heat was oppressive and the
stench from the rotting vegetation near the river made her
nauseous.

The wagon was turned slowly, for the heavy-footed work
horses were in no hurry to leave their cropping of the rank grass
near the river. The road was narrow, obviously cut from the
thick vegetation that kept it nearly as dim as the river had been,
but it was a good road—hardly bumpy at all—and Elena found
herself relaxing in spite of the strangeness of the land.

The road angled up at once and, as they climbed out of the
dense growth, fields spread out on each side and she could see
that this was indeed a working plantation, for gangs of the huge
blacks were busy in most of the fields, chanting as they worked.
Strangely enough, the singing stopped the moment the men
became aware of the strangers, and Elena felt a chill when the
dark eyes were turned their way. Here there was no flash of white
teeth in a grin, no sign of friendliness at all.

"They look sullen," Mimi said, shivering, though it was very warm now they'd moved out into the sun.

"Perhaps they were not well treated by your husband's uncle," Elena suggested.

"But Andre..." Mimi began, then stopped as the driver suddenly drew rein.

An old black woman appeared out of the brush and made her way slowly across the road, looking neither to the right nor to the left. Their driver watched her but said nothing. Only when she'd disappeared on the far side did he slap the reins on the horses' backs and urge them to move again.

"Who was that?" Mimi asked.

"Grandma Karame," the driver said, his tone reverent.

"Your grandmother?" Mimi asked, plainly skeptical, for the driver appeared to be at least as old as the woman.

The man shook his head. "She *mamba*, good kind. Everybody call her Grandma. She mother of your Tante Derra."

Mimi opened her mouth to ask for more details, but Elena noticed that she closed it again—obviously not sure what a *mamba* might be, but not wanting to ask a slave. They rode on in silence till suddenly they rounded a small stand of trees to see the plantation house rising before them.

For just a heartbeat it was like being back in France, but then the image paled a little and she realized that—though the garden was French in its layout and care—many of the flowers that bloomed were unfamiliar. The house, also very like those she'd seen in France, was subtly different, too. Before she could think or comment, however, the door opened and a tall, graceful black woman emerged.

"I bring, Tante Derra," their driver called. "Ladies here."

The woman came forward without hurrying, curtsying with grace when she reached them. "Welcome to Highland," she said in only slightly accented French. "We've been waiting for you." She snapped several orders to the driver which seemed to galvanize him into action at last. He climbed down and assisted first Mimi, then Elena, to the ground, then turned his attention to the children and the unloading of the few belongings they'd brought with them.

Elena studied the woman with interest, trying to guess her age but finding it difficult. She was very handsome, perhaps in her middle years, and obviously well in control of the plantation house. Servants appeared and were directed to carry the things in while Elena, Mimi, and the children were shepherded smoothly into the dim coolness of the parlour.

"Would you like tea now, Madame?" the woman asked Mimi.

Mimi looked around, then nodded. "Thank you very much."

"Tante Derra," the woman said. "That is what everyone calls me."

"I presume you managed the household for my husband's uncle," Mimi said, her voice more businesslike now that she was actually in the house and safe.

The woman nodded. "He was gone often for long periods, and he had no wife to watch over it."

"I would appreciate it if you would continue to do so," Mimi said. "I'm sure I will be making changes, but for now caring for the children and helping them to adjust to this new land will take much of my time."

"I hope you will find happiness here," Tante Derra said. "Now some tea and cakes, and perhaps some fruit."

"That would be most welcome," Mimi said. "The children..."

"I ordered milk and cakes for them, and some of the fruit, too," the woman said. "Do you wish them here, or shall I have them served in the playroom? One of the maids could stay with them if you wish to rest before seeing the rest of the house."

Mimi smiled. "That would be lovely," she said with feeling, and Elena could only nod her agreement. Though Josette and Serge were good children, the long weeks on the ship had made them all rather tired of each other's company. It would be a pleasure to have the quiet time in the lovely room with its shuttered windows and the fresh scents of flowers everywhere. They settled back together to await the promised tea, suddenly feeling very content.

That first afternoon seemed to set the pattern for their days. The vast house was well cared for by a large group of black girls under Tante Derra's watchful eyes. Meals were prepared and served flawlessly; there was always someone to watch over the children so Elena had little to do other than to prepare their lessons and work with them a few hours each day. The rest of the time she read the books from the large library and relaxed, awaiting the birth of her child with more peacefulness than she'd known since its conception.

Mimi had little more to do. For nearly three months they saw only each other and the servants and slaves that lived on the plantation. Then suddenly the invitations began to arrive, and Elena watched rather sadly as Mimi and Andre left for several days at a time to visit some of the more distant plantations where they were to meet their neighbors.

With them gone there was only Tante Derra to talk to, and Elena soon began to regard the older woman as a close friend. It was just as well she did, for when the baby chose to arrive a month early Mimi was far away and it was Tante Derra who soothed her, and the wizened but strong Karame who finally delivered the small, squalling bundle of life.

"You have a fine, strong son, little lady," Karame said in her gentle voice. "He is small now, but he will be a good man, a leader of men, the pride of his family."

Elena looked down at the red face and the flailing tiny fists, and for a moment she remembered the night in the grove, the horror and the pain; then another memory intruded and she was in Jamie's arms. She closed her eyes against the pain of the second memory. How could he be the pride of his family? she wondered bitterly. How would he even grow to manhood without a man's guidance?

"Don't doubt my mother's words," Derra said softly. "She has great powers. She is *mamba* of this whole area. Everyone turns to her for what they need, for what they must know."

"I'm very grateful to her for helping me, for both of you taking care of me. I don't know what I would have done, with Mimi being gone."

"He would have come," Derra said, smiling down at the baby, her fingers gently quieting him so that he slept in the crook of Elena's arm. "It is the way of the world. You believe Grandma Karame and rest now. You must produce milk for your son so that he will grow strong and well, and for that you need sleep."

The next six months passed in a haze for Elena. Louis—as she christened her son, in memory of her father—seemed to thrive, and was quickly a favorite of the slaves as well as the LaCroix. The circumstances of his conception had long faded from her mind and she held him tenderly, crooning lullabys in French or Spanish, caring little for anything but his future. Still, when she took him out in the morning sun, she found herself studying his eyes and speculating. Would they be dark like

Hernan's? Or hazel-green, as were her own? Or could they possibly change to the rain-cloud grey of the eyes that still haunted her dreams from time to time?

Her heart leaped with joy and relief when she could finally be sure that the indeterminate shade of his baby eyes had truly changed to the same steely grey she'd thrilled to in the dark alley of Mallorca when they first met hers.

As Louis needed her less often, however, Mimi began to intrude in Elena's happy world. "You cannot remain hidden away here forever," she said firmly.

"I'm not hiding," Elena protested. "I have my son to take care of."

"Derra can see that Louis is properly cared for," Mimi said with a dismissing wave of her hand. "It's time for you to go with us to some of the local balls and parties. If you're to find a proper father for Louis and a husband to love you, you'll have to meet the men of St. Domingue."

Elena opened her mouth to protest, to tell Mimi she couldn't marry anyone, that her heart still belonged to the father of her son, but something in the older woman's face stopped her words. She remembered again Jamie's words about the fiancée he'd left behind and was returning to marry. She sighed.

"What party did you have in mind?" she asked.

"There is a ball at the de la Mer plantation," Mimi said. "He's just come back to the area after a time in France. His plantation is the largest around and he is alone there. I heard he lost his wife in childbirth."

"What is he like?" Elena asked, not really interested but aware that she must try to find a husband for Louis's sake, if not for her own.

"Very handsome, in his late thirties, powerful, and quite a charmer. I danced with him at the last ball and I think Andre was a bit jealous. He does have a reputation with the ladies, but of course there are so few unmarried women in this area... He asked that we bring you, Elena. It seems he has learned we have a lovely young woman hidden here."

Elena smiled at that. "Is his plantation far away?" she asked.

Mimi shook her head. "We shan't even have to spend the night, so you won't have to worry about Louis. I'm sure Derra can care for him for one day, can't she?"

Elena laughed and agreed, her mind already busy with plans

for what she would wear. The ball would be fun, she decided, suddenly realizing that she'd been lonely in spite of her absorption with Louis.

The next week passed quickly as she worked on a piece of green silk, fashioning a gown for the ball with the aid of several of the maids—who were more talented with a needle than she was. The final effect shocked her a little as she stood in front of her looking-glass the afternoon of the ball.

The gown fit well, leaving her creamy shoulders bare and clinging suggestively to the swelling curves of her breasts. Her waist was tiny again, but it was more than that, she realized. The person who looked back at her was no longer a girl. Though she was just past eighteen, the eyes that stared back at her were older and her face had lost its girlishness. Her hair, bleached a little by the tropical sun, was once more long, and it strained at the careful molding the maid had done. One red-glinting tendril had been allowed to drop to her shoulder.

What would Jamie think if he saw her now? she wondered idly. Would he forget his English bride and seek to marry her? Or would he remember only that she was no longer innocent, and take her as a man claims someone he wants but doesn't respect?

The idea chilled her, and she turned abruptly from the mirror, then jumped as she found Derra behind her. "I am sorry, Madame," Derra said, but there was no smile in her eyes. "I had to come to speak to you before you leave for the de la Mer plantation."

"What is it?" Elena asked. "Not Louis..."

"The little one is quite well and happy," Derra said. "It is that my mother wished you to be warned. You must be careful tonight. It would be best if you did not go, but if you do you *must* be careful."

"What are you saying?" Elena asked. "It's just a ball at the next plantation. I've promised Mimi and Andre that I'd go with them."

Derra bowed her head, stopping Elena's words.

"Guard yourself well, Madame," she said. "There is danger there for you. That's all I can say."

Chapter 29

ELENA SAT ALONE after Derra had gone. The glow of her excitement about the evening had faded, though she firmly told herself it was nothing but native superstition. The blacks on St. Domingue were haunted by all sorts of demons and pagan beliefs, she assured herself, and she was being foolish to even listen, much less let it spoil her fun. She'd almost convinced herself by the time Mimi tapped on her door and called her to come and join them for the short drive to the de la Mer Plantation.

The plantation house was lovely and had been decorated with flowers and small lanterns for the party. A fine band of musicians played in one corner of the huge ballroom, and Elena was soon being swirled about the floor by a succession of men who outnumbered the women by at least five to one. It was fun, truly enchanting, and she was soon enjoying herself immensely.

Their host, Francoise de la Mer, paid her special attention, leaving his other duties to dance with her and escort her to the heavy-laden table of food that had been set out for the guests. "It is such a pleasure to meet you at last, Madame Elena," he said, looking down at her, his handsome features arranged in a very proper smile, though he held her a little too close and his eyes seemed always to be seeking to see beneath the bodice of her gown. "I have heard so much about you."

Elena laughed, a little embarrassed. "But where would you hear about me?" she asked nervously.

"From your friends, of course," he said. "It has been a disappointment to all of us that you've not joined our parties before."

"I have been very busy with my new son," Elena said.

"I hope I will be allowed to see you much more often," he went on. "You are far too lovely to hide yourself away with only the company of children."

There was more, much more through the evening, and Elena found herself growing more and more uneasy with each passing compliment. It was painfully obvious to her and to everyone else that he was paying her court and, though she knew she should be pleased and flattered, Elena felt only a growing weariness.

Once, when she excused herself to go upstairs and rest for a moment, Mimi followed her. "Isn't it wonderful?" she said, smiling broadly. "You're the belle of the ball, Elena, just as I knew you would be. In fact, Monsieur de la Mer has already been hinting to Andre that he would like to pay serious court to you. What do you think of that?"

Elena shivered in the warm night. "I don't think I'm ready to even consider anything like that," she said fearfully.

"But you *must* consider it," Mimi said. "You cannot go on trying to raise Louis by yourself. And what will you do when Josette and Serge no longer need you? I mean, you are welcome to stay with us, but I know you would not be happy to just live as a guest. And there is your future to consider. You are a lady, Elena, and you belong in a proper home where you can live as you were raised."

"I know you're right," Elena admitted, "but Monsieur de la Mer..." She let it trail off, unable to give a name to her misgivings.

"He is from a powerful family, and you can see how he lives. Andre has been most impressed with the way he's made his plantation flourish. He questions some of his methods, but that is of no interest to you." she shrugged. "I don't understand these things, but I do know that every unmarried woman has watched you with envy tonight. You would do well to use this opportunity if you can."

Elena nodded obediently, and then with Mimi's help secured the thick russet waves of her hair, which were now falling loose from their moorings. "You think it would be wise?" she asked finally.

"The other men who might be interested are either much older or without anything to offer you. You would be rich if you married Monsieur de la Mer."

With that in mind, Elena returned to the ballroom and, when Monsieur de la Mer presented himself to her again, she smiled up at him and tried hard to flirt, though the long months alone had almost made her forget what little she knew of the art. He, however, responded joyfully, growing ever more free with his compliments and hinting more and more broadly at his intentions.

It had grown quite late when he asked her to dance still another time. Elena, weary now from the dancing and from the hour—she was more used to going to bed when Louis did than to staying up past the rising of the moon—rose slowly. "It's so warm in here," she said in mild protest.

His eyes warmed instantly. "Perhaps a breath of air, Madame?" he suggested. "The gardens are as lovely in the moonlight as at dawn, and I have several varieties of flowers that open only after the sun has set. Would you care to see them?"

For a moment Elena hesitated—remembering the warning Derra had given her—then she shrugged her reservations away. The gardens opened just beyond the French doors, and there were always couples venturing out that way for a few moments of privacy. They would not be alone. "That would be pleasant," she said quietly.

His fingers were hot on her arm as he guided her firmly through the throng of people and out the door to the sweet-scented garden. The paths were marked by fine white sand, and they had no difficulty following them between the dark shadows of brush.

"I've told you already of my pleasure at having you as my guest, Madame," he said. "To have you join me here is even more delightful."

"It was kind of you to invite me," Elena said. "I am, after all, only an *institutrice* in the LaCroix household."

"I'm sure you are much more than that," de la Mer said, not at all put off by her words as she'd hoped he would be. "Andre himself has told me that his wife considers you a younger sister, and that they were godparents for your son at his christening."

"They have been extremely kind to me," Elena agreed, somewhat ashamed of her words since they did reflect on Mimi and Andre.

"I understand that your life has been difficult, coming here, bearing your child without a husband. But now that the child is old enough for you to leave him on occasion, I propose to change all that."

"Pardon?" Elena said.

"My dear lady, this is not the society of France. We do not stand on ceremony here. I knew from the first moment I saw you that you must become Madame de la Mer, and I mean to see that it happens soon." He had stopped as he spoke, and before she could say anything Elena found herself clasped in his embrace.

"Monsieur," she protested against his lips, but he paid no attention. His kiss was hard and demanding, hurting her mouth till he parted her lips to explore the softness inside. She tried to twist away, but his arms bulged with muscles and he held her easily, twining one hand in her hair to keep her mouth his prisoner while he pressed her soft body against him.

"I mean to have you, Elena," he said, "and you're no shy virgin to be wooed and won with hours of tender words and caresses. You've known a man's love—your child proves that—and I intend to know what kind of a woman you are before I take you off Andre's hands."

"No," Elena squeaked, sobbing a little at the pain as she wrenched her hair free of his strong fingers. "Let me go!"

He laughed. "When I'm ready, and not before."

"I'll scream," Elena gasped, looking back toward the well-lighted house, which seemed much further away than it had a moment ago.

"You do and I'll ruin your reputation so that no man will have you," he said with smiling cruelty. "You came with me willingly, remember? You've been casting warm glances at me all evening. What will people say if I tell them you led me out here, that you're trying to force me to marry you? If I tell them to ask questions about the father of your son?"

Elena stiffened at the malice in de la Mer's tone when he

mentioned Louis. The abrupt change in the man shocked and confused her as much as it frightened her. "My husband was killed," she said, aware even as she spoke that her tone held no confidence in the words; the attack had been too unexpected. "I came here to try to forget the tragedy."

His chuckle was mocking. "Of course you did," he said. "And to bear his son away from those who might ask too many questions. My wife would have no trouble making everyone believe such a story, I'm sure. But I have heard whispers since my return. Marry me and you son will be properly educated, perhaps even sent back to France to study, if you wish. I would be happy to settle a good sum on him, too."

"My son and I are not for sale," Elena snapped, anger flooding back. "I don't care what you believe about me. Let me go. I'm going back inside!"

She tried to pull away, but he was quicker and stronger. "You are mine, Elena," he said, "and I will have you now, here, like the serving girl you claim to be. I don't wait for anything, as you'll soon learn. Perhaps I, too, shall give you a son, but at least I will marry you and give him my name."

His hands were cruel claws as he pulled her to him, forcing more kisses on her, then his hand moved to her shoulder and caught at her gown, trying to force it down, to free her breasts for his eagerly seeking lips. Visions of the night in the grove filled Elena's mind, and she became that frightened child again. Sobbing in terror, she lashed out with a foot and heard him grunt in pain as her toe connected with his shin.

"*Bitch!*" he snarled, lifting his hand to strike her.

It was the opportunity she had hoped for. She jerked free of his other hand, leaving a part of the green silk in his fingers as she half-ran, half-fell into the bushes, fleeing in terror. For a moment she seemed to be alone in the darkness, but then she heard him crashing along in her wake, cursing horribly. "I'll have you!" he shouted. "You won't escape me, bitch!"

It was like running in thick mud or waist-deep in the sea. Bushes and roots seemed to snare at her, and she had no idea where she might be going. The moon was lost in the thick growth; she could scarcely run. Panting and exhausted, she nearly fell when she stumbled at last into a small clearing.

"This way," a soft voice said, and Grandma Karame suddenly appeared before her like a dream. "Under the bush.

Cover your face and arms with your skirt and be very still."

She was holding up a heavy vine and Elena, too exhausted to think, dove under it obediently. The vine dropped at once, thick fleshy leaves settling against her unpleasantly. She scrambled to cover herself with the flaring skirt, making sure her white petticoats were well hidden, and then she lay still except for the panting breath she could not control.

Peering out by lifting the hem of her skirt, she could see beyond the vine. Karame dropped to the ground and lay still, then de la Mer burst into the clearing, his face twisted and demented. "Where is she?" he demanded as Karame scrambled nimbly to her feet.

"Girl knock me down, master," the old woman whined in the pidgin French of the slaves. "Why girl want to hurt old lady?"

"Which way did she go?" de la Mer demanded, not even looking at the old woman.

"That way, master," Karame said, indicating what appeared to be a path leading from the far side of the clearing. "Girl run that way."

De la Mer was off without a backward glance, and Elena could soon hear him crashing through the brush again, still alternating between curses and pleading offers of love and friendship. Shivering with the aftermath of her terror, Elena crawled out from under the vine as Karame held it up for her. "How can I ever thank you?" she gasped.

"He is a devil," Karame said calmly, again speaking excellent French. "I have nursed the girls from his slave pens after he has taken them. He is worse than any he-goat, for his joy is in giving pain. He cares nothing for the children he sires. Before he made his trip back to France, he sold his own sons to the men who make them creatures to serve the needs of other men." Karame spit into the dust. "It is for that reason that I warned you to stay away."

"I should have listened," Elena admitted. "But I didn't know."

"There is no time to talk now," Karame said, looking around. "When he doesn't find you, he may return." She waved a hand at the shadows and a huge black man moved slowly out into the light to stand and wait, not even looking at them. "He will take you back to the plantation," Karame said. "It will be a long walk, but that cannot be helped."

"Mimi and Andre..." Elena protested.

"I will see that they are told you've gone home," Karame said, her dark eyes glancing at Elena. "You could not return as you are."

Elena followed her gaze and gasped. Her gown was half torn away, her creamy skin covered only by the fine cloth of her undergarment. She tried to cover herself, but Karame shook her head.

"Just go," she said. "You will be safe with him, and Derra will take care of you once you are home." She paused, then added, "We will talk again, I think, for this man is not one to yield his will easily."

Though she was still shaking, Elena followed the strange-looking man obediently as he led the way into the bush. He moved stiffly, looking neither to the right nor to the left. He seemed almost unaware of her behind him, neither pausing when she stumbled nor responding to her few questions about where they were and how he could find the plantation in the blackness of the bush at night.

When they reached the clearing that surrounded the plantation house, he stopped, and when Elena moved ahead of him he turned and disappeared back into the bushes, not seeming to hear her invitation to stop in the plantation kitchen to rest—not even acknowledging her heartfelt thanks. Derra, however, had heard her, for the front door opened before she reached it and she was helped up to her room without a word.

"De la Mer?" Derra asked as she removed the destroyed green silk gown.

Elena nodded. "Your mother saved me. She hid me, then sent me back here with a man. I don't even know who he was. He didn't talk or look at me, just led me through the brush and trees till we got to the house. He wouldn't even come in for some food or rum."

Derra sighed. "He would have no use for such things, Madame," she said. "He's one of my mother's servants. One of the walking dead."

"What?" Elena gasped.

"They serve my mother when she needs them, then return to their resting places. I told you, she is a powerful *mamba*."

"You can't believe such things," Elena protested. "You've had instruction in the Christian ways. You know such things just aren't possible."

"Was it possible for my mother to know in advance that you

would be in danger tonight?" Derra asked. "How could she be there to protect you, if she didn't have special powers? And where is this man you say brought you safely home? My mother lives alone and has no man to help her."

Elena shook her head, then the whole terrible evening swept over her and she began to cry. Derra comforted her without further words, soothing her so that she slept at last, too weary even to dream.

In the morning, however, the nightmare began with her waking to find Mimi in her room. The small French woman looked very bright-eyed and excited, although Elena knew she and Andre had returned very late and couldn't have had more than a few hours sleep.

"I thought you'd never wake up!" Mimi said. "And you've so much to tell me, I'm sure."

"*Tell* you?" Elena blinked at her, remembering at once her terror and the flight from the cruel, grasping hands and demanding mouth of Francoise de la Mer. "But I . . ."

"Now don't you play the sly puss with me." Mimi said, settling herself on the side of Elena's bed. "Your handsome suitor has already let out your secret, so you might as well confess. What happened in the garden to make him so eager? Tell me your secret so I can give it to Josette when she's old enough to seek a husband."

"I don't know what you're talking about," Elena said, though deep inside she had a terrible feeling she did know—and that it would be unbearable.

"I'm talking about your coming marriage to Francoise, of course," Mimi said. "He announced it to the entire company and we all drank a toast to you as his bride-to-be."

For a moment the bed seemed to spin and Elena closed her eyes. "He is wrong," she said without opening them. "I would rather be dead than marry him. I agreed to nothing last night. I fled the party to escape him, that's all."

"*Elena!*" Mimi's horrified tone brought her eyes open.

"I mean it," Elena said, but with less confidence. "He can't force me to be his wife."

Mimi gnawed on her lip for a moment, then sighed. "Perhaps not," she said, her tone full of doubt, "but what is left if you refuse? You saw how the men deferred to him. There is no one in the area who will pay you court if de la Mer forbids it. He's so powerful, Elena! He holds notes on most of the plantations, and..."

"Is there no one who'll try to stand against him?" Elena asked. "Am I the only one to see what a horrible man he is?"

Mimi only shrugged, her face lined with worry.

"I shall never be his bride," Elena said, but even as she spoke, she was worried about how she could escape the trap she seemed to have stumbled into. "There must be a way," she murmured, but she lay alone for a long time after Mimi left and no answers came to her.

Chapter 30

JAMIE SAILED FROM English Harbour with a mixture of relief
and dread. He had no fear of what might lay immediately ahead.
Indeed, he looked forward to the promise of battle and the
testing of his men and their training—but beyond that, his future
seemed to hold little promise.

Mr. Rathbone had agreed with Sally that she must make the
journey to Port Royal in one of his trading ships, so that she
would be there to welcome Jamie once their attack on Porto
Bello was accomplished. No amount of protesting on his part
had been able to sway either one of them, and he'd left her
planning what she'd take with her to her aunt's house. Jamie
sighed and changed his position at the rail, remembering what
Sally had said when they discussed the matter.

"The way you protest my going to Port Royal, I'd almost
believe you have another woman there waiting for you," she'd
said, tossing her golden mane.

"How should I have managed that?" Jamie asked, smiling.
"You know I've never been there."

Mr. Rathbone had come to his rescue, too, telling her she was speaking foolishly, but Jamie had seen the questions in his father-in-law's eyes and wisely stilled any further protests. "I only worry about your safety," he'd assured her.

"My sister will watch over her till you arrive," Mr. Rathbone said. "She's been asking me to let the children visit her for years, so now will be a good time."

"Missing her already?" Percy asked, snapping Jamie's mind back to the present roughly.

"She's a sweet girl," Jamie said a little stiffly. Though he'd managed to forgive Percy—once he'd realized his friend was innocent of the deception—he still felt uncomfortable with him.

"Far better than her sister," Percy agreed.

"That's not the way it looked to me," Jamie said, a little angered. "At least *you* seemed very fond of the fair Rebecca."

"Aye," Percy said with a sigh, "that little minx was a surprise to me. She seemed such a proper little lady I was even considering the fatal leap. There is a girl at home my father would like to see me wed. Her father's lands adjoin ours, and she's an only child."

"So you'll go meekly home when this is over," Jamie said, shaking his head. "I'll wager she hasn't long golden curls or violet eyes to bewitch you."

Percy nodded, but his eyes held no real regret. "Her hair is the brown of fall leaves, and her eyes are like the sea on a sunny day. She's far from Rebecca in beauty, but I know she'll be waiting for me when I return, just as you know your Sally will be waiting. With Rebecca, I suspect a man would never be sure."

Jamie looked at his friend more closely, surprised by the words and the way they were delivered. It was a side of Percy he'd never suspected existed. "Is that why you didn't talk to her father?" he asked at last.

Percy nodded. "I've seen too many of my friends watching their wives at every social gathering, wondering always if the man she's talking to is just a friend or if she's seeing him on the sly. You've had a taste of that from the girl you escaped, so you should understand."

Jamie thought of Amelia and felt again the humiliation and fury that had possessed him once he knew her game. "I couldn't live that way," he said heatedly.

"Nor could I," Percy said. His smile came easily. "Give me a plain and faithful wife and I'll find the brighter moments for myself. There are always fair wenches for the wooing, and if a man takes care he can enjoy them all."

Jamie looked at Percy with surprise—which he hastily concealed, realizing that Percy's was the accepted morality. "You're right, of course," he said, not adding that he couldn't quite bring himself to think that way. It was, he decided, the way his uncle had raised him. In their home a man married one woman and she was enough for him.

"It's a shame your bride is so determined to follow you to Port Royal," Percy went on, his eyes on the sea as the large ship strained against her sails, creaking and groaning in the rising wind. "I've heard it's a city full of lovely women and we can have our choice once we've taken our treasure."

"You'll be envying me," Jamie said, with more hope than confidence. "While you suffer in pursuit, I'll be having a home and a loving wife to take care of me."

Percy laughed and shook his head. "We'll see," he said. "We'll see."

Jamie watched him as he strolled forward to talk to one of the ship's officers, then turned his attention back to the sea. He felt better for having talked to Percy, and was glad the tension between them had disappeared. They would be a long time together now, and Percy's friendship was far too precious to him to be destroyed by a violet-eyed witch who'd cast her spell on them both.

Jamie sighed and went below, seeking to forget all women in a discussion of sea battles with the old man who mended the sails and served as ship's tailor, now that he was too old to climb the rigging as he had since he was a lad. Elena, Sally, Rebecca . . . none of them had a place in the world they sailed to now.

They reached the coast of Panama the night of November 20, and the next morning assembled for the attack. It was only then, in the morning light when they could see clearly what lay ahead, that Jamie felt the first cold fingers of fear. Porto Bello was not, at first sight, a promising victim.

It was a good bay, and the British fleet had driven a number of the *guarda-costa* vessels into the anchorage. On the north side of the bay, near the entrance of the harbour, stood a mighty fortress called the Iron Castle. It had an impressive battery of guns, which Jamie could see were nearly level with the water.

On the other side of the bay and about a mile farther up on a hillock was the Gloria Castle, with its two bastions toward the bay and a line of eight guns pointing toward the entrance of the anchorage. Above the Gloria Castle was a third fort, the stoutly-built Fort St. Jeronimo. In the distance, at the bottom of the bay, forming a half-moon along the shore, was the town of Porto Bello.

"It doesn't look so easy, does it?" Percy asked, his voice losing some of its confidence. "I mean from what our informants said. I'd pictured a sitting duck."

"I only hope they were correct," Jamie murmured.

"It looks like we'll find out soon enough," Reggie observed, joining them at the rail. "It seems *Hampton Court* is to take the lead."

"We are to sail into the harbour, shelling the Iron Castle as we pass it," Percy said.

"I wonder if he will want my sharp-shooters," Jamie mused, looking to the Vice-Admiral Vernon, who stood peering at the city.

"You'd be wise to have them ready," Percy said. "If he calls for them, I wager he'll want them in the rigging quickly."

Jamie went below and gave the necessary orders, then came back to the deck as the *Burford* took its place in the now-moving fleet as they sailed for the narrow inlet to the bay. Reggie stood with Jamie, but Percy had already gone below to the first gun deck, which was under his command for this first assault.

Hearing sounds from below, Jamie shook his head. No matter what came of the attack, he had to admit he much preferred being where he was, where he could see more than the narrow view from the gun ports. He wouldn't have to watch the sweating, half-naked men as they swabbed, loaded, and fired the cannon that lined the sides of the fighting ship. Nor did he want to think of the powder boys carrying the small but dangerous charges of powder up from the magazine for each firing.

The breeze was strong and true and the ships moved with dignity toward the harbour entrance. *Hampton Court* in the lead, closely supported by the *Norwich* and *Worcester*. All seemed to be going smoothly, then suddenly, as the *Hampton Court* began to fire its first round, the wind slacked, then dropped to almost breathlessness.

Shouts came from the Captain of the *Burford* and from the

Vice-Admiral. Sailors swarmed into the rigging setting all sails. Other men began dipping water from the sea and raising it by the bucketful to be thrown on the slack sails so that they would hold the slightest breath of wind. The *Burford* moved again slowly, creaking under her full compliment of sails as she inched toward the battle.

Ahead of them puffs of smoke rose from the Iron Castle, and there were a few marks on the walls as the first cannonballs struck. However, there was also a splintering and tearing in the mast of the *Hampton Court* as the returning fire from the Castle struck home.

Norwich and *Worcester* drifted into position, and the air was full of the thundering of cannon as they added their fire to that of *Hampton Court*. Jamie watched, fascinated. The ships bucked and rolled as the cannon were fired, and whenever an answering round struck, there were screams. For a moment a small fire flared on the deck of the *Worcester*, but it was quickly extinguished and the firing continued unabated. His head began to pound with it, the air became heavy with the smoke and the stench of powder, then suddenly it ceased.

Commands were shouted, and groups of marines began to file up on the deck. Boats were readied as the *Burford* moved majestically toward the forbidding walls of the Iron Castle. Was it all over so soon? Jamie wondered, moving to stand with the men he'd trained, waiting only for the order to go ashore with them and secure the obviously surrendering fort.

As if in answer to his question, the silent guns of the Iron Castle began to bellow again, and the first cannonball came streaking into the rail of the *Burford*. Wooden splinters, some of them huge, filled the air. One struck a man, nearly cutting him in half as he fell, shrieking, to the deck. Another marine spun, caught by a splinter driven like a lance into his shoulder.

Shouts filled the air, and in a moment the deck heaved beneath them as the first of the *Burford*'s cannon answered the fort's fire. "Get your men into the rigging, McDonald!" Vernon shouted, somehow managing to be heard above the din of the battle.

Heart pounding even as his stomach wrenched at the sight of the dying man writhing on the deck, Jamie shouted the order and was proud of the way his men scrambled into the lines, their protective ropes hooked in the waists of their trousers. Most of them were in position and priming their loaded weapons even before Jamie reached his position on the lower crosspiece of the main mast. At a signal from Vernon, he gave the order for his men to commence firing down at the Spaniards, who were busily manning the few active cannon of the Castle.

There was a return of fire from the Castle and, even as he watched, Jamie saw one of his men hit. The man's musket dropped into the heaving sea, but the rope held him as he slumped against it, blood rushing from a wound in his side.

Jamie stood where he was, sickened at the sight; then his mind woke to action. He began working his way along the mast till he could reach the man, Davy Crane.

A quick examination showed that the wound, though ugly, was treatable. Jamie looked around and spotted one of the younger sailors and shouted to him for help. The man scrambled up the lines to take a position above the wounded man, steadying him as Jamie freed him, then sharing the burden of Crane's weight as they carried him down to the sheltered area of the deck where Reggie was working over the injured.

"Reggie, can you help here?" Jamie shouted above the continuing din of the battle.

Reggie turned from his bandaging of a head cut and snapped an order to the apprentice who was assigned to help him. In a moment the marine's clothing was stripped from the wound, and Reggie was packing it to stop the bleeding. Only when the blood slowed to a trickle did he look up.

"Your foolish rope saved him," he said with a grin. "Once this battle is over, I'm sure I can clean the wound. He's healthy enough to live to fight more Spaniards."

"Then I'd best get back to my men," Jamie said, suddenly remembering he had other duties.

Reggie lifted his head. "I doubt there'll be much more to do up there," he said. "The cannon have stopped again. Vernon ordered the deck marines into the landing boats a few minutes ago."

"My men!" Jamie gasped, thinking they might have been ordered into the boats in his absence, but a glance up into the rigging showed they were all still in place, though they fired only rarely now.

Jamie scrambled back to his post on the mast and watched as the small boatsful of men neared the walls of the castle. There had been no breach of the thick wall in spite of their mighty firing, but the sailors quickly scrambled on each other's shoulders to climb through the embrasures from which the lower cannon had been fired, and the top men in turn assisted the more heavily-armed marines into the Castle.

From his higher post there was plenty to watch, and Jamie soon forgot his mission as he surveyed the scene. Men appeared and disappeared about the Castle. The fleeing defenders and the determined marines prowled the building for hours, till at long last the British flag was raised above it to signal that the capture was complete.

Shouts from the ships filled the air, now well cleared of the smoke of battle, and the men were ordered down from the rigging to the deck where they were quickly assembled for the Captain and the Vice-Admiral to account for those killed or injured in the attack. Evening was already settling over the water.

Everyone smiled as the losses were assessed. The *Burford* counted three men dead, five wounded. Once dismissed, Jamie made his way down to the part of the hold where Reggie had set up his hospital. Here the lanterns burned bright and the air was filled with the sounds of injured men. Reggie looked up, his face marked with weariness just as his clothing was stained with blood.

"What can I do for you?" he asked, accepting the mug of rum Jamie handed him.

"I wanted to see how Davy is doing," Jamie said.

"He's feeling badly just now, but the wound is good and clean. If he escapes the fever and the cut doesn't start to bleed again, he'll be strong enough to fight again in jig time."

"We only lost three men," Jamie said, "and the Castle is secured."

"There are two more forts to be taken," Reggie said, moving to check one of the men, this one with burns on his arms and chest.

"If they're no better defended than this one, they'll be no trouble," Jamie said calmly. "Lt. Broderick returned and said most of their cannon were useless because they had no gun carriages. They were low on ammunition and had so few men they couldn't have defended it from a much smaller force than we have. The Spaniards must have thought we'd let them sleep forever."

"How did Percy fare?" Reggie asked.

Jamie laughed. "He's talking like an old seadog now. You'd think it was his guns won the day."

Reggie joined his laughter. "And we all know it was your sharpshooters," he teased.

Jamie relaxed. "I almost lost one," he said. "My youngest man kept loading and firing, but without priming. He had six charges in his musket before I realized what was going on. If he'd remembered what he was doing and fired properly, he'd have been blown apart." He shook his head. "He's still on deck, turning greener and greener as he draws the charges out."

"Everyone will be easier next time," Reggie said. "My apprentice spent half his time leaning over the rail after he saw the first man die." He sighed. "It's hard to believe wood can do such terrible things when it's struck by a cannonball."

Jamie looked around the crude hospital and became aware again of the sleepy groans and moans. "Well, I'll leave you now," he said. "Will you be coming up for dinner?"

Reggie's gaze followed his. "If young Rob gets back soon, I'll be up. If I'm not, would you have someone bring me a plate later? I'll be spending the night down here, I'm sure."

"Thanks for looking after Davy," Jamie said. "He's got a wife and three sons at home."

"Your hooked lines saved him," Reggie said. "If he'd gone into the sea, he'd be feeding the fish now, that's for sure."

"I just wanted them to have both hands free to load and fire," Jamie said. "I guess I never really thought about anyone being hit."

Reggie nodded. "We all learned a lot," he said, then added, "See if you can cheer Percy up after he gets through with his bragging."

"What do you mean?" Jamie asked. "When I saw him he was fine."

"The second ball got one of his powder boys," Reggie said. "Killed him outright, but Percy still dragged him to me. There was nothing I could do. Well, you know how he goes on about those lads. My guess is he's put it out of his mind for now, but later on, when the celebrating is over, he'll remember and it will go hard with him."

Jamie nodded, remembering how his friend had spent much of his time on the voyage from England with the frightened powder boys, telling them stories, and on clear nights, teaching them about the stars as his father had taught him when he was a boy. "I'll do what I can," he said, though he felt inadequate at the thought.

As he climbed the narrow companionway to the deck, Jamie found his taste for battle disappearing. If they attacked tomorrow as they had today, what men would fall? What if Percy and Reggie were killed or wounded? What if one of the deadly splinters should find him in the sails or on the deck with his command? To fight man-to-man with a sword or knife, to see his enemy and hate him, that was one thing; but the flying cannonball gave no quarter, made no mistakes.

He sighed, telling himself that what he was feeling came from his empty belly and the dissipating of the rum-glow he'd had earlier. Tomorrow he would do whatever was ordered and soon Porto Bello would be theirs.

Morning found the Spaniards in a new mood. A white flag hung outside the walls of the city and, before the noon meal, the governor of Porto Bello had surrendered, accepting the terms dictated by Vice-Admiral Vernon. The two remaining strongholds—Gloria Castle and Fort St. Jeronimo—took a little more convincing, but they soon yielded, too.

Treasure began to flow from the city to the ships to be shared out among the victors and, though the town itself was not to be plundered, the harvest was a rich one. Even the sailors brightened at their shares, and Jamie glowed at the idea of recovering the money he'd used to purchase his Commission.

All brass cannon were brought to the ships while the iron guns were spiked or otherwise destroyed, and the marines went about the business of trying to level the mighty fortress. They proved stubborn, resisting all but the mightiest of explosions, and it was not till the sixth of December that they were able to leave the harbour, finally secure in the knowledge that the *guarda-costas* could no longer shelter there in safety.

They sailed out in greater numbers than they had arrived, taking with them all the ships that had been in the harbour, including three of the hated *guarda-costas*. As they stood at the rail, Percy sighed.

"What's the matter?" Jamie asked. "Don't tell me you found a dark-eyed lady you can't bear to leave?"

Percy laughed. "No such luck," he confessed. "I was just thinking I'd like to be the one to take the news of this victory home to London. Can you imagine the celebrating? We've won the first victory of this war. We've made the Spaniards cry out and surrender."

Jamie nodded. "I wonder what my father will say," he said, thinking rather sadly of the damp, cold world he'd known all the years of his life and now missed sorely. "If Ian is right, he'll probably be bragging about me now."

"Where do you think we'll go next?" Percy asked.

Jamie shrugged. "Perhaps to Port Royal to leave the wounded and to get new reports, or maybe we'll find one of those fat galleons laden with gold. Now *that* would be a prize to take, wouldn't it?"

Percy agreed and they talked on of future prizes, dreaming of their riches. But even as he spoke, Jamie thought of Elena and wondered about her. Was she even now preparing for the Christmas season with her family in Le Mans, or had she left there, perhaps found a new home with a husband?

He winced with the thought and his own realization that he had a wife awaiting him in Port Royal. It burned him with shame to acknowledge that the months hadn't faded his memories of Elena at all. If he closed his eyes he could see her easily, head back, eyes stormy and full of pride. Or as she'd been in his dream, all soft and gentle, warming beneath his fingers, her breath quickening with his, her body responding with eagerness even as she tried to deny it with her lips. And her shuddering surrender... Aching with a longing that no forceful concentrating on Sally's willing charms could ease, he followed Percy below, wondering if he'd ever be able to forget Elena and live as honor told him he must.

Chapter 31

THE JOURNEY TO Port Royal passed quickly. As they neared the port itself, however, Jamie began to wonder about Sally. Would she be waiting for him? Or would her trip have been delayed for some reason? He couldn't honestly decide whether he hoped it had or not.

Strangely enough, he found himself thinking of her more often as the days after the battle crawled by. Though he had no illusions of loving her, memories of her warmth and loving ways were a balm against the emptiness that came whenever Elena intruded into his thoughts. More than that, her passion excited him and he longed to hold her in his arms once more.

As soon as the *Burford* was docked and he'd seen that Davy was taken ashore under Reggie's watchful eye, Jamie took the address Sally had given him and sought out public transport to take him to it. The streets were crowded with all manner of people and animals—rather like a market day in the Highlands, except that the people here were dark-skinned and the goods they offered were exotic to his eyes.

The house was a fair-sized one, set back from the street and sheltered by a beautifully blooming tree. When the cart stopped, Jamie hesitated, not sure whether he should dismiss the driver or not. Then the front door opened and a golden-haired girl called his name. Jamie tossed the driver a coin and leaped down, scarcely taking time to lift his belongings from the cart before Sally was there, throwing herself into his arms.

"I thought you'd never come," she sobbed, nearly drowning him with tear-wet kisses. "We saw the sails hours ago, and we wanted to go to the harbour to meet you but Aunt Helena wouldn't allow it."

"She was right," Jamie said, holding her close and enjoying the sweet, clean scent of her hair and skin even as she cuddled into his arms. "The harbour is no place for a girl like you. I came as soon as I could, just as I promised."

"I know you did, but I've missed you so." She hugged herself to him like a second skin, and his desire for her flared at once. "I've been here nearly three weeks, and we were so afraid you wouldn't be here for Christmas."

"I'm sure we'll be here that long, perhaps longer," he assured her.

"How nice for all of us," a voice said at his shoulder and Jamie stiffened, lifting his head from Sally's and turning to see Rebecca standing beside him.

"What are you doing here?" he demanded, his pleasure fading the moment his eyes met hers.

"Is that any way to welcome your loving sister-in-law?" Rebecca asked, her violet eyes mocking as they met his.

"Father refused to let me come alone," Sally said, her tone making it plain she was no happier about the arrangement than he was.

"I couldn't let my poor innocent little sister travel to this wicked city without me," Rebecca murmured, her tone so filled with irony no one could miss her meaning. "Besides, I promised we'd see each other again, dear Jamie, don't you remember?"

Hot answers rose to his lips, but he controlled them, aware that Rebecca was enjoying his discomfort. "Of course," he said with a firmly forced smile, "and you must forgive my ungraciousness. It's just that I'd thought to be alone with my wife and ... I am naturally delighted to see you again, Rebecca, and most grateful that you came with Sally."

The shock in her lovely face was his reward, and he savored it for a moment before turning his attention back to the girl in his arms. He kissed Sally with long and deliberate passion, well aware of Rebecca's furious gaze. He'd teach her to mock him, he thought furiously.

Once inside, things moved swiftly. He was introduced to the tall, raw-boned Aunt Helena, then escorted up a broad staircase to the second floor rooms that he and Sally were to share. They were beautiful, the sitting room well-furnished with comfortable sofas and chairs and carved tables and shelves that held a surprising number of books.

The bedroom contained a magnificent four-poster bed with matching chests and tables, and both rooms were riotous with flowers that filled the air with their perfumes. Sally led him about, telling him she'd chosen the material for the bedspread and matching canopy and draperies herself and supervised its preparation for this day.

"I'll do the same for our own house when you wish to choose it," she said, her eyes searching his face. "That is, if you wish to choose one. My aunt assures me it is unnecessary, and says she would be much relieved if you would agree to stay here as long as you are at sea with the fleet."

"Your aunt is too kind," Jamie said.

"She is very lonely since her husband died," Sally went on, perching on the high bed. "He left her a great deal of land and money, but she must remain here to watch over her holdings. She misses the family, and I think it would be a kindness to accept."

"Is that what you want?" Jamie asked, forcing himself to dismiss Rebecca from his mind.

Sally put her head to one side, her blue eye regarding him for a moment before she answered. "When you are here, I should like best to have you alone in our own little house," she said with a gaze that set his blood boiling, "but when you are gone, I should die if *I* had to live alone."

"Then we shall stay here," Jamie said, leaving her long enough to go out and secure the door of their sitting room. "This will be our own private hideway, and we'll pretend the rest of them don't exist." He joined her on the bed, silencing her half-hearted protests with his lips as he made love to her.

In spite of the doubts he'd entertained, both when he sailed from English Harbour and when he reached Port Royal to find

Rebecca in residence, the weeks of his stay in Port Royal were some of the happiest he'd known. Sally was everything she'd promised to be: warm, loving, full of laughter and fun, teasing him when he became too solemn.

Rebecca troubled him surprisingly little once he made it clear he meant to have no part of her cruel games. He was far from immune to her almost tangible sensuality, but he hid the fact from her by turning always to Sally.

Percy came calling and took Rebecca out for drives as before, and Jamie watched him sometimes—wondering if they played out their sensual games in some other cove—but he dared not ask, for even his anger and disgust couldn't quite overcome a longing to participate. Rebecca might be little better than a tart in the streets, but her allure was so strong she could make any man forget everything else, at least for a while.

The shares from the taking of Porto Bello were rich, and Jamie felt well able to entertain his friends during the holidays. He offered rich gifts to Sally and her aunt, and even purchased an amethyst necklace for Rebecca, matching her eyes as closely as he could. Her tears when she opened the gift shocked him, for he sensed that they were real and not just another of her artifices.

Jamie spent little time at the harbour, going down only rarely to drill his men to make sure they didn't lose their ease in the rigging. He went also to visit Davy in the rooms where Reggie kept watch over the still-recuperating injured. The young marine had survived the wound well enough, but once on his feet it was plain he would never have the speed and agility necessary for his service. Jamie reluctantly advised him to take his share of the treasure and return to his family in England.

"But I'll have nothing left once I've bought my passage," Davy protested. "How'll I feed and care for them, sir?"

"What have you been doing here, to keep yourself busy?" Jamie asked, aware that the man was right.

"Mending nets and sails," Davy said, waving a disparaging hand at the pile of them in the corner of the room. "I thought to earn my keep that way. And I try to help the surgeon with those worse off than me." He smiled. "He says I've got a knack for it."

"Then why not earn your passage to England?" Jamie suggested. "You've made friends here. Let them ask among the ships that come and go from here; they'll likely find someone who'll offer you a berth for your work."

Davy brightened at once. "If I could take my full share home, it might be enough to get a small farm," he said. "That's been my dream always, but a man such as myself generally has small hope for it."

"I've another favor to ask of you," Jamie said. "I would like you to carry a message from me to my father. A personal letter I'd rather not send through official channels. Would you do that for me?"

Davy looked up at him, his eyes bright. "I would swim across with it for you, sir," he said, his voice so soft Jamie had to move nearer to hear the words. "I owe you my life."

Jamie cleared his throat uncomfortably. "In battle all men owe their lives to each other," he said sternly.

"You brought me down," Davy reminded him.

"And Reggie cleaned and cared for your wound," Jamie said. "And the shots you fired before you were hit may have saved other lives."

Davy continued to look at him and Jamie knew the man wasn't hearing the words. "Anyway," he said, "I'll bring you the message in a day or so, and I'll give you my father's address in London. If you'll take it to him, I'm sure he'll reward you properly."

"I need no reward, sir," Davy said. "Just doing it for you will be enough."

Jamie ignored the words, embarrassed by them. As soon as he could, he left the make-shift hospital and went back to his rooms to write the letter to his father.

In the rush of his wedding and leaving English Harbour, he had not taken time to write and tell his father of his marriage. But now he knew he must. The weeks in Jamaica had changed his feelings. Though he realized he would never love Sally as he loved Elena, nor desire her as he was forced by his own senses to desire Rebecca, he did care for his wife and wanted her place in his family made secure in case something happened to him.

Jamie wrote slowly, carefully, telling his father of the Rathbone family and detailing his wedding. He included many details of the raid on Porto Bello, then finished with the simple statement that he hoped that his father would have forgiven him for his past indiscretions, and the hope that he wouldn't find too much difficulty in the announcement of Jamie's marriage. He carefully avoided any mention of Amelia Starburough, though she was in his thoughts as he blotted the pages and read them over before sealing them carefully in a water-tight packet.

"Will your father be very angry?" Sally asked, coming in to watch the final process.

Jamie shrugged. "He's been angry with me for a long time," he said without rancor. "Perhaps this news will change that."

"I wish I could have met him before the wedding," Sally said.

"He might have frightened you away," Jamie teased.

"Not even if he has two heads and breathes fire," Sally said, coming to cuddle in his arms and pull his mouth down on hers. "I knew that first night that you were going to be mine; I vowed it the first moment you walked into the house. You didn't see me, but I knew."

"I'm glad you did," Jamie said, holding her close. "I'm grateful you did what you did, Sally."

Her tears spilled over, damping his shirt front. "Do you mean it?" she asked. "Do you really mean it?"

"Of course I do," Jamie said, startled at her response. "Why wouldn't I?"

"She would have married you when Percy refused to offer for her hand," Sally said. "She won't admit it now, but I know she would have."

"Then you saved me from a great deal of sorrow," Jamie said, denying the sharp pang her words brought him.

Sally's eyes regarded him for a moment, as though she sought to see into his very heart, then she nodded as though having reached a decision. He expected her to say something, but she only took his hand and placed it on her breast, then lifted her lips for his kiss. As he claimed her more than willing body, Jamie wondered who possessed whom, but in the fever of passion it hardly seemed to matter.

Once the new year dawned in the tropical islands, a restlessness gripped him. Though he spent his time as before, he found his thoughts going more and more often to the harbour where the *Burford* seemed to tug at its moorings, as anxious to be free as Jamie was. Percy and Reggie echoed his feelings, talking more and more of the other cities that dotted the coasts of the new world—and less and less of the parties and entertainments they'd found in Port Royal.

When the word came that they were to sail again, they were all relieved. Only Sally seemed to react badly when Jamie told her.

"But you can't leave me now," she protested, her eyes wide and fearful.

"You'll be perfectly safe here," Jamie said, tousling her hair. "You've known all along that I would be sailing before long. We were just lucky to be in port for Christmas."

"But I need you here," Sally protested, her blue eyes filling with tears.

"You have your aunt and Rebecca," Jamie reminded her. "That's why we didn't find a place of our own, remember? I don't think we'll be gone long. This is to be our home port, so we'll be returning here after our next raid."

"Where will you be going?" Sally asked, her expression telling him his words weren't mollifying her.

Jamie shrugged. "We haven't been told," he said.

"I can't let you go," Sally said, her arms slipping around him and clutching him tight to her. "You belong with me now."

"What on earth is wrong with you?" Jamie asked. "You weren't like this when I sailed from English Harbour. We were just newly wed then; we're an old married couple now."

"When you left there it was different," she said, her eyes skittering away from his.

"How was it different?" Curiosity spurred Jamie, and he caught her chin in his hand and forced her head up. "What is it, Sally? Has something happened? There isn't any trouble between you and Rebecca, is there?"

"Rebecca?" Sally looked surprised, then shook her head. "I think she's finally given up trying to steal you away from me."

"Then what is it?"

"A woman needs her husband with her when she's carrying his child," she said softly.

Jamie opened his mouth to say something more about his mission in the Caribbean, but the words died as what she'd said suddenly reached him. "When she's *what*?" he gasped.

Sally smiled up at him shyly.

"Are you sure?" he demanded. "Have you seen anyone?"

"As sure as I can be this early," Sally said. "I wouldn't have told you yet if you weren't thinking of leaving me, but..." She stopped, her expression sober. "I don't want you to go, Jamie.

What if something should happen to you? What if you're captured and can't come back to me for years? I couldn't face it alone, Jamie. That's why you have to stay here and let the ship sail without you."

"*My baby?*" Jamie just looked at her, scarcely hearing her words. "A son, no doubt. I wish Davy hadn't sailed already. I'd like to put that in the letter to my father—might make him feel better about everything."

"Jamie, *please* say you'll stay with me this time." Her fingers clutched at him.

He drew away instinctively. "I can't, Sally, you know that. I have a commission in the Royal Navy. I'm assigned to the *Burford*, and if I stayed with you I would be deserting."

"If you go, you're deserting *me*."

"I'll be back long before the baby is due," Jamie reasoned, reaching out to her as he would to a restive horse. "You're just upsetting yourself, and you shouldn't do that."

"You don't want to stay with me," Sally said, accusingly.

"Don't be foolish," Jamie replied.

"I've seen it in your face these past few weeks," she interrupted. "You want to go to sea and attack the Spanish. You're *tired* of me!" She began to cry.

Jamie comforted her, but even as he held her his eyes were drawn to the window and the distant forest of masts that marked the fleet. His words of sympathy and love were strained, for she was right. When the day came to sail, he left with a happy heart, glad she would be well cared for in his absence but pleased to be on the sea once again. He had a son's future to build, he told himself. That was more important than sitting around Port Royal holding Sally's hand because she was afraid for him.

Chapter 32

THE NEXT WEEK was like a slow nightmare for Elena. De la Mer came to call several times, smiling and unfailingly courteous when Mimi and Andre were present, but when they were alone he was like an animal. Elena shuddered at the memories. Her arms bore the marks of his fingers, black with bruises wherever he touched her—and he seemed to enjoy touching her.

What was worse was his insistence on seeing Louis, even holding him. Her heart stopped each time the big, cruel hands approached her small, helpless son, yet she dared not anger him by trying to keep him from the infant. It was torture, and she sensed that de la Mer was enjoying it immensely.

It was not till late in the evening, nearly ten days after the terror of the ball she'd attended at his plantation, that she was given a little reprieve from her suffering. They were sitting in the parlour of the LaCroix home when de la Mer sighed.

"You are going to have to set a date, *ma cherie*," he said. "I know you are shy, but I grow impatient to have my little bride at home."

The words were spoken with tenderness, but the hot eyes ravished her and Elena felt her skin crawling at the suggestion. "But I..." she began, searching wildly for an excuse to delay longer, to give herself a few more moments to find some means of escape.

"You will have three weeks to think about it," de la Mer said. "I must travel to my holdings on the far side of the island, but when I return I'll expect your answer." He smiled with his lips, though his eyes remained cold. "And I'm sure the day named will be soon, won't it, *ma cherie?*"

The threat was there, and Elena could only nod—her mouth too dry for words to form. *Three weeks!* Her mind raced. Long enough? She couldn't be sure, but she could hope. Somehow she had to find a way to escape the living nightmare de la Mer had planned for her, even if it meant leaving St. Domingue and the LaCroixs.

The first day after de la Mer left, Elena merely moved about the plantation and enjoyed the sense of freedom that came from knowing he was gone. Even the air itself felt lighter, and the sun seemed especially warm and pleasant. She was so content with her walking that she was late returning to the house. Derra was waiting for her when she entered.

"You must hurry, Madame Elena," she said softly. "Madame LaCroix has told me there will be a guest for dinner and she asked specifically that you be in attendance."

Elena stiffened. "Not de la Mer?" she gasped. "He was to leave today."

Derra shook her head. "It is not the evil one, Madame. An older man came to speak with Monsieur LaCroix this afternoon, and it is he who will remain to dine."

Elena let her breath out in relief. "Thank you, Derra," she said. "I'll go up and change now."

Elena found herself looking forward to the evening, mainly because it was a treat to have someone new to talk to and because she felt liberated by de la Mer's absence. When she descended the staircase, she found Mimi and Andre in the drawing room with a smiling grey-haired gentleman. He rose to greet her warmly, and Elena felt his admiring eyes often through the early hours of the evening.

After the dishes had been cleared away and the gentlemen had had their cigars and liquor, Monsieur Carnac—as the visitor had been introduced—crossed to Elena with a smile. "Madame de Vere," he said with a courtly half-bow, "Monsieur LaCroix has told me how lovely his gardens are and has credited you with much of the planning, so I wonder if you might be interested in showing me through them this evening."

Elena got up willingly enough, a little surprised at the words, but perfectly happy to spend some time alone with the gentleman from Port-au-Prince who was, she'd learned, to be their guest for the next several days. "I'm afraid I can take little credit for the gardens," she said as they stepped out into the flower-scented night. "I made a few suggestions, that's all."

"You are too modest," Monsieur Carnac said. "Though such efforts really wouldn't be necessary from one so lovely. It is my observation that women of your beauty need never do anything but smile."

Elena laughed. "I'm afraid I would be quite a disappointment in your scheme of things, Monsieur," she said. "I'm acting as *institutrice* for the LaCroix children, and I have a son of my own to care for. I have little time to sit about and smile."

"That could be changed." The words were spoken softly, but Elena sensed that the intent was far from casual.

"What do you mean, sir?" she asked, pausing in the moonlight near one of the little benches that were scattered about the garden.

"Perhaps we could sit there and discuss it," Monsieur Carnac suggested, gesturing at the bench.

Elena allowed herself to be seated, her curiosity burning now. Monsieur Carnac smiled at her benevolently for a few moments, then reached out and picked up her hand. Surprised, Elena made no move to pull away. His hands, though showing the first signs of age, were warm and strong as he gently caressed her fingers.

"After you ladies left us this evening, I inquired about you, Madame," he said quietly, "and Monsieur LaCroix has told me a little of your background and your present situation."

Elena tensed. "What do you mean?" she asked.

"I know that you are a widow with an infant son." He smiled. "A very lovely widow, I might add. From Monsieur LaCroix, I understand you've attracted the attentions of Francoise de la Mer—attentions which, according to Monsieur LaCroix, you do not enjoy. Is that true?"

Elena's heart leaped with hope. She'd made it plain to Mimi that she hated and feared de la Mer, but she'd never been sure how much Mimi had told Andre. "It is very true," she admitted. "I am terrified of the man, but he insists I must marry him, and he is so powerful..."

"I have heard about his ways," Monsieur Carnac said. "My son has a plantation on the far side of the valley, and the stories of de la Mer's cruelty to his slaves have reached even that far."

"I fear for my son's life," Elena said quietly. "For myself, I think I would choose death before accepting his proposals, but Louis is so young..."

"Please, don't think there is no other choice," Monsieur Carnac said.

"What do you mean?" Elena asked, her hope rising even higher. "Is it possible that you would help me to leave here, perhaps escort me to Port-au-Prince? From there surely I could escape him and perhaps find another post as an *institutrice*."

"That is the least I am prepared to offer," Monsieur Carnac said softly, his hands caressing her with more firmness.

"I don't understand," Elena said, suddenly unsure.

"You are still a child, Madame," he said gently. "In spite of the child you have, you are no older than my youngest son, and I fear you know little of the ways of the world."

Elena tossed her hair back. "I know more than you realize," she said, thinking painfully of all the things she'd been trying to forget in the peace of St. Domingue—before she'd met Francoise de la Mer.

"My journey here had several purposes," Monsieur Carnac went on, seeming not to have heard her words at all. "First, I came to see my son and to meet my grandson. Second, I had contracts to see to. I represent many of the *planteurs* in their trade dealings. However, my last purpose was an even more personal one. I have been alone for nearly two years since the death of my wife, and I had thought that I might seek companionship among the lovely ladies."

Elena swallowed hard, understanding for the first time why he'd been so interested in her. "What are you saying?" she asked, caught between fear and hope.

"That I would be willing to take you from here as my wife, Elena de Vere. I can offer you a great deal. My endeavors have been profitable, and I am considered a man of some standing in

Port-au-Prince—powerful enough to give you protection against de la Mer's anger if you choose to accept my offer." His face, handsome and hawklike in the moonlight, eased a little. "I am not expecting love, my dear," he went on more gently. "At my age a man has become more realistic. However, I think you might learn to hold me in some affection, and that—plus your fidelity—would be sufficient for me. In return I will raise your son as my own and see that you are well provided for at my death."

Elena swallowed hard. "You shock me, Monsieur," she managed after a moment of seeking for words. "I had no idea that you would... We've just met and..."

His chuckle stopped her. "I'm not asking for an answer tonight, *ma cherie*," he assured her. "I simply thought it would be well to speak at once and give you as much time as possible to consider my proposal. I understand you have only three weeks before de la Mer's return, and I suspect it might be wise to be far from here by then."

Shuddering, Elena had to agree.

They sat in silence for several minutes, then Monsieur Carnac spoke again. "If my proposal is unacceptable, I will still offer you my protection for the journey to Port-au-Prince. It is my plan to leave within the week, and once in Port-au-Prince I can make arrangements for you to sail from this island, if you wish."

"You are most kind," Elena said, humbled by his offer. "Far kinder than I deserve."

"You think on what I've said," he replied, getting to his feet. "We'll talk further tomorrow. Now I think we should return to the LaCroixs. They must be wondering what there is to see in the moonlight that could hold our interest for so long."

Elena laughed with him as she realized that they'd been sitting on the bench for a long time. "I'll look forward to tomorrow," she said, meaning it. Though Jean Carnac was outwardly far from the man of her dreams, she sensed his warmth and kindness. She went inside feeling far better than she had since the night of de la Mer's ball.

The next few days passed quickly and pleasantly. Jean, as she was soon calling him, proved to be a romantic suitor, bringing her flowers and small gifts of perfume and jewelry. His kisses were gentle but ardent, and she knew he would be a tender lover when the time came. To her surprise, she found herself looking forward to the day she would become his wife. It was only after she accepted his offer of marriage that she began to have doubts—not about him, but about her own worthiness to accept what he offered.

As the second week began, she knew she owed him more than future fidelity and the affection she already felt for him. Even though it might jeopardize her future, she knew she must tell him the truth—both about herself and about Louis. With that in mind, she suggested a picnic for the following afternoon.

As they drove out in his carriage, Elena watched the thick, tangled brush and trees on the side of the road. "You seem troubled today, *ma cherie*," Jean said. "Have you had a change of heart, now that our wedding day is so near?"

"I haven't," Elena said, "but you may, Jean. There are things you don't know about me, things I must tell you before I can let you go through with our wedding."

Elena stole a glance at Jean and saw that he was smiling. "What grave sins have you committed, little girl?" he asked, gently.

Elena took a deep breath. "To begin with, my name is Elena de Vere Flambeau, and I was raised in Spain, not France." She went on slowly, carefully, leaving out nothing—not her violent rape in the olive grove or her second experience with love on the ship going to France. She told him of her days in Le Mans with the Flambeau family, and her violent expulsion from the family as a result of Hernan Valdez's letter.

"I'm not surprised to learn your son had no legal father," Jean said when she paused in her narrative. "I guessed as much. It is often thus when a young girl has a son and speaks only rarely of her husband."

"There is more," Elena said, feeling the blood in her cheeks as she went on to tell him about Raul and the rooms he'd taken her to. She kept her eyes down, not wanting to see the change in his face, the disgust she was sure would replace his kind acceptance of all she'd told him before. When she finished, he said nothing for a long time and she felt her hopes and dreams draining away.

Had she destroyed everything? she asked herself. Had she doomed herself and, more importantly, Louis? Had she been a fool to be so honest and lose her only hope of escape?

"Do the LaCroixs know about this?" Jean asked, his voice suddenly toneless.

"Of course not," Elena said, her heart dropping completely.

"Mimi knows Louis has no legal father, but I dared not tell them the rest."

"Yet you've told me."

"I couldn't allow you to marry me without knowing," Elena said, her head down. "I'll understand if you wish to withdraw your proposal, all I ask is that you allow me to travel with your party to Port-au-Prince. I won't trouble you once I'm safely away from here, I promise. I don't want to make trouble for anyone; I just can't stay here and allow Francoise to harm my son."

Jean wound the reins loosely about the front of the carriage, then turned to her, his eyes grave as they searched her face, forcing her to hold up her head and meet his gaze. Elena endured the scrutiny, fighting back her tears as she looked at his dear face and realized that, in a very special way, she had come to love this man.

"You look like such an untouched child," he said, shaking his head. "I never cease to marvel at the strength of women, did you know that? Men may fight the battles and conquer the land, but it is the courage of women that makes it all possible. You have that courage in full measure, *ma cherie*, or you would have followed in your friend Celeste's footsteps long ago."

Elena sighed. "There have been times when I've wished I had done that, and ended all the misery before it began. Then I look at Louis and for him, I would endure anything."

"And since that time, since you fled from your cousin?"

"There has been no one," Elena said. "I had no desire for anyone, Jean. I didn't even want to go to the ball where I met de la Mer, but Mimi insisted. She said I must marry for Louis's sake and I knew she was right. My son will need a father when he grows a little older."

"And he shall have one." The words were spoken quietly, but firmly.

"What?" Elena just stared at him, startled. "What are you saying, Jean?"

Jean reached out and gently smoothed back the waves of her hair. "I've had two wives, Elena, and to be honest, when I was younger I had a mistress or two, also. I've seen much of love and of people. There are pure virgins I'd not trust past the wedding day and whores who have the capacity for faithfulness. What happened to you was ugly and cruel, and I'm amazed you survived it so well. I'd like to guarantee that you won't suffer so again—and as my wife, you'll have all the protection you need, both now and later."

For a moment she just looked at him, searching the lined face and looking deep into the dark eyes that met hers so honestly. "You're sure?" she asked, unable to believe her own ears.

"I know I've been happier in this past week than I've been in years. You make me feel young again, Elena—young and strong and in love. I won't discard that because you were forced into a situation where you had to endure a kind of life you should never even have had to know about. You left that life behind you when you came here with the LaCroixs, and I think we can safely forget it now, don't you?"

Elena could only nod, her heart bursting with love as tears overflowed her eyes and ran unnoticed down her cheeks.

"In a day or so you will be Madame Carnac. That is the only thing the world will need to know." Jean pulled her close, and his kiss was like a benediction. "From now on we will think only of tomorrow and the years ahead," he said firmly. "The past can sleep alone."

He picked up the reins with one hand, but the other arm stayed around her shoulders and Elena cuddled close to his side, weak with relief and pleasure. She would love him forever, she vowed, love and honor him and never give him cause to doubt her. Whatever years remained to him—and she hoped they would be many—she would make as happy as she could. Her devotion would be small payment for the trust he was willing to place in her.

Chapter 33

THEY DROVE FURTHER than Elena had expected before they found exactly the spot Jean was seeking. However, when he lifted her down from the carriage and handed her the basket of food and the blanket to spread on the ground, she was glad she hadn't complained of the distance, for the area was beautiful.

Exotic flowers bloomed in dizzy profusion about the small clearing, and a little stream bubbled happily over the rocks, dropping a few feet at one end in a miniature waterfall that caught the light and filled it with rainbows. Elena carried the basket and blanket to the grass near the little falls, putting the bottle of wine in the water to cool after she spread the blanket.

Derra had packed a fine meal of cold meat, fruit, bread, and cheese, and there was even a box of delicate French pastries for later—to end the meal on a sweet note. Elena unpacked everything, setting it out as attractively as she could while Jean unharnessed the horse and tethered it to graze on the far side of the clearing.

They ate hungrily, talking easily of the wedding that would be performed two days hence. Once the food was gone, Jean poured glasses of wine and they leaned against a fallen tree trunk and sipped it, discussing the future.

"We won't spend all our time in Port-au-Prince," he said. "There are other islands where I have dealings, and I'd like very much to take you with me when I must make my visits." He smiled down at her. "I have a couple who manage my home, and they will see to Louis's care when you must be away. She raised my last two sons almost from the cradle and did it well, so she can be trusted implicitly."

"I'll be happy to go with you," Elena said. "I've had little chance to enjoy traveling, but I think I might, with you as my guide."

He kissed her tenderly. "I'll show you only the happy places," he said.

They lay dreaming side by side till the afternoon shadows became long across the clearing. Only then did Jean sigh and begin to slowly rise. "Best I move my old bones,"he said with a mocking smile in her direction. "When I'm with you I forget my years."

"You'll always be young to me," Elena said. "As young as your heart."

"When you're near that's young indeed," he said gallantly, though she noted that he limped a little as he moved away from her and toward the side of the clearing where the horse grazed.

She shouldn't have let him lie so long on the wet grass, she told herself. If he wouldn't care for his health, she must think of it. From now on she would, she vowed sternly as she rose and turned her attention to picking up the remains of their lunch and stowing it in the now nearly empty basket. She was humming to herself and folding the blanket when she heard a strange sound behind her.

"Are you almost ready, Jean?" she asked, not looking around as she assumed it was he coming back to get the basket now the horse was harnessed.

There was no answer, so after a moment she put the blanket down on the basket and turned to see where he'd gone. The scene before her was like something out of a nightmare.

The horse stood between the shafts of the small carriage, ready to go, but Jean was not at his side. He was moving toward her, but slowly, backing in her direction while a mountainous black man moved toward him, mad eyes rolling, a huge cane knife raised above his head.

Jean tried to speak—she heard his voice, low and firm, though she couldn't catch the words. The black man continued forward, then suddenly he leaped at Jean and the cane knife came down, catching Jean at the side of the neck and disappearing in a red fountain.

Elena stumbled forward, then the horror of it banished everything and she slumped to the ground, the spinning earth turning to blackness around her. She didn't even feel the grass that welcomed her.

She revived slowly as though her mind was not anxious to face what had driven her into darkness. She opened her eyes, felt the grass beneath her cheek and the pain of her arm as she lay on it. For a moment she wondered where she was, then it returned to her in terror and she stirred, looking around in fear.

At first the clearing seemed totally empty. The only sound came from the stream and, in the distance, the rattle of harness as the horse grazed. Elena sat up carefully, looking around again for the hideous black man, but he was nowhere to be seen.

Could she have dreamed it? she asked herself, getting cautiously to her feet. "Jean?" she called timidly. "Jean, where are you?"

Nothing moved except the horse, who took a step, then went on cropping the lush grass of the clearing. Elena looked across the clearing and saw something in the grass on the far side. Unwillingly, she moved toward it, not really looking; drawn, yet terrified of what she might find.

She didn't allow herself to look until she was quite close to the mound in the grass, then for a moment her mind refused to accept what she saw. Screams filled her ears, pounded in her head as she stared down at what had once been a man and now was nothing but hacked flesh. She ached to escape into darkness again, to faint rather than see what had been done to Jean, but no such release was allowed her this time. She turned and ran toward the carriage, seeking to escape that way.

"Where are you going, Elena?" The voice was cold and hard and it stopped her in her tracks, banishing even the horror she'd just witnessed.

Elena turned toward the trees in time to see Francoise de la Mer emerge from their shelter. Mounted on a lathered bay stallion, he was smiling at her.

"*You!*" she gasped.

"Are you going back to your friends, my dear Elena?" he asked.

"*You* did this!" The horror of it sent chills through her, yet she felt no fear at the moment, only a rage so great she longed for a sword or knife so that she could attack the man before her.

"How could I have done it?" de la Mer asked, not even looking toward the spot where Jean lay. "Everyone knows I've gone to the far side of the island. There are plenty of men over there who will be glad to swear I never left their plantations."

"You killed him!" Elena hardly heard his words.

"A mad slave killed him," de la Mer said calmly. "You saw that yourself."

"On your orders."

The smile faded from de la Mer's face and the dark eyes grew hot with evil. "How I'd like to take you now," he said. "How perfect it would be to claim you here, beside his body. You are mine, Elena de Vere, and I *will* have you—so you remember that. Jean Carnac was a fool to think he could take what I wanted just because I was gone for a few weeks; but other men will learn from his mistake. There's no one left to help you get away from me, little Elena, no one who would dare."

"I'll never be yours," Elena snarled, her own fury blazing beyond fear. "I'll tell everyone what you've done; I'll *make* them believe it."

"Talk of it, Elena, and you'll pay," de la Mer said. "You've a son, remember? Think what a maddened slave could do to little Louis, with just a knife drawn across his belly."

Elena gasped and reeled back against the carriage, sick at the picture his words evoked. "No!" she gasped. "No!"

"Tell *any*one you've seen me here and I'll know it. No one has any secrets from me. There is nowhere you can run to escape me, nowhere you can hide your child that I won't find him and take my revenge."

Elena sank to the ground, her knees refusing to support her. "Please, no, *not* Louis. *No.*"

"Go back to your friends and tell them of the death of your old lover. But make sure that it is just the act of a mad slave and nothing more, if you want your son to live to see our wedding day."

Elena cringed from the words, unable even to protest.

"There will be a wedding day, Elena," de la Mer said, his tone heavy with menace. "If you do anything to escape me, Louis will pay—even if he has to follow you to the grave." His eyes bored into her. "Not even your death could save him."

Elena cringed from his glare, just as de la Mer jerked back on the reins—making his stallion scream in rage and pain as he rose on his hind legs, flailing at the air with his front hoofs.

"I'll see you soon, my bride," de la Mer called over his shoulder as he galloped out of the clearing, his laughter echoing behind him like an evil wind.

Elena collapsed into tears, sobbing brokenly for Jean, for herself, and for her defenseless son. Hatred for de la Mer burned through her, but there was nothing she could do, no way she could think of to revenge herself against him without endangering Louis.

Only when exhaustion dried her tears did she rise and, averting her eyes from the spot where Jean lay, go and get the blanket to cover him. That done, she climbed into the carriage and whipped the horse along the road to the nearest plantation, where she told a shocked neighbor about the horrible murder. That over, she collapsed completely, aware of little that went on around her for the next three days.

Everyone was kind and gentle, comforting her at the burial which took place, bitterly, on the day they were to have been wed. Elena stood at the graveside, wearing black, her heart as heavy as though she were truly burying her husband.

As she stared down into the open earth, she saw in her mind's eye de la Mer's mocking face and her aching pain flamed into bitter hatred. "You will pay," she whispered to the hated face. "I don't know how, but I'll find a way if it takes me the rest of my life."

Mimi's hand touched her arm, forcing her mind back from the brink of the grave. "You must go home now, Elena," she said softly. "You're going to be ill if you stay here any longer."

Elena looked at her friend, seeing the genuine compassion in her eyes, yet unable to feel it fully through her shell of secrecy. Mimi knew only her grief, she realized; no one here knew of the horror and the anger beyond it. She closed her eyes, willing herself not to faint again as she allowed herself to be led away from the grave and settled in the carriage for the trip back to the plantation.

"He was a good, kind man," Mimi said, "and it was a horrible way to die. But he was an old man, Elena, and he'd had a good life. Andre says he died instantly, that everything else was done later, after he was dead."

"He had a right to live," Elena said. "We would have had a good life together. I would have made him happy, Mimi."

"Of course you would have, *cherie*." Mimi patted her shoulder gently. "Of course you would have."

A week passed. Elena spent it with Louis, watching him, playing with him, savoring the very essence of him with a greed only she knew was based in fear. Each day she waited for the news of de la Mer's return; each day she dreaded the moment when she'd see him again, be forced to face him. She shuddered and wondered if she could bear it; then she looked at her son and knew she dared not fail.

In the months since Louis's birth she'd taken up riding again, and it was late one afternoon when she returned from a solitary ride to find the household in an uproar. She felt the tension the moment she walked into the kitchen and when Derra turned from the sink, she knew what had caused it even before she spoke.

"He's here, isn't he?" she asked.

Derra nodded. "He has been here for an hour, waiting for you."

Elena touched the doorknob behind her, thinking of the light-footed filly she'd just turned over to the stable boy. She fought down an almost irresistible impulse to run away on her back, to just forget it all.

"He spent an hour playing with the baby," Derra said. "He brought him several gifts."

Chills shook her. "Is he all right?" she asked, aware that her voice was unsteady. "Where is Louis?"

"He became tired, so I put him to bed," Derra said, her eyes full of wisdom and compassion. "He is quite safe."

Elena took a deep breath. "If you will tell them I've returned, I'll go up and change," she said with all the strength she could muster. "I'll join them shortly."

Derra nodded, leaving the kitchen without a word.

Elena went up the back stairs, her mind seething. What could she do? What could she say? Mimi and Andre would be present, she was sure. She closed her eyes, wishing mightily that she'd never left France, never come to this fair island.

She changed quickly, then went to the nursery to stand and watch her son sleep. His cheeks were rosy with health, and his fair hair curled damply on his forehead while his thumb lay cushioned in his mouth. For a moment she touched him with the tips of her fingers, weighing the future, wondering what she dared. But there was nothing she could see to do, no hope, no escape. Feeling defeated, she bent to kiss Louis, then went resolutely down the stairs.

Francoise was waiting for her, his face a mask of sympathy, though his eyes sparkled with enjoyment. "*Ma cherie*, I've just heard the sad news. How tragic for you. A whirlwind romance, the wedding so close! We must take care with these slaves. They cannot be trusted. I hope the madman was captured?"

Elena met his eyes coldly, enduring the touch of his hands only by gritting her teeth. "No trace of him was found," she said quietly. "It seems he's still roaming the countryside, perhaps seeking another victim."

Something flickered in the dark eyes and his fingers tightened on her shoulders, bruising her flesh till she winced with the pain.

"What a horrible thing to say," Mimi said, her eyes worried as they moved between Elena and Francoise.

"Perhaps you've been under too great a strain," de la Mer said, removing his hands. "You must be calm, Elena, accept what happened as the will of God. You were not to marry the merchant from Port-au-Prince, that is all."

"I doubt God had anything to do with what happened," Elena said, moving away from him as quickly as she could and settling herself on the sofa beside Mimi. "But please, let us speak of something else. The memories are too painful."

De la Mer moved to the mantel, leaning on it, glass in hand, sipping wine as he looked at her, his eyes burning her flesh as surely as a torch would have. "Shall we speak of the future?" he asked. "I recall that we were making plans ourselves before your old friend swept you off your feet."

"I can't think of the future," Elena said, keeping her eyes down with an effort. "I'm in mourning for Jean. I can think of nothing else just now."

A heavy silence filled the room and she heard de la Mer moving about, his tread harsh, seeming to shake the whole room. Her flesh crawled as he moved behind her, and she could feel the hair rising on the nape of her neck even before his fingers touched her. A scream rose in her throat, but she controlled it, holding steady, not betraying her terror by jerking away from him.

"The entire population of the valley mourns with her," Andre said quietly. "Jean Carnac was well-liked and the manner of his death was so dreadful."

The cruel finger tightened for just a moment, then relaxed and slipped away. De la Mer paced the room again, his whole body radiating his fury; then he seemed to get himself under control and sat on the chair opposite her.

"We must keep up appearances," he said softly. "How long do you propose to mourn for a man you knew less than a fortnight?"

Elena gasped at the crudeness of the words, darting quick glances at Andre and Mimi. They showed the same shock; but neither spoke. For a moment she hesitated, wondering how much she dared, then she took a deep breath. "I should think six months would be an appropriate mourning time for a man I was to marry," she said.

"Three," de la Mer said, getting to his feet again. "Three months of mourning, and then we set the wedding date, *ma cherie*. And this time I won't be leaving the area, so don't look for other lovers."

Mimi's gasp was even louder than hers. Elena saw her open her mouth to protest, then close it at a gesture from Andre. Francoise stood at the mantel, watching all three of them, his lip curling slightly.

"Thank you for your hospitality," he said, setting his glass down. "I shall be seeing you again—soon." His eyes stabbed at her. "I assume your mourning will at least allow me to call on you often, though of course you won't be going out."

There was nothing she could do but nod her assent. Andre escorted him to the door while Mimi and Elena sat together, Mimi holding her hand, her face so stricken Elena knew it must greatly resemble her own. When Andre returned, Mimi turned to him in anger.

"How could you allow him to treat Elena that way?" Mimi demanded.

Andre shook his head. "We had a little talk before you joined us, Mimi," he said. "It seems that on his trip he managed to buy a number of the notes my uncle signed before his death. Taken singly, I should have been able to settle them in a year or so, but all together they are ruinous. If he chooses to demand payment, we will lose everything. We would leave this plantation with nothing. We couldn't even buy paswage back to France."

Mimi swore, but Elena only shook her head. "I'm sorry," she said. "I seem to bring trouble to everyone who comes near me."

"He made it clear that he would hold the notes without troubling me if I didn't interfere in his plans." Andre sighed. "As if there is anything I can do to stop him. I've talked to enough of the other *planteurs* to know no one stands against Francoise de la Mer. I'm only sorry for you, Elena. I know you don't care for him."

"I would rather die than marry him," Elena said.

"Don't say that," Mimi cried, crossing herself quickly.

Elena smiled without humor. "Don't worry," she said, "I won't harm myself. Not even that escape is left to me."

They sat in silence for a long time. Elena sensed the sympathy from Andre and Mimi and was grateful for it. She didn't blame them for their acceptance of de la Mer's dominance; like her, they had no choice.

"If only you could have gone with Monsieur Carnac," Mimi said. "You would have been safe by now."

Elena closed her eyes, fighting her feeling of guilt for Jean's death. "I don't think anyone is ever safe when there is a monster like that in the world," she said, fighting back her tears.

"There must be a way," Andre said, frustration plain in his voice. "There must be *something* we can do!"

"You must do nothing," Elena said quickly, fear clutching at her. "Promise me you will do nothing to anger him. I'll marry him. It will be all right. Just don't take any chances, please. I couldn't bear to have you suffer, too."

"Too?" Andre's eyes probed at her.

Elena swallowed hard. "It will be all right, I'm sure. He obviously loves me and he's made many promises. Perhaps I'm just being foolish. I'll have a rich and powerful husband and a lovely future. Louis will be sent to France to school as soon as he is old enough. I am just upset because of what happened to Jean, that's all."

Andre and Mimi murmured proper words; but Elena knew they didn't believe her. It was a game, a deadly game of lies and pretence where no one would win. No one but Francoise de la Mer.

Chapter 34

THE NEXT TWO weeks were a nightmare. De la Mer called on her twice, always smiling, tender, and charming; but with eyes that devoured her and cold, thick lips that quivered when he spoke of Louis. Elena did everything she could to keep him away from Louis, but it was useless. De la Mer seemed to delight in holding the small child, in lifting him over his head. Elena shuddered at every touch, wondering what would happen when they were truly at his mercy.

Late in the second week, Derra came to Elena as she was sitting in the garden. Her face was unsmiling, but her eyes glowed. "My mother wishes you to come to her hut," she said. "She has consulted with the gods, and they are willing to help you against the evil one."

"Help me?" Elena looked up at her with hope, then quickly felt it die. "How can your gods help me?" she asked. "From the terrible things I've heard, they haven't even been able to protect the slaves on his plantation."

Derra sighed, bowing her head in sorrow. "Grandma Karame can do nothing herself against the evil one, but if you have the will and the courage to learn our ways, she can help you to do it yourself. She can give you the power to defeat him and free yourself and your son."

For a moment Elena hesitated, filled with doubt and a little fear; but the thought of Louis was enough to force her decision. Whatever de la Mer had in mind for her she might be able to endure; but none of his smiling promises about Louis's future were true, she was sure. She had no doubt that her son would meet with an "accident" as soon as she took him to the de la Mer plantation.

"How will I find her hut?" she asked resolutely, well aware that Karame lived apart from the other blacks and was not herself a slave.

"Say you are tired after the evening meal," Derra said. "Pretend to go to your room, but go instead to the edge of the trees. A man will show you the way." Derra smiled. "I will watch over Louis and keep him safe."

Still somewhat fearful at the prospect, Elena did as she was bid, somehow not surprised to be met by the same sort of escort she'd had before. He led her along the road, then off into the bushes, not stopping till he reached a post. It was dim in the bushes, but Elena could see that a fetish of some sort hung from the post as though in warning.

The man pointed to what appeared to be a path and signaled that she should follow it, then disappeared into the trees without a sound. Elena swallowed hard, longing to turn and run but also aware that she had no idea how to find her way back to the plantation road. Heart pounding, she moved cautiously along the path.

The hut was small, roughly built and little different from the few slave homes Elena had seen near the house. Only its location made it different—that and the woman who invited her inside.

"Welcome, my child," Grandma Karame said, her wise old eyes following Elena's as they took in the strange furnishings of the room, the chickens that wandered freely through the open door, and the altar set with food left for the various gods.

"I don't know why you asked me to come," Elena said, seating herself gingerly in response to the old woman's gesture. "I'm very grateful for what you did the night of the ball, but . . . ."

"It is time the evil one was stopped," Karame said, brushing aside her words. "I think you possess the power, if you will allow

me to show you how to use it." She smiled gently. "I know you
are afraid, and that you still serve your own God, but that is true
of many of my followers. Our gods understand the white man's
God and will lend their powers even to His followers, so long as
you are willing to believe and serve the old gods, too."

Elena opened her mouth, but no words came. The very idea
terrified her.

Karame continued after a few moments. "You must think on
this, Elena. Your people can offer you no help, no escape, and
the evil one will have his way. He has killed the man who tried to
save you. He will hurt you as he has his slave girls. He will abuse
you; but most of all, he will plot against your son, for he is a man
who never shares anything, and your love will always go first to
your child."

"How did you know about Jean?" Elena gasped.

Karame smiled sadly. "Little happens without my knowledge." She sighed. "The one who did it is dead now, killed by the
man who ordered the murder." She was silent for a moment,
then went on. "But that is the past. Your son is the future, and he
is in deadly danger."

Elena nodded, aware that the old woman was only speaking
the truth she'd already acknowledged. "He's so little," she
murmured.

"And he will never live to see a birthday if you marry that
man." The words were spoken so quietly that for a moment
Elena didn't quite take them in. Then she gasped in horror.

"A pillow over his face in the night? A drop of something in
his milk? Or even a window left carelessly ajar to admit
Dumballa's servants the serpents. It takes little to kill an infant
on St. Domingue, and yours will never be allowed to grow up
and rival the sons de la Mer hopes to breed from you."

Elena sat still for several moments, caught by the horrible
pictures that filled her mind. Not since the day in the clearing
had she allowed herself to imagine such things. She could
actually see de la Mer with the pillow, his evil smile as he held it
tight over the fighting—then ominously still—infant. Or the
snake slithering across the blanket she'd made for him with her
own clumsy stitches. Or . . . "What must I do?" she asked, lifting
her head and meeting Karame's eyes for the first time. "How can
I stop him?"

"You must come here every day. I will meet you at the road

tomorrow and show you the path in the daylight. I will teach you about the dark gods, the gods that have guarded our people for centuries, the ones that must now become your gods, too."

Elena shivered a little, but she set her teeth in her lower lip and nodded. "I will come," she said softly. "I will learn, and somehow I will protect Louis."

Karame smiled at her. "Go back to the post now," she instructed. "You will be taken safely home."

"Thank you," Elena said.

"You must give your thanks to the gods," Karame said, shaking her head. "I can only teach you what you must know. Whether or not it will work will depend on them, and on you."

And so it began for Elena. Her life separated, following two very different streams. When she was with Andre and Mimi and even the outwardly charming Francoise de la Mer, she was as she'd always been: a rather quiet, reserved Frenchwoman. But in the other hours, the hours she spent at the hut in the hills, she became a new Elena.

First there were the stories of the gods, told with great care by Karame. She knew which symbols, which colors, which foods were preferred by each of her ancestral gods. She told the stories lovingly, then allowed Elena to help in the preparation of the goods that were set out for the gods to enjoy. Once that became routine, she took her to a ceremonial deep in the hills where, Elena suspected, no white person had ever gone before.

There she heard the savage drumming that tore at her mind and made her forget the life she'd left behind. She danced a little with the black women, shyly copying the forms and steps till the pace grew too fast for her. Then she settled back to watch wide-eyed as the gods took possession of the men and women, driving them to frenzied motion, to speech in tones and words totally unlike those they'd used before. She saw them writhe on the ground as though dying, then sleep peacefully to rise refreshed and glowing with the knowledge that their bodies had been, for a few moments, the temples of their gods.

It was a terrifying experience to her French self; but in the night—when she thought of what de la Mer had done to Jean and what was coming as de la Mer pressed his suit and demanded that a wedding date be set—she found it more promising than the empty words of comfort Mimi had to offer.

The weeks passed, and it was fall again. Louis began to crawl about the floor smiling and giggling at her whenever she came to hold him. She was playing with him one afternoon when Derra came to the nursery.

"Grandma Karame asks that you come to her at once," she said, her usually smiling face strangely solemn.

"Is something wrong?" Elena asked, well aware that things were very different for her now. All the slaves on the plantation treated her with special attention, taking her slightest whim as an order they took joy in complying with. When she rode in her wagon or went out on horseback, even the fieldhands smiled in her direction—all of which had Andre shaking his head, though he was pleased by the way things were going on the plantation.

"She says only that tonight is the time," Derra said, her eyes full of suppressed excitement.

Elena swallowed hard, aware what the words meant. Tonight she would take part in the final ceremony, drink the blood of the sacrifice, and offer herself to *Dumballa*—the serpent god—who Karame had said would protect her as no other force could. She picked up Louis and hugged him to her till he squirmed in protest, his grey eyes stormy beneath his russet hair.

"Take good care of him," Elena said softly. "I must set the date soon, and once I do I fear he will be in danger."

Elena went forward that night without fear, climbing the now-familiar path into the hills, her ears already catching the distant sound of the drumming that called the worshipers to the ceremonial fire. Karame was waiting for her. She handed her a strangely carved cup containing a greenish liquid. "Drink this," she ordered.

Elena obeyed without question, though the rather unpleasant brew left her thirsty and a little dizzy.

"Now put this on," Karame ordered, giving her a rough white dress. "Leave all your white woman's clothing here and unbind your hair so *Dumballa* will find you acceptable."

Feeling strange and more afraid than she'd ever been, Elena did as she was told, concentrating only on the picture of her son's laughing face and the dark-visaged threat of de la Mer's cruelty. Even as she undressed she felt the world fading, and by the time she'd freed her hair and pulled on the coarse garments nothing seemed to matter. It was a dream, nothing more.

Karame led her away to the open-sided, roofed square, where

the ceremonial fire burned and the dancers were already circling and chanting among the carefully drawn signs that decorated the hard-packed earth floor. At Karame's instruction, Elena joined the dancers, feeling freer than she ever had.

As they whirled together, her true self seemed to dissolve and she became one of them. The drums spoke to her, and the violent dancing lifted her higher and higher. She didn't wince when the knife severed the neck of a pure white cock, nor did she gag on the warm fluid that was given to her. She laughed with joy when the pole in the floor writhed and became a serpent, and she gladly knelt to touch it before the darkness overcame her and even the pounding of the drums disappeared.

She woke slowly, her head aching and her body still heavy with sleep. For several minutes she just lay still, almost afraid to open her eyes as she tried to remember all that had happened in the secret ceremonial. A sound made her stir and look around. To her surprise, she found herself in her own bed and saw that Derra was standing beside her. She accepted the offered glass without a word, downing it eagerly to salve the terrible dryness of her throat.

"I told the master that you woke at dawn with a pain in your head," Derra said softly. "They agreed that you should rest through the day, since Monsieur de la Mer is to come to take the evening meal with you tonight."

Elena groaned at the thought, then asked, "How did I get here, Derra?"

"Gilles carried you, Madame," Derra said. "I put you safely to bed myself." She smiled reassuringly. "Sleep now, and I will care for the little one. No harm will come to him."

Elena wanted to protest, but a strange lassitude spread through her and she couldn't keep her eyes open. In a moment she slept again.

As she went down the stairs that evening, Elena sensed that something was in the air. When she entered the drawing room, Andre and Mimi were waiting with Francoise, but they avoided her eyes and their smiles of greeting were empty and meaningless. Francoise crossed the room to her at once, taking her in his arms with an assurance that never ceased to freeze the blood in her veins.

"You are lovely as always, *ma cherie*," he said, kissing her much too passionately, treating her as though they were alone.

Elena controlled her revulsion only with effort, neither responding nor withdrawing from his embrace and thick-lipped kiss. When he released her, he turned to look at his host and hostess. "I would like to speak to my bride-to-be, *alone*," he said contemptuously. "May we use the library?"

Mimi stirred as though to object, but Andre nodded. "But of course," he said, his voice full of frustration and barely-concealed fury.

Francoise dragged her across the entry hall and into the book-lined room, his finger biting cruelly into her arm as always. He closed the door with a sound that reminded her of barred windows and despair. When he turned to her, the false smile was gone.

"There will be no more delays," he said coldly. "You will be my bride within the week, or the whole of St. Domingue will learn the truth about you."

Elena just looked at him. "What truth?" she asked.

"That you are no more than a whore, masquerading as a woman of gentle birth. How do you think the LaCroixs would feel if they learn that their fine Elena de Vere is in truth Celeste, the discarded mistress of Raul Flambeau?"

Elena gulped a little. "How do you know that?" she asked.

"I have my ways," de la Mer said, his eyes devouring her body as though her gown was no more than a gossamer veil between them.

"If you believe that, why marry me?" Elena asked, grasping at a ray of hope.

"Would you prefer that I tell everyone? And what of your son? How will he fare when people know that he is a bastard, that even you very likely cannot name his sire? You know you cannot escape me, Elena. And you know what happens to those you ask for help."

He paused, and Elena choked on the memory of Jean's hacked body bleeding in the grass—his kind face destroyed beyond recognition. Shuddering, she held herself erect with pure will. "What do you want of me?" she asked, despairing.

"Since I've already made my feelings about you clear to everyone, I will give you a choice, which is more than your sort deserves. If you weren't so beautiful, I might not be so thoughtful. You will announce that our wedding will take place day after tomorrow, or I will tell everyone what and who you are."

"I can bear the shame," Elena said, sure that a son branded as a bastard would be safer than one accepted into the de la Mer household.

"You'll still be mine," Francoise said, his voice low and caressing, "but not as my wife. I wouldn't wed a known whore. White women can be bought and sold, too, Elena—and so can their sons."

Elena gasped, shivering from the evil in his face and the pleasure that was there, too. Even as the terrifying realization filled her mind, she was revolted by the joy his threats were giving him. In that moment she realized he didn't want her to agree to the wedding, that he would actually prefer taking her that other way, demeaning her even further.

"Which is it to be?" he demanded.

Elena swallowed hard, thinking only of Louis. "We will set the date," she said, deciding she would go to Grandma Karame in the morning and ask her assistance. Just as the old woman had told her, there seemed no one else she could turn to.

De la Mer nodded. "And you will smile as you take your vows," he said. "And you'll never try to run from me again, I promise you. What is mine, I hold."

He caught her to him, kissing her viciously, bruising her mouth and nearly crushing her ribs as he forced her against the hard length of him. He laughed when she staggered away from him, trying vainly to rub the feel of his mouth from her lips. "I'll tame you," he said. "I'll have you sobbing for my touch, begging me to take your body. I know secrets that . . ." He broke off, the thin veneer of humanness covering the beast once again. "The world will see my proper, beautiful wife, but we'll know the truth, won't we, little Celeste? When we're alone I'll show you ways of pleasure even a whore could not imagine." His evil laughter still rang in her ears as he escorted her back across the hall to announce to Mimi and Andre that they were to be wed in two days' time.

Elena slept not at all that night, pacing her room in terror, wanting to flee but knowing there was nowhere she could go, nothing she could do. For herself she cared little, but there was Louis to be considered. He must be protected. Whatever happened, he must survive!

In the morning she prepared a message to be taken to de la Mer. In it she asked only for a week's delay so that she might make more extensive plans for the wedding, so that he might find her a "pleasing bride". That done, she dressed in her simplest gown and, after spending a little time with Louis, left him with one of the maids and set off down the road. She went immediately to Karame's hut, but this time it was empty. Worried, she settled herself to wait.

Hours passed, the sun grew hot overhead, but still the small clearing remained empty and silent. Elena paced, aware that Mimi would be concerned when she didn't return for the noon meal—but not wanting to miss the old woman now that every minute was important. However, as the afternoon shadows lengthened she began to realize that Karame might be gone for a day or more. She could wait no longer.

Feeling weary and light-headed from not having eaten all day, Elena left the quiet hut and started down the path to the road. Almost at once, she heard the sound of hoofbeats. She paused and looked around, hoping it was one of the plantation work wagons on the road ahead, or even Andre—and that she could ask for a ride back to the house. She ran to reach the road before the rider could pass.

But the man who rode into view was no one she recognized, and she drew back instinctively as his dark eyes turned her way. He saw her and quickly reined in. "Madame de Vere," he said with a smile that did nothing to lighten his coarse, ugly features. "I have come with a message for you."

"A message for me?" Elena frowned.

Before she could say more, the man was upon her. A cloak was thrown over her head and her arms were quickly bound beneath it so that she was nearly smothered. Strong arms lifted her, and she was thrown across the saddle like a sack of meal. She tried to scream, but the heavy cloak made it impossible and the man's laughter told her that her struggles were not helping at all.

The ride was battering. Sometimes she slipped into unconsciousness, beyond caring where she was being taken or why. It was only when the horse finally stopped that she revived, only to be plunged into fear again. She was set roughly on her feet and steadied as her arms were freed and the cloak finally pulled away. She took a grateful breath of fresh air, then screamed as she looked up into the face of Francoise de la Mer.

"Did you really think you could put me off so easily, my charming little bride?" he asked, his face gleaming with malice. "Did you not know I would claim you, anyway—and at *my* pleasure, not yours?"

"No," Elena cried. "No, you *can't*!"

"Why not?" he asked cruelly. "Who will stop me? You could have had marriage and a comfortable bed for your wedding night. But you chose to oppose me, so I'll take you here like the slut you are." He caught her hair and turned her to face the battered shack. "I think perhaps I've chosen well," he said, laughing. "After tonight, I may not even want you. If I take you here, I can send you back to Andre and forget you, and truly you deserve no better. But you won't forget me." His fingers cut cruelly into her arms. "I'll see to that."

Elena tried to pull away, but he picked her up easily and carried her into the shack, kicking the door shut behind him. It was small, bare of furniture, the only light and heat coming from a small fire that burned in the corner of the room. De la Mer watched her as she looked around, then laughed again as he reached out and pulled her to him.

Chapter 35

HIS HANDS GRASPED at her clothing, tearing it, bruising her pale flesh. Elena cried out and he laughed more loudly. "Scream, slut," he shouted. "I'll make you scream even louder before I'm through. There's no one to hear in this part of my plantation, and Henri will stand guard to make sure no one disturbs us through this night."

He began kissing her throat, then moved his lips lower to her breast, tender at first, then she shrieked in pain as he bit her and drew blood. For the first time her terror gave way to fury. The horror of anything he might choose to do to her no longer paralyzed her as it had at first. Now hatred of him and all that he stood for pulsed through her veins like a healing tide. Remembering Jean, she began to think instead of simply not reacting.

For a moment she endured his touch, testing with her muscles the strength of his hold. The huge hands were cruelly strong, and she knew there was no way she could break their grip with her own muscles. Willing herself to courage, she suddenly went slack in his hold, pretending to faint, letting her head loll back, her mouth hang open, her eyes close.

As she'd hoped, he released her with a curse. She felt the cool floor beneath her, but he hadn't moved away as she'd expected him to. Instead he stood tall as a tree between her and the hut's only door. Not knowing what else to do, Elena rolled toward the fire, and even as she scrambled to her feet she pulled one of the sticks from it, brandishing the small flame before her with as much courage as she could summon.

"Don't touch me," she snarled, almost eager to plunge the burning end into his hateful face, to watch his skin blacken and fall away as roasting meat might.

De la Mer swore, then glanced about, choosing a loose slat from the wall as a weapon of his own. His face was full of anger, but there was something else in his eyes—a glow of excitement that was somehow more terrifying than his fury. He was, she realized, almost enjoying the battle.

Desperately, she tried to shift toward the door, aware that it offered her only hope—and even that a faint one, for Henri was beyond the hut somewhere. She had no doubt that he would delight in the chase even as his employer did. De la Mer seemed to sense her intent and swung his slat at her ever-shortening firebrand. Elena dodged the first blow and the second, but the third caught her unprepared, numbing her arm from the shoulder down. To her horror, the firebrand flew to a dark corner of the room, where it sputtered in the dust and went out.

"Now, my little fighter, we'll test your mettle on another battlefield," de la Mer said with a smile that chilled her. "When I finish with you, you'll never fight any man again, even if he wanted you once I've put my mark on that pale skin. But that won't be till dawn, and the nights have grown long."

Elena drew herself up, her helplessness finally complete but her anger still flowing. With nothing left to use against him, she fixed her eyes on him as Karame had taught her. "You will not touch me," she said, her voice low and without fear. "I am not the innocent French girl you think. I have been given the powers of the gods of Africa. Touch me and *Dumballa* will seek his vengeance against you. Leave me, white pig, or you shall die this night!"

For a moment she could see laughter in the twisted face, then something like fear flicked in the dark eyes. Hope rose like a tide, only to drop as he stepped forward, laughing even louder.

"I've heard whispers of your visits to the black witch's hut, my dear," he said almost conversationally, "but your threats don't frighten me. I've been told before that their gods will curse me for what I do; but I grow richer and the niggers cry, nothing more."

He plunged at her, his hands tearing away the last of her clothing as he flung her to the hard dirt floor.

"*Dumballa!*" Elena shouted in mortal terror. "God of serpents and protector of your priestess, save me!"

The small fire flared, suddenly hot and high, lighting the four corners of the room and casting de la Mer's giant shadow against the far wall. Something stirred beside her and came from the corner where the firebrand had died in the dust. De la Mer, who'd been tugging off his own clothing, turned to her, ready now to claim her cringing body. But before he could throw his weight upon her a cool, dry weight slithered over her arm and across her waist, closely followed by a second and a third. *Snakes!*

Elena lay still as death—recognizing the serpents as deadly—though she knew they would not strike unless provoked. De la Mer, his eyes glazed by his own lust, took a step forward and touched the first one. It rose and struck at him, its fangs sinking into his leg even before he saw it. He shrieked in terror.

Having thrown his slat away before he tore off the last of her clothing and threw her to the floor, de la Mer had no weapons other than his still-booted feet. He kicked out at the snakes, but with little success. Thoroughly roused, the three serpents pursued him across the small hut, striking repeatedly till he stumbled and fell, writhing in the agony their poison produced.

Elena lay still, numbed by the aftermath of her own terror, then the door burst open and Henri came stumbling in, his heavy musket at the ready. He looked at her, and for a moment lust flickered in his small eyes. Then he saw his master's body on the far side of the room.

"What have you done to him?" he demanded, not at first seeing the serpents in the dimming light of the dying fire.

Elena gathered her strength slowly and forced herself to get up without trying to cover her nakedness. "He is dead," she said quietly.

"You killed him." The musket moved toward her again.

"The serpents killed him," Elena said. "The fire must have disturbed their sleep and they came out. He tried to kick them away."

Henri turned toward his fallen master and paled as at last he saw the snakes. He stepped back, his eyes glazing. "You called them," he said. "I heard you yelling some of that mumbo-jumbo like my woman does. *Dumballa*, that's who you called on. You're a witch, and you killed him."

Elena swallowed hard, not sure what to do. To deny her powers might leave her open to another attack, this time by the overseer; but to admit to it might be even more deadly. She shuddered, not sure herself which explanation might be true. She had called on *Dumballa* in her terror, had felt the bodies of the snakes as they crossed her skin, but still . . .

The eyes regarding her narrowed. "You'll be killed if I tell," he said. "You killed a big man on this island and you did it with witchcraft. If the white folks find out you've been studying with that old *mamba*, they'll kill you, you know that?"

"And if you tell them, *Dumballa* will find you," Elena said, looking toward the corner where the largest of the snakes was stirring again.

"You get me money," the overseer said. "Lots of money, enough to get off this stinking island and back to France to live in style."

"Where would I get that kind of money?" Elena gasped, shocked at this turn of events. "I'm just an *institutrice* for the LaCroix family."

"You have the powers," Henri said, backing slowly toward the door. "Three days, white witch. You give me money, or in three days I'll lead all the *planteurs* to this cabin and tell them what I heard. They'll burn you at the stake." He laughed hysterically.

"You can't do this," Elena protested.

"My woman has powers, too," he called over his shoulder. "She'll protect me from your curses, so just get the money. I'll meet you here in three nights. Forget and they'll come after you with torches."

He was gone, and in a few moments Elena heard the sound of hoofbeats heading away from the hut, then there was only silence. Shivering with the cold and the shock of what had taken place, she gathered the remnants of her gown and covered her bruised and weary body with them. A glance about the hut told her the snakes had followed Henri out into the night. Too sick to care, she wrapped herself in de la Mer's cloak and set out, not sure where she was but aware that she couldn't stay in the hut another minute.

Within half an hour she had an escort. Another of the silent men came out of the night and led her stiffly through the brush lands, following invisible paths, guiding her as she stumbled along—too weary even to ask him where he was taking her.

Dawn was just breaking when he left her at the edge of Karame's property. Elena stumbled on to the hut, then collapsed on the floor. It was full daylight when she opened her eyes again.

"Welcome back to the living," Karame said softly. "You are very brave, and we shall revere your name long after you are gone from us."

"You know?" Elena asked, somehow not surprised.

"*Dumballa* sent the message to me in a dream," the old woman said, then her smile faded. "I am sorry you must leave us now."

"But where can I go?" Elena asked, accepting the bowl of savory stew the old woman offered. "How can I just leave?"

"The overseer has already talked too much," Karame said. "He is a fool, but his words are believed and the body of the evil one will soon be found. You must leave St. Domingue before that happens."

"But how? I have so little money."

"There will be a ship at the cove this evening," Karame said. "I will take you there and you will go with the people aboard it. It is a poor trading ship, but the Captain has as his woman my niece Juanna. You will be safe with them, and with your powers you will find a new life."

"But Louis..." Elena protested. "He is so little yet!"

"He will not be safe without your protection, and the white *planteurs* will kill you when they know the circumstances of de la Mer's death. They are the masters here, but they fear us. From behind their fine walls they hear our drums, and they are afraid." Karame's face changed, hardened. "And they have reason," she said coldly. "They shall pay one day for all the evil they have done to my people. It is well for you to be far from here, Elena, for even your powers could not protect you then. I shall show you; close your eyes."

The images came at once. Elena saw burning plantations, destruction everywhere. Butchered bodies of men, women, even children. She cringed at the sight. "Not here," she wailed.

"Not in my lifetime," Karame said calmly, "but my children and their children will see it."

"Must it be so?" Elena asked, quieting as the pictures faded.

"The future is as it must be," Karame said. "But we must think of now, the present."

Elena sighed and nodded. "I must talk to Mimi," she said. "I can't just disappear without telling her."

Karame nodded. "It will be safe for a little time yet," she said. "You can go back to the plantation now. Tell Derra what you want packed and it will be waiting at the inlet tonight. Come back along the road before the afternoon shadows grow too long and we will go to the inlet together."

Elena nodded obediently, trusting the old woman as she had not trusted anyone in a long time. She walked back to the plantation slowly, not even thinking in her weariness.

Her visit with Mimi was painful. Once they were seated in the small sitting room, she began to tell her the whole story, watching the dawning horror in the older woman's face as she described the events following Jean's death—the moments with de la Mer in the bloody clearing.

"If only I could have helped," Mimi murmured. "You should have told us."

Grimly, Elena described de la Mer's threats to Louis following the murder. "I couldn't tell you," she said. "He would have destroyed your life here, or even had you killed if you tried to help me escape him."

"But to face what he planned, *alone*." Mimi shook her head. "We had no idea how evil he is, Elena. I knew you were reluctant to marry him, but..." She looked uncomfortable. "We weren't even worried when you didn't come home yesterday afternoon. There was a message delivered, saying you were at de la Mer's plantation making wedding plans. I was surprised, but with the wedding tomorrow I assumed you knew what you were doing." She paled. "Where have you been?" she asked. "What happened to you? Where is de la Mer?"

More slowly, Elena described her kidnapping and the horror of finding herself at the hut with Francoise. Then she went back and explained her relationship with Karame and the means of her escape. The shock in the familiar face told her more than any words could have. Horrified though she was at what Elena was describing, Mimi was even more shocked at the method of Elena's salvation. Despite the honest affection between them, Elena could almost feel Mimi drawing away from her. Her heart ached at the desertion, but she could understand it.

"I'm leaving," she finished quietly. "You can see that it will be impossible for me to remain on St. Domingue. I thank you so much, Mimi, for all you've done for me. I would have died in Le Mans without your kindness, and I'm sorry I can't repay you now."

"How will you get away?" Mimi asked. "They are looking for de la Mer now—that's where Andre has gone. Once he's found and the overseer speaks, they will come for you."

"It will be safer for you if you don't know," Elena said honestly. "I'll take Louis and disappear, then you can truthfully tell him you have no idea where I've gone, or how."

Mimi nodded, and her eyes warmed again as though the horrors Elena had described were already fading from her mind. "I'll give you some jewelry," she said. "Wherever you go, you can sell or trade it for what you and Louis will need."

"I can't let you," Elena said.

Mimi shrugged. "Then I shall give the jewels to Louis," she said. "I am his godmother, so I have that right. He must have the best, Elena, for he's like my own son. I will miss both of you so much." Her dark eyes clouded with tears. "What shall I do without you to be my *amie*?"

Elena hugged the older woman and their tears mingled for a moment, then Elena drew away. "There is something," she said, her body chilled by the memory. "Perhaps there is a way I can repay you."

"What do you mean?" Mimi asked, growing grave as she seemed to sense Elena's change of mood.

"I was told something by the witch woman who guided me, Mimi. She sees the future more clearly than you and I can see what is in front of us. She told me there is trouble coming to this island, and the whites will be destroyed by it."

"What?" For a moment Mimi looked shocked, then she laughed. "That's slave talk," she said.

"I don't think so," Elena said. "I believe her. Please, listen and be warned, Mimi. Sell this plantation and go back to

France. You know you'd be happier there, and when the trouble comes you'll all be safe."

Mimi's smile faded and their eyes locked. "You know we sold everything when we left Le Mans," she said. "We cannot return now."

"Then go to the colonies north of here," Elena pressed. "Anywhere away from this island, Mimi. You must protect Josette and Serge's future, and your own." Elena paused, sensing the doubt still filling Mimi's mind. "You must believe her," she said. "She made me see it, Mimi. In my head I saw this very house burning. There were bodies on the grass and in the garden, horribly maimed bodies destroyed as Jean was destroyed."

"No!" Mimi shook her head violently.

"She warned me about de la Mer," Elena said. "She saw what would happen before I went to the ball at his house. She knew what happened at the hut. She knew what happened to Jean when no one else did. She saw the truth, and she was sorry, too."

"But Andre is kind to our slaves. He's not like de la Mer and so many of the others."

Elena closed her eyes, then wished she hadn't, for she saw the dead and dying once again. "A flood covers the fields of all men equally," she said, "and this will be like a flood of death. Promise me you'll leave here and find safety," she begged. "Warning you is all I can do to repay you for your kindness."

Mimi hesitated for a moment longer, then nodded. "I'll do it, Elena," she said. "I'll persuade Andre somehow." She shuddered, then hugged Elena again. "And you must take care. Guard yourself and Louis well, and perhaps someday . . ." She turned away. "I'll get the jewelry."

Gilles drove her to the inlet, stopping the old wagon only once when he assisted Grandma Karame into it. As they rode along, Elena looked about sadly, remembering her ride along here a little more than a year ago when she'd first landed on St. Domingue. Mimi had been beside her then and Louis had stirred in her womb, impatient to be born. Drained and exhausted by all that had happened, she couldn't even cry. She dozed a little as they waited at the inlet for the arrival of the ship Karame had summoned.

Juanna was a beautiful girl, clearly at least half white— perhaps more. The Captain was a swarthy Spaniard, dubious at first and then plainly pleased when Elena spoke Spanish to him and offered some of her small cache of coins. She and Louis were rowed out to the ship with the small cargo that was being loaded and, as the moon lit the scene, they rode the night winds away from the inlet.

Elena, shaking with fatigue, put Louis to bed, then went out on the deck where Juanna was leaning on the rail and staring out over the sea. "Where are we going?" she asked. "I didn't even think to ask before."

Juanna regarded her with soft dark eyes. "From what Grandma Karame said, you are a powerful witch," she said. "You may need your powers. We go to Cartegena, and the Spanish there are no more kind than the French on St. Domingue."

Elena sighed. "I know all about the cruelty of the Spaniards," she said quietly. She stared at the coast of St. Domingue, aware that—as before—she couldn't go back. For a moment she envied Karame's power to see into the future, then she was glad she couldn't. To know what lay ahead might be too painful a burden, and now she must deal with the present. Thanking Juanna for her help in getting settled on the ship, she excused herself and went back to her tiny cabin to sleep. The nightmares of St. Domingue stayed behind, and she slept well.

Chapter 36

THE DAYS AT sea were pleasant at first, but as they dragged on with little action, Jamie began to find them dull. They shelled the forts at Cartegena, but only from the sea—not daring to venture far into the well-guarded harbour.

The best hours came when they entered the river Chagre and demolished the Castle of Lorenzo. Treasure flowed into the holds again and, even though they were soon pursued by a Spanish fleet and forced to return to Port Royal, their hearts were far from heavy. The shares would be generous, and Jamie found himself looking forward to holding his bride in his arms once more.

His mind was full of plans as he rode through the thronged streets of Port Royal and up the familiar lane to the house Sally shared with her Aunt Helena. However, when he unloaded his belongings from the public carriage, no one came racing out to greet him.

Well aware that the entire city had known of their arrival long before the ships were anchored, Jamie approached the house with a bit of anxiety. He was relieved when the door opened and Rebecca stood before him, her smile as seductive as ever. "Welcome home, Jamie," she said, making it sound like a personal invitation.

"Where's Sally?" he asked, fears rising in his mind. "Is something wrong?"

"She's upstairs lying down, as usual," Rebecca said, her rosy lips pouting at him. "She couldn't be bothered to come downstairs to wait for you, and after all this time, too."

"She's all right? The baby . . . ?"

"She's pregnant, that's all." Rebecca turned and led the way into the dim, cool entry, calling to one of the servants to go out and bring Jamie's belongings inside. "You would think no woman had ever carried a child before. That's all we've heard since you left. I just hope she gets some life back now you're home." She faced him and her eyes were wide with malice. "I can't imagine that you'll be content to spend all your time listening to her talk about her baby."

"*My* baby," Jamie corrected her, fighting the rising tide of desire that he felt being so close to Rebecca. "I'd better go up to her."

He tried to move past her, but Rebecca moved quickly to block his path with her warm body. Her arms went around him, and before he knew what was happening her full lips were fastened to his and he found himself kissing her with the pent-up passion of his months at sea.

Just as quickly she spun away from him, laughing lightly. "Just consider that your welcome home," she said. "It may be the best one you'll get." She was gone before he could frame a reply.

Jamie climbed the stairs slowly, some of the joy of his homecoming stolen by Sally's strange lack of welcome and the frightening tide of his response to Rebecca's overtures. He sighed, wishing mightily that Rebecca had taken his advice and returned to English Harbour before his return. Now he suspected she would stay till after the baby was born.

He opened the door of the sitting room. "Sally? Sally, I'm home!" he called, looking around hopefully.

"In here." The tone was mildly friendly, without excitement.

Jamie walked toward the bedroom frowning, then forced himself to smile as he stepped through the door. "How are you, darling?" he asked, crossing to the high bed. "Have you been ill?"

The girl who looked back at him, then offered her cheek for his kiss, was a stranger. "So you finally remembered me," she said, sliding up on the pillows, her blue eyes cold.

"I've thought of you every day," Jamie protested, shocked at the change. Her face was thin and sallow, and her shoulders seemed almost bony. "I've been anxious to know how you are; I've been worried."

"I'm pregnant," Sally said. "That's what you wanted to know, isn't it? You're going to have your heir."

"But what about you?" Jamie asked, seating himself on the side of the bed and reaching out a tentative hand to touch her hair, which fell in lackluster tangles about her face. It seemed darker, the shine gone. "What are you doing up here? Have you been ill?"

"Did you really expect me to come racing to welcome you? Or is that what you'll always expect? Is that why you married me, so I'd be here when you get tired of the sea and the excitement of battles? What am I, a convenience so you don't have to pay for someone to love you?"

Anger flared in Jamie's heart and he lifted his hand. "Stop it," he shouted, barely controlling an impulse to slap the bitter expression from her face. "You know I had no choice about going with the ship. I explained that to you before and I'm not going to do it again. Now I'm home, so let's see if we can't make up for the months I was away."

His hands were a little rough as he tried to gather her in his arms, but he meant the words. She was his wife, and he cared for her. Perhaps it wasn't love, but he did care—and he had come home to her. Her body was limp as a corpse, and the lips he touched were totally unresponsive. He tried for several moments, seeking to ignite the flame that had burned between them from that moment in the trees near the cove, but nothing happened. His own desire fled and he let her go, moving away.

Sally's hands moved to caress the small mound of her stomach. "You left me alone," she said, "but I'm not alone now, Jamie. I don't need you now; I don't even want you. I cried for weeks after you left. I wanted you so badly, and I *needed* you. You taught me what it was like to love and then you went away. Well, now it's *your* turn to wait and need *me*. Go back to sea, Jamie. I don't want you now."

The words were delivered viciously, like blows, and Jamie

could feel them imprinting themselves on his face. Fury rose like a floodtide. "If that's what you want, I'll be happy to leave," he snarled, leaping to his feet. "I won't be going back to sea for a while, but I'm sure there are other places where I'll be more welcome. There are others who might be glad I'm home."

He was halfway to the door when her cries caught at him. He turned back, ready to snarl more angry words, but he was given no chance. Sally had thrown back the covers and was half-running, half-stumbling after him. He caught her, shocked by the lightness of her body as he lifted her in his arms.

"I'm sorry," she sobbed, tears flooding over her cheeks. "Oh, Jamie, I'm sorry. I do want you. I love you so much. I just couldn't bear it. Even when they told me the fleet was coming, I kept thinking it would only be for a little while. You'll just be here long enough to love me and make me want you so desperately I can't live without you, and then you'll be gone again!"

Relief rushed through him and he found her lips, stopping the tide of words as he carried her back to the bed. Her response was wild, her hunger a match for his own, yet when it was over and he lay spent beside her, he knew that something had died during the long months while he was away. He looked at her and saw that her eyes held the same knowledge.

"I'm glad you're home, Jamie," she said, reaching out to caress his cheek. "I hope you'll be able to stay a long time, long enough for our child to be born."

"I think I might be here that long," Jamie said, caressing her too-thin shoulder. "The Spanish have sent a fleet to hunt us since our invasion of Chagre. I think they mean to keep us here in the harbour so that their cities will be safe."

"Please hold me," she whispered.

Jamie gathered her to him gently, rocking her a little as he would a child. A sense of loss cut at him, mingling with guilt and sorrow. She seemed so small and young to be carrying a child, and so changed and subdued now that her single burst of anger had been spent. He held her till she slept.

The pattern of their days was soon set. Sally truly tried, rising each morning, dressing, coming downstairs to eat. Then, as the day progressed and she withdrew more and more, the afternoon would find her once more in the high bed.

She gained weight after his return, and her hair shone clean again, but the glow of her youth was gone. She slept poorly, her restlessness finally driving Jamie to ask Helena to open for him the bedroom on the far side of the sitting room. It was smaller, but there he could sleep without being disturbed by Sally's periodic wandering.

For himself, there was plenty to do, and for that he was grateful. Using the shares of the treasure he received, he sought investments, buying land in Port Royal. A sugar plantation was first, then a series of warehouses near the docks. A store, then another, all with tenants and managers to be found and tested before they could be accepted with trust.

Jamie found it challenging, fascinating to watch the money grow and build. His fortune seemed to rise even faster than his child swelled, and he was pleased—it was for his son or daughter that he made the investments.

To his surprise, he soon found both Percy and Reggie consulting him and, after a little hesitation, asking his help in investing their own shares. "I never would have dreamed it to look at you," Percy said. "Perfect gentleman, he looks, but he has the mind of a merchant. Probably end up owning the lot of us, Reggie, what do you think?"

"I think we'd be wise to let him handle our money," Reggie said. "I for one have nothing to show for the shares I received from the taking of Porto Bello, and if we're here for another few months I may manage to waste away most of the Chagre treasure as well. We'll have to sack most of the cities of the Spanish coast if I'm to go home with enough to set myself up properly."

Jamie laughed. "So you've finally realized there's something besides clubs and taverns and riotous living!"

"Oh, no," Percy said, waving a hand, "I'm not looking for anything beyond that, my man. I just want to be able to continue to afford it. Can you show me how?"

Jamie shook his head, laughing easily, enjoying himself. "No hope," he said, "but perhaps I can protect you a little. I've heard there's a good property inland a ways that is to go on the block; if you two are willing to pool your shares, you just might be able to get it."

They spent three days together at the mansion some earlier settler had built on the plantation, then returned feeling very pleased with themselves. They drank celebration toasts for a while in the club where Reggie and Percy had rooms, then Jamie finally rose.

"Best I be getting back to the house," he said with a reluctance he hated to admit even to himself. "Sally will be anxious to hear all about the plantation, and I should check on things at home. Aunt Helena has been turning more and more of her interests over to me to handle, too, and there are several things to be discussed."

"How is Sally these days?" Reggie asked.

"Uncomfortable," Jamie said.

"When is your son and heir due to arrive?" Percy asked, his expression teasing.

"Another couple of months," Jamie said with a sigh.

"And how is the fair Rebecca?" Percy asked. "I've seen precious little of her this time."

"I hardly see her either," Jamie said, keeping his voice casual only with effort. It was true, Rebecca did seem to be avoiding him much of the time, but when he did see her the result was troublesome. His desire for her hadn't diminished, and it took all his self-control not to respond to the seductive glances she turned his way when they did meet.

"Give her my regards, when you see her," Percy said, "and tell her I'd like to call one afternoon, perhaps escort her on a drive out to see the plantation."

"I'll tell her," Jamie said dryly, well aware of what Percy had in mind and both hating and envying him for it.

He was weary as he mounted his horse and turned him toward the house where Sally waited. He didn't urge the horse to any speed, only too well aware that his welcome would be the half-hearted offer of a meal and his own cold and empty bed. Not that it was her fault, he told himself firmly. The child was his and Sally was in no condition to welcome him with open arms.

The house was dark when he reached it, and the servants grumbled a little when he roused a boy to care for his horse and demanded a decanter of wine from one of the serving girls. He drank it slowly, aware that he didn't need any more after what he'd shared at the Club's victory party with Reggie and Percy. They'd drunk more than enough toasts to their winning of the plantation and the glorious future their investment promised.

Jamie downed a second glass, wishing it would make him sleepy, but it seemed to have no effect. Finally, numbed by the wine, he made his way slowly up the stairs and along the hall to his own room. As he pulled off his boots he looked out at the dark sitting room and the door on the other side.

Was Sally awake? he wondered, thinking he'd like to hold her, share his news with her. He padded halfway across the sitting room before he stopped and turned back. She'd made it plain enough that his business interests were of no concern to her, and now that she had trouble sleeping the night through he knew she'd hate him if he awakened her.

Was he being a fool by not taking a mistress? he asked himself as he stripped away his clothes and lay down naked on the bed. Percy had suggested it himself, even offering to help him find a suitable girl; but he'd only turned away, treated it as a joke. An occasional tavern girl, or perhaps a willing serving maid, but he wasn't positive about making a permanent arrangement.

He closed his eyes, remembering how it had been with Sally, wondering if it would ever be that way again. As he drifted closer to sleep, another face slipped into his mind. Green eyes blazed at him and tangled russet curls fell about a proud face. Elena, he thought. Dear God, what had become of her?

Suddenly he felt a warmth beside him. The bed shifted to accommodate another body, and warm arms slipped around him as sweet full lips sought his. It was like a dream coming true. Ripe and willing flesh pressed to his, then writhed and curled to his caresses.

Her kisses were all the wine had not been, raising his passion in a rush, driving him wild as he claimed her. Elena, his mind cried, Elena, you've come back. He drowned himself within her, then slipped peacefully into sleep.

The room was grey with dawn when a feather's touch awoke him. Delicate fingers caressed his body, arousing him once more. He pulled her close, devouring her with kisses before he even opened his eyes. It was not till later, when his passion was once more spent, that he came fully to awareness.

With shaking hand he smoothed back the cloud of golden hair and looked into mocking violet eyes. "Good morning, Jamie," Rebecca said, making no move to cover her sprawled, voluptuous body.

"*You!*" Pain knifed at him, an agony of disappointment that the girl before him wasn't the Elena of his dreams. "What are you doing here?" he demanded, pulling on his discarded clothing as fast as he could.

Rebecca smiled. "Do I really need to tell you what we've been doing?" she asked.

"Get out," he said, his spent passion a guilty pain now.

"Why should I?" Rebecca asked, stretching like a lazy cat.

"Do you want your sister to find you here?"

"She doesn't want you, so why should I care?" Rebecca moved languidly toward the edge of the bed, her ripe body mocking him.

"What of your Aunt Helena?" Jamie asked, fighting his own weakness. "Shall I call her in to drag you out of my bed?"

Fury rose in Rebecca's face. "Do you think she'd feel kindly toward you for it?" she spat at him. "I'll tell her you forced me here."

"Kicking and screaming through the halls with my wife sleeping only a room away?" Jamie turned from her, sickened both by her and by himself. "I'm sure she'll believe that, especially when I mention some of your other adventures."

A snarl of fury brought his eyes around, and Jamie winced away from the hatred that flowed at him. For once Rebecca's beauty was hidden by the twisted anger that gripped her. "You wanted me," she cried. "You wanted me last night and this morning, and you knew I wasn't poor, swollen-bellied Sally crawling into your bed."

"I took a warm body that was offered," Jamie said, hating her for his own weakness. "I didn't know or care who you were, and I still don't. Now get out, and don't come back here unless you want to be exposed for the slut you are. I know about Percy, and I'm sure finding the names of others would be easy—and I'll use them, I warn you. Try this again and I'll have you shipped back to your father in disgrace."

The delicate skin darkened to a fuchsia and her eyes blazed, but when she opened her mouth no words came. She glared at him for a moment more, then wrapped her robe about her and left him—her golden head high, her sweetly rounded body still visible and desirable beneath the soft material of her robe.

Jamie dropped back on the bed, sickness burning in his throat. Vivid memories swept over him, accusing him. It did no good to protest that he'd had too much to drink, or to pretend to himself that he'd thought it was Sally. Even the dim memories of his waking dream of Elena were no excuse for what had happened.

He'd wanted Rebecca for too long, and now the *fait accompli* sickened him. He turned over to rest his head against the coolness of the pillow, then winced away, finding it sweet with the scent of violets—Rebecca's scent.

"Jamie? Jamie, are you home?"

Sally's voice brought him up in a flash, and a glance at the tumbled bed told him he dared not allow himself to be found there. "Coming, love," he called, hurrying out and closing the door behind him.

"I thought I heard voices," Sally said, looking sleepy-eyed as she lay on the couch in the sitting room. "I came in here to wait for you last night. I must have fallen asleep." She smiled up at him, offering her lips.

Jamie kissed her with a passion born of guilt, then thrust all thoughts of Rebecca from his mind, vowing not to think of her again. Sally was his wife, and she would soon be bearing his child. Till that time, he must think of no other woman—not even one so far in the past as Elena.

Chapter 37

THE DAYS PASSED with the slowness of a death march. Jamie spent as little time in the house as possible, but when he was there he made sure he was with Sally. He scarcely saw Rebecca; whenever he did, he was only too aware of the mocking hatred in her eyes. If Sally hadn't been so near term, he would have moved out to the plantation house he'd bought.

As it was, Jamie sought and found a middle-aged couple to live in the renovated house on the plantation, and set about buying new furnishings, rugs, and draperies, making it ready for Sally and himself once the baby was born. It was time, he thought grimly, *long* past time they had a home of their own... one without Rebecca.

He came to love the plantation more with each visit. In spite of the still strange and exotic landscape, something about it reminded him of the Highlands he'd loved. It was home to him as the house in Port Royal had never been, and he spent many nights there with the Tylers, planning the future of the plantation.

There were many changes and improvements he longed to make, and only a shortage of ready money kept him from spending all his time working on it. He scarcely cared for his other holdings as he built the plantation as a home for his soon-to-be-born heir.

As he sat in a tavern, having just returned from taking Reggie and Percy on a three-day tour of his plantation, he was busily listing the things he meant to do when Reggie interrupted. "What makes you so sure you're building for a son?" he asked.

Jamie shrugged. "If this is a daughter, the next one will be a son," he said.

"What does Sally think about living out there?" Percy asked. "It's a long drive from dressmakers and shops, you know."

"She'll love it when she's seen it," Jamie said, ignoring the twinge of fear Percy's words produced.

"You mean she hasn't seen it?" Reggie asked, sounding shocked.

"I took her out there when I first bought it," Jamie said, "but the house was in sad need of repair and everything was wild and overgrown, so it was no wonder she didn't like it. She's going to love it as much as I do when she sees what I've done with it."

"I should think she'd rather have done the furnishings herself," Percy said. "My mother used to adore redoing things. It was my father's only complaint. Every three or four years she'd decide to make one of our houses totally new." He laughed. "Our tenants adored her, since they always fell heir to a good bit of the furnishings of whatever house she'd grown tired of."

Jamie shook his head. "Sally's been too ill with the child to do anything like that, and I mean to move them out there as soon as she's regained her strength after the baby comes."

"Why so soon?" Percy asked, frowning a little. "We'll be sailing before too long, you know; that is if that cursed fleet of Spaniards ever gives us a moment to slip away. You won't want to be leaving her alone out there, will you?"

Jamie moved uneasily in his chair, remembering the way Rebecca smiled at him now. It was obvious that she had something in mind, and he would have liked to get Sally away from her immediately had it been possible. "She'll be safe enough out there," he said, "and it's time she had a home of her own to manage. I think living with her aunt has been bad for her, kept her a child when she should be a grown woman in her own right."

He was aware of curious stares from his two friends, but neither of them said anything beyond calling for another round of drinks. Jamie, relieved, changed the subject to the prospects for sailing once again, and his plans for the treasure he felt they would capture once they escaped the watchful eyes of the Spanish fleet.

It was late when Jamie returned to the house, but he found a lamp burning in the sitting room and Sally was lying on the couch, dozing fitfully. She sat up when he entered, her expression cold. "Where have you been?" she demanded, angrily.

"With Reggie and Percy, of course," Jamie said. "Why?"

"I don't believe you." The words were cold.

Jamie frowned at her. "Why not?" he asked, sensing that something had happened. "Why should you doubt me? You'll be seeing them tomorrow evening, so you can ask them yourself."

"You were out at that place again, weren't you?" Sally didn't change her tone and her eyes were still stormy.

"The plantation? Yes, that's where we spent the last three days, but you knew that. I told you before we rode out there that I'd be gone three or four nights. What's the matter? Has something happened?"

"Are you truly furnishing it and making it into a grand house?" Her eyes skittered away from his.

Jamie studied her for a moment. His work on the house had not exactly been a secret, but he hadn't mentioned it, not wanting to disturb her now that the baby was so near term. "Yes, it's true," he said at last, aware that lying would only upset her since she'd obviously heard something. He settled himself on the couch at her feet and reached out to take her hands, holding them firmly even when she tried to pull away. "I've been fixing it up for a very special reason," he said.

Sally's lips quivered, and he was surprised to see her eyes filling with tears. "You would tell me that," she said, "flaunt it before me when I'm like this." She glared down at her monstrous belly.

"Flaunt it?" Jamie shook his head in honest confusion. "I thought only to surprise you once the baby is here and we can travel out there together."

"What?" She ceased trying to pull away from him. "I don't understand."

"I've been furnishing it for *us*, Sally—for you and the baby and me. I want that to be our new home as soon as we can move out there. I didn't tell you because I knew you weren't feeling well, and I thought you might worry about my spending so much money. What did you think I was doing?"

For a moment the wide blue eyes turned his way, then they dropped and he could see a blush rising to darken her cheeks. "I heard you were preparing it for your mistress," she murmured, head down, the words so muffled he could scarcely hear them.

"My *what*?" For a moment he felt an urge to laugh, then a flash of anger swept over him. "Where did you hear such a thing?" he demanded. "Who told you that story?"

"I don't remember," Sally said, her very tone betraying the fact that she was lying.

"I have no mistress," Jamie said, deeply glad that he could tell her the truth. "You're my wife, and I want only to have you out there with me, that's why I've been working so hard on it. I want it to be our home."

"You don't have a mistress?" Tear-wet eyes searched his face.

"I don't need one," Jamie said. "I have you."

She dissolved into tears and he held her gently, loving her as much at that moment as he had in their wildest bursts of passion. He had no doubt about who'd told her he had a mistress; only one person would have been so cruel—Rebecca. He longed to charge her with it, threaten her again, but he controlled his temper, reminding himself that he would soon be free of her brooding, tantalizing presence.

"You'll love the plantation," he said, hoping he was right. "The house is far grander than this one, and I've engaged a fine couple to live in it and take care of things for us. Once we've moved in, I hope you'll be able to invite some of your family to come and visit, perhaps your little sister Ruth might like to come and live with us, and your mother might make the voyage, too— to see her first grandchild."

Sally clung to him. "I'll be a good wife again, Jamie," she whispered. "I do love you, and once our baby is born everything will be the way it was, I promise. You won't need a mistress then, I swear it. I'll make you happy."

"I'm happy now," Jamie assured her, and was surprised to find he meant it. Holding her and feeling the lusty kicking of his child against his own belly was enough for the moment; he was too content even to hate Rebecca for the trouble she'd been trying to make for him.

The next few days passed smoothly. Sally asked him often about the plantation, and he was glad to tell her about the house and its furnishings. She seemed to accept without question his decision to move, and for that alone he forgave Rebecca her lies. She'd done him a favor, in spite of her evil intentions.

The summer burned on with the usual tropical storms, and Jamie was often away from the house in Port Royal, caring for his other properties and helping Percy and Reggie see to the development of their plantation. He sensed a growing restlessness in Sally but paid little attention to it, assuming it was caused by the nearness of her delivery, for they both reckoned the baby was due in September.

There was another restless presence in the house, too. Jamie felt, rather than saw, Rebecca as she roamed through the place. He felt her eyes following him as he moved through the entry, and when he looked up he would see her standing on the landing above or he would enter the library and find her sitting there, watching him, her violet eyes unreadable.

Twice when he returned to the house after spending a night or two at the plantation, he thought he caught the scent of violets on his pillows, but there was no proof beyond an occasional long golden hair—and he could never be sure it wasn't Sally's. Still, it left him uneasy, and he found himself more and more reluctant to return home.

A storm was brewing as he rode through the crowded streets toward the house on an early September evening. He'd just left Reggie and Percy at their club, having spent the past three days with them on a buying trip into the interior of the island, and he was too tired even to notice the heaviness of the air, the brooding clouds that were piled near the distant horizon.

The house was surprisingly well-lit when he rode in, and he was angry to find there was no one in the stable to take his horse. For a moment he considered just leaving the beast and searching out one of the boys who were supposed to care for the horses, but the poor animal looked so tired he sighed and unsaddled the horse himself, seeing he had food and water before he left him.

There was no one in the rear of the house when he let himself in, so Jamie climbed the narrow backstairs to his own room without looking around for the servants, eager to change from his stained and sweat-damp clothing before he faced his wife or her family. He stripped quickly, enjoying the damp wind that had sprung up and was blowing through his open window.

There was fresh water and he washed hurriedly, hungry now that he was home.

Dressed once more, his hair combed and smoothed, he crossed the sitting room, calling Sally's name. There was no answer, and when he peered into the big bedroom they'd once shared he saw that the bed was made and she was nowhere to be seen. A little surprised, he made his way down the front stairs, looking around for the servants.

"Jamie?" Aunt Helena came out of the living room, her face paler than usual. "What are you doing here? Where are the girls?"

"I was just going to ask you that," Jamie said, sensing something in the older woman's voice. "Where is Sally? It's not the baby, is it?"

"You didn't see them?" Helena staggered slightly as though his words were a blow.

"See them? Where?" Jamie just blinked at her. "I've been back in the hills for the past few days. Where is she?" he demanded, suddenly afraid.

"You weren't at the plantation?" Helena looked paler than ever, and so frail that Jamie took her arm and guided her to one of the ornately carved benches that edged the entry.

"What do you mean 'at the plantation'?" he demanded.

"But I thought . . . Rebecca told me they were going to drive out to the plantation to surprise you. I tried to discourage her, but Sally was so excited. She said the road was good and she could rest there."

Jamie was on his feet without listening to another word. "Send someone to the Club to tell Percy and Reggie," he snapped at the woman. "Tell them to follow me out there. There's a storm brewing, and I have a feeling it's going to be a bad one."

"Where are you going?" Helena called, her voice rising with hysteria.

"To get my wife," Jamie shouted over his shoulder, fury and fear propelling him through the kitchen and out to the stable.

Aware that his own horse was too weary to make another journey, he saddled the young colt he'd purchased recently and only begun to train. The beast was half-wild and the storm and wind added to his excitement, but Jamie felt no fear. The colt was young and strong and fast and that was all he cared about. Vaulting to the saddle, he set his spurs in the colt's sides and plunged out into the rising wind.

He rode like a madman, paying little attention to the condition of the road he followed. He saw few people on the way, and by the time he neared the plantation the storm was roaring like a living thing, tearing at him, trying to whip him from the saddle as the leg-weary colt stumbled into the stable yard.

A boy ran out of the stable as Jamie pulled the tired horse to a stop and threw him the reins, shouting instructions as he ran for the house, not even looking back. Once inside he paused, aware of his own panting breath and the rainwater that ran off him in rivulets.

Mrs. Tyler came around the corner of the kitchen, her face grave, then stopped, shocked to see him. "Lord bless you, where did you come from?" she gasped when she found her tongue.

"Is my wife here?" Jamie demanded, not answering her question.

Mrs. Tyler nodded. "They're upstairs, the both of them," she said. "I finally got your little wife to lie down, but the *other* one! She's like a cat, pacing and complaining and wanting to leave. I warned them about the storm, but she keeps insisting they go."

She stopped speaking, and above the sound of the storm Jamie heard Rebecca's voice. "Well, *I'm* not going to stay here another minute. If you want to lie where he's kept his mistress all these months, go ahead. But *I'm* going back to Port Royal. I'm not afraid of a little rain."

Sally's voice was softer, a low rumble of words Jamie couldn't distinguish. He hurried through the dining room, heading for the front hall where the stairs came down, eager to assure himself that all was well.

"You can't go, Rebecca," Sally was protesting as he stepped through the wide doorway into the dimly lit hall. "Please don't leave me here alone. I don't feel well and I'm afraid."

"You're always afraid and sick," Rebecca taunted. "That's why your husband has to have other women. He's even come scratching on my door like some starving puppy, and if you don't shut up, one night I'm going to let him in." Rebecca pulled away from Sally and started toward the stairs, her head high, her eyes sparkling in the light of the candles at the top of the stairs.

Furious, Jamie stepped to the foot of the stairs. "I wouldn't enter your room and you know it," he snarled. "I'd sooner crawl into bed with a nest of vipers."

There was a moment of stunned silence, then Rebecca caught

her breath. "Oh, wouldn't you now," she began, overcoming her shock and tossing back her blond hair. "I seem to . . ."

"Jamie!" Sally's voice rose over Rebecca's and she moved forward in a rush, passing her sister, hurrying for the stairway, her face glowing; then suddenly she faltered and fell, screaming, down the stairs.

It was like a nightmare. Jamie ran to her side, aware of other screams but seeing nothing but the crumpled, too-still form at the foot of the long staircase. He knelt beside her, lifted her head. Only when he saw that she still breathed did his own heart seem to beat again.

"Is she . . . ?" Rebecca wavered above him.

"You did this," he said, looking up at her. "You brought her out here and now you've tried to kill her. I'll never forgive you for this. I'll see you rot in hell for it, do you understand me, Rebecca? I'll destroy you for what you've done!"

Sally's moan brought his attention back to her, then the front door was thrown open and Percy and Reggie were in the room. Servants appeared from all sides, and after a brief moment of confusion Reggie took charge. At his orders, Sally was carried gently back up the stairs and Percy took Jamie into the sitting room and forced a large glass of brandy on him.

"I have to go to her," Jamie protested, his eyes turning to the door to the great hall. "Dear God, I have to be with her."

"Reggie's with her now," Percy said. "He can do what you can't."

Jamie shook his head but accepted the words, knowing his friend was right. A lifetime seemed to pass. Mrs. Tyler appeared and disappeared several times, taking things up to the bedroom where Reggie worked over Sally; but each time he tried to question her she only shook her head. "She's not moved or spoke, but the baby is coming," was all she could tell him.

Outside the storm raged, and inside Jamie paced the room he'd planned and decorated for Sally. Only once did he hear anything, and that sound stopped him in his tracks. A baby's thin wail carried down the stairs, and then there was silence—an endless, heavy silence from the room where he felt his own heart rested.

Hours later Reggie came down, his face grim. While Percy fixed him a glass of brandy, he took Jamie's hand. "You have a son," he said, "and I think he'll make it. Mrs. Tyler was able to find a young woman who's just lost her own child, and she'll nurse him."

"Sally?" Jamie could scarcely force the word out.

"She had no chance, Jamie. I'm sorry," Reggie said. "It is a miracle that she survived long enough to give her child life."

"She's dead?" It was a sob.

"She was near death when we carried her upstairs. She never woke from the fall; she was beyond pain, I'm sure. She clung to life long enough for me to deliver your son, then slipped quietly away."

Jamie turned from them, shamed by the tears he felt on his face and seeking release in the fury that filled him. "She killed her," he shouted. "As surely as if she'd pushed her down those stairs, that vengeful bitch!"

He was halfway out of the house before they stopped him, and so mad with pain he turned on them, fighting till someone's fist banished it all and let him sink into merciful darkness. When he woke, his head pounding from whatever Reggie had given him, it was dawn and a baby's crying filled the house.

Jamie stared down at the tiny, red-faced infant, marveling as the little mouth sought blindly for the rosy brown nipple the wet-nurse offered, then fastened itself firmly to the swollen brown breast. His son. The words filled him with awe. The girl smiled up at him sadly.

"He is strong, master," she said softly. "He will thrive as my own little girl did not."

"You will guard him with your life," Jamie said, shaking with the new emotion that flooded through him. "He'll be yours to care for, and you'll have nothing else to do, is that clear? Mrs. Tyler will help you."

The girl nodded and cuddled his son even more closely as she bent to kiss the pale fuzzy head. "I will love him, sir," she said simply.

Jamie turned to Mrs. Tyler and saw that she was nodding her approval. "I have to go into town," he said.

"We will care for him, sir," she said, "don't you worry. The poor little lamb will have all the love and attention he needs. I've not had a baby to love in ten years, but I raised eight of my own. He'll be safe enough."

"Thank you," Jamie said. "Thank you very much."

All the way to Port Royal, escorting Sally's broken body through the new-washed day, he rode in silence, plotting his revenge against Rebecca. She would pay for this, he vowed. He'd see her branded a tart in every home in Port Royal. He'd publish her affairs, list the men who'd tasted her charms, let everyone know she was worse than the whores who sold themselves on the docks.

He reached the house at last and dismounted stiffly. Helena met him at the door, her swollen eyes telling him the messenger had already arrived with the news of Sally's death. "The baby?" she asked, her eyes searching his face.

"He'll live," Jamie said. "He's with a wet-nurse at the plantation."

"You won't bring him here, to me?" She looked crushed.

"Where is Rebecca?" he asked, brushing aside her question.

Her face changed, hardened. "Gone," she said coldly. "She came out of the storm and gathered her things, then left without a word. She didn't even tell me about Sally."

"Where has she gone?"

Helena shrugged. "One of the servants said she sailed on some merchant ship. Its captain had called on her a few times, but I don't know."

Jamie stood for a moment, his dreams of vengeance breaking up around him and leaving the raw wound of his loss open to the air once again. He was scarcely aware when Helena helped him inside.

Grief rode with him through the months that followed. Fergus, as he'd christened the baby, grew strong and healthy, but even his rosy presence couldn't ease the sense of guilt and loss that haunted Jamie. He was grateful when, at long last, the new ships came sailing into the harbour and they could prepare to sail once again. He'd had more than enough of Port Royal, and the thought of battle lifted his spirits as nothing else could. Leaving Fergus in Mrs. Tyler's capable hands, he sailed on the *Burford* with a strange sense of hope.

Something lay ahead, something more than treasure or the glory and agony of battle. He lifted his face to the wind from the sea and smiled. Whatever it was, he was anxious to find it.

Chapter 38

THE VOYAGE WENT SMOOTHLY. Captain Diego proved to be a fatherly man in spite of his gruff exterior, and he was plainly very taken by little Louis—spending what seemed to Elena a vast amount of time with the little boy. When she mentioned it to Juanna, the dark woman laughed with a note of sadness.

"He would like a child of his own," she said in Spanish. "I had hoped to give him one, but we've been together over five years now and never once have I even suspected." She shrugged. "All of Grandma Karame's potions have failed."

"Have you really lived on this ship for five years?" Elena asked, a little shocked at the idea.

Juanna smiled. "*Mi Capitan* has a small house in Cartegena. But mostly he wishes me to be at his side, and I don't mind. I've seen nearly all the islands of the Caribbean Sea, and I have friends on most of them. It is a good life."

Elena sighed. "I would like to settle somewhere. I was happy on St. Domingue, but..." She forced a smile. "Perhaps Cartegena will offer what I'm seeking," she said, not ready to go into what had happened, though she suspected that Karame had told her niece something of the circumstances.

"And what do you want to find there?" Juanna asked.

"A position, I suppose," Elena said. "I was an *institutriz* for a French family, and that was a good life. At least Louis and I were safe, or would have been."

"There are a number of Spanish families who might be interested in an *institutriz*," Juanna said. "I will discuss it with *mi Capitan*. Perhaps he will know someone to ask."

"I would be grateful," Elena confessed. "I'm afraid I can't live long anywhere without an income, and there is Louis to be cared for."

Juanna nodded. "Don't you worry," she said. "*Mi Capitan* will find something for you. He's not going to put you ashore and abandon you, that I can promise."

"You've been so kind already," Elena said.

Juanna's face changed and hardened. "My dearest friend was one chosen by the evil one," she said. "When he finished with her, she could bear the touch of no man. She killed herself rather than live with the shame she felt. To know you brought his death is to make you like a sister to me. I tell you truly, if there is anything I can do to help you, you have only to ask."

Elena felt the warmth of the words and read the genuine feeling in the girl's eyes with a glad heart. "He deserved to die," she agreed quietly. "He would have forced me to marry him and then killed my son. He had already ordered the murder of a kind man whose only crime was to offer to marry me and take me away to safety."

Elena told her painfully of Jean's goodness and his horrible death. That moment of closeness and trust set a pattern, and by the time they neared Cartegena, Juanna had more or less taken Mimi's place as Elena's friend and confidant. The day before they were to land, she came to Elena's cabin with a smile.

"*Mi Capitan* has an idea," she said. "There is a family Diego knows. He served the old man for a number of years in Spain before he came here to seek his fortune. The son of that man is in Cartegena now with his wife and baby. *Mi Capitan* heard that the woman who was caring for the child is to return to Spain, so he will mention you to this man as a replacement. The child is, I think, not too much older than your Louis, so if the family is kind they may be right for you."

Elena felt her heart lift at the suggestion. "I would be most grateful," she said. "The sooner I can find a home for Louis and me, the better I will feel."

"He will contact the man as soon as we reach the city," Juanna promised.

They sailed into the well-protected harbour of Cartegena without incident, and once the ship was secured and the cargo sorted for unloading *Capitan* Diego bid them wait while he went into the city to seek the man who might have a position for Elena.

"Don't worry, Senora," he said with a kind smile. "My old *patron* was a fine man, and his son will be, too. If I can leave you under his protection, I will know little Louis has nothing to fear in his future."

"You've been more than kind," Elena told him. "I don't know what I would have done..." A wave of his hand stopped her words, and the *Capitan* was gone down the gangplank before she could begin again.

It seemed a very long day on the deck of the small trading ship. The city beyond teemed with life, and Elena stared longingly at the buildings with their tiled roofs and the narrow streets. In the distance she could see the spires of the great cathedrals of the city, and on occasion she heard their bells.

It was near sunset when *Capitan* Diego returned, and his wide grin answered Elena's questions even before she found the words to ask them. "I have sent word to the *hacienda* of my *patron's* son, and he has replied that he does indeed require the services of a nursemaid and future *institutriz* for his young son. I am to take you to his townhouse tomorrow, where he will come to talk with you. How will that be?"

"*Capitan* Diego, it's like the answer to a prayer," Elena said. "I don't know what I should have done without your help."

"I am helping both you and the son of my *patron*. What more can I ask? If you are, as I suspect, exactly what he has been seeking, he will be grateful—and his patronage here in Cartegena can be very helpful." The *Capitan* laughed. "My ship is not large, but the cargoes I carry from port to port bring much happiness to my Juanna and me."

"Come, I will help you prepare your belongings," Juanna said. "If the visit tomorrow goes well, you will probably wish to leave for the country at once."

Elena nibbled at her lip. "I'll hate to say *adios*," she admitted.

Juanna shrugged. "We come often to Cartegena, Elena, so it will only be *hasta manana*."

The next day dawned damp and rainy, and as the time to leave the ship drew near Elena fussed over Louis, afraid the winter rains might give him a fever. "Leave the boy with Juanna," the *Capitan* said at last. "She can care for him till you are ready to return."

Juanna nodded. "Please do," she said. "I would love to have him to myself the whole afternoon, and you'll be able to talk much more easily without a restless child."

Though she hated to leave Louis for even an hour, a glance at the grey world beyond the ship told Elena they were right. She agreed reluctantly, and followed Diego hurriedly to a small, covered carriage. They plunged into the tumult of the streets, crowded even in the rain.

"I have other business to take care of," *Capitan* Diego said, "so I will not be able to wait with you. But I will return to the townhouse before sunset to make sure you have taken the position, or to take you back to the ship if you choose to seek employment elsewhere."

"Where else could I look?" Elena asked, frightened now.

The *Capitan* shrugged. "I'm sure there are other well-placed families seeking someone of your training. Or you might even be able to find a husband with fair speed. If you only had some relatives here, someone to take you in for a few months and introduce you to the proper society of the city . . ." His eyes were appraising. "You are a fine looking young lady, so finding such a man would not be difficult. It is only that I do not move in such circles that makes it hard for me to help you."

Elena shuddered a little, remembering the horror that had followed the last time someone suggested she marry. "I have no desire to marry," she said coldly, knowing she would not likely find another man like Jean Carnac.

Capitan Diego glanced at her curiously, but asked nothing further. Quite soon the carriage stopped outside a walled courtyard. The heavy gate stood open and the *Capitan* escorted her inside and up to the heavy wooden door. His firm knock was quickly answered by a stern-faced old woman.

"This young lady is to await your master," *Capitan* Diego said. "Perhaps she could have some tea and a place near a fire."

The woman nodded, and Diego left Elena with a quick, fatherly pat on the arm, promising once again to return before sunset to make sure she was safely settled. Elena followed the woman along a wide corridor and through the door into a small parlour. A fire had been built there and the woman nodded toward it. "I will bring you something hot to drink," she said in Spanish.

"*Gracias,*" Elena said, moving quickly to warm her hands and to stare into the fire. Though she hadn't been aware that she was cold, the house seemed dank and her nerves left her fingers icy in spite of the flames. She removed her cloak carefully, shaking the dampness away from the rugs and the hearth, then smoothed and patted the neat knot of her hair, hoping she looked far less frightened than she felt.

The maid came in with a silver tray and settled it on the table, then left, plainly not willing to serve Elena, though she had obeyed the *Capitan's* request. Elena smiled to herself, then went to sit by the tray and pour herself a cup of tea. It was only when she moved the cup that the tray caught her eye. It was carefully etched with a crest, and there was something extremely familiar about it.

For a moment Elena just stared, then her hand began to shake so that she had to put the cup down, nearly cracking it in her agitated state. She looked around for a moment, then located the bell pull to call the maid back. The woman came slowly, giving Elena time to regain her composure.

"Please," Elena began, "what is the name of the man who owns this house, the man who is to come and talk to me?"

Dark eyes regarded her suspiciously, but after a few moments hesitation the woman sighed. "This house is the property of Senor Hernan Valdez. Why?"

Elena said nothing for a moment, her worst fears confirmed. Finally, she forced a smile. "*Gracias,*" she said. "That will be all."

The woman eyed her with further suspicion, but left after a moment. Elena paused only long enough to pick up her cloak before leaving the warm haven of the small parlour and starting back along the dimly lit corridor to the front door.

Even as she scurried along she tried to think. What could she do? Had the *Capitan* told Hernan her name, or where she could be found? She reached for the door handle, but before she could clutch it the door was thrown open and she was face to face with Hernan Valdez.

For a moment she was paralyzed. His dark eyes met hers, and she knew at once that he didn't fully recognize her, for there was confusion in his gaze. It was long enough. Gathering her courage, she tried to move past him, but he shifted his stance to block the door.

"Well, well, and who might you be, pretty little girl?" he asked, his eyes ravishing her as his hands had once.

Shuddering, Elena stepped back one step. "*Beast!*" she cried. "*Killer!* Attacker of virgins! You're worse than any animal. You should have died for what you've done to me and Celeste!"

For a moment he looked baffled, then she saw the dawning horror in his face. "*Elena!*" he gasped, just as she swung at his stomach with all her strength. The blow landed well, doubling him over, and she fled past him into the rain-swept afternoon.

The miles she'd walked on St. Domingue had hardened her muscles and she ran easily, through the gate and into the street, dodging her way along, hardly daring to glance back till she turned a corner from one narrow street to another. When she looked back her heartbeat jumped wildly. Hernan was coming along the street after her, his longer legs devouring the distance at a frightening rate.

Terrified, she ran on, looking desperately for a place to hide. Finally the sanctuary came into view. A huge cathedral reared above the surrounding walls and Elena raced up the stairs, through the handsome double doors and into the incense-scented silence of the vaulted room. Stopping, she looked around, then moved quickly along the wall to a narrow staircase carved in a small recess. Tiptoeing and controlling her panting breath with great effort, she climbed up into the shadows, then dropped onto the stones, too exhausted to go further.

Only when she stopped did she hear sounds from beyond the hidden stairway. Someone was moving about the altar area, humming softly the tones of a chant. Sudden tears filled her eyes and she longed to go back down the stairs, to approach the priest and beg him to hear her confession and free her from the burden of the pagan rites she'd learned from Karame.

But could she ever be clean again? she asked herself. Would even a kindly God be able to forgive her for calling on *Dumballa* that night in the cabin? And what would a priest say? What could she do to atone for it all?

"Father, may I speak with you?" Hernan's voice broke the stillness, causing her to start so that she nearly fell down the steep steps.

"Of course, Senor. How may I help you?" The voice was thin and sounded old.

"Did a woman come in here?" Hernan demanded. "About so tall, with darkish hair and green eyes? Wearing a cloak, and running."

"I've seen no one for an hour, Senor Valdez." The priest's voice had changed, making it obvious that he'd recognized Hernan and was now more than willing to help him. "What is the trouble?"

"The woman is a thief," Hernan said, his voice hard with anger. "She played on my pity, asking for help. Then, when I bent to assist her, she took my purse and fled into the streets."

"I hardly think a thief would come here for sanctuary," the priest said. "You would be better to look to the *taberna*. When people drink, they often welcome such as that in their midst."

Hernan seemed about to reply sharply. She could hear the harsh sound of his indrawn breath in the stillness of the cathedral, but then he seemed to think better of his anger and said only, "Thank you for your help, Father. If she should come here to you for sanctuary, be warned that she is not to be trusted."

"I shall be careful, my son," the old priest said, and in a moment the silence of the cathedral told her that Hernan had left.

Elena stayed where she was, trying to think. What could she do? The first thing was to fetch Louis, she decided, Louis and their belongings. But it had to be done quickly, she realized, for Hernan was no fool; once he was sure he'd lost her in the streets, he would go looking for the man who'd brought her to him. *Capitan* Diego would be easily fooled into helping him, she was sure.

She had enough money to hire a public carriage to take her to the ship, but once she was in it her mind whirled with fear. Seeing Hernan had been terrifying, but the implications of it were even more frightening. Cartegena was no haven now. She must somehow find a way to escape from the city and seek her future somewhere else.

When she went cautiously aboard the ship, she found Juanna in her cabin with Louis sleeping peacefully in his bunk. "So soon?" Juanna asked, looking startled. "Did the man bring you back for your belongings?"

Elena bit her lip, considering her few alternatives, then made her decision. She had little money, and no idea how to sell the jewelry Raul and Mimi had given her. Also, with no friends in the city, she would be all too vulnerable to Hernan's inquiries. He would be sure to seek her in the city's *posadas*, and eventually he would find her. Taking a deep breath, she told Juanna as much as she dared about Hernan, sparing herself nothing, even describing the way he'd taken her in the grove and then tried to kill her.

"Your mother?" Juanna suggested. "Perhaps I could get word from you to her."

Elena shook her head. "She would have no power to protect me. You know the laws are only for the man. Besides, she's not strong, and she's believed me dead for nearly two years. The shock might be too much."

"But what can you do?"

"I was wondering if you would help me hide somewhere in the city till I can get another ship out of the harbour. Hernan is sure to go to the *Capitan* to help him find me and I must hide well."

Juanna shook her head. "Once he knows the story, *mi Capitan* will protect you and little Louis. He owes the man nothing."

Elena shook her head, though she longed to accept the girl's offer. "Hernan would destroy him if he knew," she said. "The *Capitan* will be safe only if he doesn't know where I am. I only ask you because I have nowhere to go and know no one in the city. For myself I might even choose the waters of the harbour and be done with it, but there is Louis to consider."

Juanna glared at her. "Do not speak so," she said. "You have survived other dangers. I have *amigas* here." She considered for a moment, then her dark eyes glinted merrily. "In fact, I know just the place. Your enemy will never seek you there, and you will be given shelter gladly once Camille knows what you did to de la Mer. She was one of his first victims, and lives as she does because of it."

"Then we must go quickly," Elena said. "Before Hernan can come to the ship to find me."

"We'll go at once." Juanna began gathering the already-packed boxes and trunk. In no time at all they were in another wagon, heading through the clearing afternoon toward the crowded, narrow streets of the city. Elena closed her eyes, wondering if she would escape this city alive—or if her luck had finally run out.

Chapter 39

ONLY AFTER THEY were safely away from the ship did Juanna speak again, and this time her face was very grave. "Before we go to Camille, there is something you must know," she said. "Her business is..." Juanna's golden brown skin flushed deeply. "She cares for the girls who entertain men," she said at last.

Elena said nothing for a moment, not really understanding at first, then suddenly she spoke. "You mean it is a *brothel*?" she gasped.

Juanna nodded. "Camille lives in a small house behind the main building, and she allows no man to touch her. She hasn't been able to endure the touch of any man since her weeks with that evil one. But she had to live, and without a husband her choices were few. I visit her whenever I am in Cartegena, but I know she is lonesome and would offer you protection and shelter."

Elena felt a strong desire to refuse, but after a glance at the busy streets she knew she couldn't. Whatever her feelings, she dared not expose Louis to the dangers of the streets, and if Hernan should find her with Louis the dangers would seem petty. She shuddered to think what might become of her son once she was killed.

"There are a few other people I know," Juanna was going on. "Most of them work for the wealthy Spaniards, though, and I'm afraid having a white lady as a guest would be too exciting not to gossip about."

Elena nodded. "If your Camille will have us, I shall be very grateful," she said. "I can understand only too well why she feels as she does. If he had succeeded with me, I would have chosen to do what my friend Celeste did, for his treatment could never be forgotten."

Juanna nodded. "I left the island to escape him," she said. "I was lucky to find *mi Capitan*."

"What will you tell *Capitan* Diego?" Elena asked.

Juanna smiled. "While we are here in Cartegena, only that you feared the man and didn't want to accept the post so you hired a carriage to take you to someone else you discovered was in Cartagena. I'll tell him the truth once we've sailed for another port. For now, I'll let him think it was a French person you met on your way back to the ship—a friend of a friend."

Elena reached out and took the girl's hand. "You are the dearest of *amigas*," she said softly. "I can never thank you enough for what you are doing for me."

"Perhaps we shall sail together again," Juanna said. "I know people on every island and in all the ports, so when you escape leave word with Camille and I'll find you again. All right?"

Elena nodded, tears in her eyes at the thought of parting from still another *amiga*. Was she never to find a home, a haven for herself and Louis?

"There's the place," Juanna said, pointing to a rather large old building surrounded by a wall with a narrow, discreet gate on the side. "You wait here. I'll go talk to Camille."

It seemed hours, but Elena and Louis were moved in and settled in the small house at the rear of the large building before nightfall. Camille, who was darker-skinned than Juanna but still showed signs of white blood, welcomed Elena warmly, though her downcast eyes told of her shyness. The room was clean and comfortable, and dinner was a tasty stew.

The sounds from the big building kept Elena awake the first night, but as the days passed she soon learned to ignore them. Camille became more friendly, and Elena's life settled into a rather quiet routine. She went out only in the early morning hours, and only then with her head carefully covered so that her face and hair were hidden. With Camille's help she sold the jewelry for prices far higher than she'd dared hope, and through Camille she made discreet inquiries about ships leaving the port.

"I'm afraid there is no way you can go now," Camille informed her about two weeks after she'd come to live behind the *Casa de Flores*—or House of Flowers—as the brothel was called. "The man you fear has several agents on the waterfront watching all who seek passage out of the city."

Elena sighed. She'd gradually told Camille the whole story of how she'd come to Cartagena, and why she feared Hernan Valdez so greatly. The other woman had nodded, seeming unsurprised by Elena's past. Not even her days as Raul's mistress had brought shock. Her only comment was, "You are wise, Senora, and fortunate. Many of my girls have come to me destroyed by just such experiences. They leave their children with their families or friends and work here to make enough to care for them."

"And you?" Elena had asked, noting the love Camille lavished on Louis. "Have you never wanted a child, Camille?"

The dark eyes changed and tears filled them. "I had a daughter. The evil one kept me till I was carrying his child. She was a beauty, even when she was no older than Louis. I lived because of her, stayed on the plantation to care for her and protect her, but when she was five he took her from me. He sold her to a man who uses children in houses like this one. I ran away then, trying to find her, but I never did. I can only pray she died before she could become like the poor girls in the *Casa de Flores*, for he would not protect her even as much as I can protect the girls who work for me."

Elena shuddered. "I wish you could have seen him die," she said quietly. "He was in agony, Camille, and in terror."

The dark girl smiled. "Perhaps I shall go home someday soon now. With all I have earned here, I can buy a small piece of land and live in peace."

"I hope you do," Elena said, envying the girl and ashamed of herself for it. "You deserve great happiness."

"So do we all," Camille said. "But now I must go back to work."

Elena watched her go and swallowed a sigh. They were safe

here for the moment, but for how much longer? She stood at the window, watching the arrivals as they were admitted through the side gate. Her glance was casual, her interest only slight, and that only because there was so little else to occupy her mind in the early evening hours.

Suddenly a familiar form caught her eye. She leaned forward, pressing her face against the light curtain that concealed her from the outside world. It couldn't be, she told herself, and yet her heartbeat quickened. Frightened, yet hopeful, she wrapped herself in a shawl and crossed the shadowed rear court to the back door that Camille used. Inside she found a small boy and sent him to find Camille and ask her to come speak to her.

Camille looked shockingly different. She was dressed severely, but her hair was up and her truly pretty face was carefully emphasized with cosmetics. "What are you doing here?" she demanded. "You could be in danger. There is a man here from the Valdez *hacienda*. If he should see you the monster will find you."

"An older man called Carlos?" Elena asked.

Camille nodded. "He comes here about once a month," she said. "I had forgotten, or I would have warned you."

Elena swallowed hard. "I must see him," she said. "Could you arrange it somehow?"

Camille looked shocked, then her eyes narrowed. "You wish him to know you are here?" she asked.

"He served my father before Hernan came to our *hacienda*," Elena explained. "He serves Hernan because he is bound to the *hacienda*, but he would never betray me, I'm sure."

Camille bit at her lip, then smiled. "I will tell him there is a special girl, just for him," she said. "You will go with the boy to a certain room. He will lock you in and then give me the key—that way you'll be safe to wait for this Carlos."

"Bless you," Elena said.

The room was small, and Elena found herself embarrassed— even though she was alone in it with the door safely locked behind her. The bed dominated, its bright drapings and soft cushions almost obscene in their welcome. There were wall-hangings and paintings everywhere, even on the ceiling above the bed. She blushed at the sensual scenes depicted, wishing fervently that she'd asked to have Carlos brought to her room in the cottage.

When the sound of the key came, she was so nervous she almost screamed. She turned away from the door, covering her face in case someone might be passing in the busy hallway.

"Well, well," Carlos said, "let's see you, *mi muchacha*. Camille tells me you are very special."

Elena swallowed hard and dropped the shawl, turning to face the old man. "*Buenes noches*, Carlos," she said. "It's been a long time."

For a moment the eyes were full of lust, going over her body, then the words seemed to reach him and his eyes came to her face. For several heartbeats the eyes contained only confusion, then he paled and staggered back.

"*Por Dios!*" he gasped. "Senorita Elena! But you are dead!"

Fearing for him, Elena forgot her own shyness and hurried to his side, easing him down on the gaudy bed. "I'm not dead, Carlos," she said. "It was Hernan's story. He tried to kill me, but he failed and I escaped him. Only now I am in great danger."

The old man paled, then his color returned and he struggled to understand. "Senorita what happened? How did you come to be in this place? Why did he say you were dead?"

Elena raised her hand and then, keeping her voice as calm and steady as she could, she told him the whole story, leaving out only the details of her escape from Mallorca, her time with Raul, and the exact reason for her leaving St. Domingue. He listened with ever more angry silence.

His swearing, when she finished, was more fearful than anything she'd ever heard, and he apologized afterward. "I would cut out his heart with my own hand," he said.

"No," Elena said. "He will be punished, but not by you. You would only suffer for it."

"But why did you come to me here?" Carlos asked. "You should not be in such a place. Your poor mother would be disgraced."

"How is my mother?" Elena interrupted. "That's what I wanted to know."

"She is gone," Carlos said. "After the Senor claimed to have been robbed, he decided she should go back to Spain to have her child. She and the little Senor left with Dona Isabella over a week ago."

"She is expecting another child?" Elena was surprised. "And Dona Isabella is still with them?"

"Only for the journey." Carlos hesitated, then sighed. "She

found the Senor with one of the maids. It was like Celeste again, and I think she realized it. She said nothing to him, but decided at once to return to her family's *hacienda* and then to enter a convent. She was staying only till he could find someone to care for the child. Then, when he decided your mother and the boy must return to Spain, she said she would travel with them and care for them as her duty."

"He sent them home because of me," Elena said. "He must have been desperately afraid I would go to mother and tell her what he did to me."

"You must get away from here," Carlos said.

"How?" Elena asked. "He has the harbour watched. I have little money and nowhere to go."

"You are in terrible danger. He has told everyone the lie about a woman robbing him, and he described you well. I just didn't realize it till now. There is a reward for you—he has it posted wherever the rabble gather. They would cut the throats of their own mothers for what he is offering for you. You must get away, even if you have to walk out through the jungle."

"I have a son," Elena said, mentioning Louis for the first time.

"Seed of the monster?" Carlos almost spat the words out.

Elena shook her head. "He is not Hernan's child."

The eyes that touched her changed slightly, but Carlos asked no questions. "There has to be a way," he said.

"It must be by sea," Elena said.

"That could be dangerous," Carlos said. "There are rumors of a British fleet in the area. We may even be attacked."

Elena sighed. "Perhaps if we are, I'll be able to escape," she said, not really afraid. "Even Hernan will lose his taste for vengeance if his lands are in danger."

Carlos shook his head, his face sad. "It is well your mother cannot see you now," he said.

"To her I shall always be dead," Elena said, her own sadness heavy inside. "She's safe with him. And only the wind knows where I shall be taken next."

"I'd like to help you," Carlos said. "Just tell me what you need."

"Just come again," Elena said. "Just visit me and tell me about my mother and all the people I knew. That helps, Carlos, more than you know."

He shook his head. "It is not enough," he said. "I shall go

back to the *hacienda* and think. There has to be a way. And we'll find it, that I promise you. Just be brave, Elena. God will help us."

Her tears were still falling when he left the room, giving her the key. "I will tell Camille to come for you," he said. "You should not be here. There is no safety in the halls. There are too many men who don't know a lady when they see one."

"Guard yourself, Carlos," she called after him. *"Vaya con Dios."*

She went back to the small house with more hope than she'd known in a long time. Carlos had little power, but he was a man and he would guard her secret, she was sure. He was someone who cared, someone who might be able to help her out of the trap she'd hidden herself in.

Chapter 40

THE DAYS WENT on, slow and each much the same as the last one. Elena's hope began to fade. In spite of Camille's generosity and kindness, Elena's money was disappearing much too rapidly and she grew more and more fearful of the future.

It was a sultry night. Louis had been fretful through the day, but was finally settling down to sleep. Elena sat in the window, still hidden behind the light curtain but trying hard to catch a breath of fresh air from the sea. The early flurry of arrivals was over, and the habitual late crowd had not begun to arrive yet. The courtyard was peaceful.

Then suddenly the evening's quiet was broken by shouts and noises from the big house. Elena had long since learned to pay little attention to such sounds, but this time they continued too long and the screams of the girls were added to the men's voices. Uneasy, she glanced toward the gate and was surprised to see that Pablo wasn't at his usual post. She sighed and started to move away, sure he must have been summoned inside if a man's strength was needed.

Just as she turned, however, she saw a flash of movement and

recognized Pina, one of the regular girls, as she burst out the
back door of the building and came racing across the courtyard,
her bright gown flying to reveal the golden-skinned body
beneath it. Knowing something must be wrong, Elena hurried to
the door to meet her.

"You must come," Pina sobbed. "The man has gone mad.
Pablo tried to put him out, but he struck him so hard . . ." She
stopped to sob. "Pablo is bleeding and he doesn't move. Now the
man has taken Camille!"

"What?" Elena gasped. "What are you saying? Who has
taken Camille?"

"Senor Hernan Valdez." Pina's expression didn't change.
"He is mad with drinking. Camille didn't want to let him in, but
he was with two of her good customers." She shrugged. "He is
loco, that one. When he's like that he does evil things to the girls
and no one will go with him. He says if he can't have the girls, he
will take Camille. She is prettier anyway."

The name had already frozen the blood in her veins, but the
mention of Camille broke the ice with a blaze of broiling anger.
"He will not harm her," Elena snarled, running to the kitchen
and picking up the long-bladed knife Camille used so expertly
when she prepared their meals. "Go and bring the *policia*. I will
stop him from hurting Camille."

The girl was still whimpering her protests when Elena raced
across the courtyard and into the big house. She hesitated only a
moment, then followed the sounds of the girls' screams through
the twisting corridors of the *Casa de Flores*. Most of the girls
were huddled together in a bright-colored knot outside the door
at the top of the stairs, and it was from behind that door that the
pitiful cries were coming.

Leaving her fear behind, Elena ran up the stairs and pushed
the door open. The scene was just as she'd imagined: the room
was very like the one where she'd met Carlos, but now it was
being used quite differently.

Camille lay on the brightly-draped bed, her dark clothing a
pile of rags on the floor. A thin trickle of blood ran from the
corner of her mouth, and there were several bruises on her face.
Now, however, as Hernan moved to claim his prize, she lay still,
her face frozen in a kind of terror that even Elena couldn't
imagine—though she knew the evil de la Mer had been capable
of doing.

"Leave her alone, Hernan," she said, her voice sounding strangely serene in her own ears. "You don't really want her, you know. I'm the one you want."

For a moment she was afraid the words wouldn't be enough, but the handsome head lifted and the reddened eyes turned her way. For a brief second memories of her own night of terror filled her mind, then she pushed them ruthlessly away, keeping the knife concealed in the flared skirt of her gown.

"*Elena!*" he gasped. Camille was quickly forgotten, though she lay naked before him.

Elena faced him as though they were alone in the room. "Why did you tell everyone I stole from you?" she demanded. "*You* are the thief. You took my innocence, my home, my family, even tried to steal my life from me. You are filth, Hernan, a killer and a defiler, but you won't have your way this time, not with Camille."

As she'd known he would, he lunged at her, fury in his face, his eyes half-mad with drink and frustration. Elena stood still till his fingers caught at her shoulders, then she lifted the knife and tried to use it. His elbow caught the blow, deflecting it slightly, but she felt the impact as it struck his side and his shriek of pain filled the air.

For a moment she stood over him, the knife still in her hand, blood flowing freely to stain her skirt and wet her bare feet. There were sounds from behind her, and in a moment strong hands caught her arm and took the knife from her now-nerveless fingers. "Bind her arms," a man ordered. "Put her over there." Elena was dragged to one side as the man, in the garb of the local *policia*, knelt beside Hernan.

"Senor Valdez," he said. "What happened?"

After that, everything happened so quickly Elena really had no clear recollection of the separate events. Only small flashes of it stayed in her mind. She saw Camille, dressed once more, talking earnestly to the *policia*, but couldn't hear her words. Another man had come—a higher official of the *policia*, or so Elena assumed—though of course nothing was said. He and a hastily summoned physician were busy with Hernan while the original policeman stood watch over her.

She was still waiting in the hall when Hernan was carried out. He was pale, but looked much stronger than she'd hoped he would be when he ordered the men to stop before her. "You'll pay for this," he said. "When my strength returns, I'll make you pay. For now, you'll be well cared for. Don't think of escape, dear Elena. Remember, I'll have your child—the son *Capitan* Diego told me about."

The words brought her first sob, and the vicious fury in his eyes frightened her more than anything else could. She tried to pull free of her bonds, of the men holding her, but she couldn't. He was carried out, laughing triumphantly before he lapsed into groans of pain.

"What will happen to me?" she demanded of the man who held her.

The man shrugged, his expression telling her he truly didn't know. "It will be decided by the *Capitan*," he said. "He is in charge here."

She was roughly hauled down the stairs and carried out the door before she could speak to anyone else. Once outside she was hurled into the bottom of an old wagon and covered with what felt like grain sacks. "Lie still or die," she was ordered, and she felt a sharp pricking in her spine.

It was a nightmare journey, never-ending. Sometimes she wondered if she was being taken to the *hacienda* after all, but she dared not lift her head or even shift her position to ask. She could only lie still and wait. By the time the wagon finally stopped, she was so battered and weary she scarcely cared where she was.

Rough hands dragged her from the wagon and held her as she stumbled on legs long numbed and useless. "Where am I?" she asked.

"Fort St. Joseph," the *guarda* said, his eyes appraising. "And a welcome addition, I might add. It's a pity our orders are so explicit. I fancy we could work out much better terms for you, if you were willing to be cooperative." His eyes made his meaning clear and Elena shivered, wishing her arms were free to cover her breasts as they strained against the bodice of her gown.

"Don't cringe away, little girl," the *guarda* said bitterly. "You've nothing to fear from me. You come well protected. It seems someone has very special plans for your future." His laughter was anything but reassuring.

The cell was small and dark, the only opening a grill in the door that opened from the corridor.

Elena was untied, then thrust roughly inside. She fell on

damp and musty-smelling straw, and before she could scramble to her feet the door was locked and the *guardas* were gone—taking the weak but welcome glow of their lantern with them and leaving her in absolute darkness. Terror haunted her as she listened to the shifting of the dirty straw and heard the distant, disappearing sound of footsteps. Once it died away, she was alone in the blackness.

For the first few hours she almost welcomed a terror bordering on madness. Her screams echoed painfully in her own ears and she crashed into the wet walls as she stumbled about in her fear. Then exhaustion overcame her, stilling her cries, and she dropped once more to the floor. There was no one to hear her, she realized, no one to care. This was a fort, not a prison, and the *guardas* had left her long ago.

With silence came a kind of acceptance and relief. Only her fear for Louis penetrated the trancelike calm. What would Hernan do to the little boy? He would know at once that the child was not his. He might, in fact, even recognize the grey eyes that even now had the power to haunt her.

"Louis," she sobbed, "Oh, Louis, how am I to help you?"

Time passed slowly, though she had no way of knowing how much, or even whether it was day or night in the world beyond her prison. Her long hours of darkness were broken regularly by the arrival of food and fresh water. She was given two blankets, and once she was taken from the cell long enough for the old straw to be raked up and fresh put down. When that happened she dared to ask, "What is to become of me?"

The young man guarding her only shrugged. "My orders are to see that you live, Senorita, nothing more."

"Whose orders?" Elena asked.

He shrugged again. "I do not ask questions," he said. "You have a powerful enemy, for this is not a prison. And with the British fleet beyond our port, you should not be here."

"The British fleet?" Elena's senses sharpened slightly. "Are they going to attack?"

The man laughed. "They shelled our forts once and sailed away. I doubt they will do more this time, though it is rumored that the man who leads the fleet is already bragging of how he will spend the treasure of Cartegena."

"And if they come?"

"You will die."

Elena swallowed hard.

The man laughed, reaching out to caress her arm with his faintly damp hand. "Don't be afraid," he said, "I would have much better plans for you than the touch of a knife. You are wasted in this darkness." His eyes devoured her, and after that Elena preferred the dark solitude to the times when he brought her food or water.

The other man was older, more taciturn. Still, the time came when he was very late, and his face was much graver than usual when he opened the heavy door of her cell. "Wasn't sure you'd still be here," he said, setting down the bowl of stew and half-loaf of bread that was her unvarying diet.

"Where would I go?" Elena asked, smiling a little shyly.

"Thought perhaps you'd been moved, that's all." The man's face didn't change as he picked up the crusted empty dishes and prepared to leave.

"Please, why would I be moved?" Elena asked.

Dark eyes turned her way, studying her gravely without the lust that always sparked the other *guarda's* gaze. "I know nothing of why you're here," he said.

"But you just said . . ." Elena began.

"'Tis the ships outside the harbour I was thinking of," the *guarda* said.

"Ships? What ships?" Elena felt a surge of hope.

"Some British dog has come sniffing around again. Seems he had some luck and took Porto Bello as she lay like a fat lady in the sun. Now he's turned his greedy eyes on our gold and brought his fleet here to try to steal it."

"The British are invading?" Elena swallowed hard, remembering that Carlos had warned her it might happen, and remembering too what the other *guarda* had said about her not surviving the attack. "But . . ."

"I'm sure there'll be orders to move you back into the city," the *guarda* said, going to the door. "Since you're to be cared for so special, it's not likely you'll be allowed to fall into enemy hands." His eyes went over her again. "Not that you'd enjoy it, I'm sure. I've heard what they do when they plunder a town."

Elena shivered. "When do you think they'll attack?" she asked.

"They didn't give me their plans," he said without humor, "but you'll be hearing the guns. Even down here you'll hear the guns." He sighed, then went out, taking the lantern with him. In the darkness he left behind, she could hardly find her way to her water and bread. The food didn't touch the icy emptiness in the pit of her stomach, though she ate every bit of it. The once ominous silence was now more welcome as she leaned back to consider what he had said.

What did it mean, this threatened invasion? What would happen to her if the British took this very fort? Would they attack her as she'd heard, or would the fact that she was a prisoner give them pause. Would they perhaps allow her to escape?

And if she escaped, what of Louis? She could not leave Cartagena without her son, that she knew well. She smiled in bitter amusement at herself—a fool who thought worriedly about leaving Cartagena while the door was still locked and she lived in darkness. How much more likely it was that she'd be found dead in this cell or, perhaps more frightening, be taken like a bound animal from it and transported to the *hacienda* of Senor Hernan Valdez. She had no illusion about surviving a visit like that, and—knowing the man—she was sure that death here would be preferable and far quicker.

"Oh, Louis," she whispered. "Louis, if only I could hold you again." She cried for the first time in many days. And even as the first teardrops fell, she heard a distant sound like thunder and then louder thunder from above. The stones trembled with the sounds that went on and on and on...

Chapter 41

JAMIE STUDIED THE distant fortifications of Cartegena with definite misgivings. When they'd shelled the port city before, he'd complained that it was insulting without purpose, but everyone had laughed. Now he wondered how much fortifications had been improved because of the previous brush with the fleet. This was, he suspected, a far more difficult target than Porto Bello had been.

He cast an eye over the more than one hundred ships of the fleet, glad of the reinforcements that had joined them during their months at Port Royal. They made an impressive sight, but beneath the exterior promise he already sensed trouble brewing between the Vice-Admiral and General Wentworth, who was to have charge of the land forces of the proposed invasion.

Not that he really cared how the battle went, he thought, still despairing. Then he remembered his son—born too soon, but clinging to life with surprising energy. For him, Jamie must survive.

His gaze returned to the city. Two narrow peninsulas protected the entrance of the harbour, and the entrance was so narrow that only one ship could pass through it at a time. On one side it was guarded by the square fort St. Louis, with its four bastions, and the smaller forts St. Phillip and St. Jago.

Across the narrow entrance was the Baradera with a battery of fifteen guns. There was also a small, flat island on that side, and on it was the fort St. Joseph with twenty-one guns. The entrance itself, called the *Bocca Chica* was guarded by a boom or underwater barricade, designed to rip the bottom out of any ship foolish enough to sail past the cannon. Beyond all that protection four large ships of the line waited, all turned to give broadsides to anyone who survived the perilous *Bocca Chica*.

They began at dawn, sailing sternly toward the forbidding forts. The outer battery, the Chamba, was first to fire, but the guns of the *Princess Amelia* soon silenced it. By noon the ships *Norfolk*, *Russel*, and *Shrewsbury* were anchored very close to forts St. Jago and St. Phillip, their cannon blazing so viciously that it took little more than an hour to reduce the forts to the point that the Spaniards abandoned them.

Cheering marines were rowed ashore to take possession, and for a while everyone was laughing and talking about another Porto Bello and speculating eagerly on what the shares of the treasure might be from this city—reputed by some to hold more gold than any other Spanish port. The laughter turned to concern, however, as the *Shrewsbury* swung free of a cut cable, exposing her stern to the pounding of the Spanish ships within the harbour.

"If she holds, I'll be the whole night mending the damage to her men," Reggie muttered as he stood with Jamie on the deck watching the battle. "That is, if she survives the day."

"She'll hold," a stern voice said behind them, and Jamie nodded, agreeing with the Vice-Admiral.

"Captain Townsend won't give ground," Jamie said, having met the man a number of times in Port Royal.

The long afternoon proved him correct. The battle raged till the air was blue with smoke and burned their eyes and lungs. Reggie, having proved himself the most able surgeon in the fleet, was soon summoned away, and Jamie was left alone to stare at the shore and wonder when he would be called upon to lead his men against one of the forts.

He stood with patience. Sally's death had aged him. He felt very much a man now, aware of his responsibilities. He felt differently about this battle, about wars in general. For the first time he'd begun to realize that some of what his father had told him so long ago made more sense than this slaughter for gold.

Nightfall ended the battle and he reported to his commander for a short report before going below to the area that was Reggie's hospital. Seriously injured men from other ships were being brought aboard, and a few stomach-wrenching moments were all he could bear of it. Men without arms or legs, men burned almost beyond recognition but screaming in agony, men blinded or shattered.

Jamie went back up on deck and stared at the city, wanting to hate the Spanish for what they'd done but not really able to. He'd heard too many stories at Port Royal; he knew what the invading men would do to the people of the city if they didn't surrender their gold as willingly as the people of Porto Bello and Chagre had. In the heat and excitement of battle the glory remained, and he had felt the glow of it; but afterward, when the price was counted in pain and death . . . He was not so sure then.

A face filled his mind, a face the love and sorrow of the past year hadn't dimmed. Did Elena ever think of him? he wondered. Had she changed? He sighed and looked up at the stars, promising himself—as he had so many nights before—that he would go to France once he had got his son safely to England. All he needed to do was make a friendly call on the Flambeaus, a polite inquiry after the girl he'd claimed to know so casually and then he would know.

He shook his head, wondering if he would ever be able to forget her. The compliant and lovely Sally had done her best, and so—in her way—had Rebecca, but all their kisses, even the miracle of having a son, hadn't touched the core of him as the mere dream-memory of his Elena had. The only thing that had claimed his attention for a while had been his single-minded search for Rebecca, and even that had failed before they sailed from Port Royal. Even revenge was no escape.

"You'd best come below," Percy said at his shoulder. "Tomorrow we'll be turning our attention to the big one, Fort St. Louis, and I've a hunch it won't be as easy to capture as the others were."

Jamie nodded. "Have you talked to Reggie?" he asked, thinking that the two men had become like brothers to him in his time of trouble. Without them, he wondered if he would have survived the night of the storm.

Percy nodded. "We won't be seeing much of him for a while," he said. "They had twenty killed and forty wounded on the *Shrewsbury*, and the ship is almost a wreck. Knowing our Reggie, he'll have the worst of them in his care."

Jamie nodded, thinking privately that Reggie might be the bravest of them all, for his battles had no real glory and his enemies were tireless and far more cruel than any human could be. He slept poorly that night, and woke feeling the day ahead would not be a good one.

The next three days were much alike. The shelling continued as the landing forces were readied for an attack on Fort St. Louis, but before the invasion could be mounted Vice-Admiral Vernon changed his mind. He called a conference.

"There is far too much dangerous firing from the forts on the Baradera side of the entrance," he said. "I think it would be wiser to attack the forts on both sides at once. We can try to take the ones on the Baradera side by surprise, if possible. They will think we are still attacking only fort St. Louis."

Jamie leaned forward, well aware that his marines would have a part in the assault and eager for the action. Sea battles held no joy for him, and he longed for the more usual use of sword or musket or even the fury of hand-to-hand combat with the enemy. He'd spent many hours during the last weeks in Port Royal bringing his swordsmanship back up to the standards Ian had set for him when he was a boy, and he was anxious to make use of it. Combat might fill the emptiness he felt, as nothing else had.

The weather, which had been fretful since they approached the city, was showing no sign of improving as the rainy season settled around them and the invading force was held up by the bad weather till the night of March 19th.

They landed at midnight but were sighted, and the guns began firing upon them. Moving swiftly, they gained the walls and quickly took charge of the small battery; but the alarm had been given and their task became impossible. They spiked the guns they'd taken and burned the battery, then returned to the ship with light losses.

The days began to take on a terrible sameness for Jamie. Each day different ships were sent forward to pound the walls of the forts that still controlled both sides of the *Bocca Chica*, but still they held. Losses grew heavier, and soon Reggie's hospital would hold no more and he became grey-faced and haunted as he worked over the suffering wounded. When he wasn't needed on deck, Jamie went to help him, as did Percy, though there was little they could do to ease the agony of the continuing parade of shattered men.

Then there were the sick. The rainy season had brought with it fevers and other weaknesses that struck the men down with the same violence as the firing of the enemy. None of the usual methods seem to help them and many died, shivering and shaking in their bunks.

By the twenty-fifth, Vice-Admiral Vernon decided it was time to make another try for both the forts that controlled the *Bocca Chica*. Parties were sent against the still-holding Fort St. Louis and against the Baradera forts. Jamie and his men were sent with Captain Knowles to the island Fort St. Joseph. Here they met with very little resistance, storming the fort and carrying it with no loss of life.

The Captain, well pleased, accepted Jamie's report that the guns had been silenced. "You stay here with your men," he said. "Search the place to the lowest dungeons and make sure they haven't left powder and ammunition behind. We're going to try the entrance and see if we can get into the harbour now the dons are on the run."

Jamie opened his mouth to protest, to plead with the Captain to allow him to go along and have a part in the attack, but the man was gone before he could frame the request. Shrugging, Jamie went out to issue commands to his small company of men and, once the larger force had left, to begin the routine search of the fort.

There was little to be found. Jamie ranged through the dank corridors with his lantern, looking into the open cells that lined both sides. They found supplies here and there, and signs that someone had set up a lower-level guard post. There was even a small stack of heavy trays, food bowls, and mugs, some of them dirty.

Curious, Jamie made his way down to the deepest recess of the fort, noting as he went along that there were marks of other boots along the damp passageway. Was the Captain right? he wondered. Could there be a secret magazine in the depths here? Or were there troops hidden here, perhaps waiting to mount a surprise attack from the rear once they left the fort?

A sound from the shadows ahead made him stiffen, then he identified it as a moan. Moving more cautiously, he approached a closed door, the first he'd seen in these levels. The light showed a grill, but little beyond it.

"Help me," a voice pleaded. "Please God, someone help me."

"Who is there?" Jamie demanded, stiffening at the hollow echo of his voice.

Silence was his only answer. He stared through the grill, but could make out little more than a huddled form on the far side of the small cell. He looked around and saw a ring of keys hanging on the opposite wall. Nervously, he took it down. It took him three tries to find the key that opened the lock in the door. It creaked ominously as he forced it open and stepped inside.

The creature stirred, blinking as the light reached her. Wild, filthy hair hung about a gaunt face. Damp clothing clung to a woman's figure, but the eyes that looked out at him were those of a frightened animal.

"I'm not going to hurt you," Jamie said in Spanish. "Don't be afraid, I've come to set you free."

"Free?" A hand lifted to push back the straggling hair, and suddenly the eyes focused and the pale skin seemed to grow even paler. "Jamie?" the woman whimpered. "*Por Dios*, I am already dead if I see you here."

For just a heartbeat he could only stare at the poor creature, then the glint of the light in the woman's eyes kindled and he saw that they were green. He stepped nearer, not believing his own senses as he looked more closely. "Elena?" he gasped. *Elena?*"

Her sobs were answer enough. Without another word he gathered her in his arms and carried her out of the cell, through the twisting corridors till they reached an upper level room that had served the men who'd manned the fort. There he lowered her gently on a cot and left her to get water and food for her. Only after she'd had a chance to drink and eat and wash herself did he ask her how she'd come to be in such a place.

Her explanation shocked him. As she spoke of what had happened, the letter from Hernan Valdez and the way she'd been thrown out, he began to curse. He did little else as she described what had happened on the island of St. Domingue. When she reached the part about her escape from the island he interrupted, suddenly aware of a stir outside the room where one of his men stood guard.

"But how did you get here?" he asked. "This isn't a prison, is it?"

Elena shook her head. Her hair, freshly washed, was drying

in waves about her shoulders, and she looked absurdly young in the men's clothing she'd donned after washing. "He had me kept here. I wounded him when he was going to rape Camille, and..."

"Who?" Jamie interrupted, aware that he'd missed much of her story but afraid to take the time to hear it all now.

"Hernan Valdez," Elena said, and the fires of hate burned in her green eyes once again. "He's here, outside the city. He means to kill me this time. He had me kept here until he is well enough to enjoy it."

"Well, you have nothing to fear," Jamie said. "I'll have you taken to my ship at once. The Captain may be a little upset, but as soon as you tell him that you're a Frenchwoman held prisoner by the Spanish, and my fiancée..."

For a moment her eyes glowed in a way that made him want to take her in his arms, then the glow disappeared. "I cannot," she said, lowering her head.

Anger touched him, but he pushed it away. "What is there to keep you here?" he asked, careful to keep his tone very casual, well aware that the years had changed him and might well have changed her, too. She'd given him few details of her life as she outlined her travels.

"My son," she said, not looking at him. "That was how he kept me alive in this place. He said if I died, he would kill Louis."

"He would kill a child?" The words were forced from Jamie on a tide of pain as he thought of someone else touching her, siring a child. "Surely even a man like that would stop at the taking of an innocent child's life."

Elena's head came up and her eyes blazed at him. "Hernan would do anything to hurt me," she snapped.

Jealousy swirled inside him and it took all his control to keep from reaching out to shake her, to demand to know about the child, about her life; then he forced himself to remember his own life and all he'd done since they parted. His anger cooled a little, and the feeling he'd denied so long surged back in its place. For the first time he fully accepted his love for her for what it was. Skinny, starved, half-mad from being abandoned in the dark for God knew how long, driven wild with worry over her son—he loved her as he'd never loved poor Sally or the bewitching whore who was her sister.

"Do you know where the boy is?" he asked her at last, his voice sounding slightly altered even to his own ears.

"No," Elena admitted, "but Carlos will know."

"Who is Carlos?" Jamie asked, his jealousy returning.

"He was my father's head man, and he stayed on to serve on the *hacienda* after my father died. He came here with the family." Her voice dropped. "I talked to him once before Hernan found me again. He will know about Louis. He will have protected him, if it was possible."

Jamie hesitated only a moment, weighing his feeling against the lies she might be telling him, the life she could have lived since he left her in France. Was he being a fool again? he asked himself, remembering both Amelia Starburough and his days with Rebecca in English Harbour. But the answer was beyond the cold logic of his mind. It had to do with the fact that he'd never been able to forget her, and never would if he let her go now. The eyes that met his were not flirtatious or even smiling, and her face was marked with suffering. Still, she was beautiful to him.

"Where is this Carlos?" he asked, surrendering.

"There is an estate beyond the city," Elena said. "Camille will know the way."

"Then we'll go there and get your son," Jamie said, going to the door. He summoned the Sergeant and, ignoring Elena's startled face, said to him, "This woman is a friend of mine. She is French, but she speaks excellent Spanish. I think with her help I can get into the city and examine the fortifications and see the morale of the people. I can learn more in a few hours that way than all the ships have accomplished in the weeks we've shelled the forts."

The Sergeant stirred and opened his mouth, but before he could interrupt Jamie went on. "You can take charge here, and when you are recalled to the ship—or when the Captain returns—you will tell him I've undertaken a spying mission. Is that clear?"

"But you'll be in terrible danger, sir," the Sergeant protested. "And how do you know you can trust this woman?"

"When I return I'll have knowledge that may save all our lives," Jamie said.

"Your spying may not be needed," the Sergeant argued. "I've

just had word that they've entered the harbour."

"All the more reason for me to get beyond the walls and into the city itself," Jamie said. "It must be near nightfall, and with the confusion of all that's happened we'll have a good chance." He looked at Elena. "Do you have the strength?" he asked.

She nodded, her eyes quiet now, strangely peaceful.

Jamie allowed himself a smile, sharing her feelings. "I'll use a bit of this boot black to stain my hair, then change to some of the clothing the former tenants have so kindly provided," he said. "My uniform might not be so welcome inside the city walls."

Her eyes met his, and he felt the depths of her courage. More than that, he saw the love that burned there, undimmed by what she'd suffered. He longed to hold her and kiss her, but there was no time. Memories of the stain he'd once spread on her fair skin haunted him as he dyed his hair, and he was glad that the Jamaican sun had made his own skin dark enough. Almost too soon it was time to go.

Chapter 42

ELENA SAT QUIETLY in the boat as Jamie rowed them to shore. She had little to say as they walked the long miles into the city itself; the miracle of having Jamie find her seemed enough for now. Just being out of the cell, seeing the sky and smelling the damp air with its heavy scent of flowers—it was all like a dream, and sometimes she was afraid she would awaken and find herself once more in the cell, lying on the musty straw waiting for death.

It was only when they were within the city walls, mingling with the frightened crowd, that Jamie brought her mind back into focus. "Where is this Camille?" he asked.

"She takes care of the girls in a brothel," Elena said, and cringed slightly at the look she saw on Jamie's face. There was still so much she hadn't told him.

"You know a woman like that?" he asked, plainly shocked.

"She hid me from Hernan when there was no one else," Elena said defiantly. "She suffered at the hands of the animal on St. Domingue, the one I told you about, and cared for me because I was responsible for his death."

"You lived in a place like that?"

She sensed that he was drawing away from her and her heart felt torn, but she held her head up, determined to be as honest with Jamie as she had been with Jean. "I lived with Camille," she said quietly.

Jamie stopped. "Was she one of the girls in that house?"

"Of course not," Elena said, her cheeks burning slightly at the suggestion. "She couldn't bear the touch of any man after what de la Mer did to her. She looked after the girls who worked there. She was trying to help them when Hernan took her." She stopped, not wanting to remember. "I only wish my arm had been stronger and my knife had not deflected. He deserved to die."

"Is that where we're going?" Jamie asked after a long period of silence. "To the brothel?"

Elena stopped. "You've seen the city," she said, forcing herself to set him free of whatever responsibility he might feel. One man had died because he loved her; she didn't want to risk Jamie's life, too. "You're safely inside, and I'm sure you'll be able to get out again without my help. You don't have to come with me. Setting me free... You saved my life, and I'll always be grateful, but Hernan Valdez would recognize you, too. If he sees you, you'll be killed as a spy. Louis is my responsibility. I'll find him somehow."

"And what?" Jamie's face was closed and unreadable. "What will happen to you then? You can't protect yourself, let alone a child. You're coming with me. We'll find your son, then I'm taking you back to the ship where you'll be safe." His hands touched her arm, then suddenly they were in the shadows of a balcony and she was in his arms. His lips found hers and she felt a blaze of desire that melted her body against his. When he let her go, he looked as shaken as she felt.

"We will be married when we reach Port Royal," he said. "I don't care what you've done or where you've lived. I'll never let you go again, Elena."

A part of her heart leaped with joy for a moment, then dropped. His very proposal was a surrender to his need, nothing more, she realized. His very words showed his doubts. He'd never trust her, never believe her innocence. Once he'd seen the *Casa del Flores*—heard of her life with Raul—it would be over. She had no right to expect marriage after all that had happened to her. She dropped her head. "You don't need to marry me," she said quietly. "I'm sure the bride your father chose for you is still waiting."

Jamie swore. "That match was broken long ago. Much has happened to me since I escaped that witch's clutches," he said, his face dark with anger. "Now, how soon will we find this Camille of yours?"

"Soon," Elena murmured, looking around. "The *Casa del Flores* is just ahead, behind that wall."

The gate was locked, and there was no answer to her pounding. Confused and worried, Elena gave up knocking and moved around the familiar streets, seeking someone—anyone—who might be able to tell her what had happened. It was nearly an hour before she recognized one of the scurrying figures as the girl who'd come for her help the night of her arrest.

"Pina," she called, stopping her. "Where is Camille? What has happened to her?"

The girl's eyes widened as she saw Elena's male attire. For a moment she feared Pina might faint, then her color returned. "We thought you were dead," Pina said.

"I very nearly was," Elena admitted. "Now, what happened?"

"They took your boy that night. Camille was like one demented. She closed the house and left, said she was going back to her home, that she never wanted to see Cartegena again. She sailed three days before the fleet came." Pina took a breath. "But what about you, Senora? How did you escape?"

"I haven't time to tell you," Elena said, very much aware of the girl's curious glances at Jamie and at her strange attire. "I must find my son. Can you tell me how to reach the Valdez *hacienda?*"

The directions were simple enough, and using the money Jamie supplied Elena quickly managed to rent a small wagon. They left the city just before sunrise, heading inland away from the sea. As they rode along, Elena tried to find words to tell Jamie about Louis, but he gave her no chance.

The quiet man she'd known seemed to have vanished in the many months they'd been apart. Jamie talked as though driven to it. He began with his return to London, talking of the woman he had been meant to marry. He told her about his friends Percy and Reggie and the life they shared on the ship. Then his words slowed and he spoke of a wife.

Elena felt her heart breaking as he described his marriage, the

life in Port Royal, the child he'd sired. Then she sensed a change
and he spoke more quickly, anger in his voice as he told her of his
wife's death and the woman who'd caused it.

Finally he drew a deep shuddering breath. "I have a son,
Elena," he said. "He's being cared for on the plantation, but I'll
want him with me. I cheated Sally because I didn't love her as a
man should love his wife, but I must make it up to Fergus. Can
you understand that?"

"I know what it is to love a child," Elena said softly, suddenly
afraid to tell Jamie the truth. From what he'd said, she knew he
would insist on marrying her once he knew Louis was his son—
and at the same time, she knew such a marriage was not what she
wanted. If he couldn't love her for herself and in spite of what
she'd been, she could not marry him. "If it hadn't been for Louis,
I would have killed myself long ago," she said. "I only hope and
pray we're not too late now."

They rode in silence for a while, then Elena asked, "What will
your father say when you take your son to England? Has he
forgiven you for not marrying the girl he chose for you?"

Jamie smiled. "He has forgiven me and accepted my
marriage to Sally, but I'm not going to return to England, except
perhaps for a visit."

Elena frowned. "You wish to continue on the sea?" she asked.
"Make the Navy your life?" His descriptions of the battles and
some of the ugliness of ship life made her think otherwise; but he
seemed to have withdrawn from her again, disappeared into his
own thoughts and become a stranger. She pictured herself in a
small house in Port Royal, waiting for his ship to return to the
harbour there, seeing him only when the fleet was at rest. It was
not what she would have chosen, but she was too weary to run
any longer—and she loved him far too much to insist that he
marry her.

"I've talked to several men who've been north to the English
colonies, and they speak well of life there," Jamie said, then
sighed. "I'd planned to settle down on my plantation, but after
what happened there it would be hard." He shook his head. "I
think a man could make a good home in the northern colonies,
start a new life."

"You would leave the Navy?" she asked, not sure what his
words meant. His talk about marriage had been so long ago she
was no longer sure she was included in his plans for a new life.

"I've more than enough gold to buy my way out of the Navy and to purchase land in the colonies," Jamie said, and she felt his grey eyes on her, searching her face. "I've many investments in Jamaica, and there are plenty of people who'd like to buy them."

"Is that what you want?" Elena asked, frightened by the coldness of the conversation.

He shrugged. "I've had little time to decide," he said. "And what of you? What do you want now?"

"To have my son with me and to be safe," Elena said. She met his eyes, then took a deep breath. "I . . . Raul forced me to be his mistress before I escaped from France with the LaCroixs, Jamie," she said, hating the ugliness of the words, but determined to have the worst of her past before him as soon as possible, before her weakness and love led her to live a lie rather than let him go. "I had no choice—it was his protection or the streets when my family turned me out. I couldn't even choose death, for I was carrying Louis at the time."

Jamie swore softly. "The bastard," he said. "I should have known he couldn't be trusted. I should never have left you there."

Elena shrugged. "Perhaps I should have gone back to Mallorca," she said with a sigh. "Perhaps my mother would have understood and helped me. She survived the news of my death and has a son—*his* son. She might have helped me to escape him, sent me to Le Mans in proper style."

"The man in the grove was your stepfather, wasn't it?" Jamie asked, remembering how he'd felt so long ago and wondering at his own blindness.

Elena nodded. "I lied to you to keep you from being killed," she said simply. "It's the only lie I've ever told you, or ever will tell you."

Jamie reached out and took her hand as their eyes met again. "I believe you," he said.

"Now you understand why I couldn't accept your proposal of marriage," Elena said. "After what happened with Raul you could never marry me."

Jamie's eyes dropped for a moment, but his fingers tightened on her hand. "Do you love me, Elena?" he asked. "Did you ever stop loving me?"

His eyes bored into her as he waited for her answer. "I never loved anyone else," she said softly.

"That's enough for now," he said, looking around. "Does this look like the area that girl described to you?"

Elena tore her gaze from his face, her heart pounding with a mixture of hope and fear. He hadn't denied her or pulled away. It wasn't the proposal of her dreams, the romantic love whispers of those long ago days on Mallorca; but for now, as he'd said, it was enough. She studied the landscape, then nodded. "That opening to the right must be the field road she told us about, the one that leads to the slave quarters."

Jamie watched her closely, confused. This was not the Elena of his dreams, not even the girl he'd kissed so passionately in Cartagena. She seemed so cold and withdrawn, in spite of what they'd said. As he guided the weary donkey down the road she indicated, his mind went once more to the child they'd come after. She'd told him so much, but not the one thing he wanted to know: who had fathered it?

He wished he'd dared to ask her, but something had kept him from it. Could it be Raul, her own cousin? But no, she'd said she was already carrying the child when he forced her to submit to him.

"Is the child Hernan's?" he demanded. "Is he mad enough to harm his own son?"

"Louis is not Hernan's child," Elena said, her tone so icy he feared to ask more, though his mind spun at the implications.

Who could it be? He tried to remember what she'd told him in those first minutes at the fort, but he could find no mention of a suitor or another man after he left her in France. She'd mentioned no one till the old man in St. Domingue and the madman who'd killed him.

Pictures rose in his mind. He remembered her in his arms, stripping off the boy's clothing, caressing her till . . . But that had been a dream. He shook his head a little.

If only he'd stayed in France with her, he thought bitterly. Or taken her to England with him. He'd been a fool, he thought bitterly, a self-righteous fool to believe one man's cruelty could change Elena from a proper girl to something less. He'd treated her as though it were her fault, as though she'd misbehaved as Amelia had, instead of having been brutally attacked and nearly killed.

He could feel himself blushing at the memories of their days and nights together. His shame made him want to stop the donkey and hold her in his arms and promise never to hurt her again; but when he looked at her, the remoteness of her expression kept him from moving.

He turned his thoughts to the future. The idea of marrying her and making a new life in the English colonies had been a sudden one, but he liked it. They could go to London first, of course, so that he could make peace with his father; but he had no desire to settle there. And having seen more of the world, he was no longer anxious to return to his uncle's lands either.

Jamie glanced again at Elena, seeing not the girl he remembered but a woman, her eyes filled with fear as she looked ahead. She was more than beautiful now, he thought, shaken at the idea. The bloom of girlhood was gone, and with it the look of injured innocence he remembered only too well. But even the long weeks of imprisonment and the horror she'd suffered before hadn't tarnished her delicate features, or erased the firm courage that gave her dignity even as her hair escaped from her hat and fell to her shoulders, making a mockery of her man's disguise.

"You'd better tuck your hair back up," he said, giving one curling russet lock a gentle tug. "We don't want to be reported to the master here."

Elena jumped as though his hand had burned her and he drew it back, more confused than ever. Had her kiss been a lie? Was there someone else in spite of what she'd said, perhaps the father of her son?

"What's the plan?" he asked, to escape his own thoughts. "How do we find the boy?"

"First I'll have to find Carlos," she said. "He should be in the stable area." She glanced at the sky. "It's late enough for him to have returned from whatever duties he has here."

"And me?" Jamie asked.

Her eyes appraised him. "You'd better stay hidden," she said. "Even with your dark hair you don't look like a peasant. Why don't you hide in there with the wagon?" She pointed to a small grove of trees thickly fringed with brush. "I'll come back as soon as I talk to Carlos."

Jamie took her arm again and felt his pulse quicken the

moment he touched her; even now he wanted her, he realized. "Don't do anything without talking to me first," he said. "Don't take any risks. Perhaps this Carlos can bring the boy to us. You must not be seen, Elena. This is his territory, and I can't protect you if I'm not with you."

For a moment she looked up at him and she was again the girl from the garden at Mallorca, the bewitching young girl he'd fallen in love with; then her eyes changed and grew hard. "I must save Louis," she said quietly. "He means more to me than my own life."

Jamie dropped his hand abruptly, turning away slightly. "We'll get him," he said with more confidence than he felt. Deep down, he was afraid that this entire mission might be futile. The man he remembered from Mallorca wouldn't hesitate to kill a child, he was sure, not after what he'd done to Elena. He looked at her, suspecting that she was haunted by the same fears.

For a moment he considered saying something to her, trying to prepare her for what she might find at the house, but a look into her eyes stopped his words. His suspicions were already reflected there and, he suspected, were joined by others more horrible than he had considered. He lifted her down from the wagon, holding her only a second longer than necessary. "Be careful," he said before he led the donkey into the grove to wait.

It seemed forever that he waited, listening to the insects that buzzed about the flowers that grew thick after the heavy rains of the past few weeks. The donkey grazed happily on the lush growth and Jamie's eyes burned with a need for sleep, but he was too worried to yield to it. He moved about the grove restlessly, spending most of his time at the edge nearest the stable, hoping for a glimpse of Elena. He was, however, at the wagon when a soft sound made him turn and he saw a woman slipping into the shadowed area. His hand went to the knife he wore in his belt. He had it out before a soft giggle stayed his hand.

"Don't you recognize me as a woman?" Elena asked, her eyes sparkling in spite of the weariness in her face.

"Where did you get those clothes?" he demanded, half-angry at the fright she'd given him.

"Carlos got them for me." Her smile deepened. "Louis is safe. Carlos has seen to that."

"Where is he?" Jamie asked, trying to regain his composure by tending strictly to business. "How do we get him?"

Elena's face grew serious. "He's in the main house. Hernan is taking no chances with him. That's the reason for these clothes. I'll slip in pretending to be a maid, then just scoop him up and run. Hernan is away this afternoon attending some sort of meeting—about gathering men from the outlying areas to help in the defense of the city. Carlos thinks he will be home soon and he always checks on Louis when he returns. Once he's done that, we can take Louis and have the entire evening and night before he's discovered missing."

"No one watches over him?" Jamie asked. "What of the servants?"

Elena's smile was bitter. "They have no more love for Hernan than I do. Carlos said they would protect themselves with some lies." She sighed. "I only wish I could cut his heart out before we leave. He deserves to die. Carlos told me he planned to kill Louis the day I was brought to him from the fort." She closed her eyes. "His body would have been presented to me before Hernan killed me."

Jamie shook his head. "Thank God we got here in time," he said.

The sound of hoofs on the road beyond their hiding place interrupted him, and they both moved to the edge of the grove in time to see Hernan Valdez driving himself in a fine carriage. His face was twisted with brutal anger as he lashed at the already lathered horses, then jerked them to a standstill in the stableyard.

"Carlos!" he bellowed, his voice clearly audible. "Bring me the bastard!"

Elena gasped, knowing only too well to whom he was referring. Together they hurried out of the grove, slipping as close as they could to the stableyard, hiding behind the heavy growth the rainy season had brought to life.

"The child is sleeping, Senor," Carlos said. "Is something wrong?"

Hernan's whip flared out, cutting the old Spaniard on the back. "She's escaped me again," he snarled. "The British dogs have her. I hope they tear her apart or throw her in the hold to let their sailors enjoy her. It's not the death I had planned, but better than none. Get the child."

"But, Senor, if she's gone, why bother?" The whip came again, sending him staggering to his knees.

"I want none of her blood alive to haunt me," Hernan snapped. "Now bring him here so I can dispose of him. I won't have a British bastard on my land, I can tell you that."

Jamie heard Elena's gasp of protest as from a distance, but his mind wasn't on her or even on the terrible scene before him. The words swirled about in his mind as he tried to capture them, to understand them "A British bastard . . ." Not French, not the child of some unknown lover, but *British*!

He shook his head to clear it, then turned to Elena, wanting to demand an explanation. But she was no longer beside him. Even as he turned he saw that she was running toward the house. Jerking his knife from his belt, Jamie ran after her. Explanations would have to wait!

Chapter 43

ELENA REACHED THE door just as Carlos was emerging, and when she held out her arms he handed her the sleeping child without a word. She held him tightly to her, noting even in her terror how he'd grown in the weeks they'd been apart. Not sure what she was doing, yet aware that her life depended on it, Elena began to run away.

For a moment she might have been alone, then a bellow of rage filled the air and something came whistling at her, wrapping itself painfully around her legs. She fell heavily, barely managing to turn her body so that she cushioned her son against the fall.

"Elena!" Hernan came pounding toward her, his eyes blazing with a kind of unholy joy that struck terror in her and made her struggle against the snare of the long whip he'd used to capture her. He stood over her, smiling, catching his breath. "How did you get here?" he demanded.

"I've come to take my son away," Elena said, cuddling the now sobbing child against her breast.

His laugh was ugly. Even as she freed her legs and tried to scramble to her feet, he drew his sword. "You have more lives than a stable cat, my dear," he said, "but I think I know how to end them. One sword thrust for both of you, or perhaps I'll kill the boy and then take you first. I hardly remember that night in the grove; I was too drunk to enjoy myself properly, but now my head is clearer."

"You will have to kill me first, Senor Valdez," Jamie's voice interrupted softly.

Hernan turned quickly, his sword ready. Jamie stood with his knife, his hat gone so that the fading sun touched flashes of gold from the hair he'd missed in his attempt to dye it. "No," Elena cried. "*No*, Jamie!"

"So you found her," Hernan said. "Our little family circle is complete. I'd scarcely dared hope for such good fortune. You took her off Mallorca, didn't you? Stole her away like the slut she is. And now you want her? Well, she's what you deserve. Did she tell you she lived in a whore house? That I caught her because she came to defend the honor of the Madam herself?" His laugh was ugly. "That's the woman you're fighting for, McDonald. A French whore, fresh from a whore house in the negro section of Cartagena. Some prize!"

"She will be my wife," Jamie said, his voice hard as he moved slowly away from Valdez, giving ground as the older man began flicking his sword lightly.

"I'll bury her beside you," Valdez said coldly, "and your whelp between you."

Hernan lunged, and Elena gasped as the sword missed Jamie by inches. "Let him go," she cried. "It's me you hate, not Jamie or the child. Let them go and you can kill me as you wish."

Hernan's evil laughter was her only answer, but there was movement at the house and in a moment Carlos appeared in the doorway. "Senor," he called softly to Jamie, and Elena gasped as she saw something flash in the sun between the two men. Hernan's sword licked out and Jamie's dirk spun away, but her gasp died in relief when she saw that Jamie held a sword, too. Carlos had thrown it to him.

"You'll die for this, Carlos," Hernan snarled. "When I've killed this clumsy British cur I'll deal with you. I should have done it long ago; I never trusted your loyalty."

Carlos said nothing, and Elena's heart nearly stopped as

Hernan and Jamie began circling each other—their swords flicking like serpents' tongues. Hernan had a reputation as a swordsman, she remembered that from the long ago days on the *hacienda* in Spain. But Jamie . . . Dear God, did he even know how to handle one? She had no idea.

The first moments of fear stretched out, and Elena realized the battle was nearly equal. Carlos had tossed Jamie's knife to her, and she held it firmly as she comforted Louis, whispering softly that his father had come back to them at last. As she watched, her hopes began to rise again, for Jamie was more than holding his own. Then the tide turned abruptly.

Hernan seemed to catch fire. His eyes blazed with fury and his mouth twisted as he spat obscenities at Jamie. Then he lunged at him, slashing and cutting with a violence and speed that Jamie was unable to counter. Blood spurted from Jamie's arm, and Elena could see he was staggered by the blow as he gave ground.

"Run, child," Carlos called. "Save yourself and your son."

Elena took a step, but she could go no further. Not even the need to protect Louis could pull her eyes away from the furiously battling men. Jamie was parrying the thrusts, but still giving ground, then he seemed to stumble, to go to one knee. Elena screamed as Hernan plunged in for the kill. A horrible shriek filled the air and she set Louis down, her knife ready.

Hernan staggered back and as he turned she realized it was he, not Jamie, who'd cried out. Jamie's sword had entered his belly, and even now Hernan clawed in agony at the protruding hilt as he stumbled against the wide porch of his handsome house. He clung there for a moment before sliding to the ground.

Elena heard his cries for help but ran instead to Jamie, who was swaying slightly on his feet, his good hand grasping the bleeding arm. Without thought she ripped off her petticoat and wrapped the wound to staunch the flow of blood.

"Bring him inside," Carlos said. "Let me tend that."

Only when the flow of blood had stopped did she have time to look around and think. "We've got to get away from here," she said. "Hernan . . ."

Carlos smiled quietly. "I've already arranged that," he said. "Some of the men are taking him in his carriage out along the road. He'll be found there tomorrow, perhaps the next day, the victim of the rabble fleeing the city. There are plenty who would cut his throat for the gold he carries. No one will question it."

"But what of the servants, the slaves?" Elena looked around, suddenly aware that there were several women in the big kitchen, that they had been talking and preparing food and even caring for Louis while her whole attention had been concentrated on Jamie.

"There have been other Celestes," Carlos said. "There is no one who will mourn him here."

"What will happen to us?" one of the women asked, her eyes on Jamie. "Will the English come here and kill us?"

Jamie smiled at her and shook his head. "From what I've seen, you'll be safe enough from our fleet."

"What do you mean?" Carlos asked. "The men who came this morning said the fleet was in the harbour, that the *Bocca Chica* had been opened."

Jamie nodded. "Battered ships filled with sick men," he said. "I ask you to tell no one this, but don't be afraid here. When the fleet is gone, send a message to Spain, to your mistress. My guess is that she'll be happy to allow you to run this place while her children are growing up. With their father gone, they will perhaps have a chance to grow up as fine as their half-sister."

Carlos nodded, his eyes shrewd. "I will write to her that he died honorably," he said. "And what of you, Senorita Elena? Shall I tell her about you?"

Elena considered for a moment, then shook her head sadly. "She's accepted my death, has she not?" she asked.

He nodded. "She grieved, but the birth of her son gave her the strength to go on."

"Then we'll leave it at that," she said. "Let her mourn Hernan and raise his children to be better men than their father was."

Jamie stirred. "We'd better go," he said, wincing as he moved his arm.

"No," Carlos said. "You cannot make such a long journey. It is almost nightfall, and I spoke truly about the dangers of the roads. You must wait till morning. You will stay here, at least give your wound a little rest."

Elena saw the doubt in Jamie's eyes as he looked around, but it faded as Carlos helped him to his feet. "Come along," he said. "You can rest till the food is ready. I will have it brought to you. Tomorrow will be soon enough to make plans."

Elena allowed herself to be led to the large guest room and

helped Carlos to ease Jamie down on the wide bed. "I'll stay with him," she said softly.

Carlos nodded. "Louis's room is through there," he said, pointing to a nearby door. "He is sleeping again, according to Lupe."

"Thank you," Elena said. "Thank you for so very much."

Carlos bowed slightly. "Your father gave me the chance to learn to read and write, so that I might rise above the stablemen. He was always kind to me, as you well know. I am only glad to have a chance to repay some of his kindness and to serve you. Rest well."

Elena closed the door behind Carlos, then stood irresolutely near it. Jamie lay still, hardly seeming to breathe. Should she go to him? What could she say, now that the danger was past and Hernan was dead?

"Come lie beside me," Jamie said.

Elena hurried to obey, moving carefully on the big bed, not wanting to jar his arm.

"Why didn't you tell me?" he asked. "Why did you let me think that Louis was someone else's child?"

"Would you have believed me?" Elena asked, stung by the hurt in his voice. "I heard you tell Ian you had dreamed of making love to me, but that you never touched me. That you *wouldn't* touch me, after what had happened."

He winced, but she knew the pain wasn't from his wound. "God forgive me," he said, "I thought it was a dream, a wonderful dream that haunted me from that day till now." He sighed. "I tried to forget with Sally and with others, but it was always you." He laughed without humor. "I kept telling myself you were married, a respectable French housewife with a baby or two. But *my son*. A son I never dreamed existed!" His tone changed to one of wonder.

"He's a good little boy," she said, "and growing so fast. He was born early, but he's strong." She stopped, aware that Jamie was frowning.

"How did Valdez know he was my son?" he asked.

"That's why I was so afraid for him," Elena admitted. "He has your eyes, and I knew Hernan would recognize them as soon as he saw Louis. If it hadn't been for that, he might have believed Louis was his own child. He would have been less likely to harm him."

"When he wakes up, bring him in here," Jamie said. "I want to see him."

Elena nodded. "Sleep now," she said. "We'll have plenty of time tomorrow."

His good arm slid around her and his lips found hers. "So long as you're with me," he said. "Just as long as you're here and safe."

Jamie scarcely remembered the dinner that Elena forced him to eat; his arm throbbed with determination and his whole body felt sore. By morning it was worse. He dimly sensed people working around him, cool hands touching him; but nothing made much sense. He relived the weeks in Mallorca and on the ship from there to France. He cried out for Elena and was soothed by a gentle kiss. He slept again.

The room was dim when he opened his eyes. He moved carefully, expecting the racking pains, but they didn't come. His left arm was sore and his head was light when he tried to sit up, but the room quickly steadied and he caught his breath.

"Jamie." The movement came from the shadows on the far side of the room and in a moment Elena was beside him, her fingers warm on his face. "The fever is gone," she said, sounding joyful.

"You *are* here," he said, blinking at her. "I was afraid I'd wake up back on the ship and find Reggie leaning over me, telling me it was all a dream."

"I'm here," she said. "How do you feel?"

"I'm fine. My arm's stiff, but other than that I'm all right."

Her lips caressed his gently. "You stay here while I call for some food," she said. "You haven't eaten in two days."

"Two days?"

"Your fever was high."

"Dear God, we've got to get out of here," Jamie said, fighting dizziness as he leaned over the side of the bed. "We've got to get back to the coast and the fleet. What about Valdez? If anyone finds out we're here..."

"His body was found yesterday. Everything is fine. There is so much concern about the attack on Cartegena, no one has even bothered to investigate."

"What's the word on that?" Jamie asked.

"The fleet is in the harbour," Elena said. "They are attacking the walls of the city itself now."

Jamie eased himself back against the cushions. "They won't find it easy, I'm afraid," he said, "but perhaps I can help if I return now and tell them what I've learned."

"Not before tomorrow," Elena said. "It's a long ride, and you've scarcely recovered. You were very ill."

Jamie leaned back and closed his eyes, too weak to argue with her. In spite of the danger he was aware of, he felt strangely at peace. It was enough to lie still and see Elena move about the room, to see the small boy that stared back at him with stormy grey eyes full of curiosity.

They left at dawn in the same small wagon they'd come in, Elena driving while he held the excited and wiggling little boy. The road was much more crowded. Wagons, riders, and even people on foot were moving in both directions; some fleeing the city while others were en route to fight to hold it. Jamie eyed the heavy wagonloads of supplies that were being taken to the city and shook his head.

"They won't surrender as the people of Porto Bello did," he said. "If the land forces had been successful... If there was no way into the city from the land..." He sighed. "I must tell the Admiral. Once he knows, I think he'll forgive my absence and welcome you aboard."

"And if he doesn't?" Elena asked, a note of fear in her voice.

"Then he'll just have to take us anyway," Jamie said. "We'll all leave together this time. I'm not taking any more chances with you."

Her smile was his reward, and it made him feel better. Whatever had been between them, whatever doubts she'd had, it all seemed to have vanished. The eyes that looked up into his were clear and green and glowing with a love that made him ache to take her in his arms and claim her as his wife. Only one thing worried him. He reached out and touched her cheek, then looked down at Louis.

"What about Fergus?" he asked. "I can't just forget my second son."

"Louis will have a brother," Elena said, her eyes clear and serene as they met his. "They will be playmates, they are so close in age."

"You could love him?"

"He's a part of you."

He accepted that with a great sense of relief, even dozing a little to escape the growing pain from his arm.

As they neared the city, the crowds grew worse and soon they were only inching along. Elena sighed and handed Jamie the reins so she could tend to Louis's hungry cries. "What are we going to do?" she asked as she fed the boy some of the bread Carlos had sent with them. "How are we going to reach your friends?"

Jamie shook his head, his sense of ease disappearing. "I don't know exactly," he admitted. "I thought we could just row out to the ship, but now I'm not so sure." Clouds of smoke rose over the city, and even from a distance they could hear the sounds of shelling. "Perhaps it would be wiser to go back the way we came."

"What do you mean?" Elena asked, looking confused. "Go back to the *hacienda*?"

"No, no, I mean the way we came into Cartegena. If we could walk along the shore again and perhaps find a small boat to row out to that fort where I found you ... There will be men left there to guard it, and I'm sure they can get us safely to the Vice-Admiral. In the city we'd all be in danger."

Elena looked dubious, but as soon as they could she guided the donkey away from the main road and onto the rough, less traveled path. They bounced along for what seemed hours. The sun disappeared and night came with the usual tropic suddenness. The sky was cloudy and rain began to fall. Jamie's arm, which had ached before, began to throb with a seriousness that told him he'd left too soon. But there was no turning back.

The wagon slipped in the mud, and a wheel splintered against a rocky outcropping, spilling them out onto the wet ground. His arm was beneath him and the pain was like an arrow in his brain, exploding to bring a final blackness.

When he recovered consciousness, he was swaying along on the donkey's back with Louis before him, sheltered by his slumping body while Elena's hand held them both in place. "Where are we?" he murmured.

"Near the shore," Elena said. "Wait here and I'll see if I can find someone with a boat."

"You can't," he began, but she was already gone, leaving him alone with Louis in the darkness. He dozed a little, then jerked awake at the distant sound of shots and a scream. The weary donkey stirred, but he'd gone only a few steps when rough hands dragged him off the beast. He tried to hold onto Louis, but someone touched his wound and the blackness closed in again.

He was dimly conscious of warmth and gentle hands. "Elena," he moaned, his eyes too heavy to open.

"'Fraid not, old man," a familiar voice said. "You'll have to settle for my rough ways for a day or two more."

"Reggie." Jamie sat up, then dropped back weakly. "Where is she?"

"Hey now, she's all right," Reggie said reassuringly. "She'll be down to see you in a bit. I just meant she wasn't going to be up to tending you for a day or so."

"But she's all right? She wasn't wounded by those idiots with their muskets?"

"A graze on the shoulder, that's all," Reggie said. "Didn't even raise a fever. Fortunately they weren't as well-trained as your boys."

Jamie closed his eyes. "Louis?" he said. "My son, where is he?"

"Safe with his mother, unless the good Vice-Admiral has him. Make you laugh to see the way he's taken over the ship. If you've any intention of escaping marrying that lady, you'd best start swimming right now. The Vice-Admiral has been planning the wedding himself, for the moment you're well enough to stand up."

Jamie just blinked at his friend. "What are you saying?"

"That the fair Elena has cleared your name, my friend. She even gave the Vice-Admiral all the details about the city and its fortifications. Not to mention telling me what plants and herbs to use to treat this fever that has three-fourths of the men too sick to hold muskets, let alone use them. She convinced him to break off the attack. We sail with the dawn, thanks be to God. If she hadn't convinced him, I swear we'd have stayed till there wasn't a man left with the strength to sail us to Port Royal."

"How soon will I be able to stand?" Jamie asked.

"What?"

"You said I could get married when I could stand up," Jamie reminded him.

Reggie shook his head, but he was grinning. "Pretty bride like that, you'd better rest a few days," he said. "Your arm is healing fine now, but you want to have *all* your strength back."

"I'm feeling better already," Jamie assured him. He looked across the small cabin and saw Elena standing in the doorway—her eyes glowing with the green blaze of love that warmed him as no other light had ever done.